To Callum,

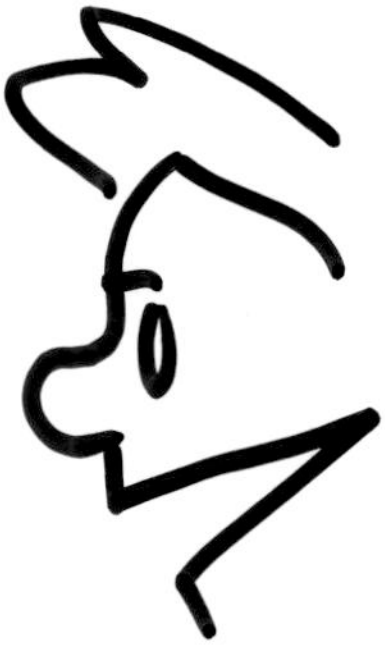

Cosmic Commandos

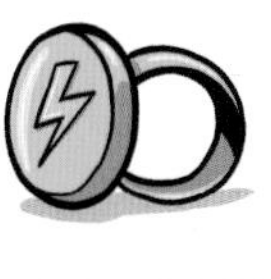

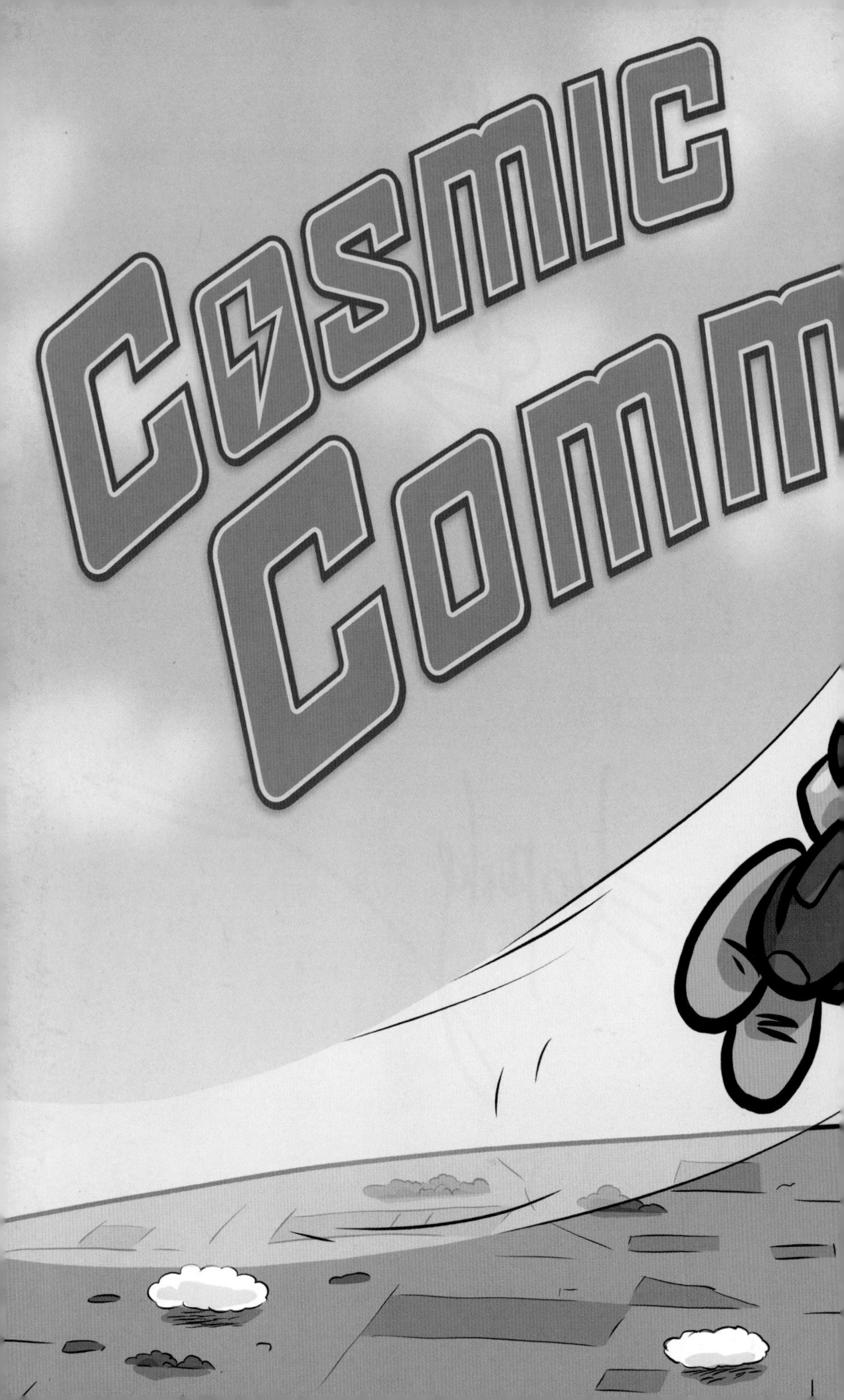
Cosmic
Comm

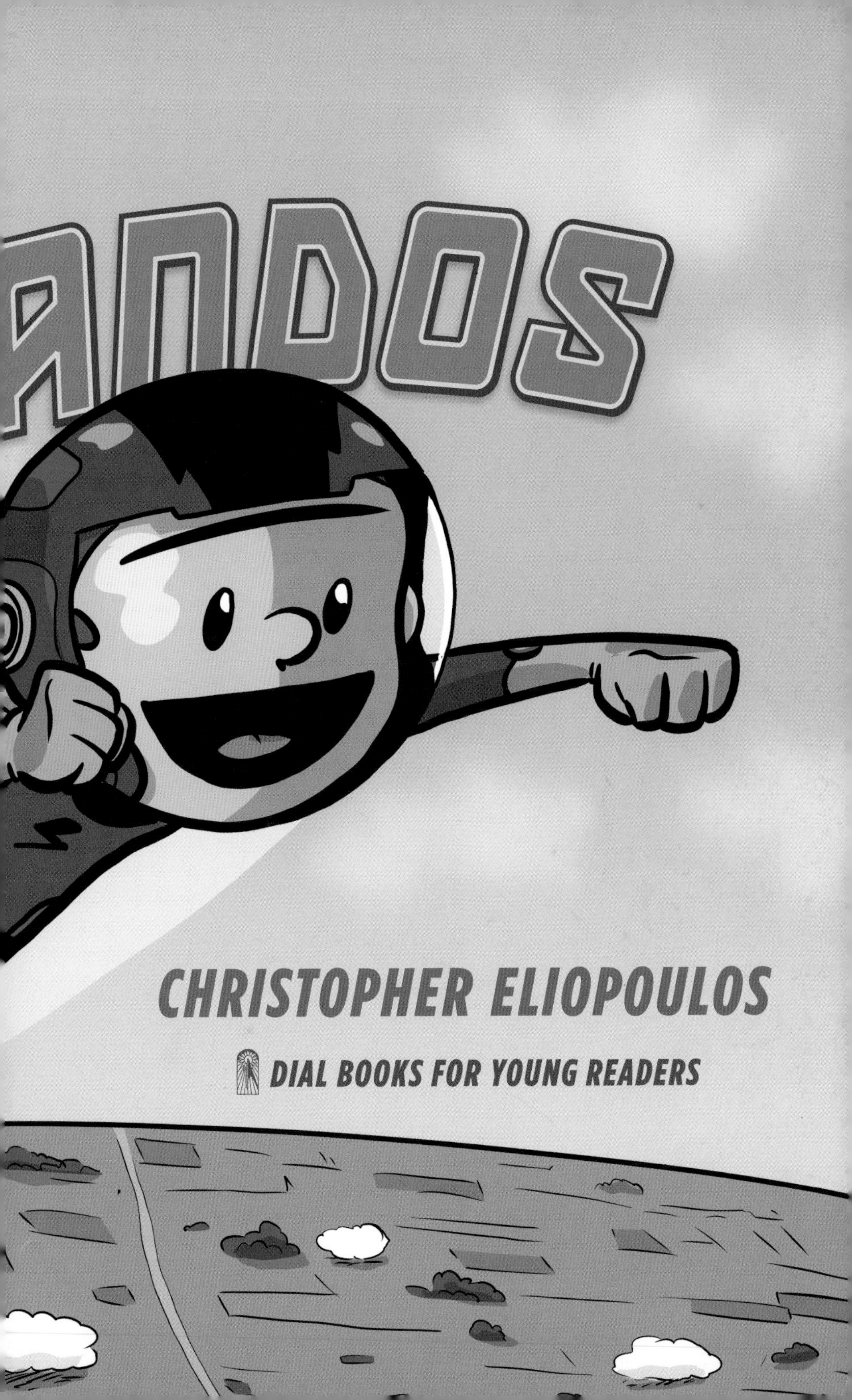
ANDOS

CHRISTOPHER ELIOPOULOS

DIAL BOOKS FOR YOUNG READERS

DIAL BOOKS FOR YOUNG READERS

PENGUIN YOUNG READERS GROUP • An imprint of Penguin Random House LLC

375 Hudson Street • New York, NY 10014

Copyright © 2017 by Christopher Eliopoulos

Printed in China

ISBN 9781101994481 • 10 9 8 7 6 5 4 3 2 1

Design by Jason Henry

The artwork for this book was created digitally.

*For Jeremy and Justin,
my heroes*

CHAPTER ONE

A STINKISH LIFE

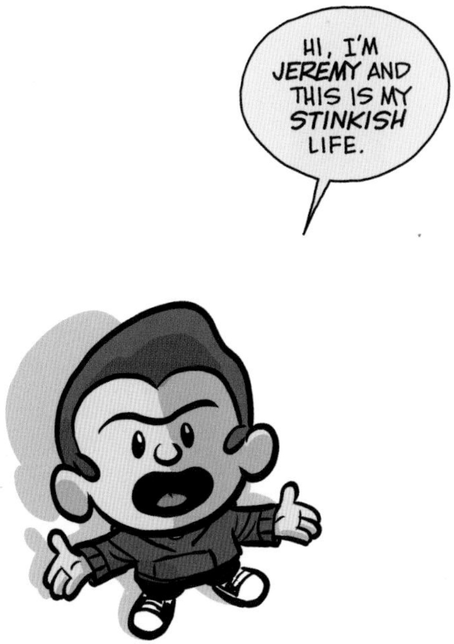
HI, I'M JEREMY AND THIS IS MY STINKISH LIFE.

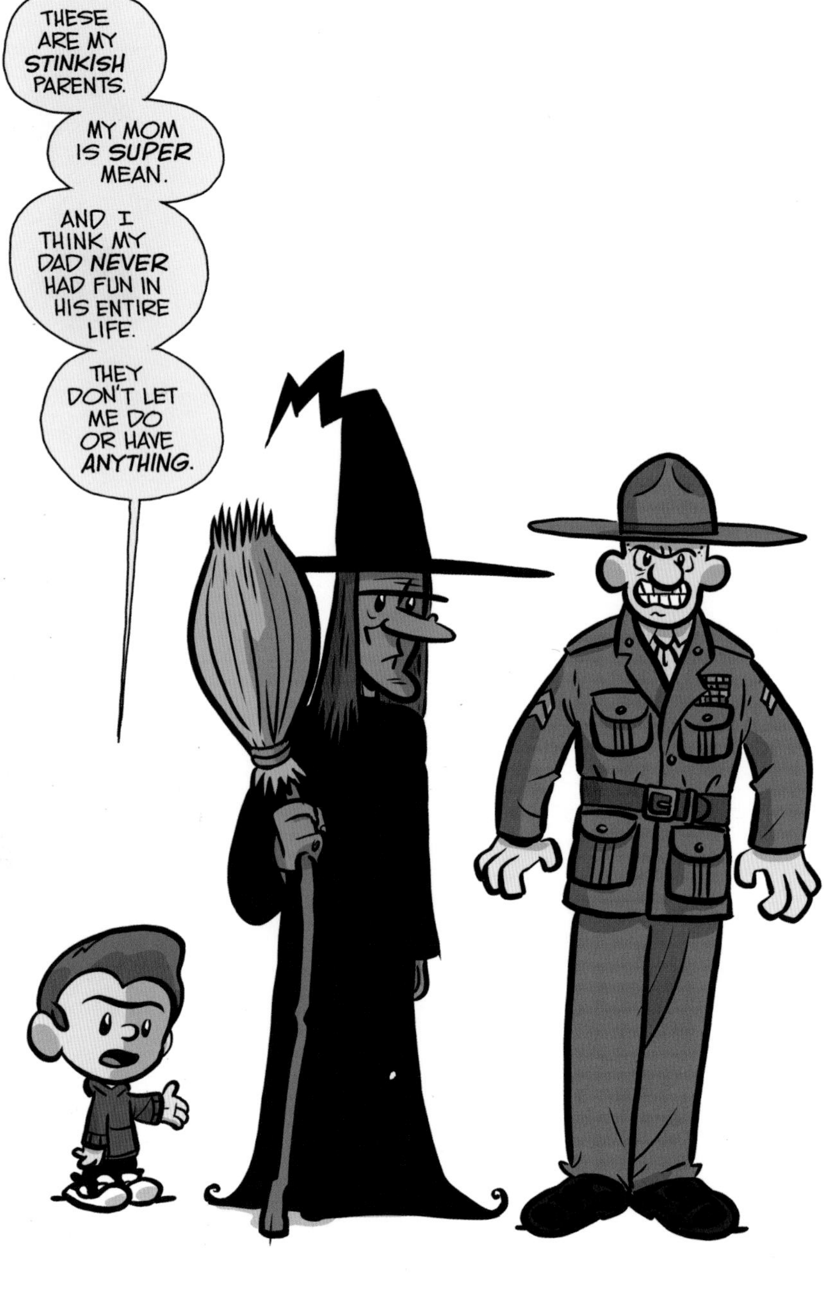
THESE ARE MY STINKISH PARENTS.
MY MOM IS SUPER MEAN.
AND I THINK MY DAD NEVER HAD FUN IN HIS ENTIRE LIFE.
THEY DON'T LET ME DO OR HAVE ANYTHING.

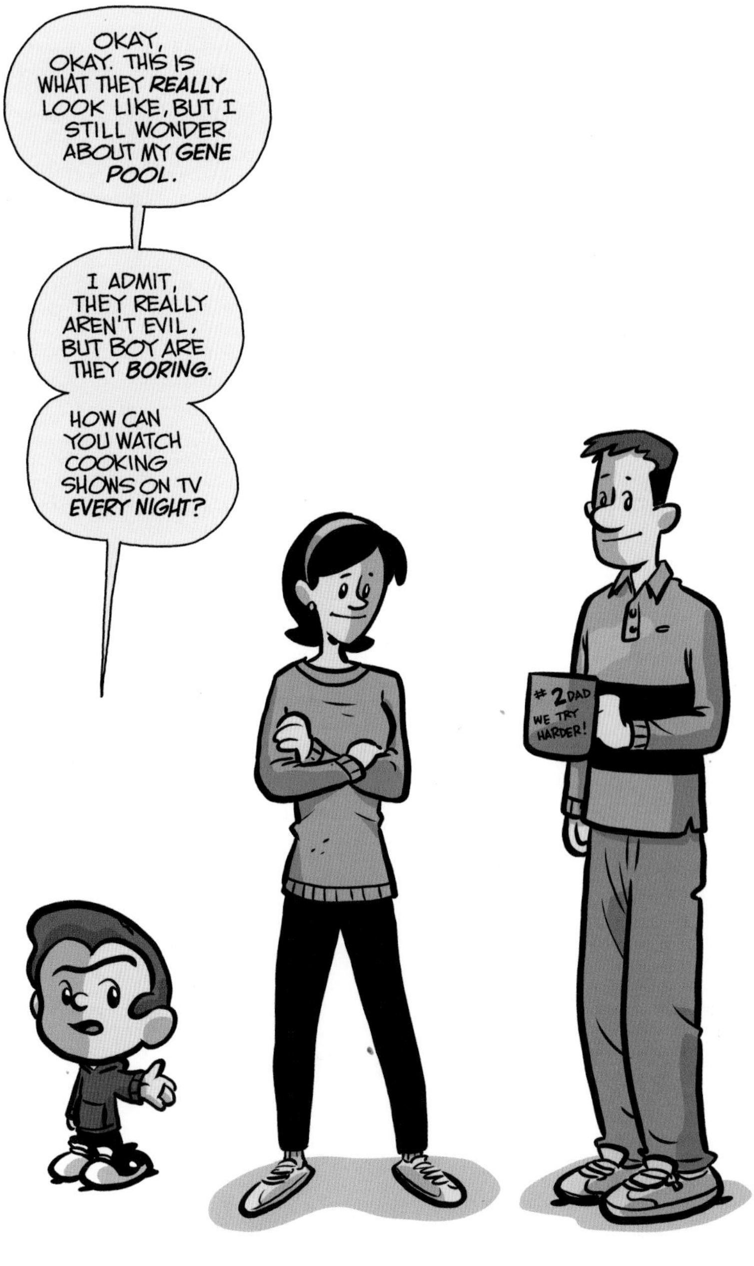
OKAY, OKAY. THIS IS WHAT THEY REALLY LOOK LIKE, BUT I STILL WONDER ABOUT MY GENE POOL.
I ADMIT, THEY REALLY AREN'T EVIL, BUT BOY ARE THEY BORING.
HOW CAN YOU WATCH COOKING SHOWS ON TV EVERY NIGHT?
2 DAD WE TRY HARDER!

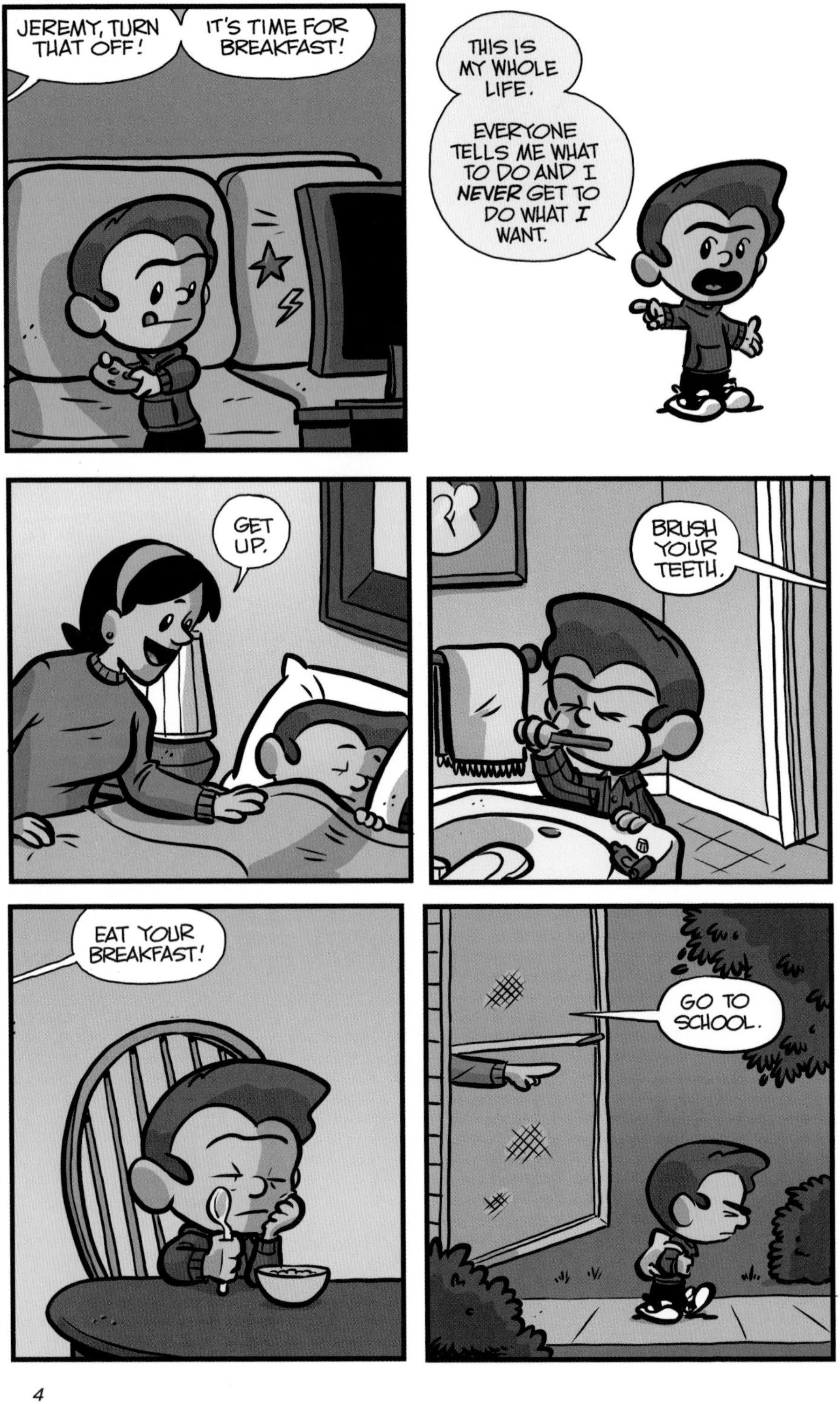
JEREMY, TURN THAT OFF!
IT'S TIME FOR BREAKFAST!
THIS IS MY WHOLE LIFE.
EVERYONE TELLS ME WHAT TO DO AND I *NEVER* GET TO DO WHAT *I* WANT.
GET UP.
BRUSH YOUR TEETH.
EAT YOUR BREAKFAST!
GO TO SCHOOL.

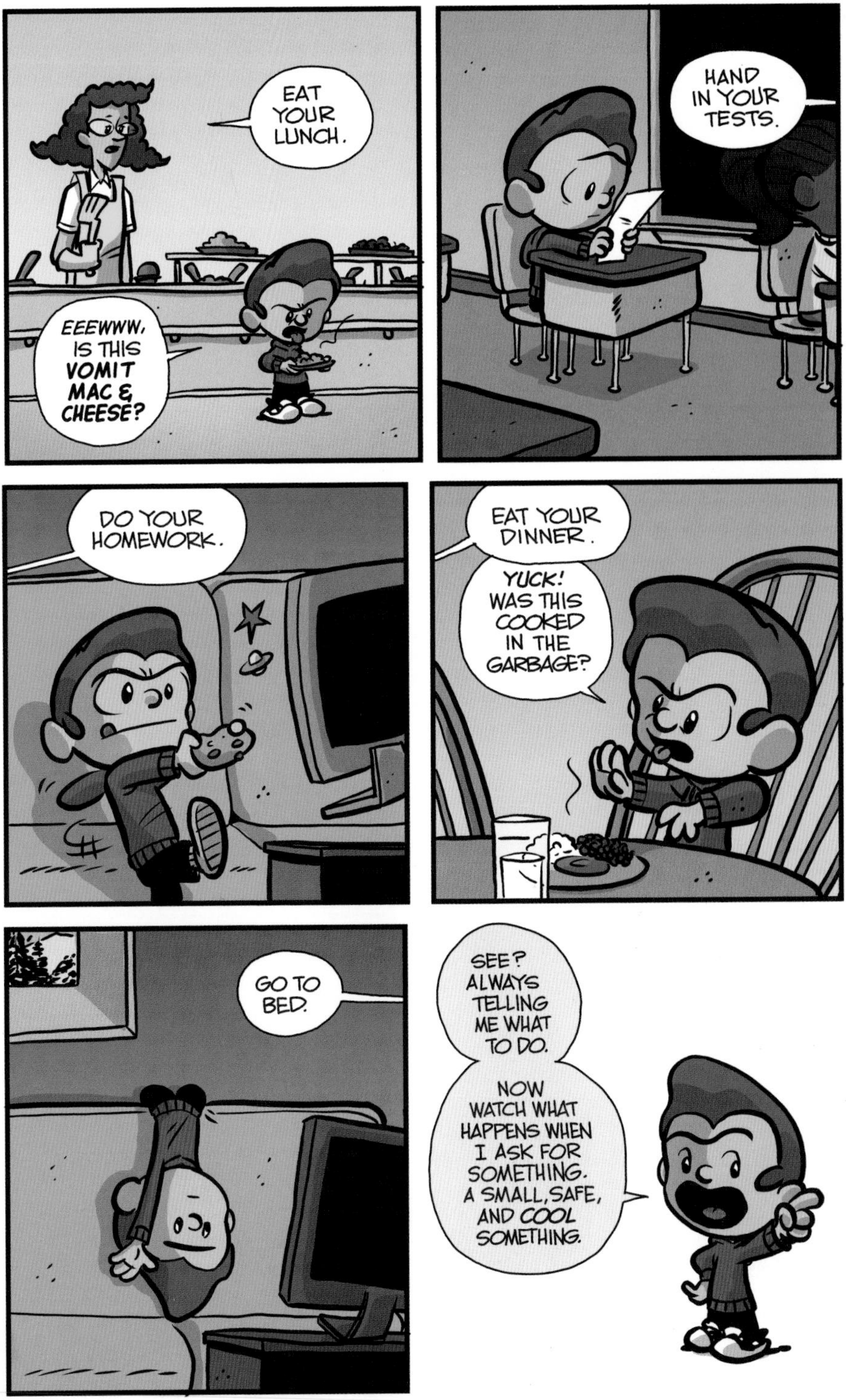
EAT YOUR LUNCH.
EEEWWW, IS THIS VOMIT MAC & CHEESE?
HAND IN YOUR TESTS.
DO YOUR HOMEWORK.
EAT YOUR DINNER.
YUCK! WAS THIS COOKED IN THE GARBAGE?
GO TO BED.
SEE? ALWAYS TELLING ME WHAT TO DO.
NOW WATCH WHAT HAPPENS WHEN I ASK FOR SOMETHING. A SMALL, SAFE, AND COOL SOMETHING.

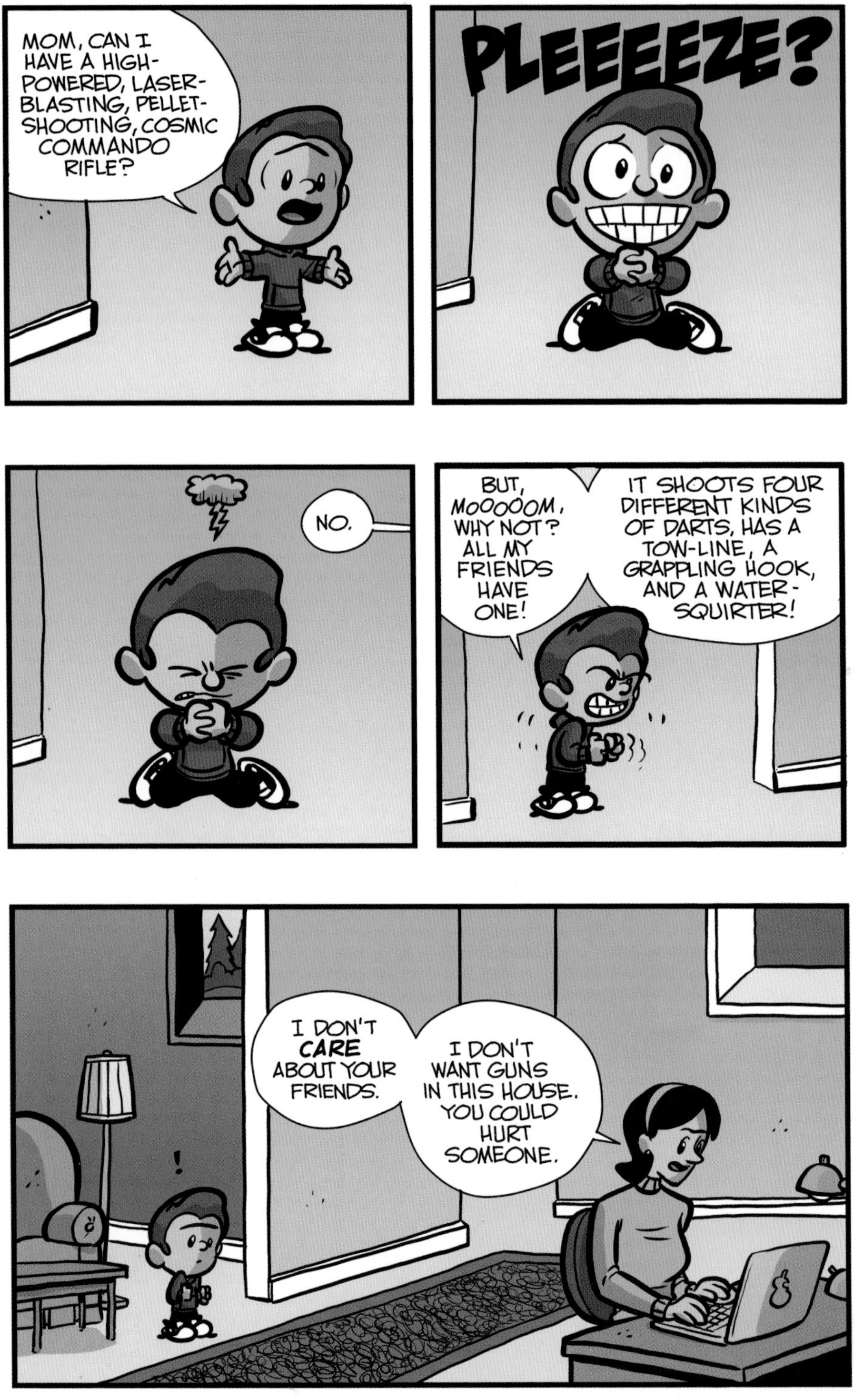
MOM, CAN I HAVE A HIGH-POWERED, LASER-BLASTING, PELLET-SHOOTING, COSMIC COMMANDO RIFLE?
PLEEEEEZE?
NO.
BUT, MOOOOOM, WHY NOT? ALL MY FRIENDS HAVE ONE!
IT SHOOTS FOUR DIFFERENT KINDS OF DARTS, HAS A TOW-LINE, A GRAPPLING HOOK, AND A WATER-SQUIRTER!
I DON'T **CARE** ABOUT YOUR FRIENDS.
I DON'T WANT GUNS IN THIS HOUSE. YOU COULD HURT SOMEONE.
!

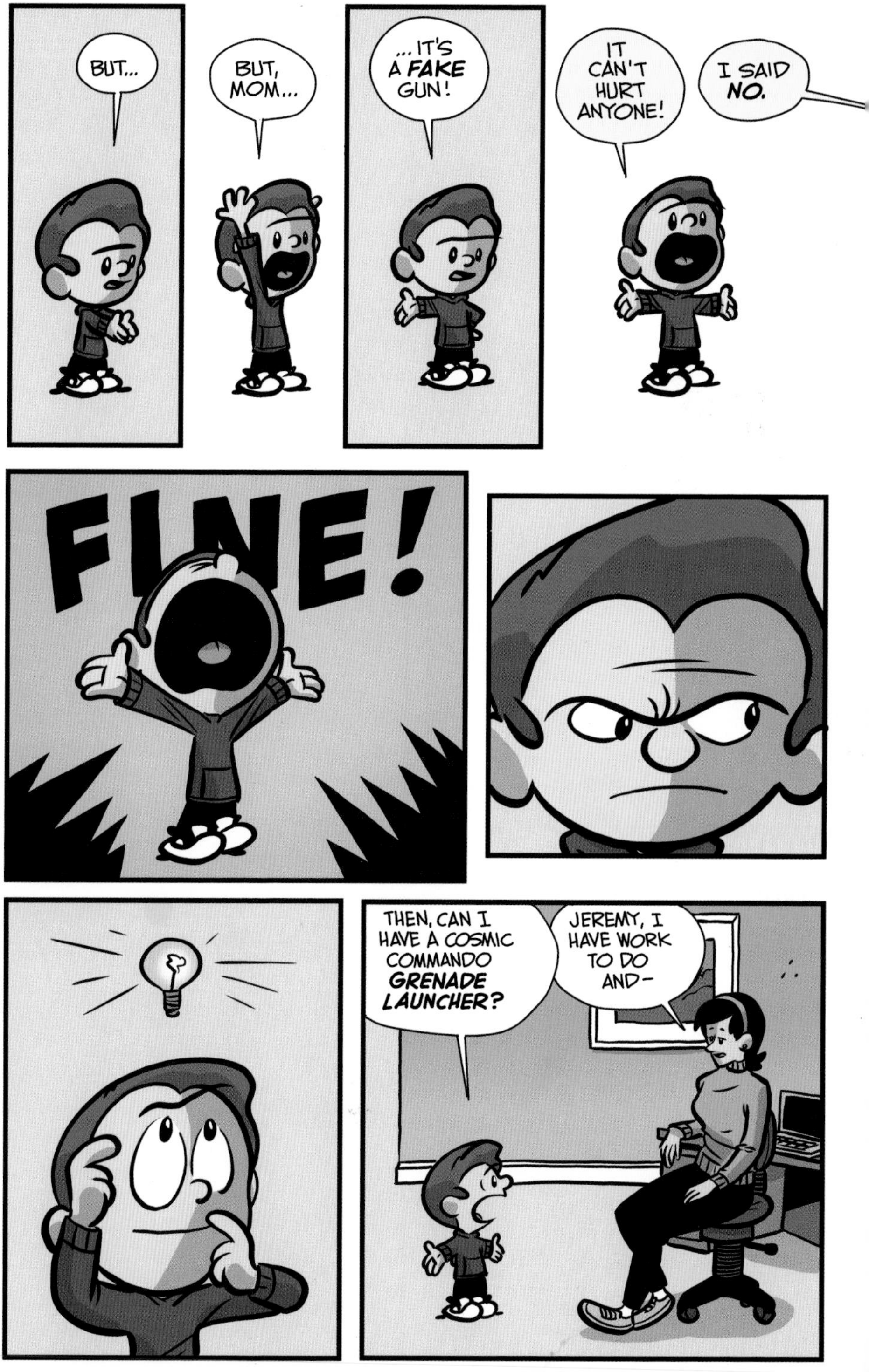
BUT...
BUT, MOM...
...IT'S A **FAKE** GUN!
IT CAN'T HURT ANYONE!
I SAID **NO.**
FINE!
THEN, CAN I HAVE A COSMIC COMMANDO ***GRENADE LAUNCHER***?
JEREMY, I HAVE WORK TO DO AND-

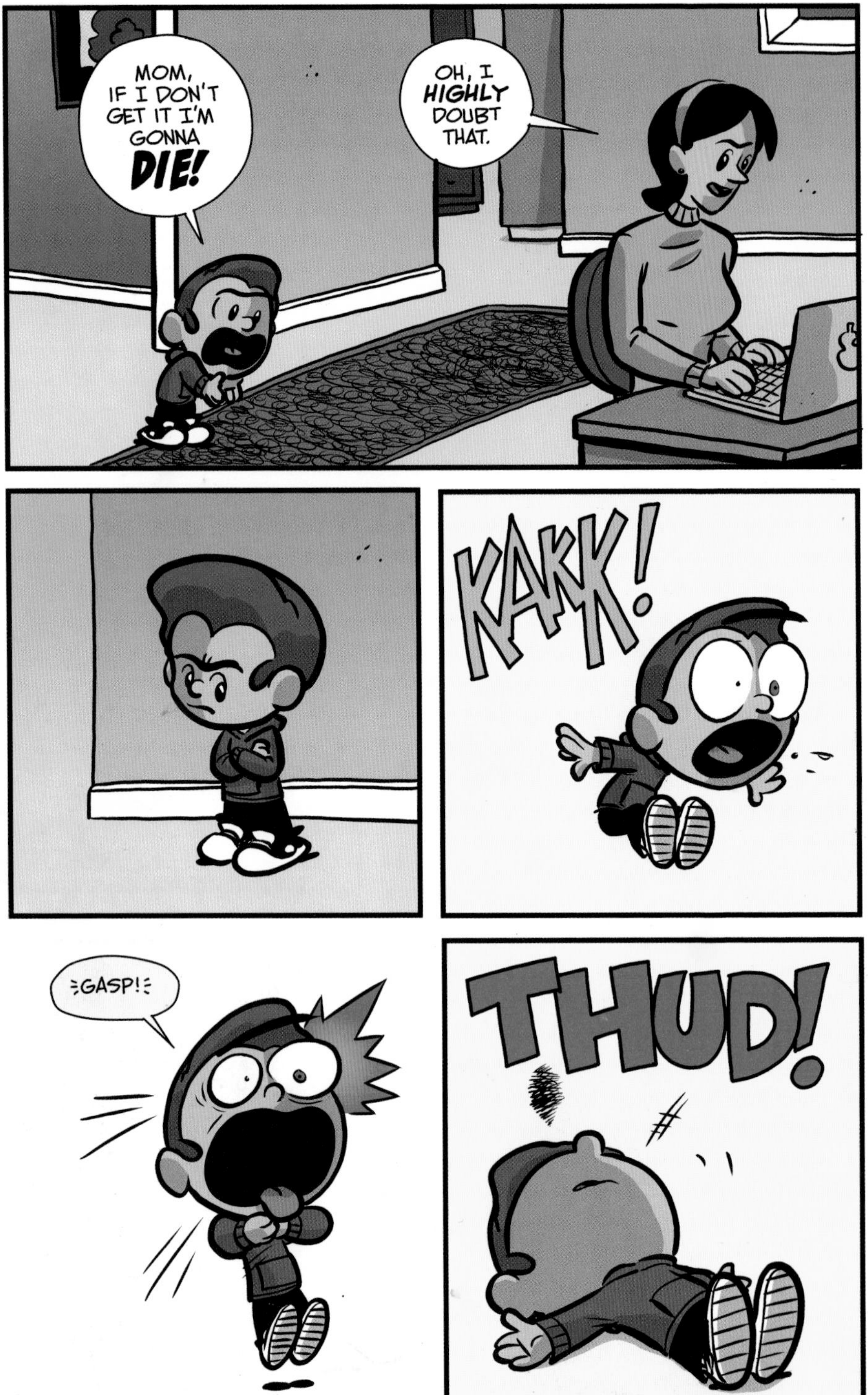
MOM, IF I DON'T GET IT I'M GONNA DIE!
OH, I HIGHLY DOUBT THAT.
KAKK!
GASP!
THUD!

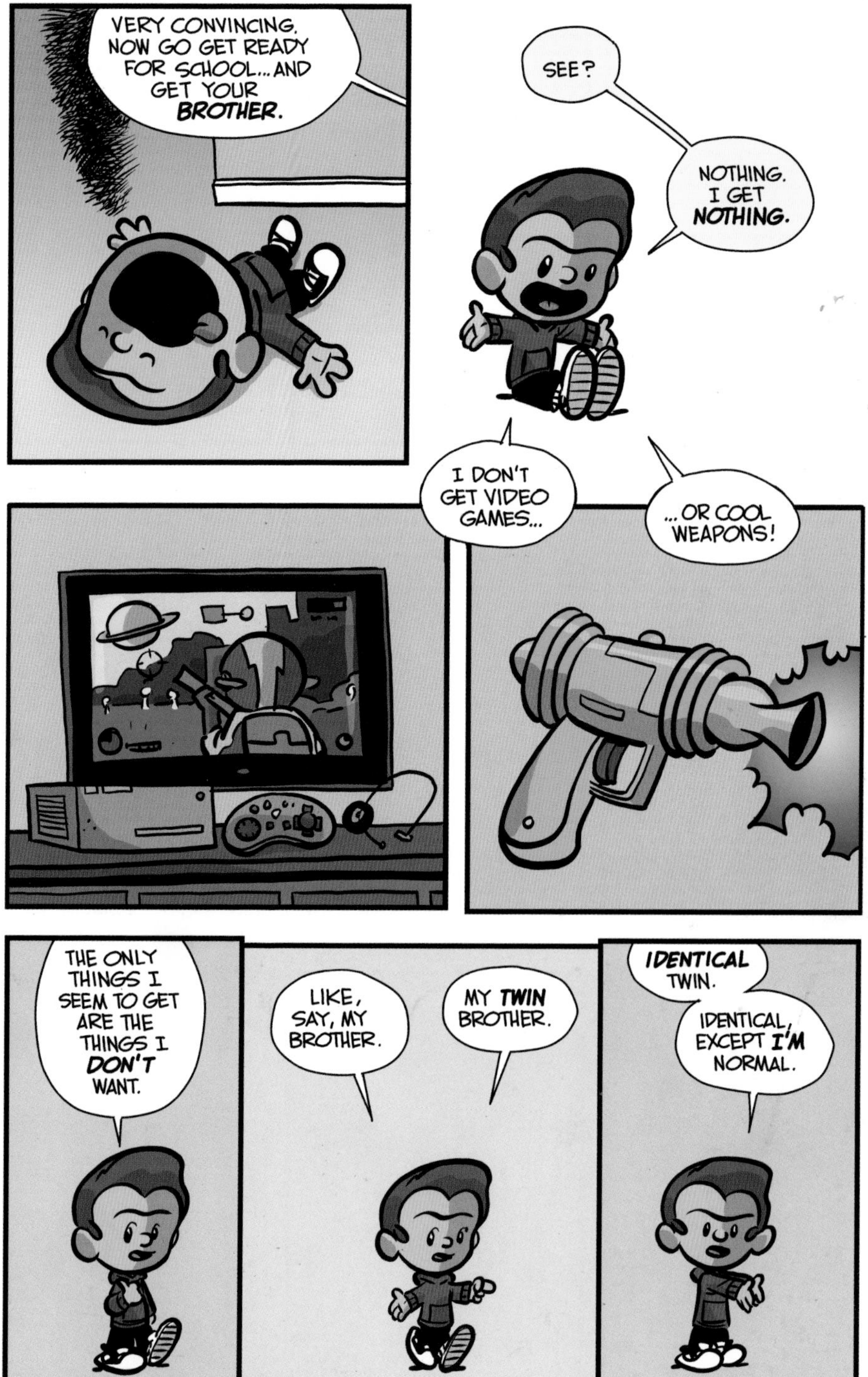
VERY CONVINCING. NOW GO GET READY FOR SCHOOL... AND GET YOUR BROTHER.
SEE?
NOTHING. I GET NOTHING.
I DON'T GET VIDEO GAMES...
...OR COOL WEAPONS!
THE ONLY THINGS I SEEM TO GET ARE THE THINGS I DON'T WANT.
LIKE, SAY, MY BROTHER.
MY TWIN BROTHER.
IDENTICAL TWIN.
IDENTICAL, EXCEPT I'M NORMAL.

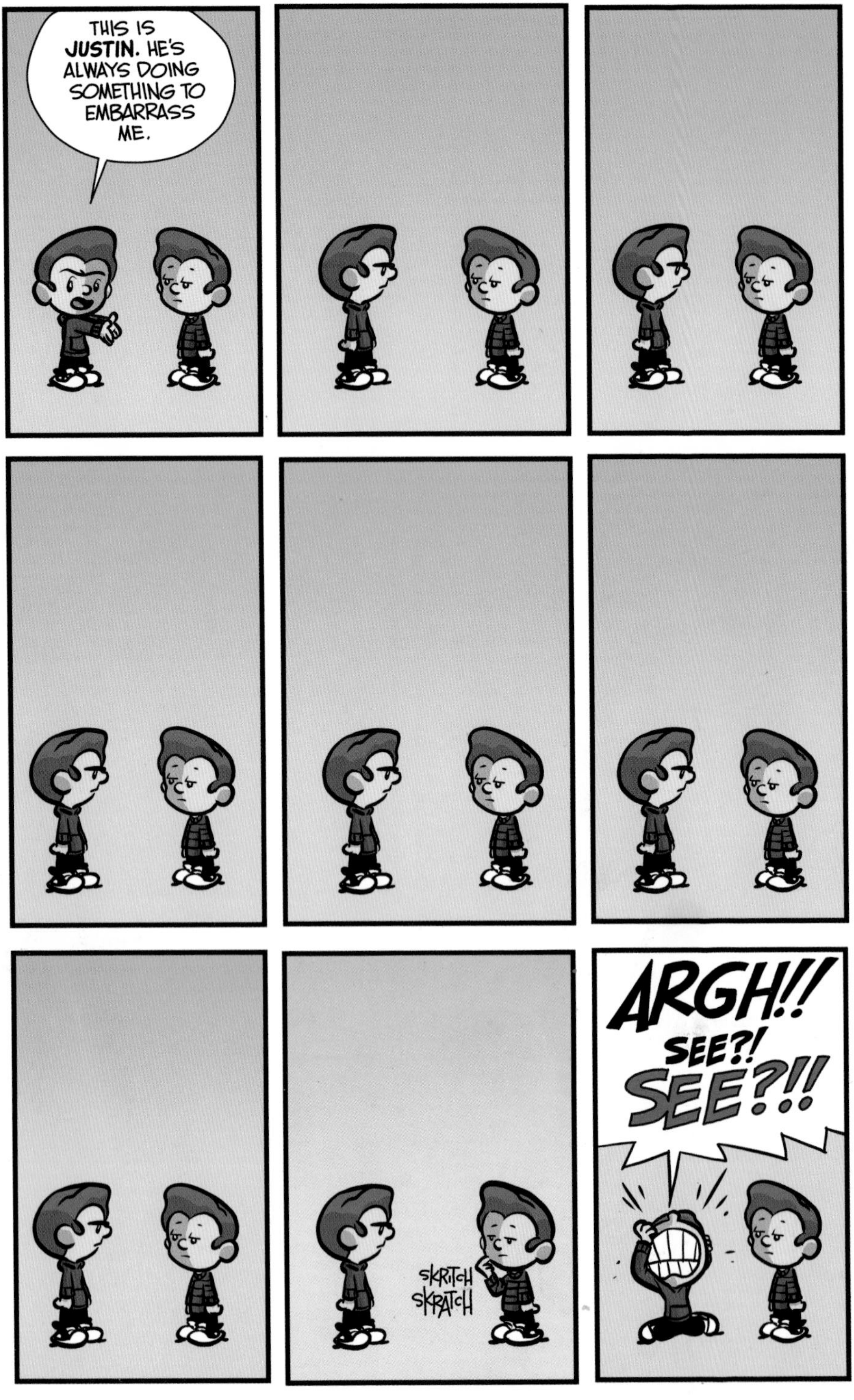
THIS IS **JUSTIN.** HE'S ALWAYS DOING SOMETHING TO EMBARRASS ME.
SKRITCH SKRATCH
ARGH!!
SEE?!
SEE?!!

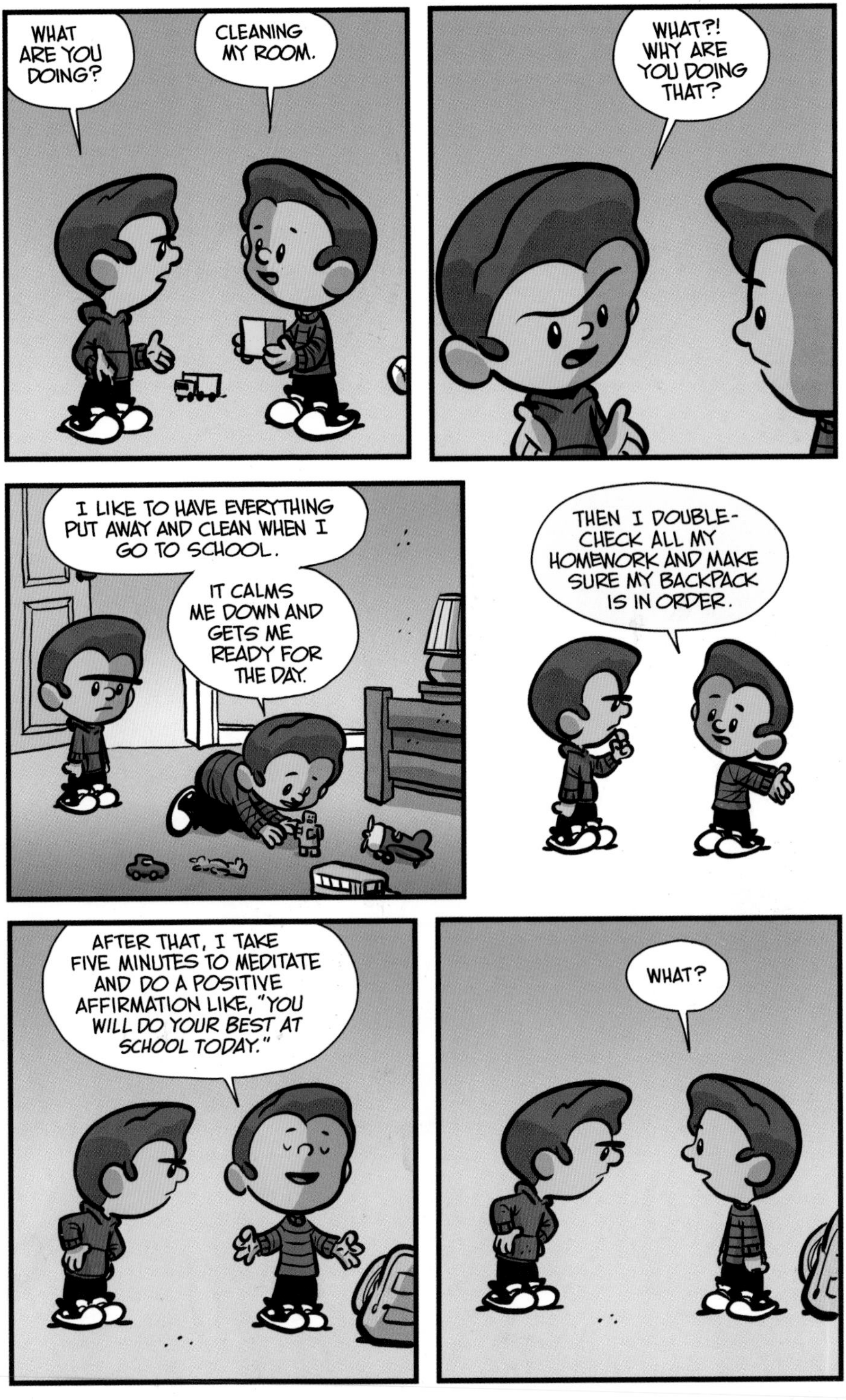
WHAT ARE YOU DOING?
CLEANING MY ROOM.
WHAT?! WHY ARE YOU DOING THAT?
I LIKE TO HAVE EVERYTHING PUT AWAY AND CLEAN WHEN I GO TO SCHOOL.
IT CALMS ME DOWN AND GETS ME READY FOR THE DAY.
THEN I DOUBLE-CHECK ALL MY HOMEWORK AND MAKE SURE MY BACKPACK IS IN ORDER.
AFTER THAT, I TAKE FIVE MINUTES TO MEDITATE AND DO A POSITIVE AFFIRMATION LIKE, "YOU WILL DO YOUR BEST AT SCHOOL TODAY."
WHAT?

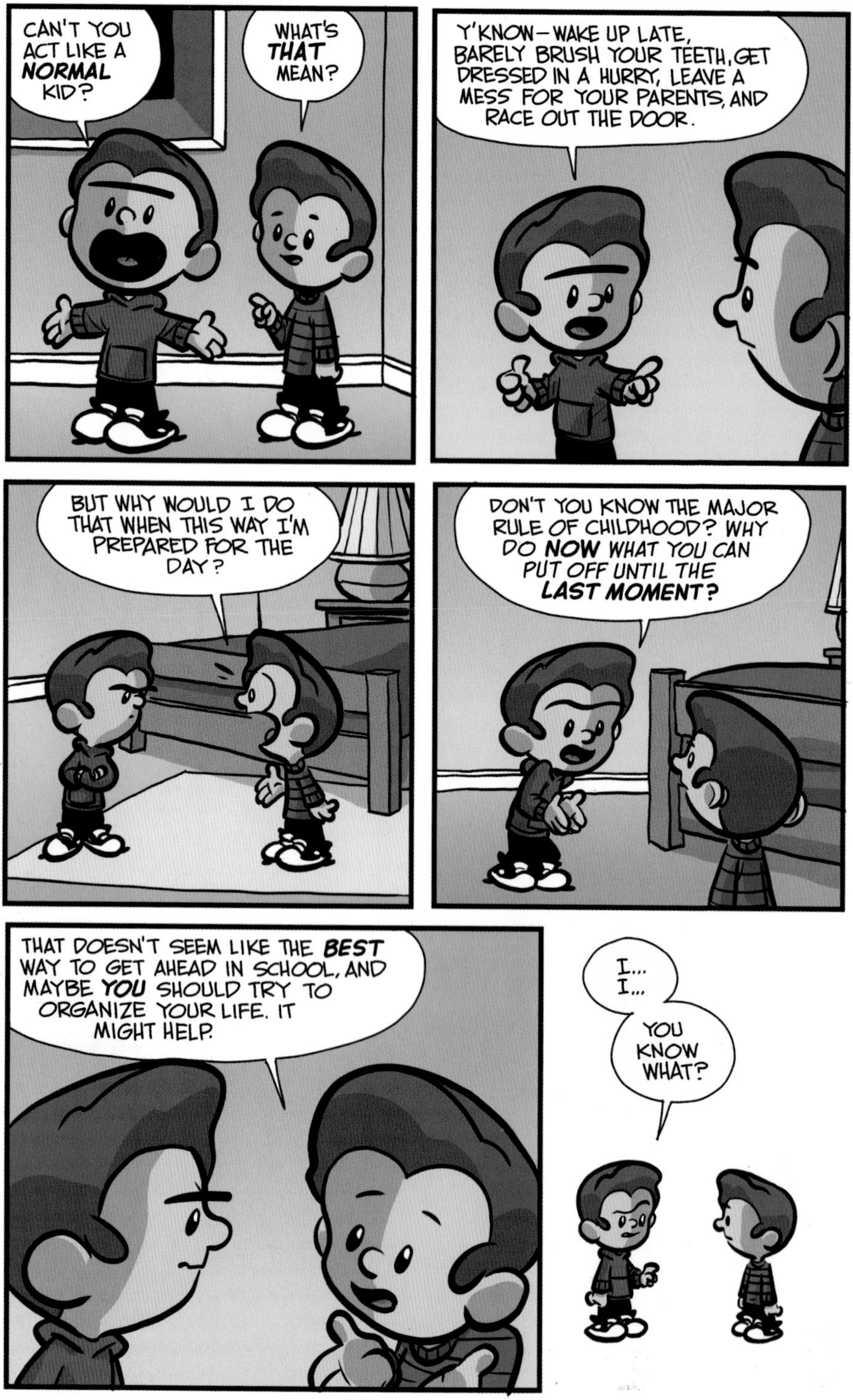
CAN'T YOU ACT LIKE A NORMAL KID?
WHAT'S THAT MEAN?
Y'KNOW—WAKE UP LATE, BARELY BRUSH YOUR TEETH, GET DRESSED IN A HURRY, LEAVE A MESS FOR YOUR PARENTS, AND RACE OUT THE DOOR.
BUT WHY WOULD I DO THAT WHEN THIS WAY I'M PREPARED FOR THE DAY?
DON'T YOU KNOW THE MAJOR RULE OF CHILDHOOD? WHY DO NOW WHAT YOU CAN PUT OFF UNTIL THE LAST MOMENT?
THAT DOESN'T SEEM LIKE THE BEST WAY TO GET AHEAD IN SCHOOL, AND MAYBE YOU SHOULD TRY TO ORGANIZE YOUR LIFE. IT MIGHT HELP.
I... I...
YOU KNOW WHAT?

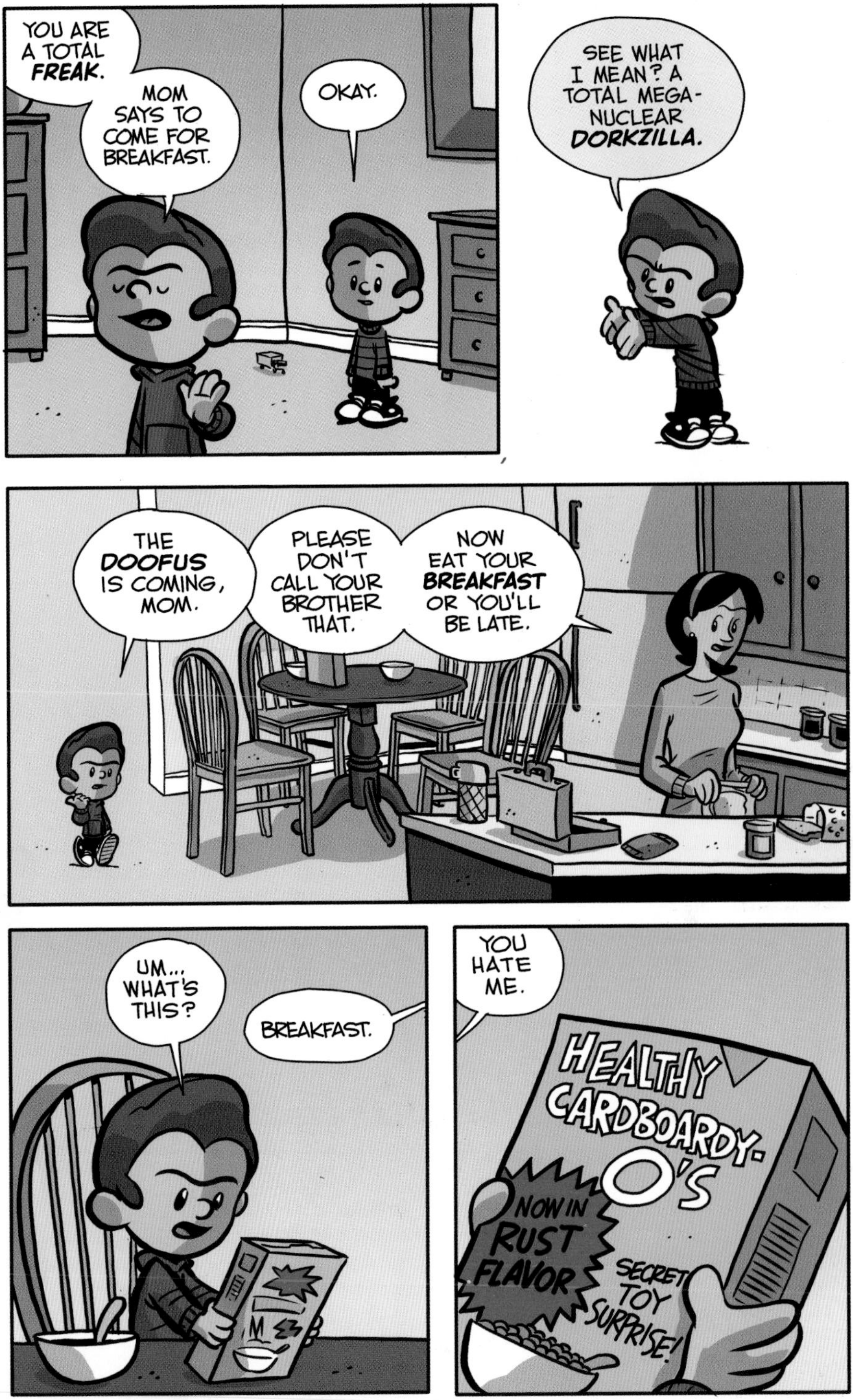

YOU ARE A TOTAL **FREAK**.
MOM SAYS TO COME FOR BREAKFAST.
OKAY.
SEE WHAT I MEAN? A TOTAL MEGA-NUCLEAR **DORKZILLA**.
THE **DOOFUS** IS COMING, MOM.
PLEASE DON'T CALL YOUR BROTHER THAT.
NOW EAT YOUR **BREAKFAST** OR YOU'LL BE LATE.
UM... WHAT'S THIS?
BREAKFAST.
YOU HATE ME.
HEALTHY CARDBOARDY-O'S
NOW IN RUST FLAVOR
SECRET TOY SURPRISE!

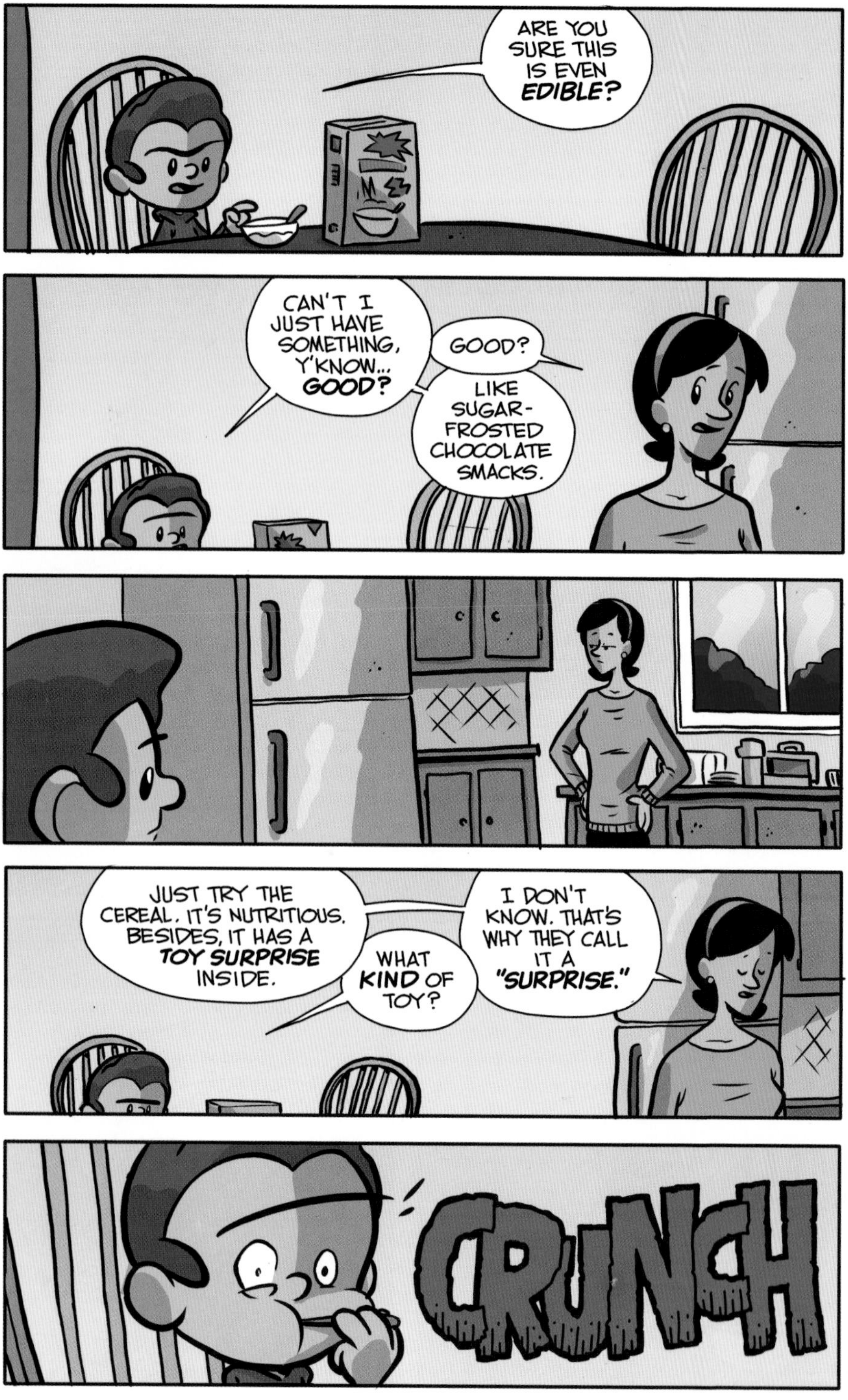
ARE YOU SURE THIS IS EVEN EDIBLE?
CAN'T I JUST HAVE SOMETHING, Y'KNOW... GOOD?
GOOD?
LIKE SUGAR-FROSTED CHOCOLATE SMACKS.
JUST TRY THE CEREAL. IT'S NUTRITIOUS. BESIDES, IT HAS A TOY SURPRISE INSIDE.
WHAT KIND OF TOY?
I DON'T KNOW. THAT'S WHY THEY CALL IT A "SURPRISE."
CRUNCH

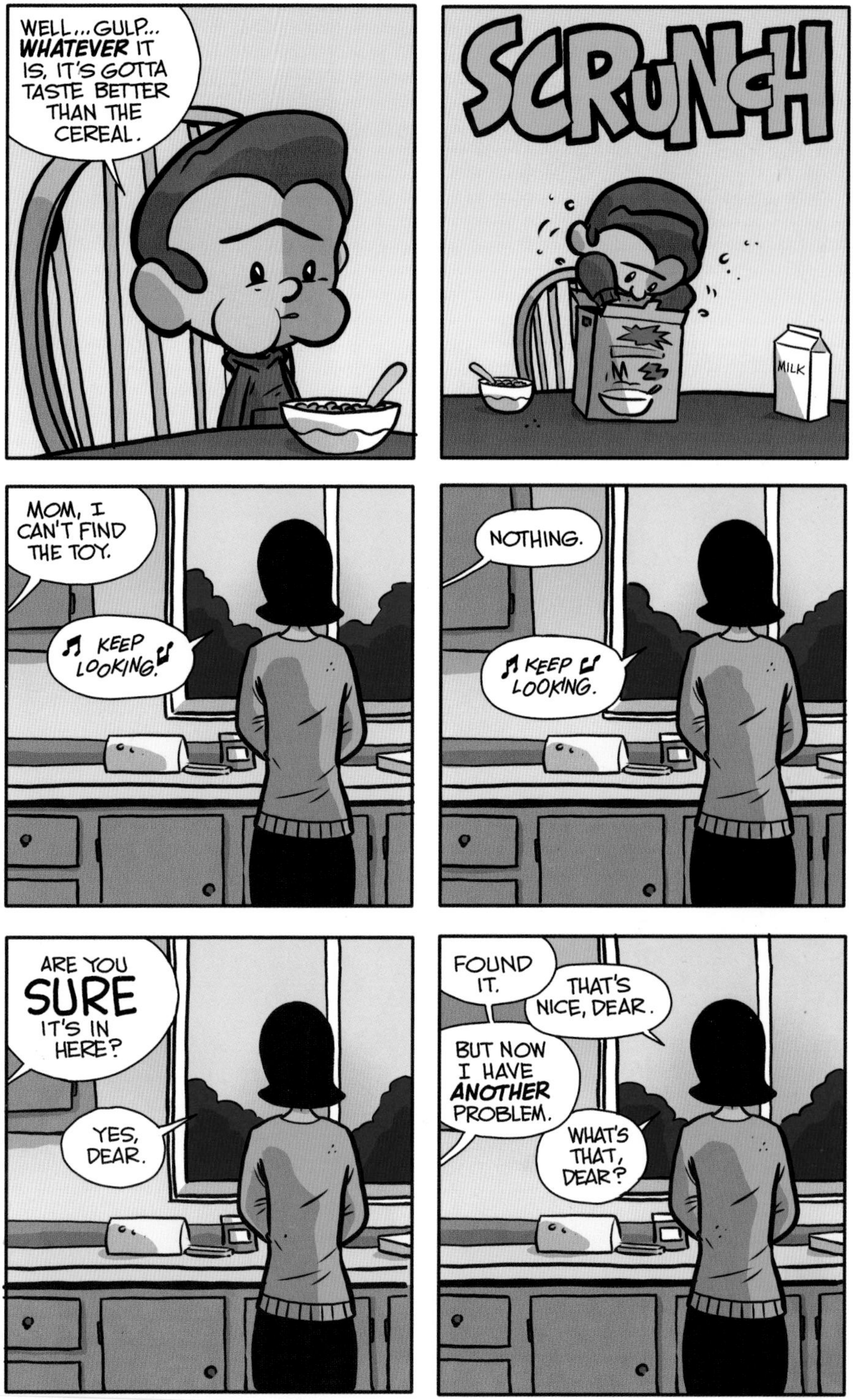
WELL...GULP... **WHATEVER** IT IS, IT'S GOTTA TASTE BETTER THAN THE CEREAL.
SCRUNCH
MILK
MOM, I CAN'T FIND THE TOY.
KEEP LOOKING.
NOTHING.
KEEP LOOKING.
ARE YOU **SURE** IT'S IN HERE?
YES, DEAR.
FOUND IT.
THAT'S NICE, DEAR.
BUT NOW I HAVE **ANOTHER** PROBLEM.
WHAT'S THAT, DEAR?

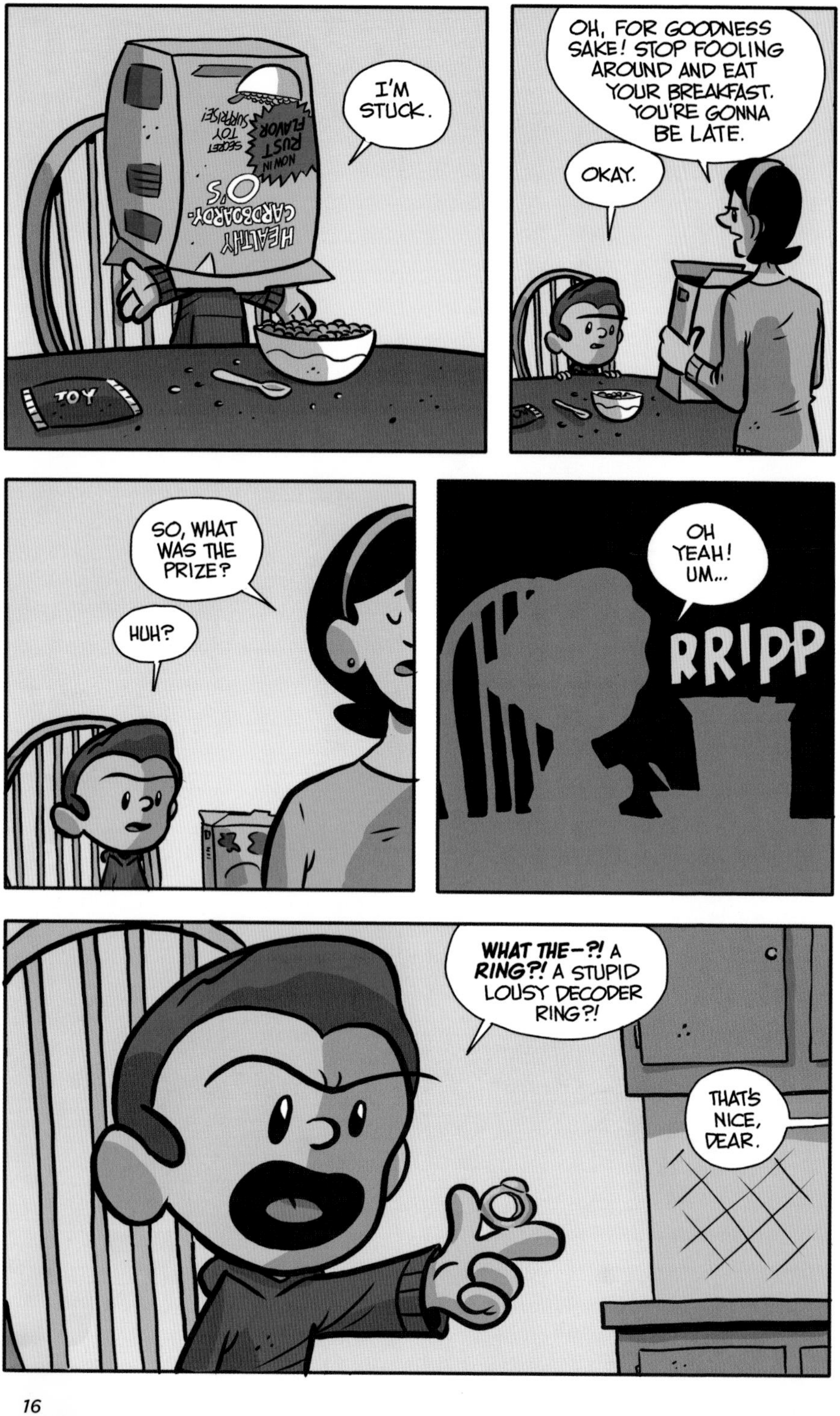
HEALTHY CARDBOARDY-O'S
NOW IN RUST FLAVOR
SECRET TOY SURPRISE!
TOY
I'M STUCK.
OH, FOR GOODNESS SAKE! STOP FOOLING AROUND AND EAT YOUR BREAKFAST. YOU'RE GONNA BE LATE.
OKAY.
SO, WHAT WAS THE PRIZE?
HUH?
OH YEAH! UM...
RRIPP
WHAT THE–?! A RING?! A STUPID LOUSY DECODER RING?!
THAT'S NICE, DEAR.

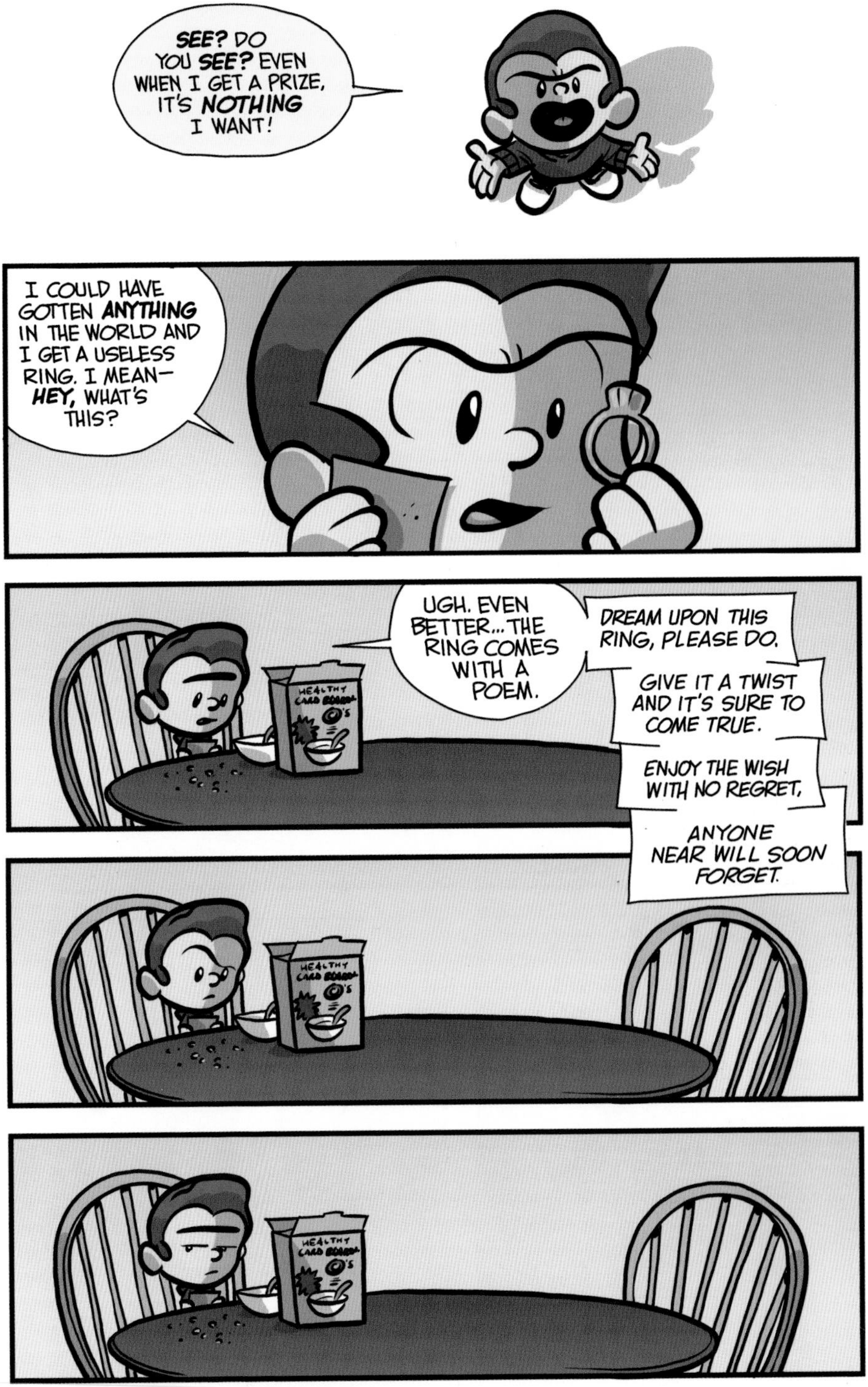

SEE? DO YOU SEE? EVEN WHEN I GET A PRIZE, IT'S NOTHING I WANT!
I COULD HAVE GOTTEN ANYTHING IN THE WORLD AND I GET A USELESS RING. I MEAN— HEY, WHAT'S THIS?
UGH. EVEN BETTER... THE RING COMES WITH A POEM.
DREAM UPON THIS RING, PLEASE DO.
GIVE IT A TWIST AND IT'S SURE TO COME TRUE.
ENJOY THE WISH WITH NO REGRET,
ANYONE NEAR WILL SOON FORGET.

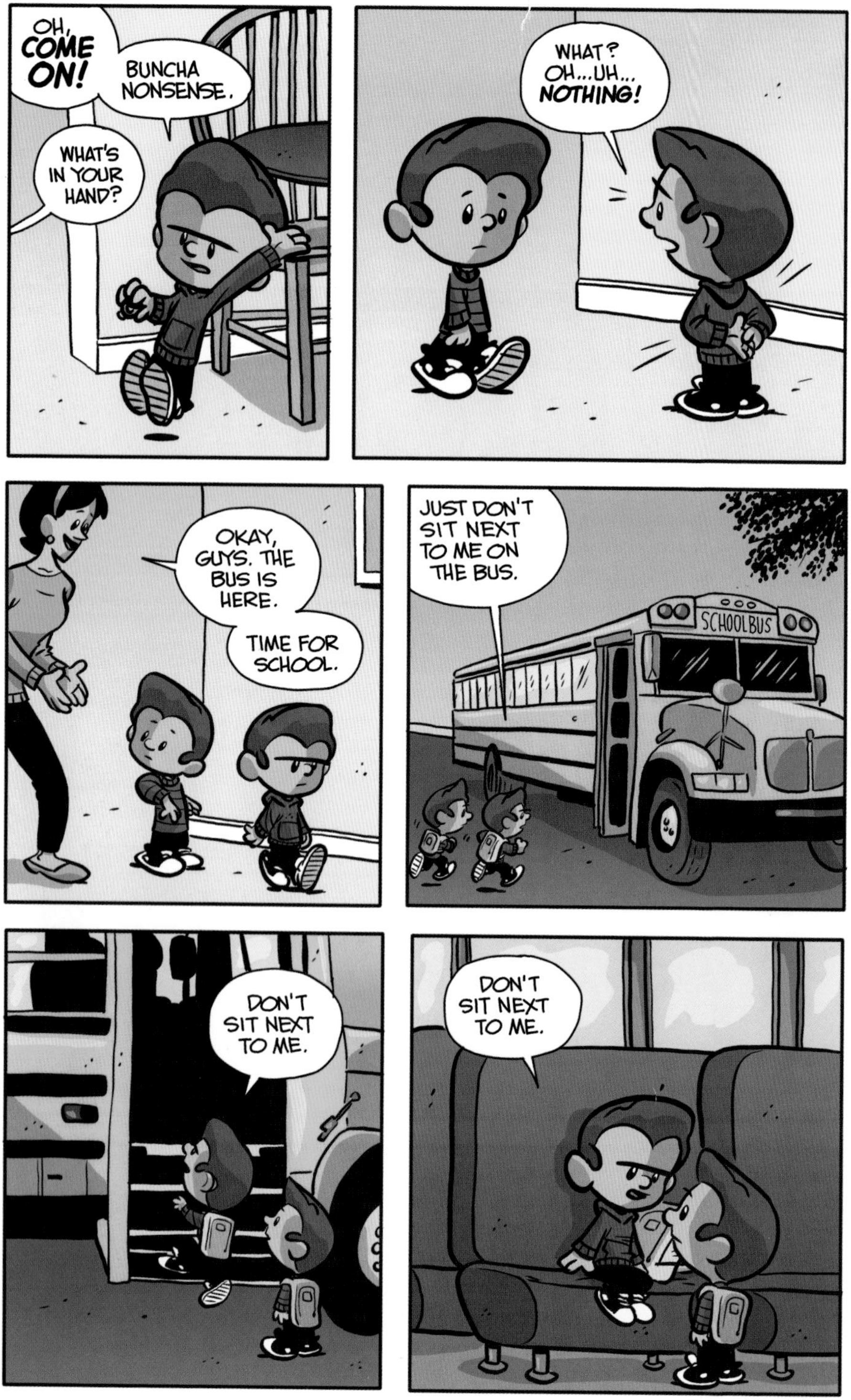
OH, COME ON!
BUNCHA NONSENSE.
WHAT'S IN YOUR HAND?
WHAT? OH...UH... NOTHING!
OKAY, GUYS. THE BUS IS HERE.
TIME FOR SCHOOL.
JUST DON'T SIT NEXT TO ME ON THE BUS.
SCHOOLBUS
DON'T SIT NEXT TO ME.
DON'T SIT NEXT TO ME.

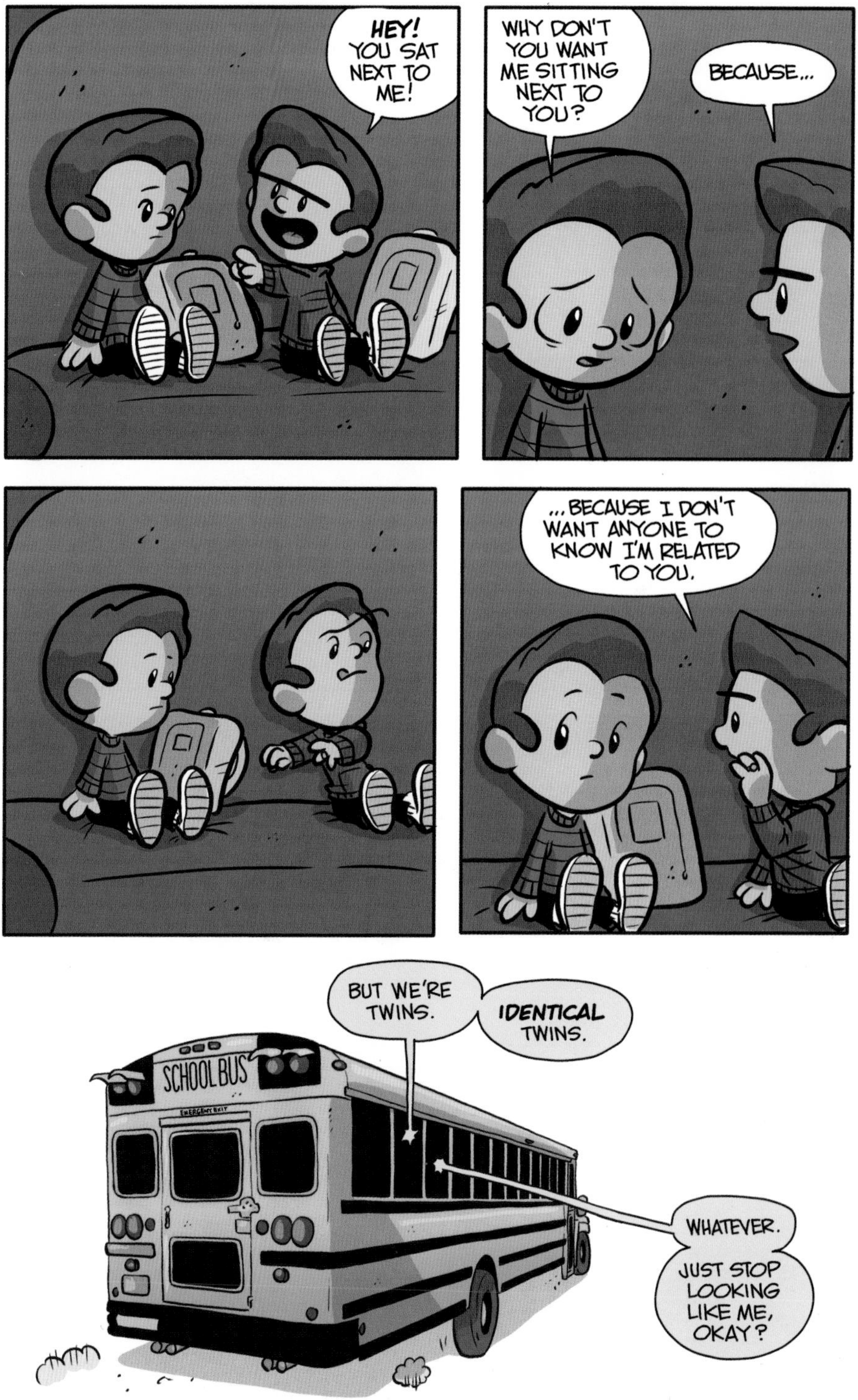
HEY! YOU SAT NEXT TO ME!
WHY DON'T YOU WANT ME SITTING NEXT TO YOU?
BECAUSE...
...BECAUSE I DON'T WANT ANYONE TO KNOW I'M RELATED TO YOU.
BUT WE'RE TWINS.
IDENTICAL TWINS.
SCHOOLBUS
WHATEVER.
JUST STOP LOOKING LIKE ME, OKAY?

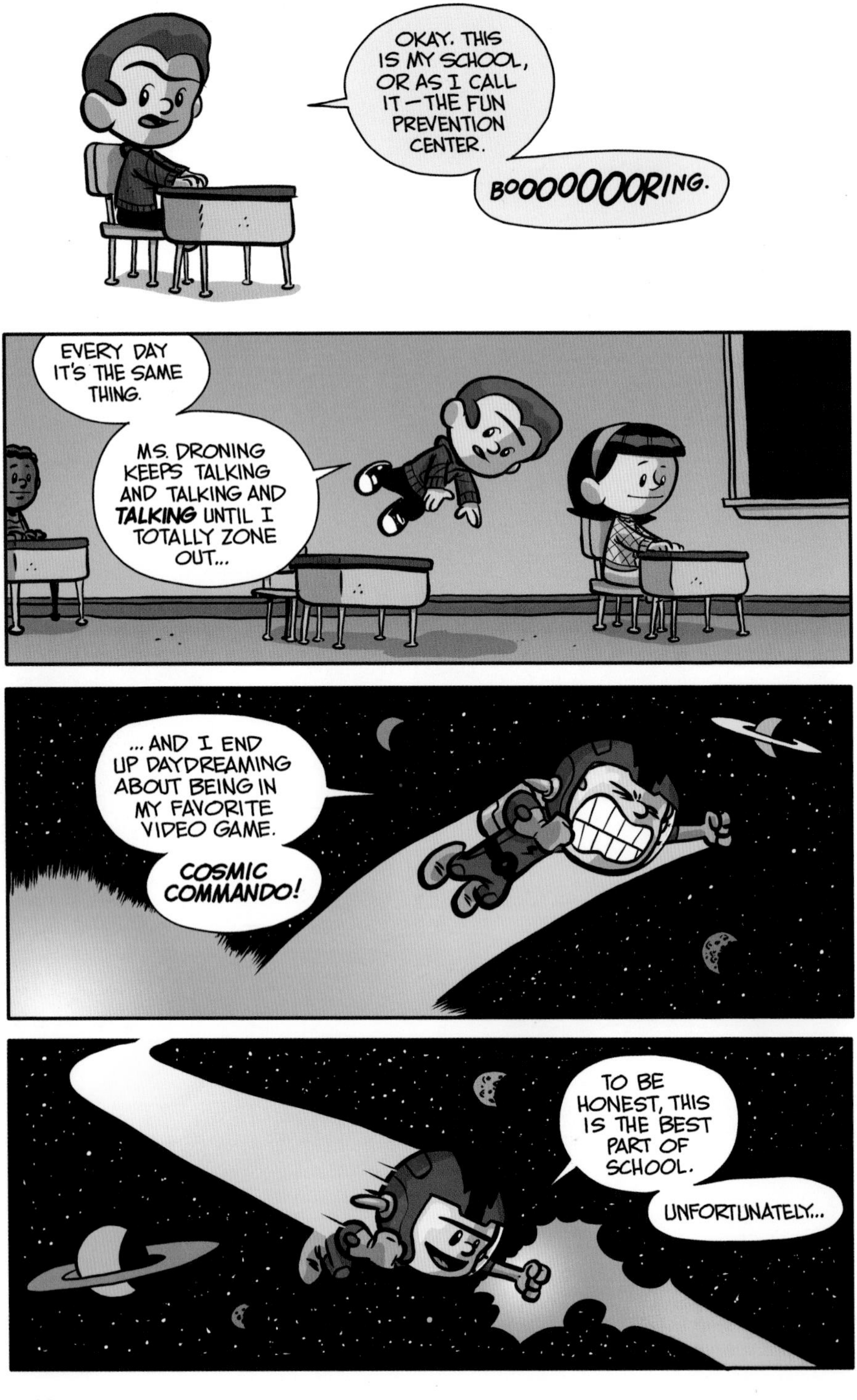
OKAY. THIS IS MY SCHOOL, OR AS I CALL IT—THE FUN PREVENTION CENTER.
BOOOOOOOORING.
EVERY DAY IT'S THE SAME THING.
MS. DRONING KEEPS TALKING AND TALKING AND **TALKING** UNTIL I TOTALLY ZONE OUT...
...AND I END UP DAYDREAMING ABOUT BEING IN MY FAVORITE VIDEO GAME.
COSMIC COMMANDO!
TO BE HONEST, THIS IS THE BEST PART OF SCHOOL.
UNFORTUNATELY...

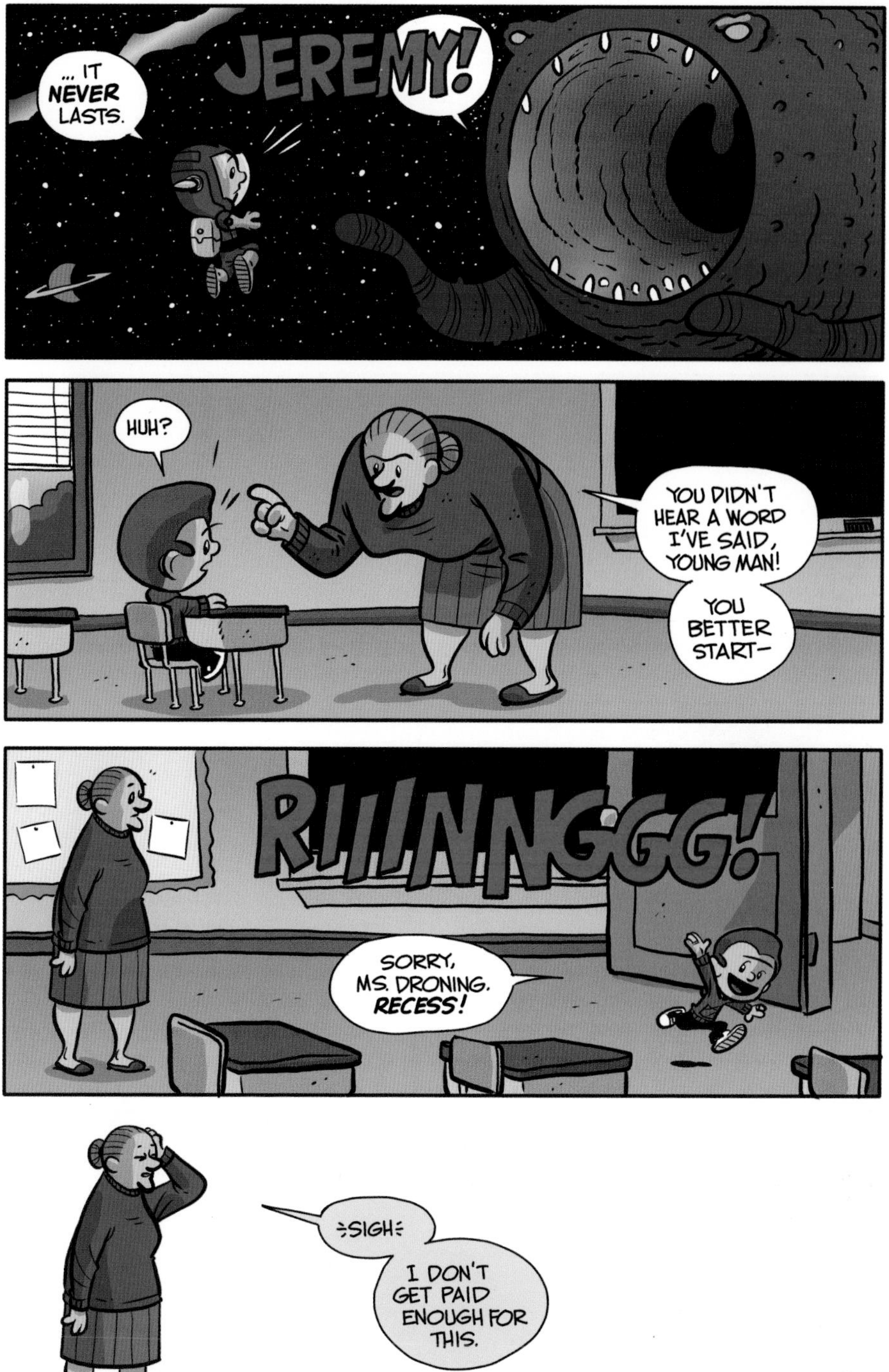
... IT **NEVER** LASTS.
JEREMY!
HUH?
YOU DIDN'T HEAR A WORD I'VE SAID, YOUNG MAN!
YOU BETTER START–
RIIINNGGG!
SORRY, MS. DRONING. ***RECESS!***
SIGH
I DON'T GET PAID ENOUGH FOR THIS.

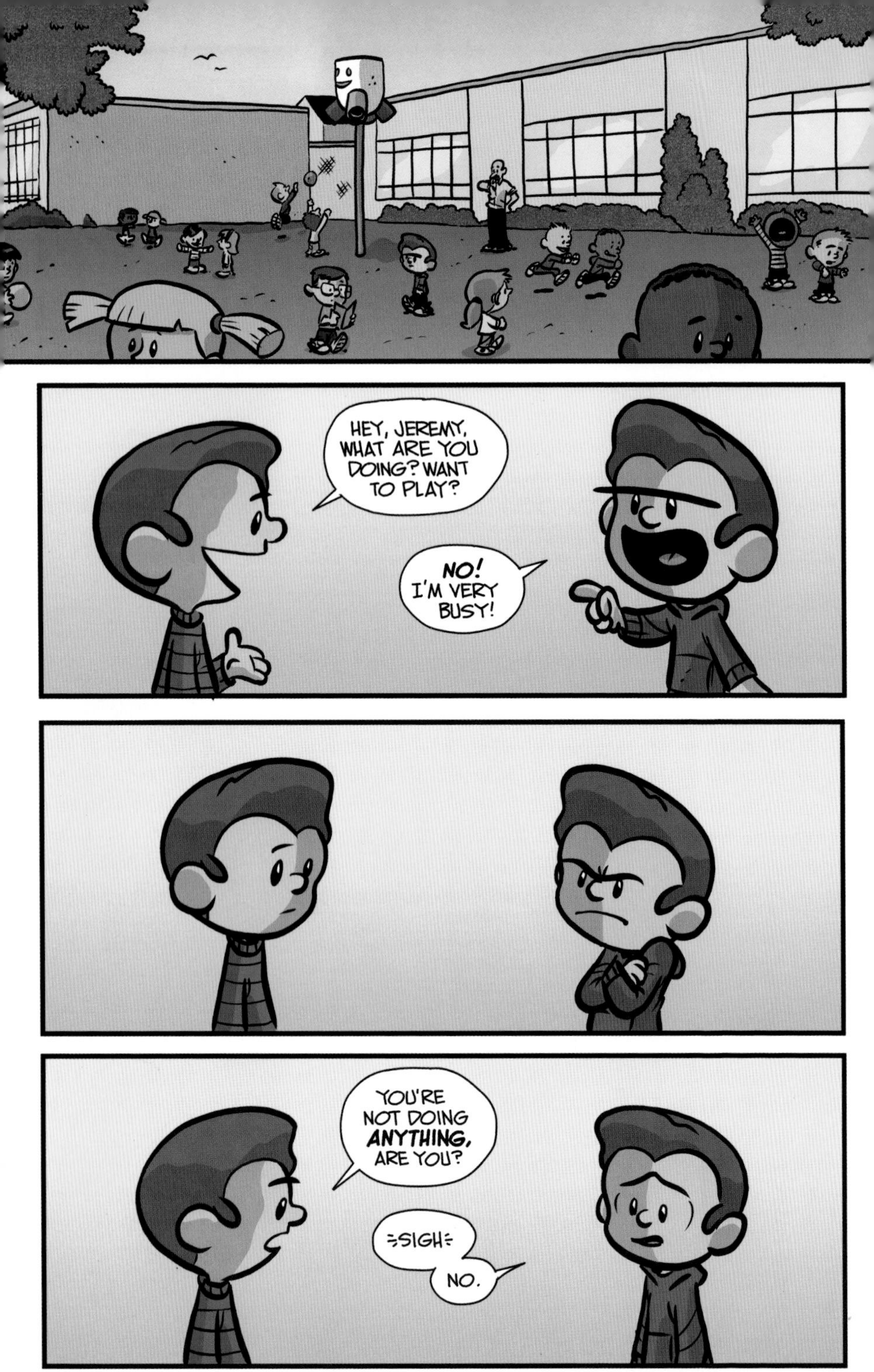
HEY, JEREMY, WHAT ARE YOU DOING? WANT TO PLAY?
NO! I'M VERY BUSY!
YOU'RE NOT DOING ANYTHING, ARE YOU?
=SIGH=
NO.

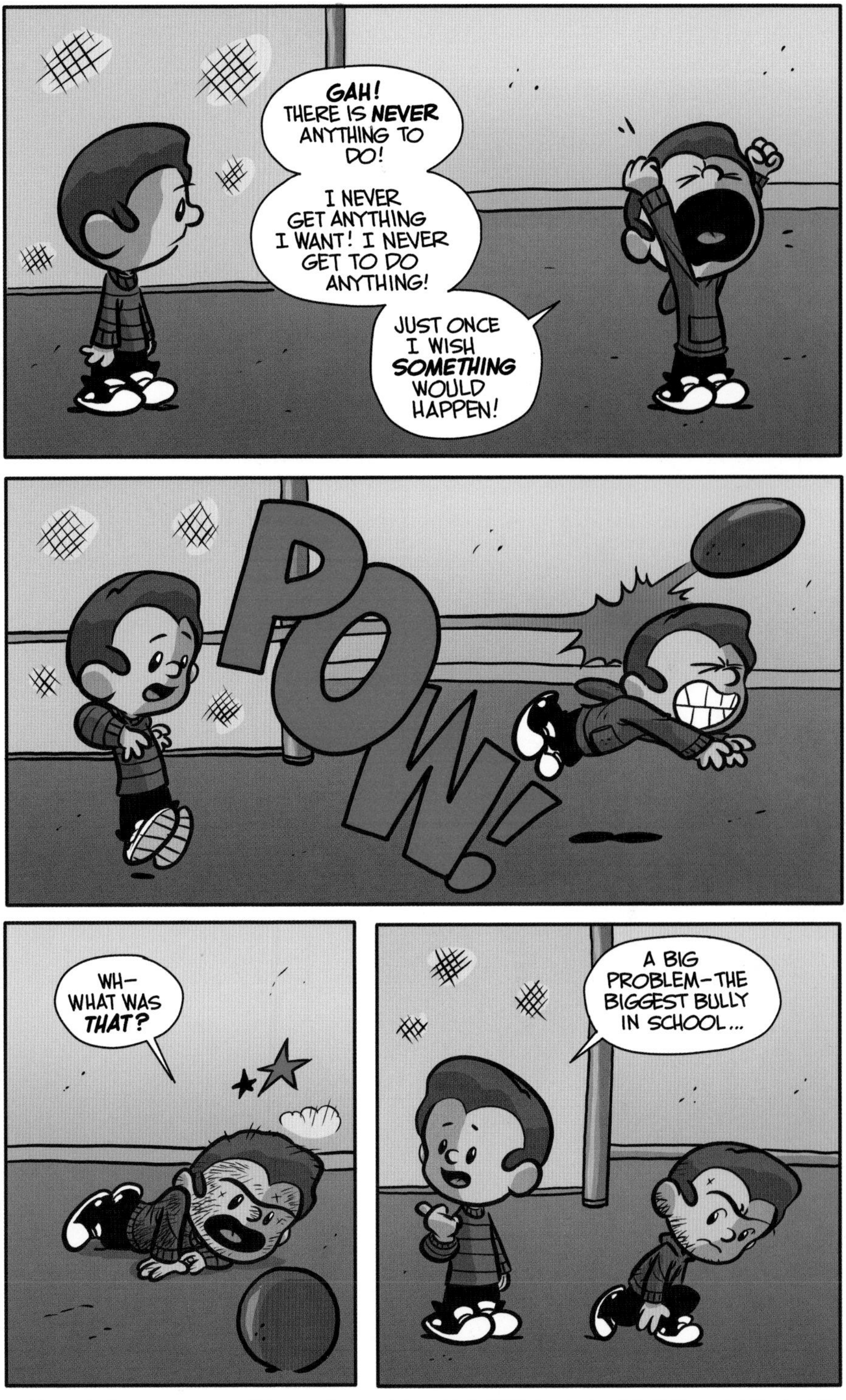
GAH! THERE IS NEVER ANYTHING TO DO!
I NEVER GET ANYTHING I WANT! I NEVER GET TO DO ANYTHING!
JUST ONCE I WISH SOMETHING WOULD HAPPEN!
POW!
WH- WHAT WAS THAT?
A BIG PROBLEM—THE BIGGEST BULLY IN SCHOOL...

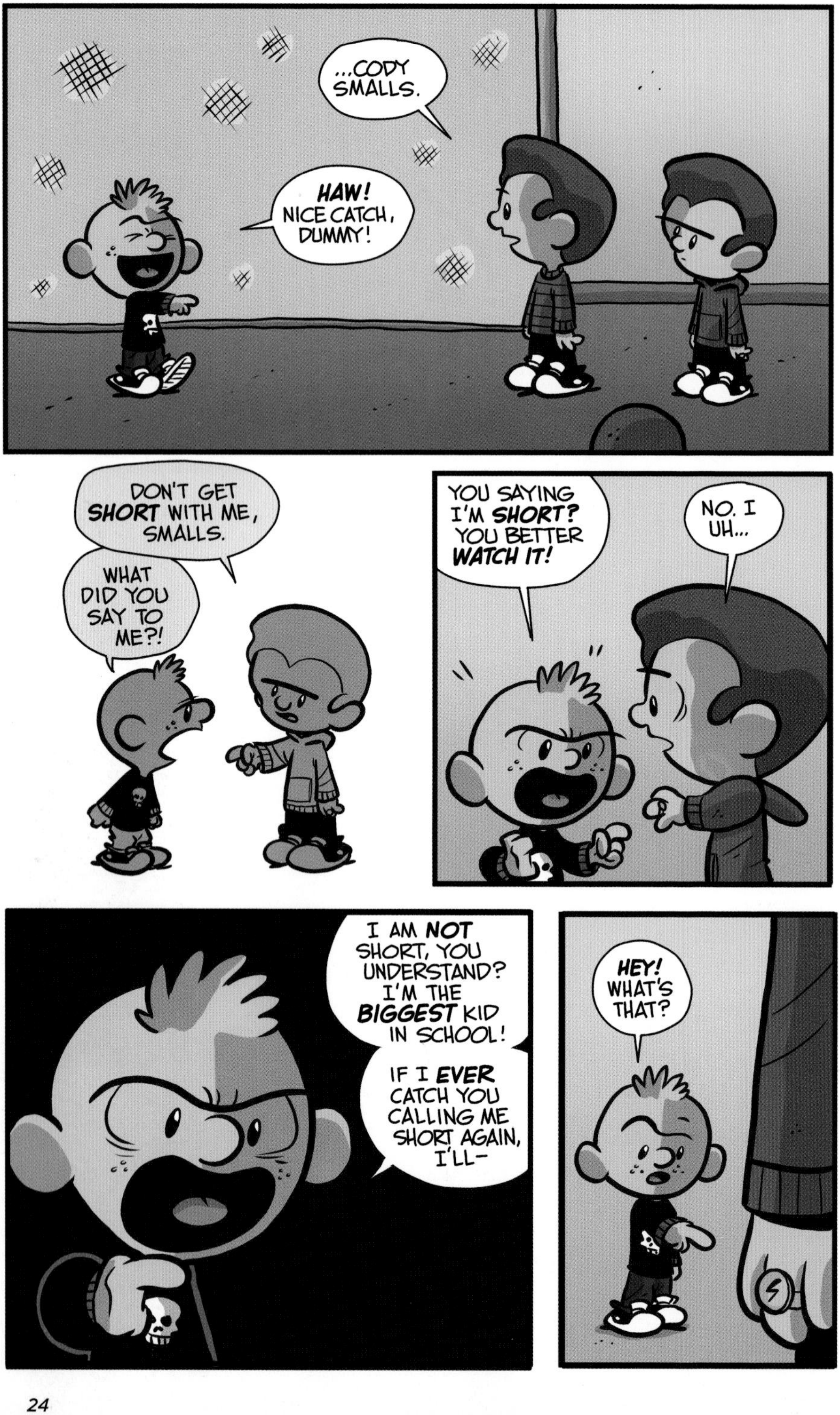
...CODY SMALLS.
HAW! NICE CATCH, DUMMY!
DON'T GET SHORT WITH ME, SMALLS.
WHAT DID YOU SAY TO ME?!
YOU SAYING I'M SHORT? YOU BETTER WATCH IT!
NO. I UH...
I AM NOT SHORT, YOU UNDERSTAND? I'M THE BIGGEST KID IN SCHOOL!
IF I EVER CATCH YOU CALLING ME SHORT AGAIN, I'LL–
HEY! WHAT'S THAT?

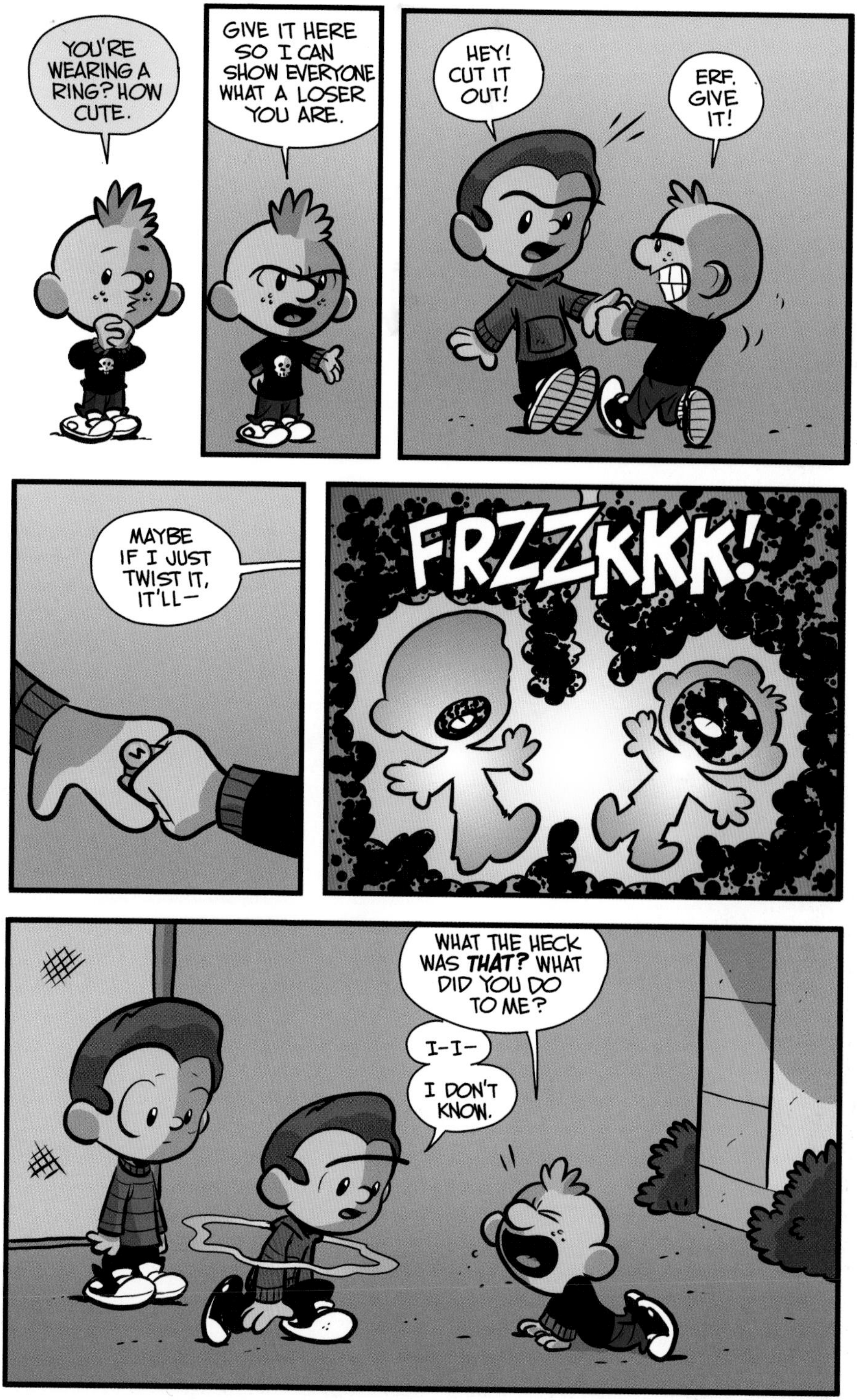

YOU'RE WEARING A RING? HOW CUTE.
GIVE IT HERE SO I CAN SHOW EVERYONE WHAT A LOSER YOU ARE.
HEY! CUT IT OUT!
ERF. GIVE IT!
MAYBE IF I JUST TWIST IT, IT'LL—
FRZZKKK!
WHAT THE HECK WAS THAT? WHAT DID YOU DO TO ME?
I-I-
I DON'T KNOW.

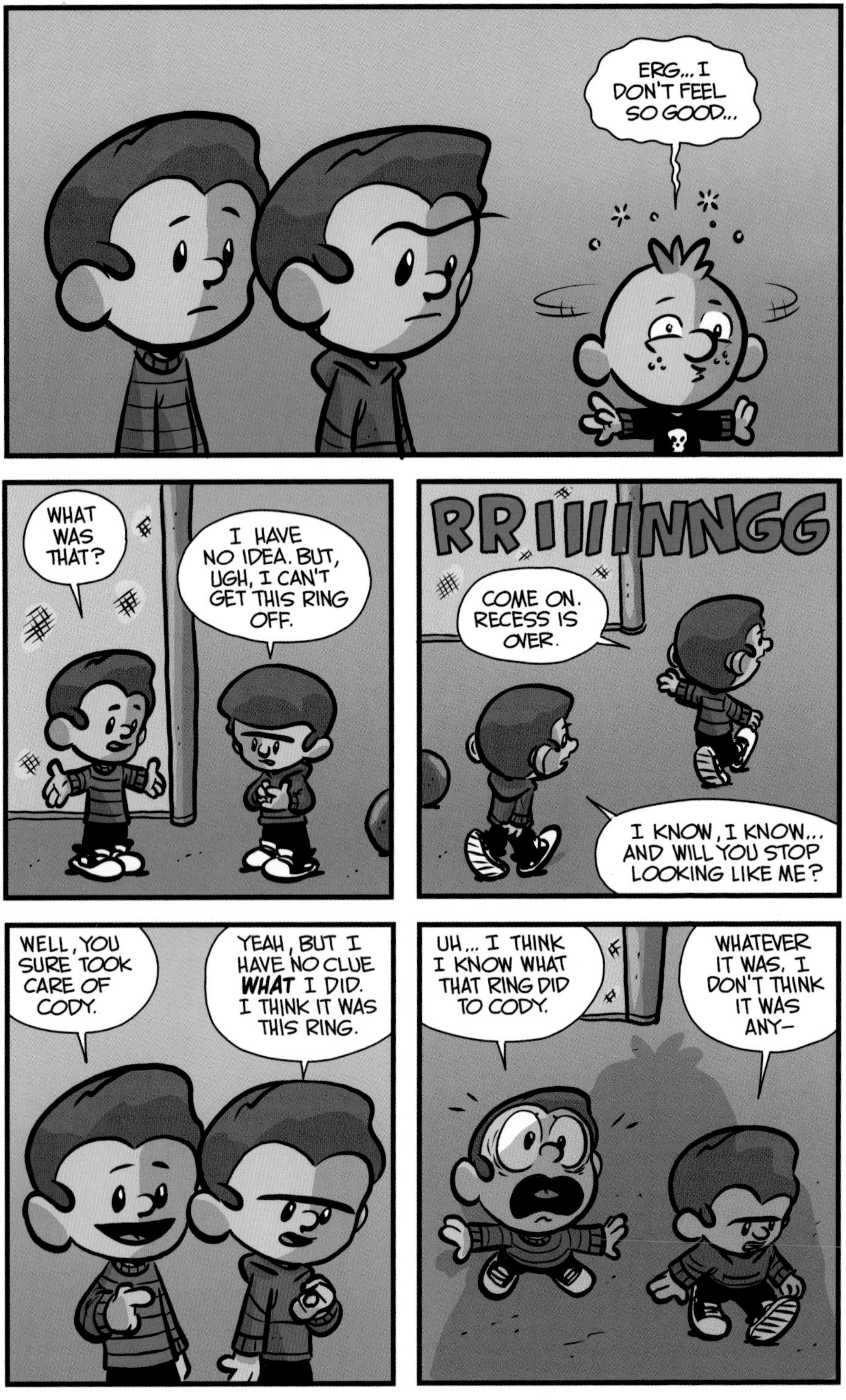
ERG... I DON'T FEEL SO GOOD...
WHAT WAS THAT?
I HAVE NO IDEA. BUT, UGH, I CAN'T GET THIS RING OFF.
RRIIIINNGG
COME ON. RECESS IS OVER.
I KNOW, I KNOW... AND WILL YOU STOP LOOKING LIKE ME?
WELL, YOU SURE TOOK CARE OF CODY.
YEAH, BUT I HAVE NO CLUE **WHAT** I DID. I THINK IT WAS THIS RING.
UH... I THINK I KNOW WHAT THAT RING DID TO CODY.
WHATEVER IT WAS, I DON'T THINK IT WAS ANY—

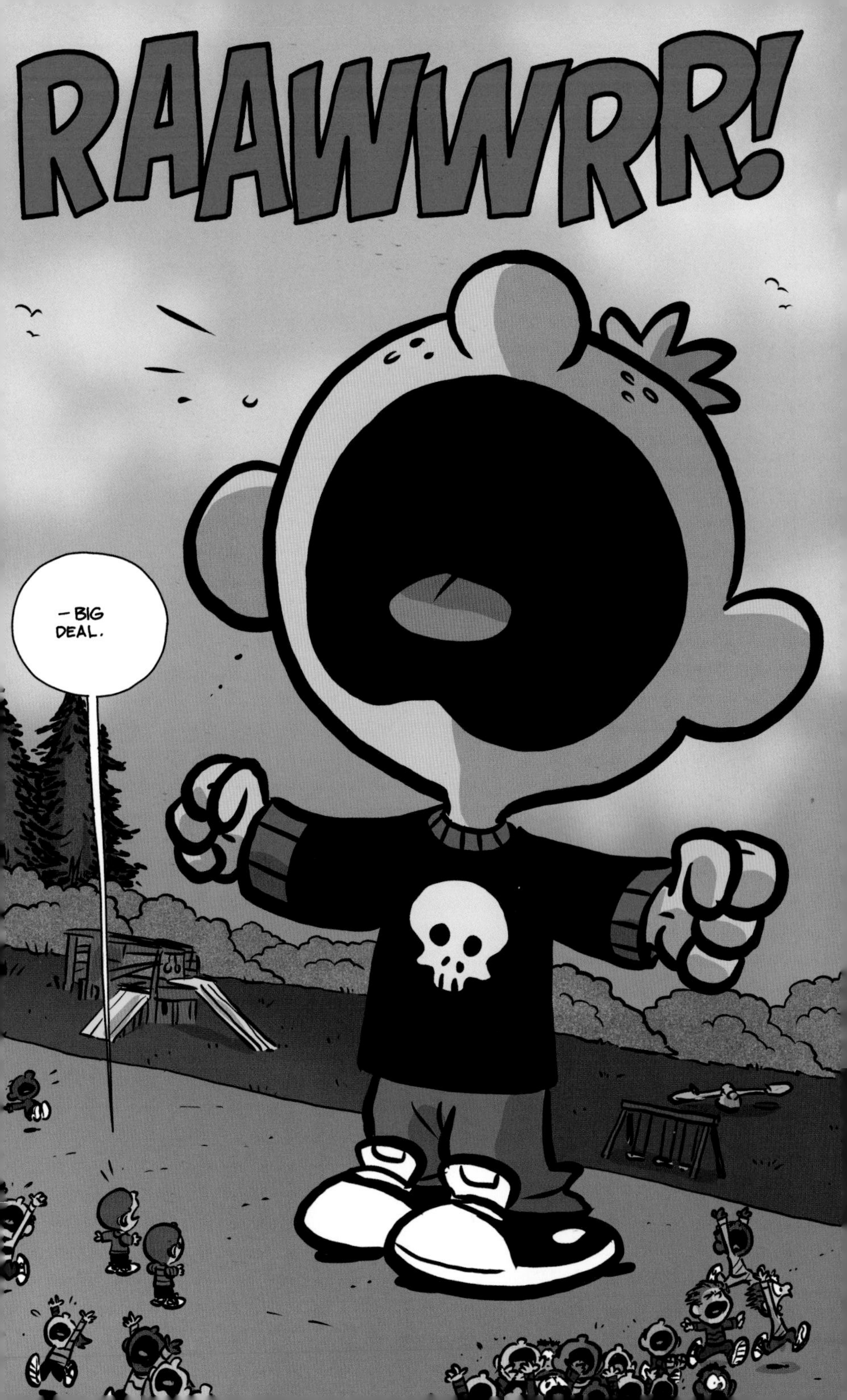
RAAWWRR!
—BIG DEAL.

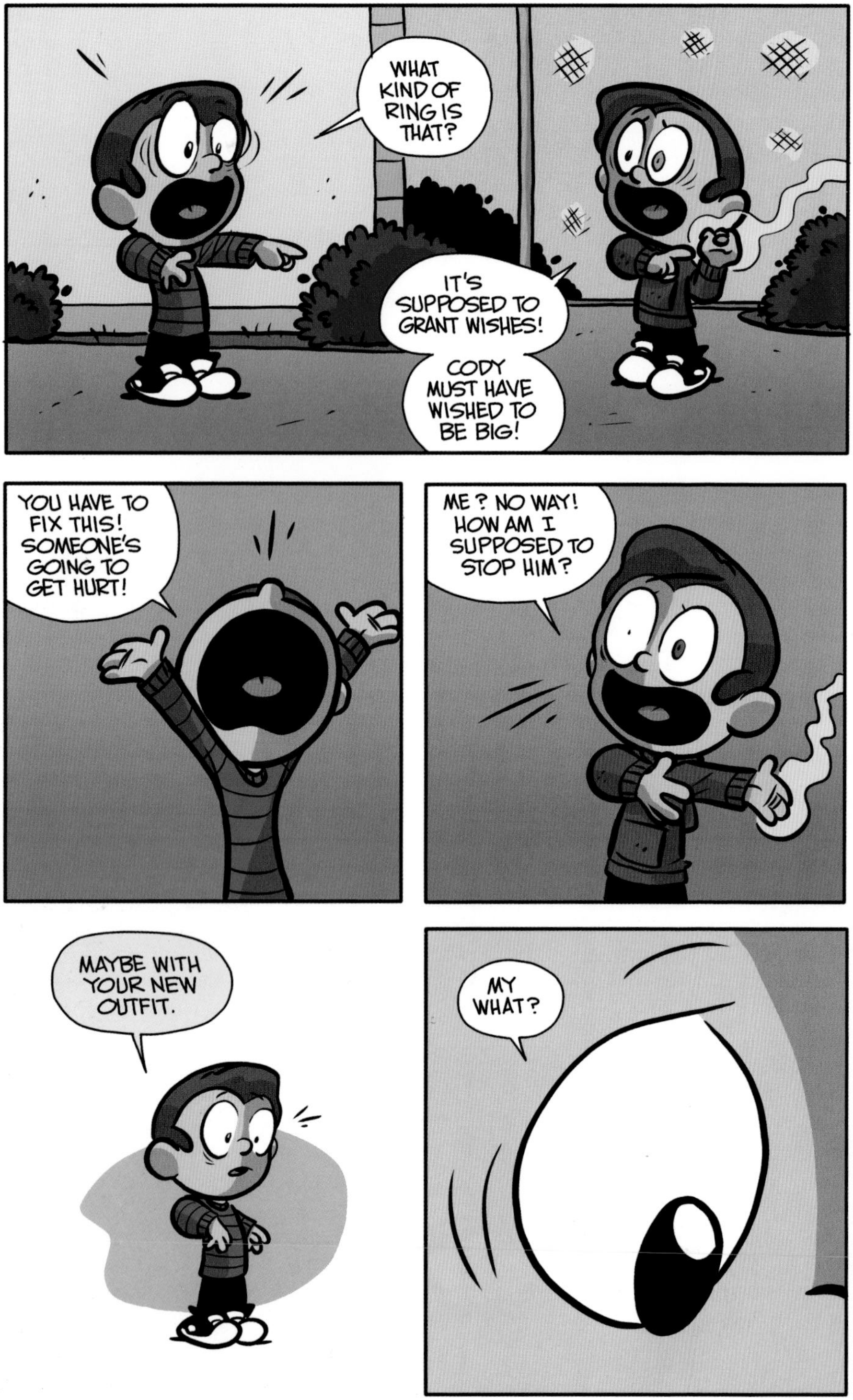
WHAT KIND OF RING IS THAT?
IT'S SUPPOSED TO GRANT WISHES!
CODY MUST HAVE WISHED TO BE BIG!
YOU HAVE TO FIX THIS! SOMEONE'S GOING TO GET HURT!
ME? NO WAY! HOW AM I SUPPOSED TO STOP HIM?
MAYBE WITH YOUR NEW OUTFIT.
MY WHAT?

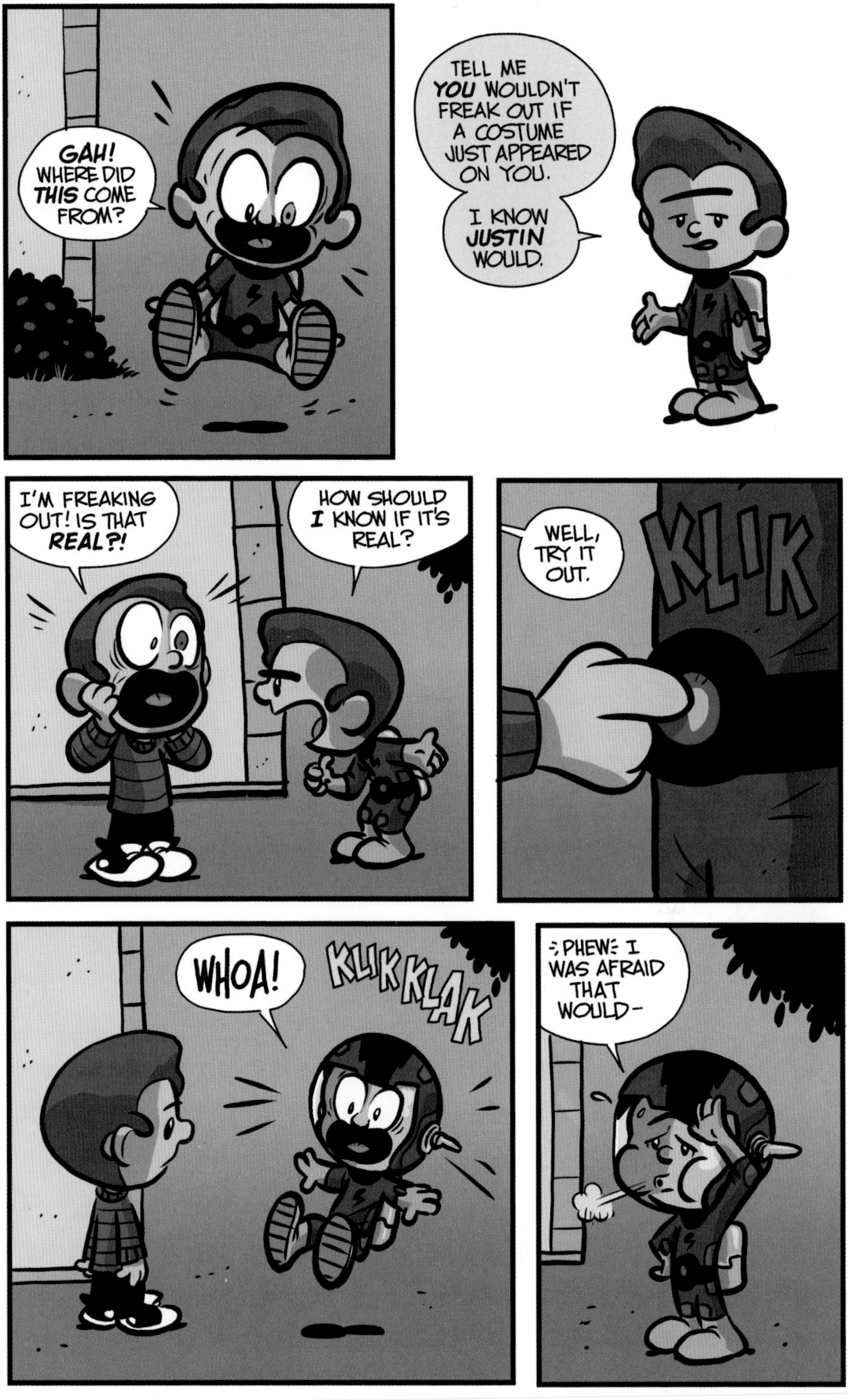
GAH! WHERE DID THIS COME FROM?
TELL ME YOU WOULDN'T FREAK OUT IF A COSTUME JUST APPEARED ON YOU.
I KNOW JUSTIN WOULD.
I'M FREAKING OUT! IS THAT REAL?!
HOW SHOULD I KNOW IF IT'S REAL?
WELL, TRY IT OUT.
KLIK
WHOA!
KLIK KLAK
PHEW! I WAS AFRAID THAT WOULD-

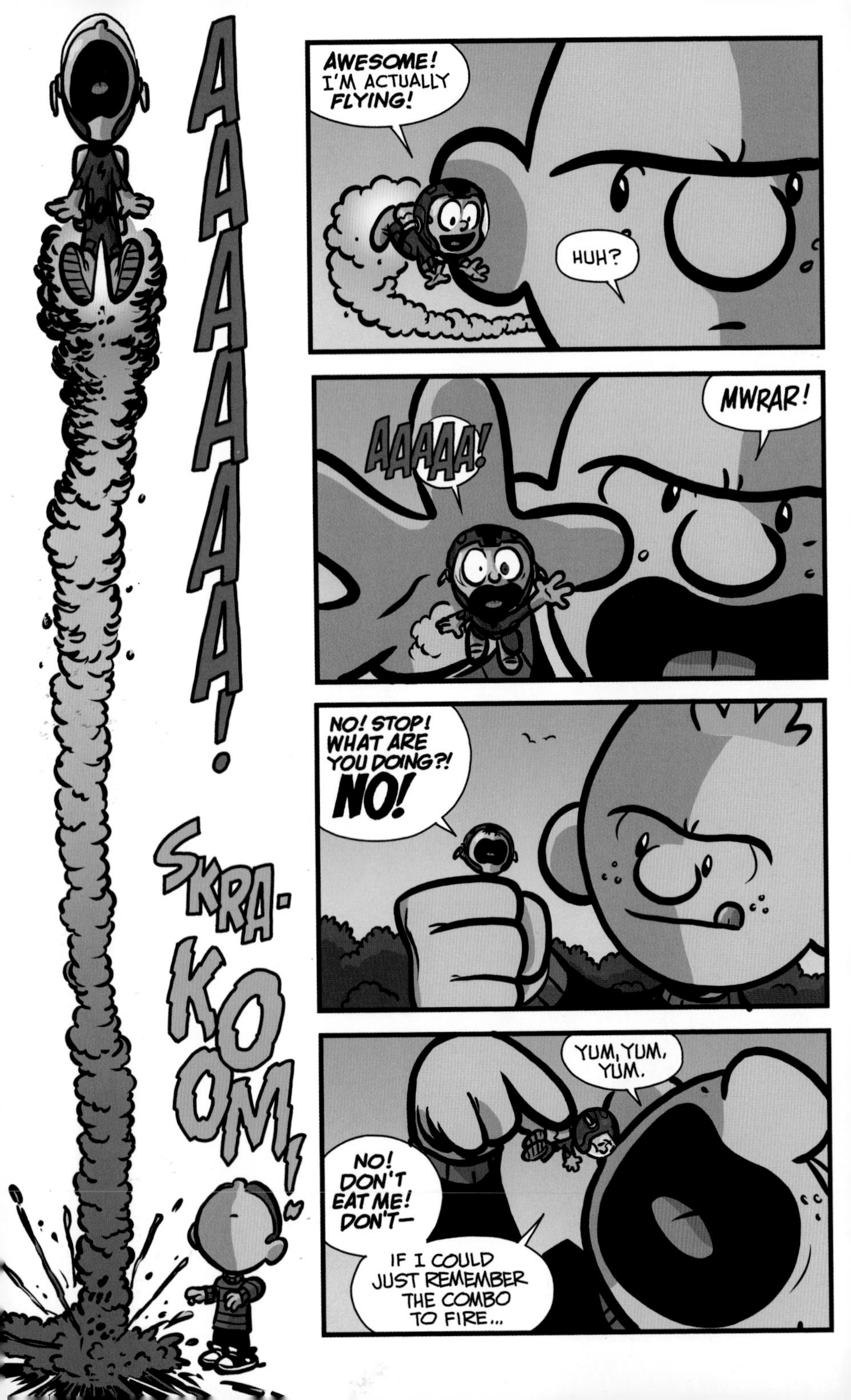
AAAAAAAA!
SKRA-KOOM!
AWESOME! I'M ACTUALLY FLYING!
HUH?
MWRAR!
AAAAA!
NO! STOP! WHAT ARE YOU DOING?! NO!
YUM, YUM, YUM.
NO! DON'T EAT ME! DON'T—
IF I COULD JUST REMEMBER THE COMBO TO FIRE...

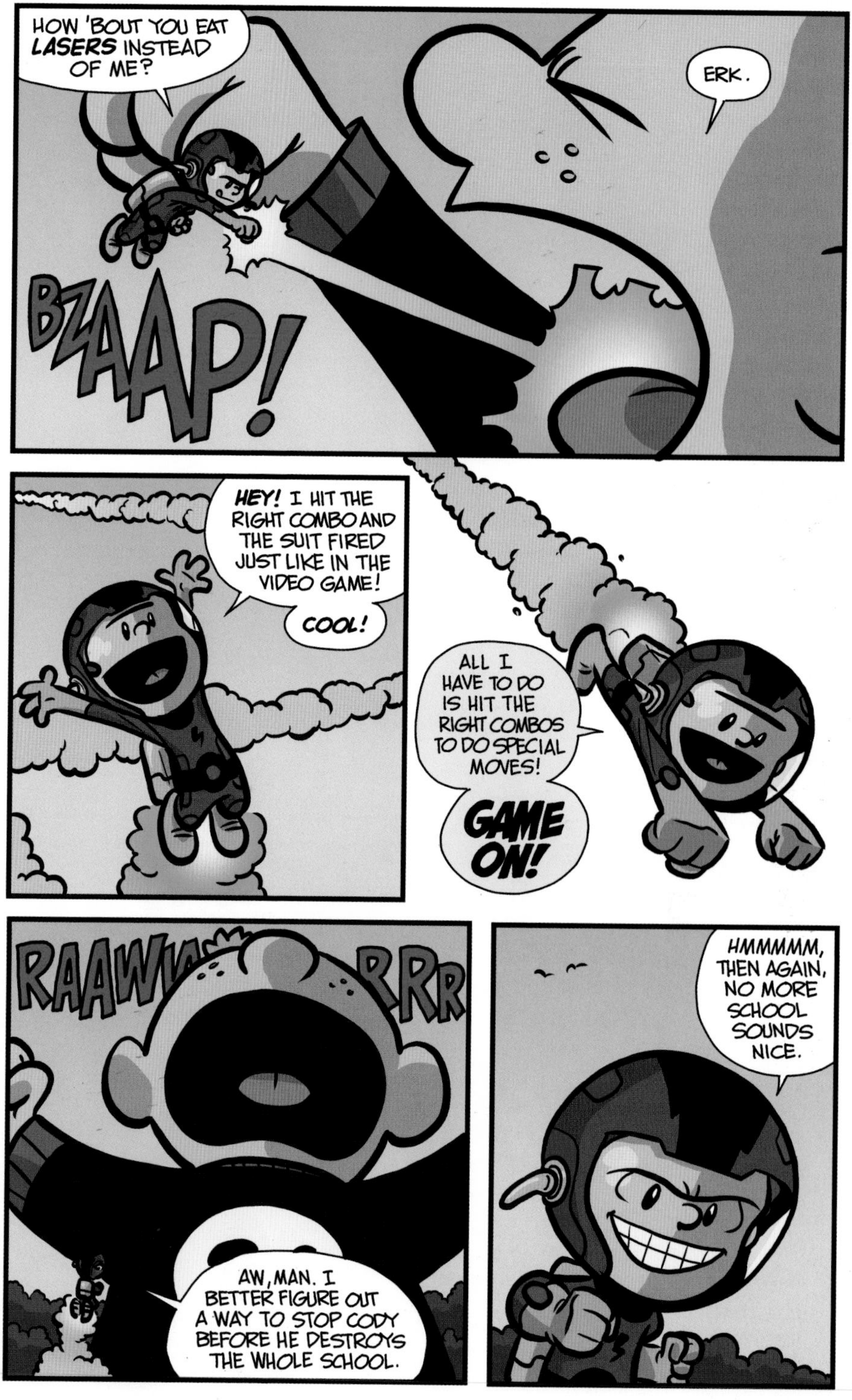
HOW 'BOUT YOU EAT LASERS INSTEAD OF ME?
ERK.
BZAAP!
HEY! I HIT THE RIGHT COMBO AND THE SUIT FIRED JUST LIKE IN THE VIDEO GAME!
COOL!
ALL I HAVE TO DO IS HIT THE RIGHT COMBOS TO DO SPECIAL MOVES!
GAME ON!
AW, MAN. I BETTER FIGURE OUT A WAY TO STOP CODY BEFORE HE DESTROYS THE WHOLE SCHOOL.
HMMMMM, THEN AGAIN, NO MORE SCHOOL SOUNDS NICE.

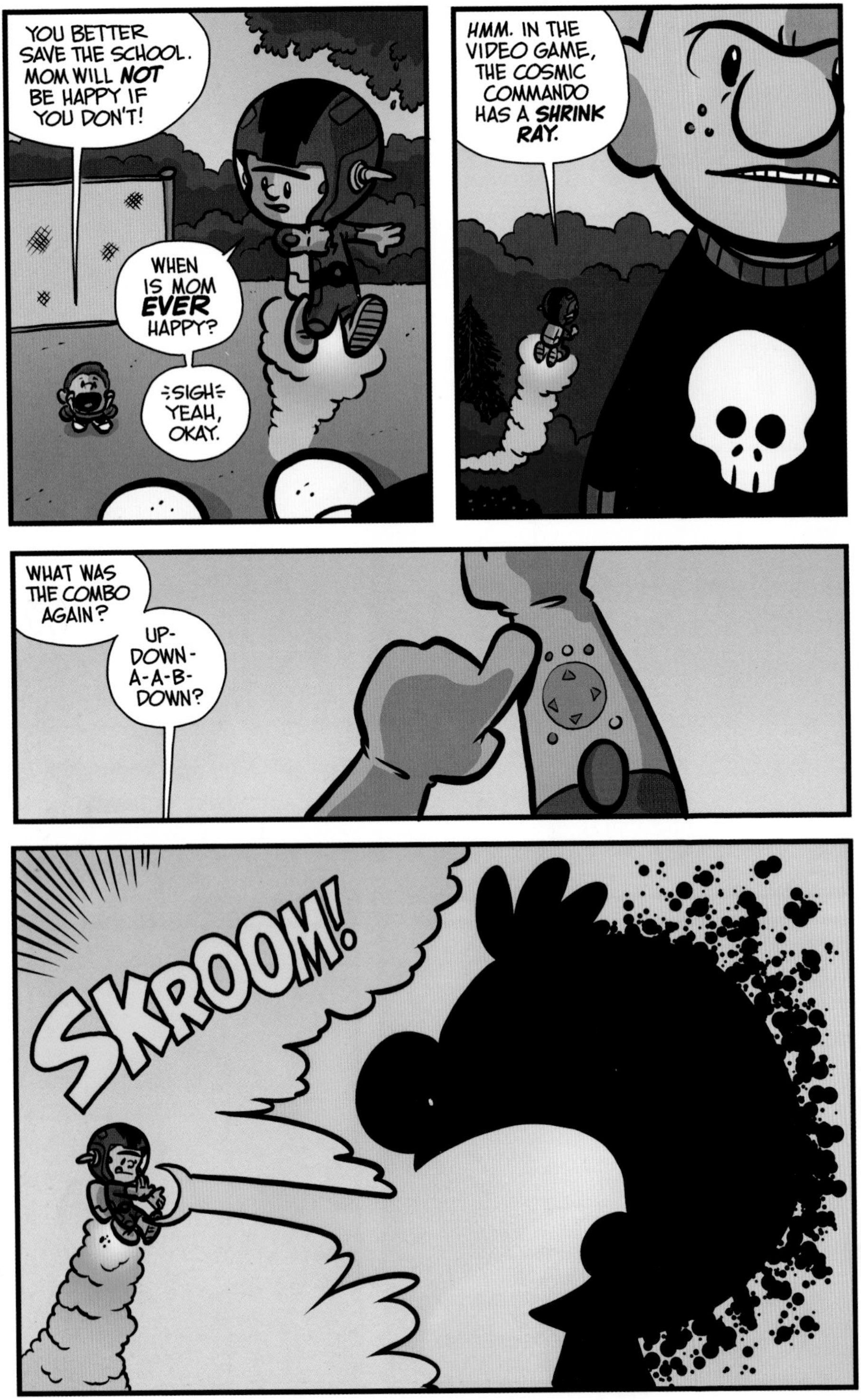
YOU BETTER SAVE THE SCHOOL. MOM WILL **NOT** BE HAPPY IF YOU DON'T!
WHEN IS MOM **EVER** HAPPY?
=SIGH= YEAH, OKAY.
HMM. IN THE VIDEO GAME, THE COSMIC COMMANDO HAS A **SHRINK RAY**.
WHAT WAS THE COMBO AGAIN?
UP-DOWN-A-A-B-DOWN?
SKROOM!

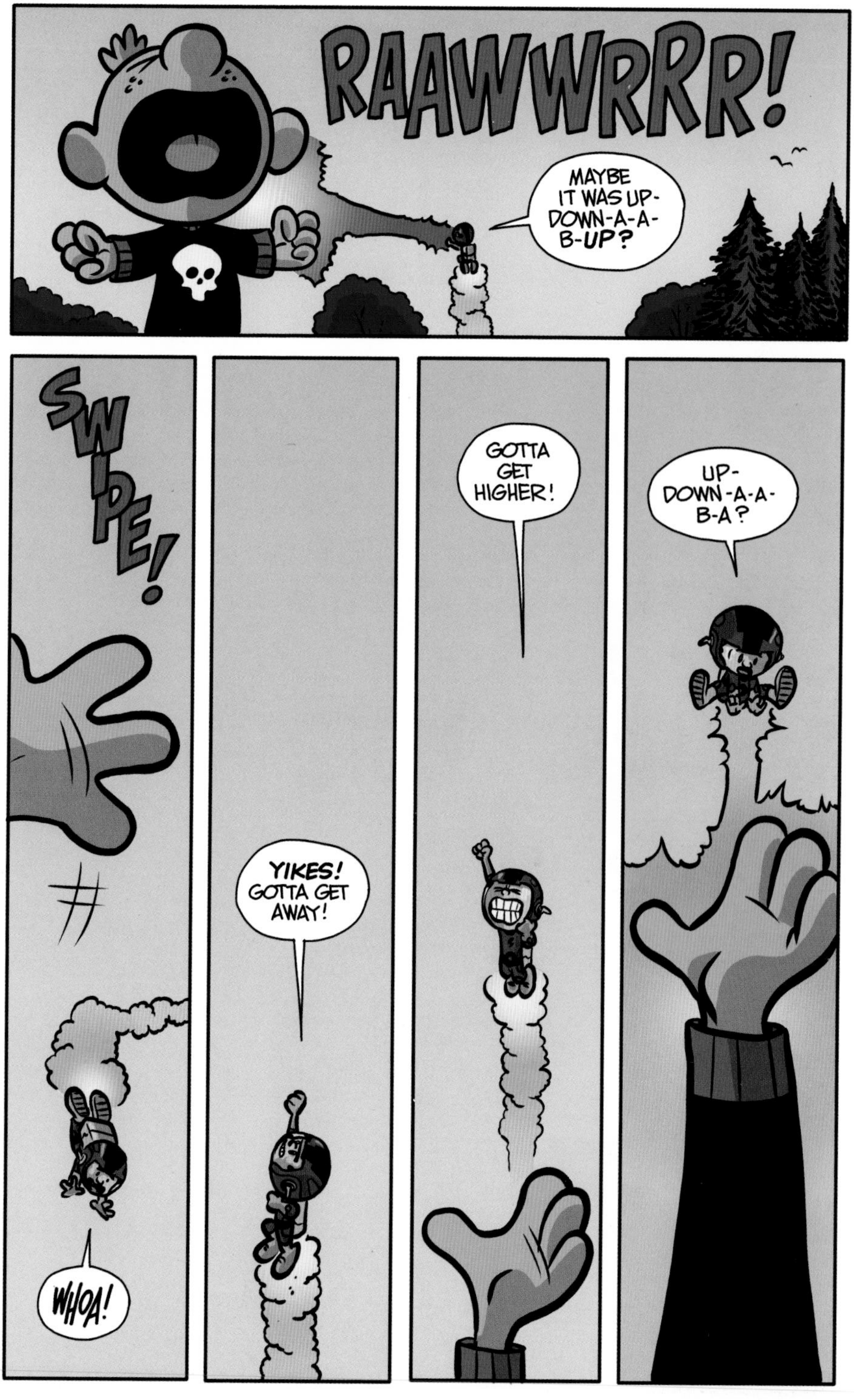
RAAWWRRR!
MAYBE IT WAS UP-DOWN-A-A-B-UP?
SWIPE!
WHOA!
YIKES! GOTTA GET AWAY!
GOTTA GET HIGHER!
UP-DOWN-A-A-B-A?

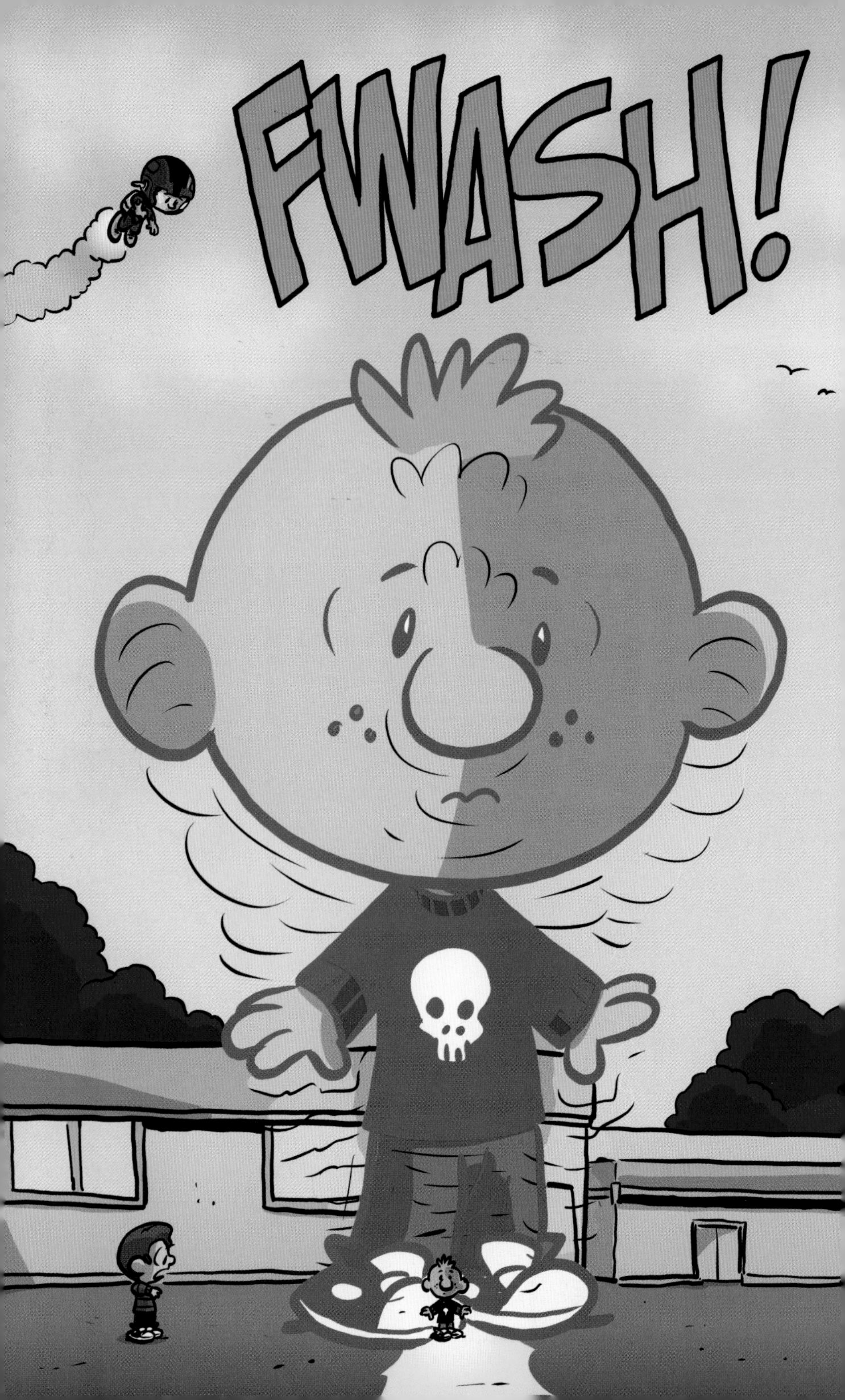
FWASH!

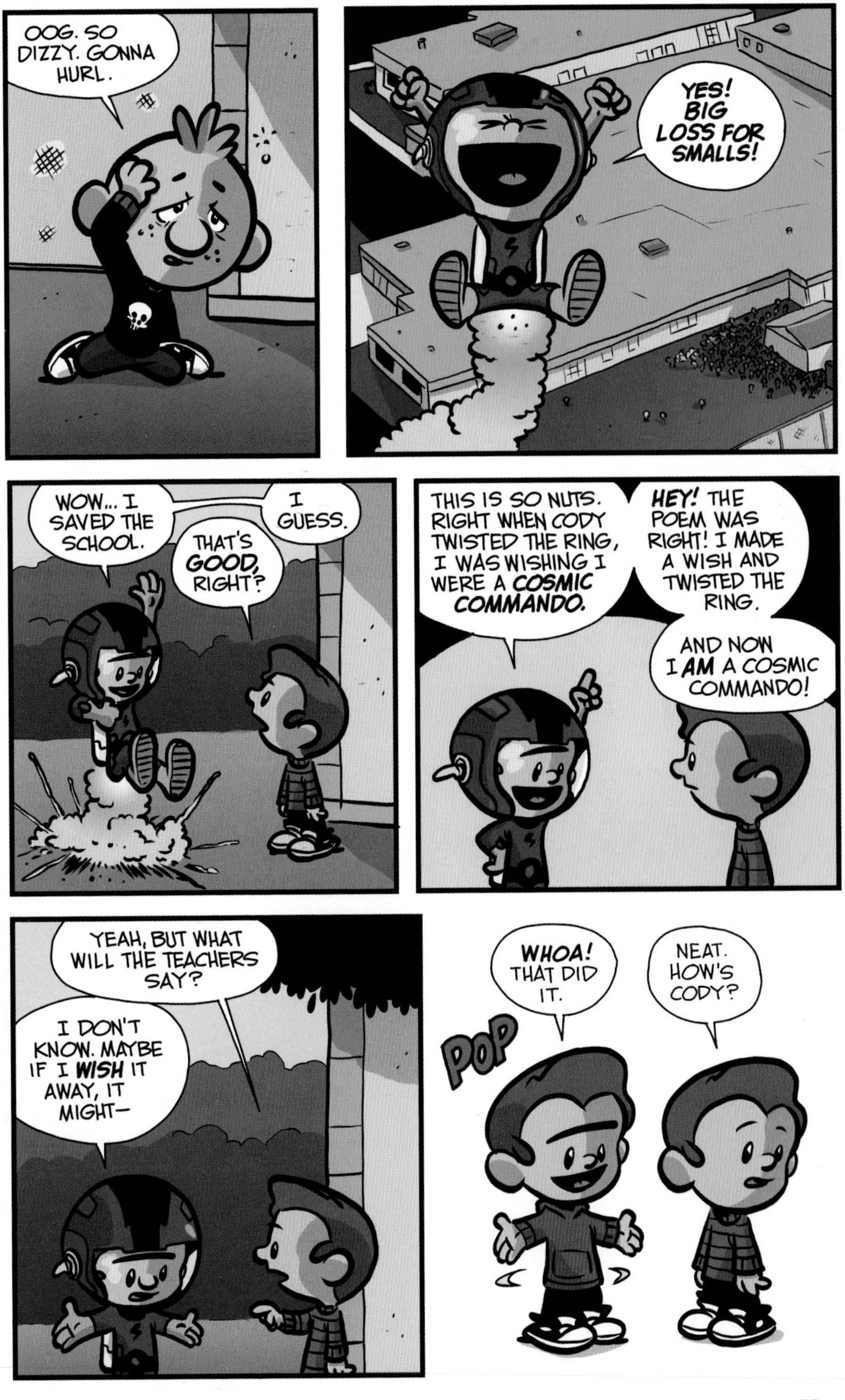
OOG. SO DIZZY. GONNA HURL.
YES! BIG LOSS FOR SMALLS!
WOW... I SAVED THE SCHOOL.
I GUESS.
THAT'S GOOD, RIGHT?
THIS IS SO NUTS. RIGHT WHEN CODY TWISTED THE RING, I WAS WISHING I WERE A COSMIC COMMANDO.
HEY! THE POEM WAS RIGHT! I MADE A WISH AND TWISTED THE RING.
AND NOW I AM A COSMIC COMMANDO!
YEAH, BUT WHAT WILL THE TEACHERS SAY?
I DON'T KNOW. MAYBE IF I WISH IT AWAY, IT MIGHT—
POP
WHOA! THAT DID IT.
NEAT. HOW'S CODY?

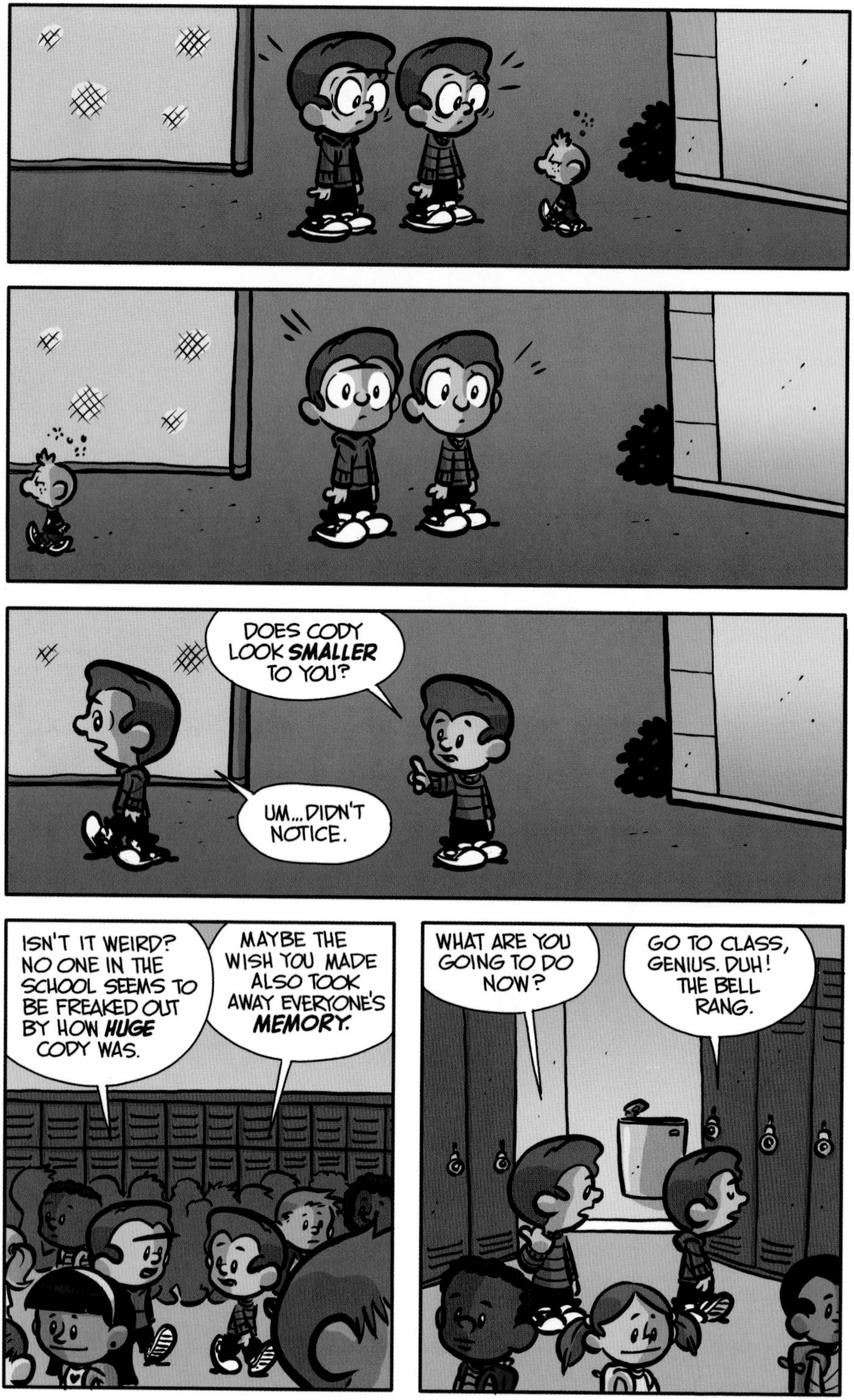
DOES CODY LOOK SMALLER TO YOU?
UM...DIDN'T NOTICE.
ISN'T IT WEIRD? NO ONE IN THE SCHOOL SEEMS TO BE FREAKED OUT BY HOW HUGE CODY WAS.
MAYBE THE WISH YOU MADE ALSO TOOK AWAY EVERYONE'S MEMORY.
WHAT ARE YOU GOING TO DO NOW?
GO TO CLASS, GENIUS. DUH! THE BELL RANG.

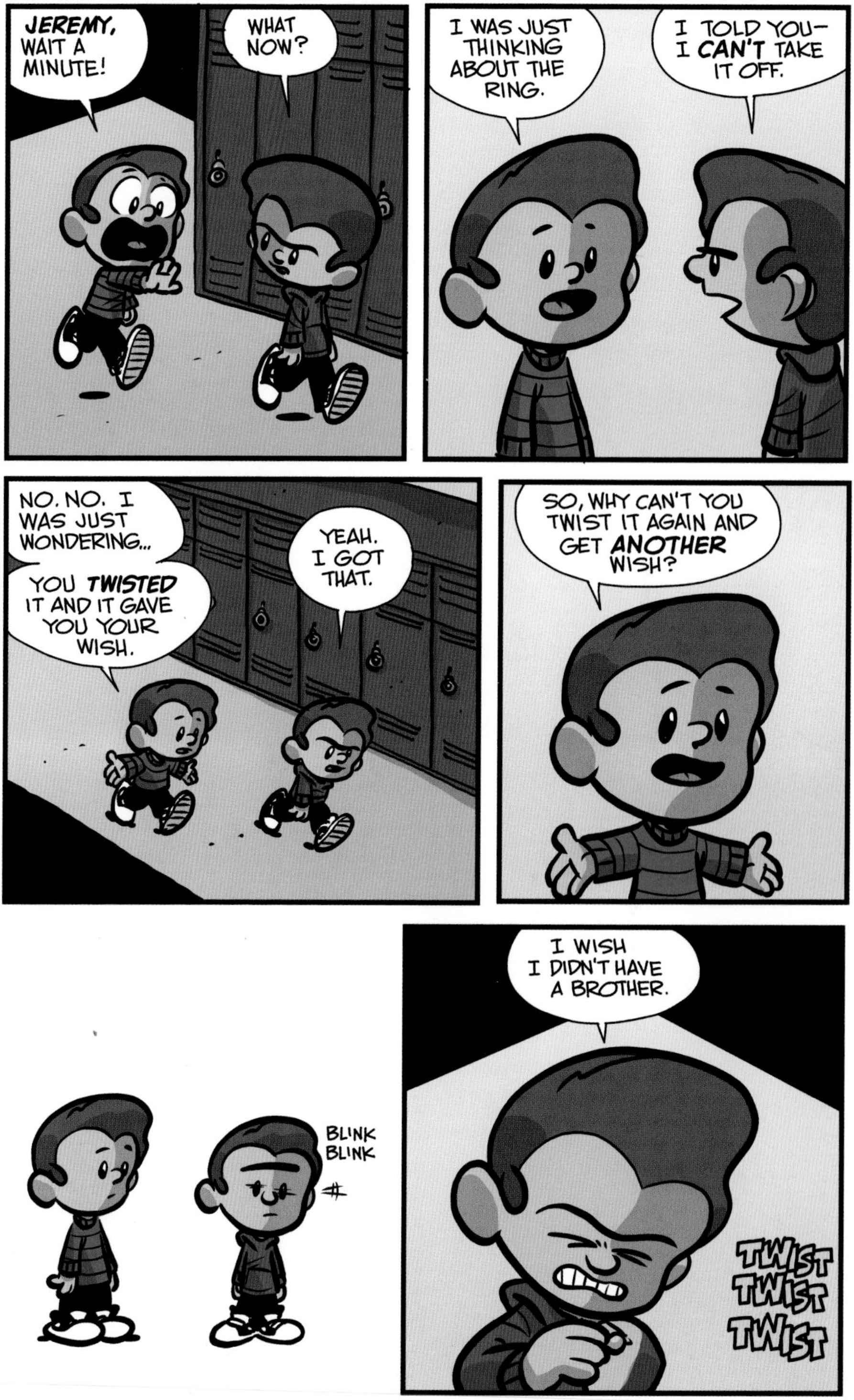
JEREMY, WAIT A MINUTE!
WHAT NOW?
I WAS JUST THINKING ABOUT THE RING.
I TOLD YOU— I CAN'T TAKE IT OFF.
NO. NO. I WAS JUST WONDERING...
YOU TWISTED IT AND IT GAVE YOU YOUR WISH.
YEAH. I GOT THAT.
SO, WHY CAN'T YOU TWIST IT AGAIN AND GET ANOTHER WISH?
BLINK BLINK
I WISH I DIDN'T HAVE A BROTHER.
TWIST TWIST TWIST

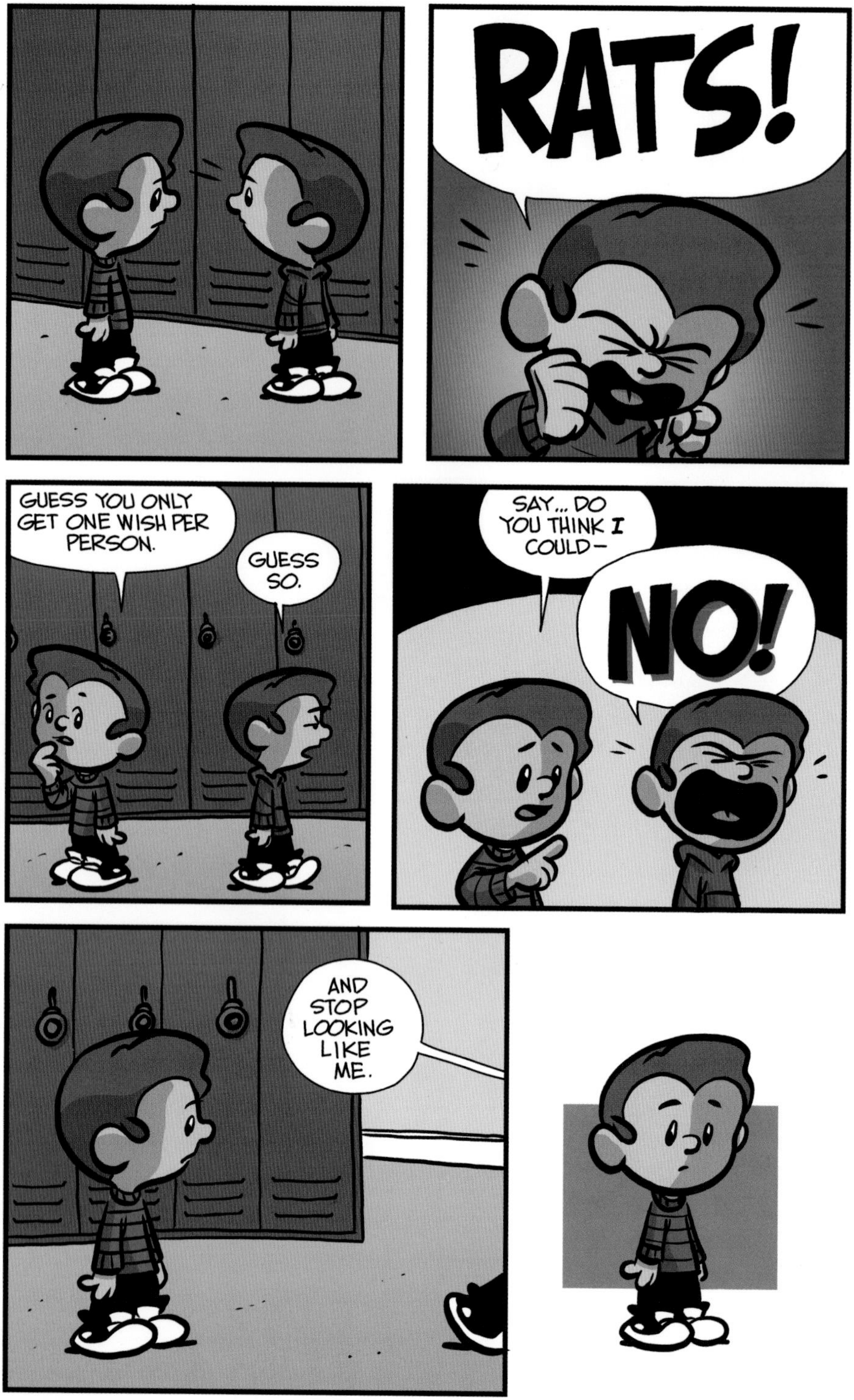
RATS!
GUESS YOU ONLY GET ONE WISH PER PERSON.
GUESS SO.
SAY... DO YOU THINK I COULD–
NO!
AND STOP LOOKING LIKE ME.

CHAPTER TWO

BROTHERLY SHOVE

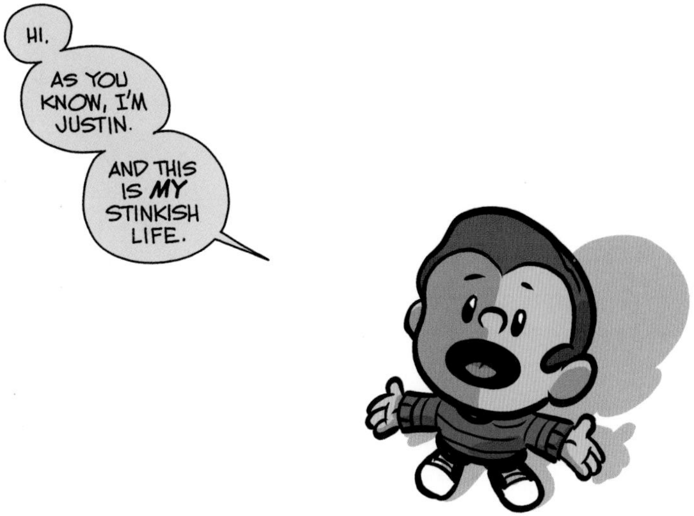
HI.
AS YOU KNOW, I'M JUSTIN.
AND THIS IS *MY* STINKISH LIFE.

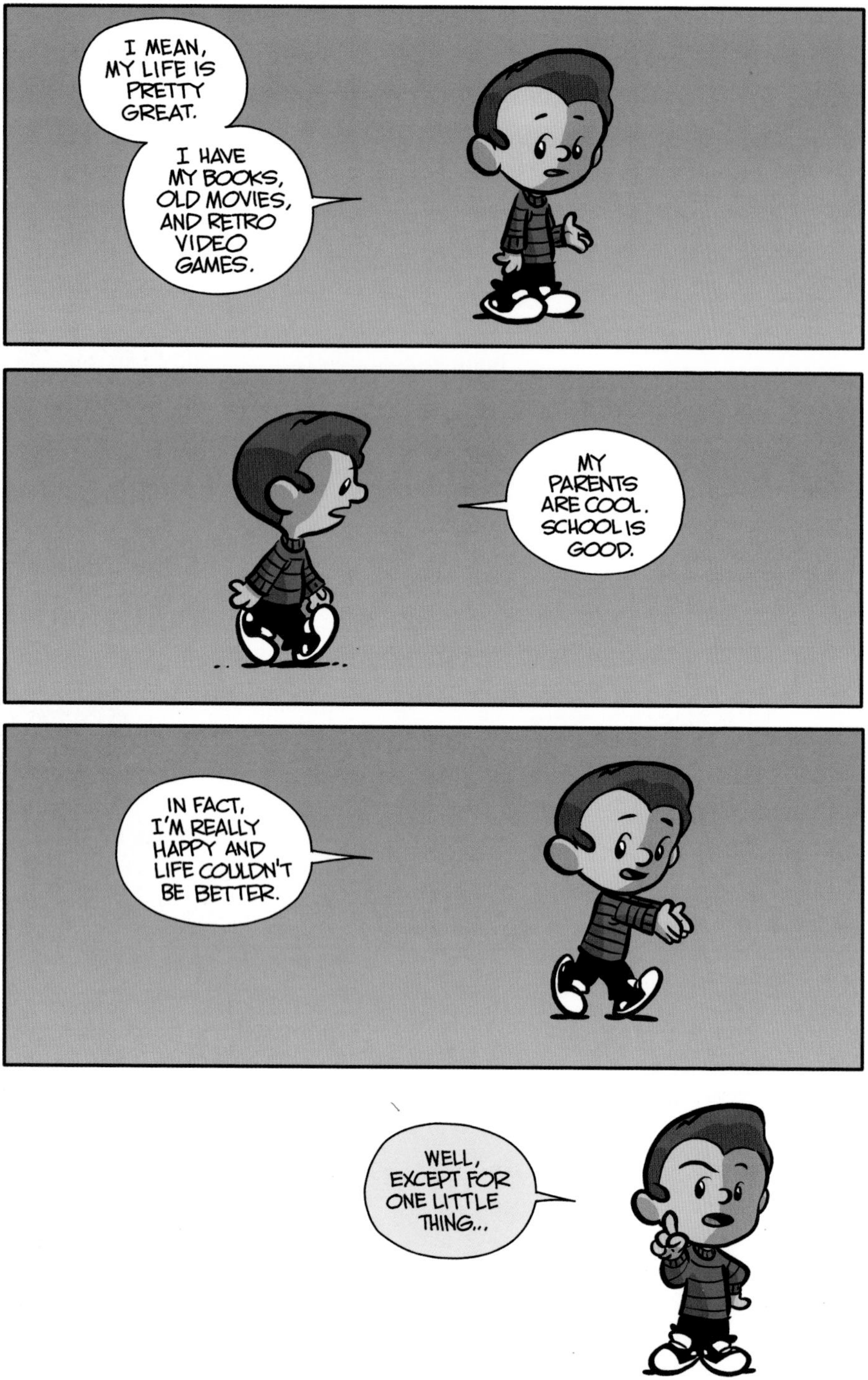
I MEAN, MY LIFE IS PRETTY GREAT.
I HAVE MY BOOKS, OLD MOVIES, AND RETRO VIDEO GAMES.
MY PARENTS ARE COOL. SCHOOL IS GOOD.
IN FACT, I'M REALLY HAPPY AND LIFE COULDN'T BE BETTER.
WELL, EXCEPT FOR ONE LITTLE THING...

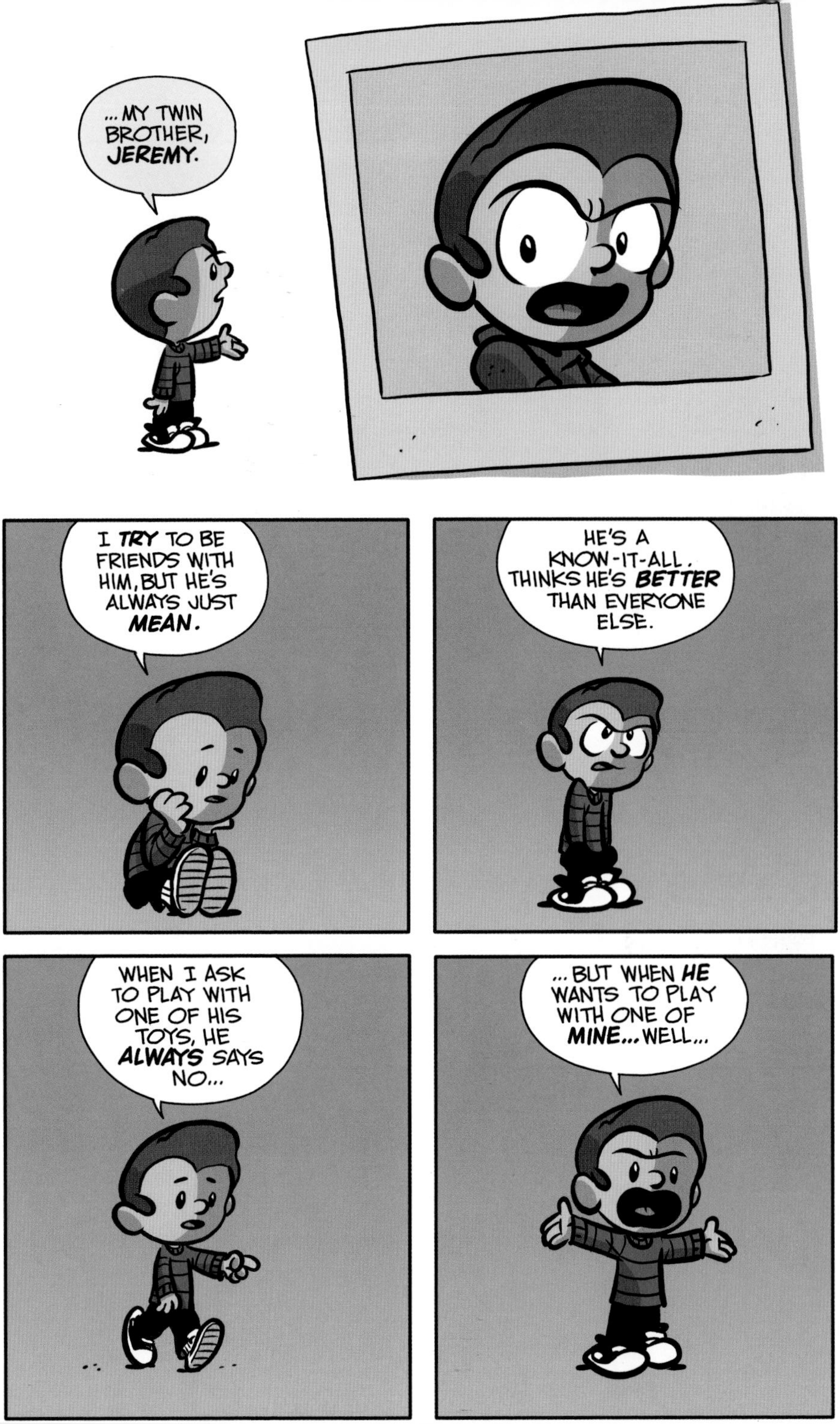
...MY TWIN BROTHER, JEREMY.
I TRY TO BE FRIENDS WITH HIM, BUT HE'S ALWAYS JUST MEAN.
HE'S A KNOW-IT-ALL. THINKS HE'S BETTER THAN EVERYONE ELSE.
WHEN I ASK TO PLAY WITH ONE OF HIS TOYS, HE ALWAYS SAYS NO...
...BUT WHEN HE WANTS TO PLAY WITH ONE OF MINE... WELL...

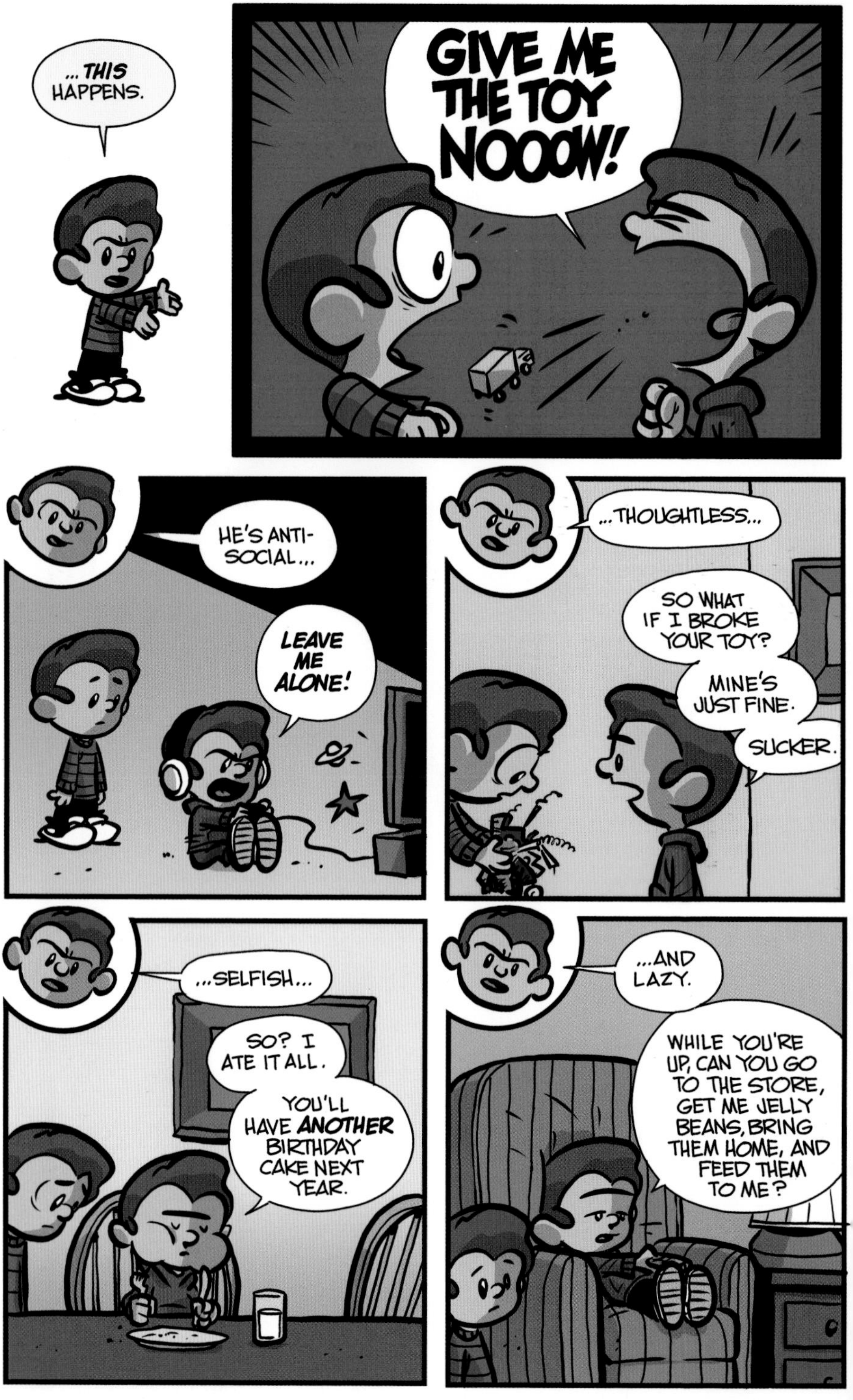
...THIS HAPPENS.
GIVE ME THE TOY NOOOW!
HE'S ANTI-SOCIAL...
LEAVE ME ALONE!
...THOUGHTLESS...
SO WHAT IF I BROKE YOUR TOY?
MINE'S JUST FINE.
SUCKER.
...SELFISH...
SO? I ATE IT ALL.
YOU'LL HAVE ANOTHER BIRTHDAY CAKE NEXT YEAR.
...AND LAZY.
WHILE YOU'RE UP, CAN YOU GO TO THE STORE, GET ME JELLY BEANS, BRING THEM HOME, AND FEED THEM TO ME?

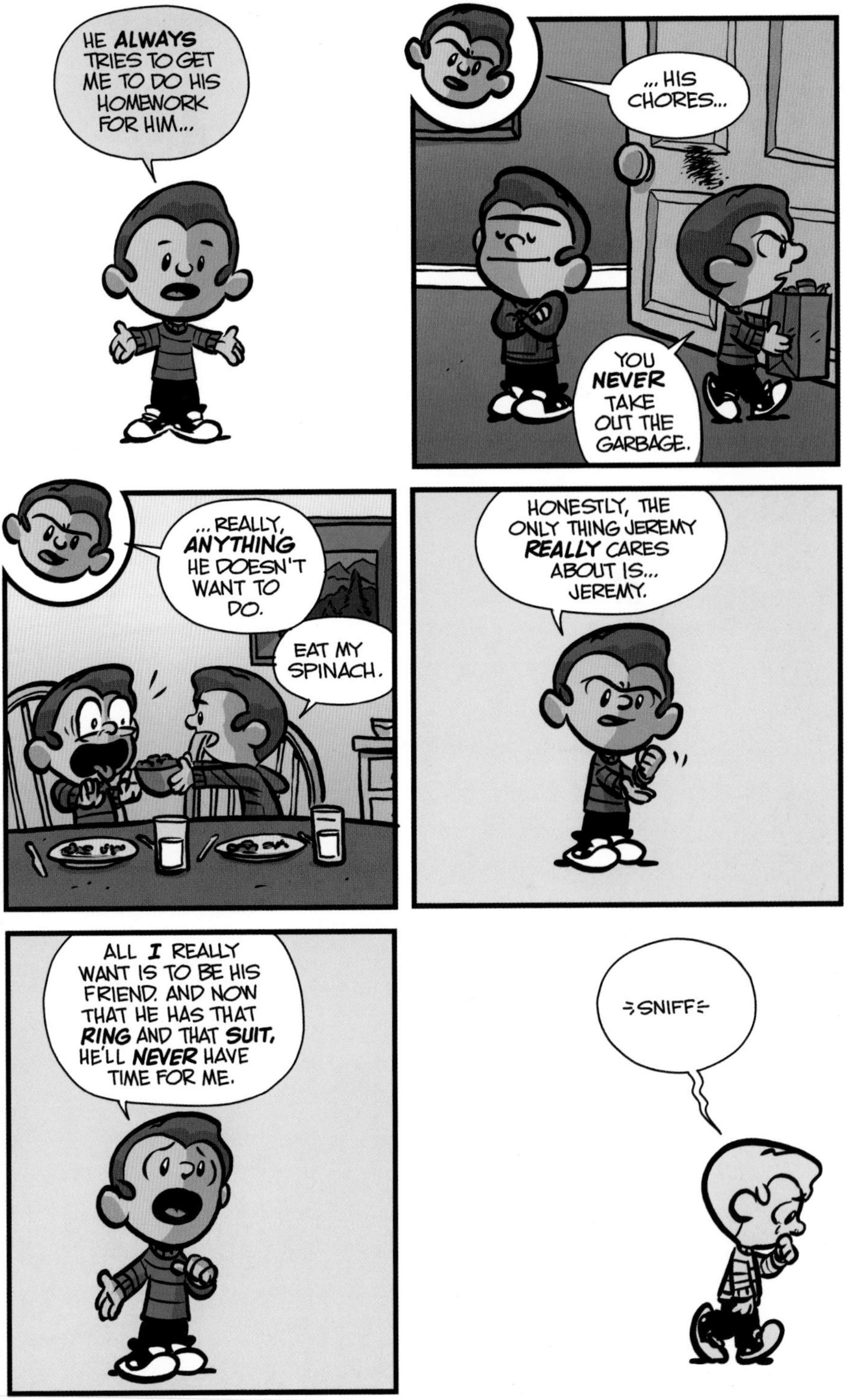
HE ALWAYS TRIES TO GET ME TO DO HIS HOMEWORK FOR HIM...
...HIS CHORES...
YOU NEVER TAKE OUT THE GARBAGE.
...REALLY, ANYTHING HE DOESN'T WANT TO DO.
EAT MY SPINACH.
HONESTLY, THE ONLY THING JEREMY REALLY CARES ABOUT IS... JEREMY.
ALL I REALLY WANT IS TO BE HIS FRIEND. AND NOW THAT HE HAS THAT RING AND THAT SUIT, HE'LL NEVER HAVE TIME FOR ME.
=SNIFF=

CHAPTER THREE

TAKEOFF!

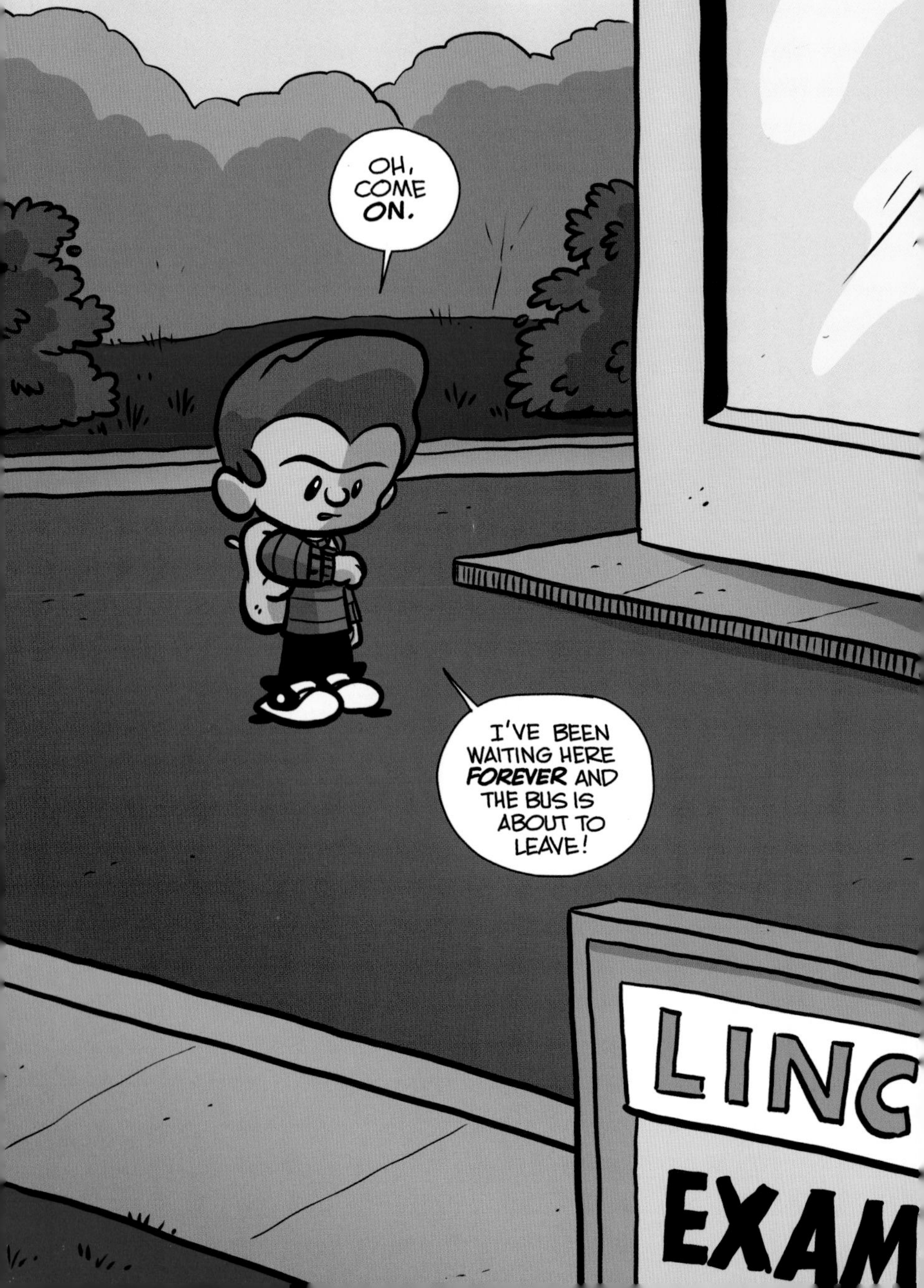
OH, COME ON.
I'VE BEEN WAITING HERE FOREVER AND THE BUS IS ABOUT TO LEAVE!
LINC
EXAM

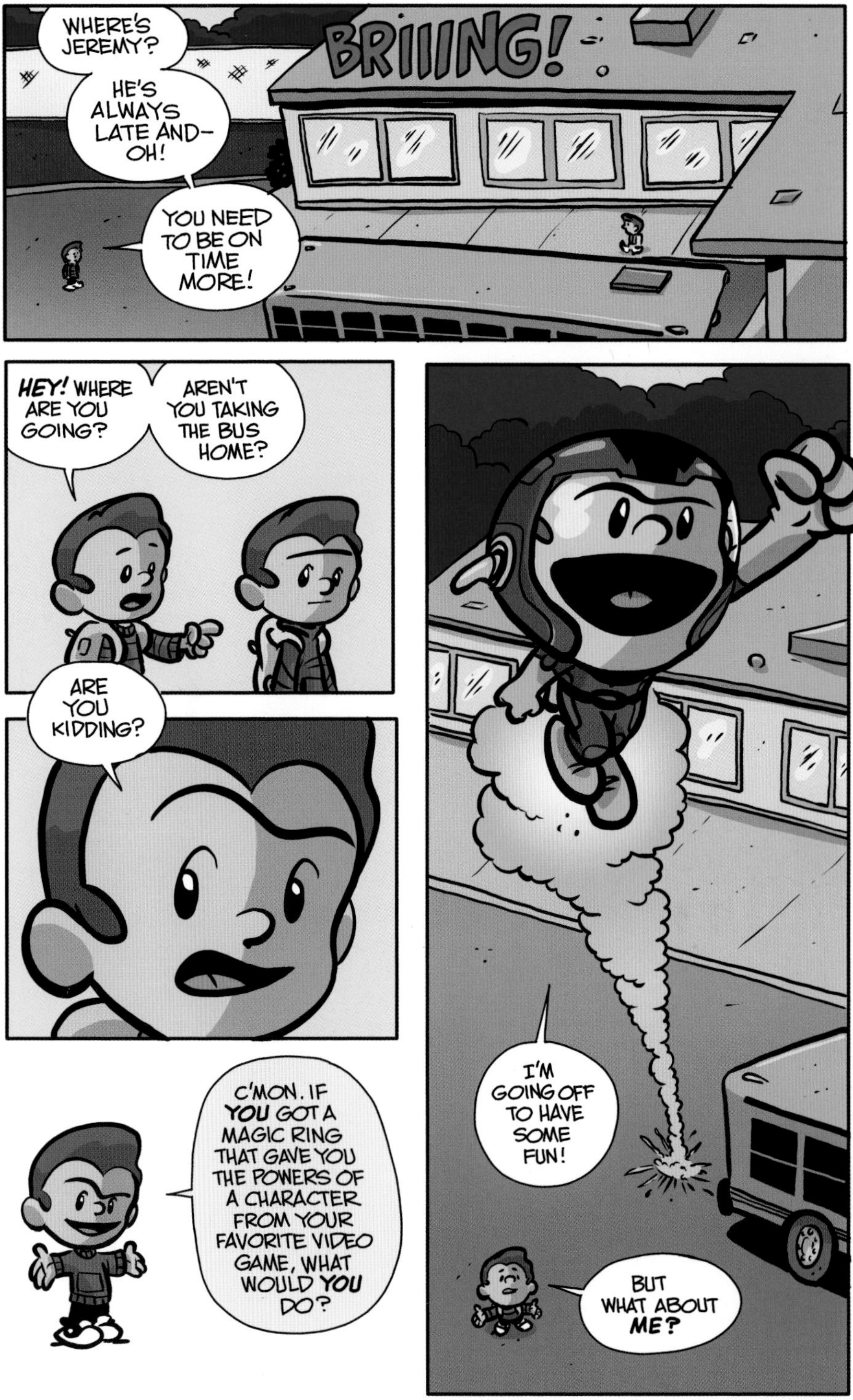
BRIIING!
WHERE'S JEREMY?
HE'S ALWAYS LATE AND— OH!
YOU NEED TO BE ON TIME MORE!
HEY! WHERE ARE YOU GOING?
AREN'T YOU TAKING THE BUS HOME?
ARE YOU KIDDING?
C'MON. IF YOU GOT A MAGIC RING THAT GAVE YOU THE POWERS OF A CHARACTER FROM YOUR FAVORITE VIDEO GAME, WHAT WOULD YOU DO?
I'M GOING OFF TO HAVE SOME FUN!
BUT WHAT ABOUT ME?

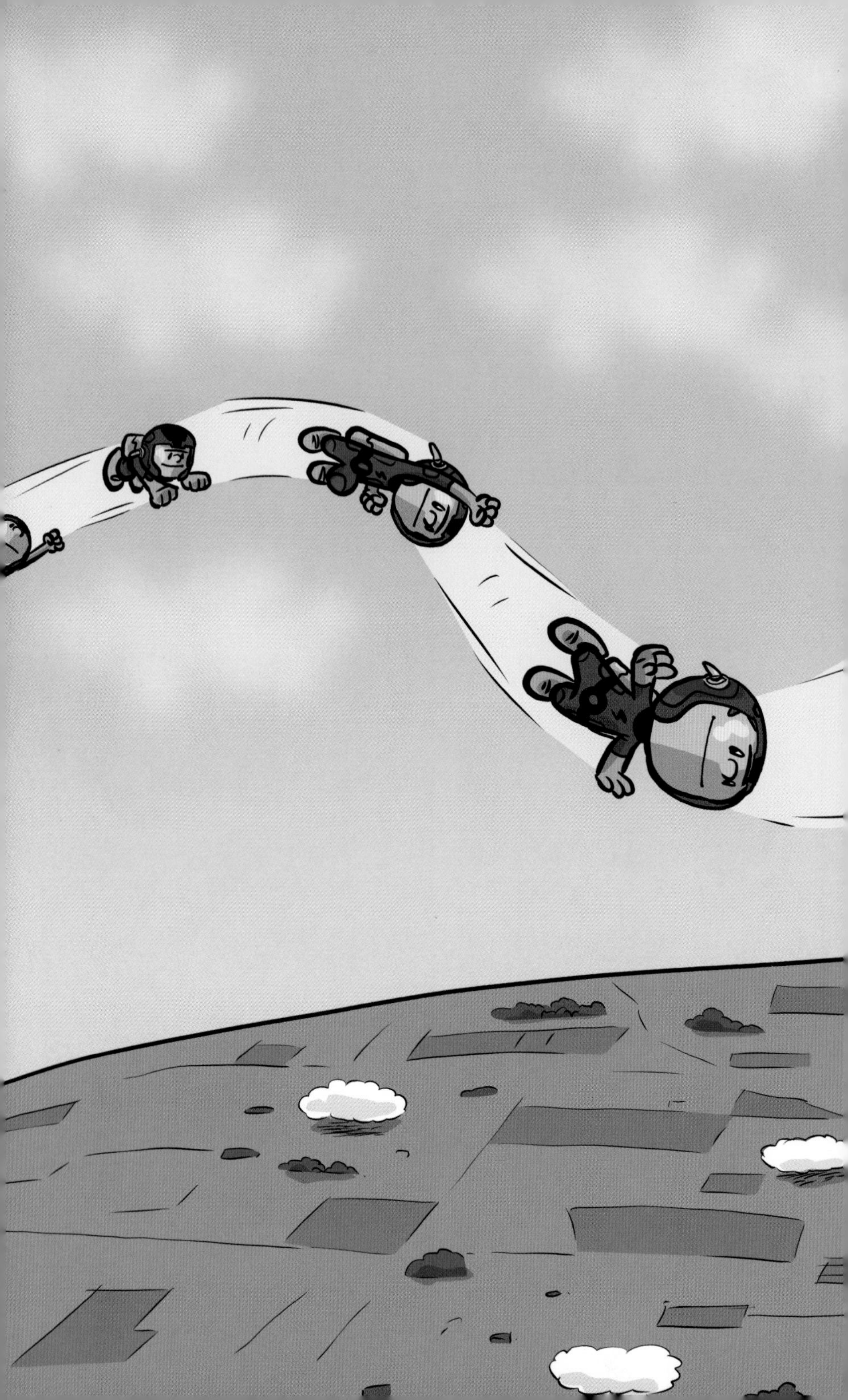

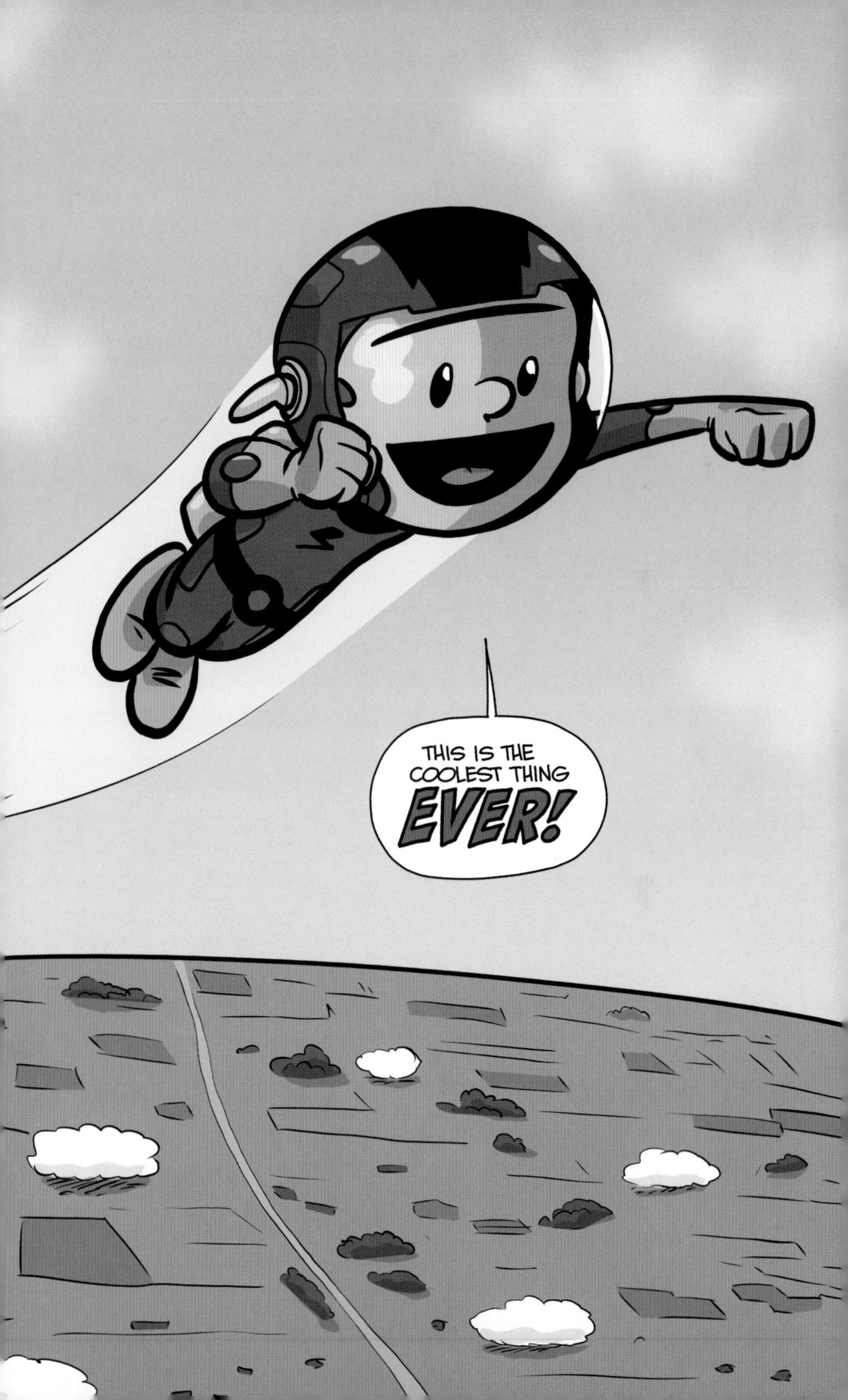
THIS IS THE COOLEST THING EVER!

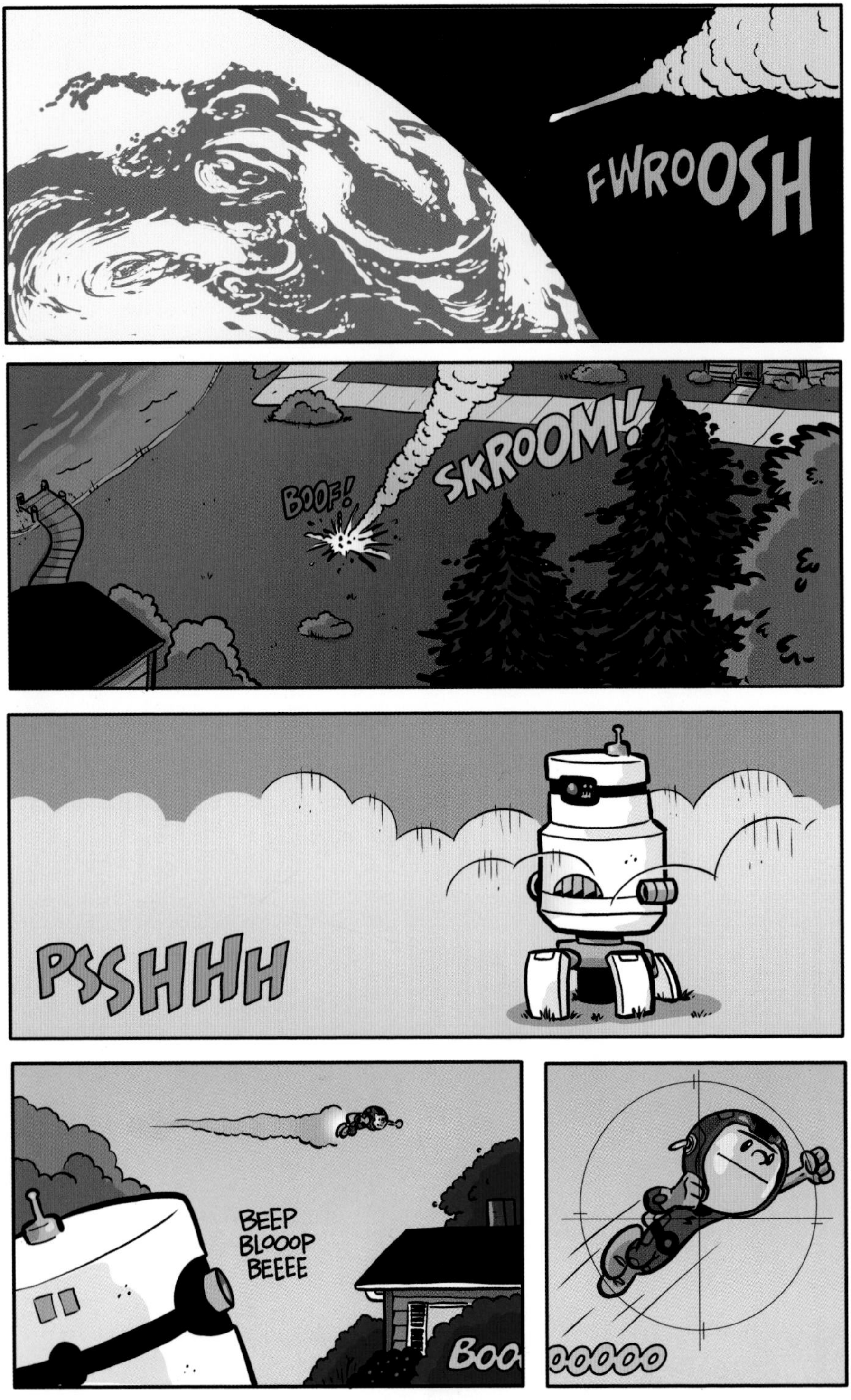
FWROOSH
BOOF!
SKROOM!
PSSHHH
BEEP
BLOOOP
BEEEE
BOOOOOOOO

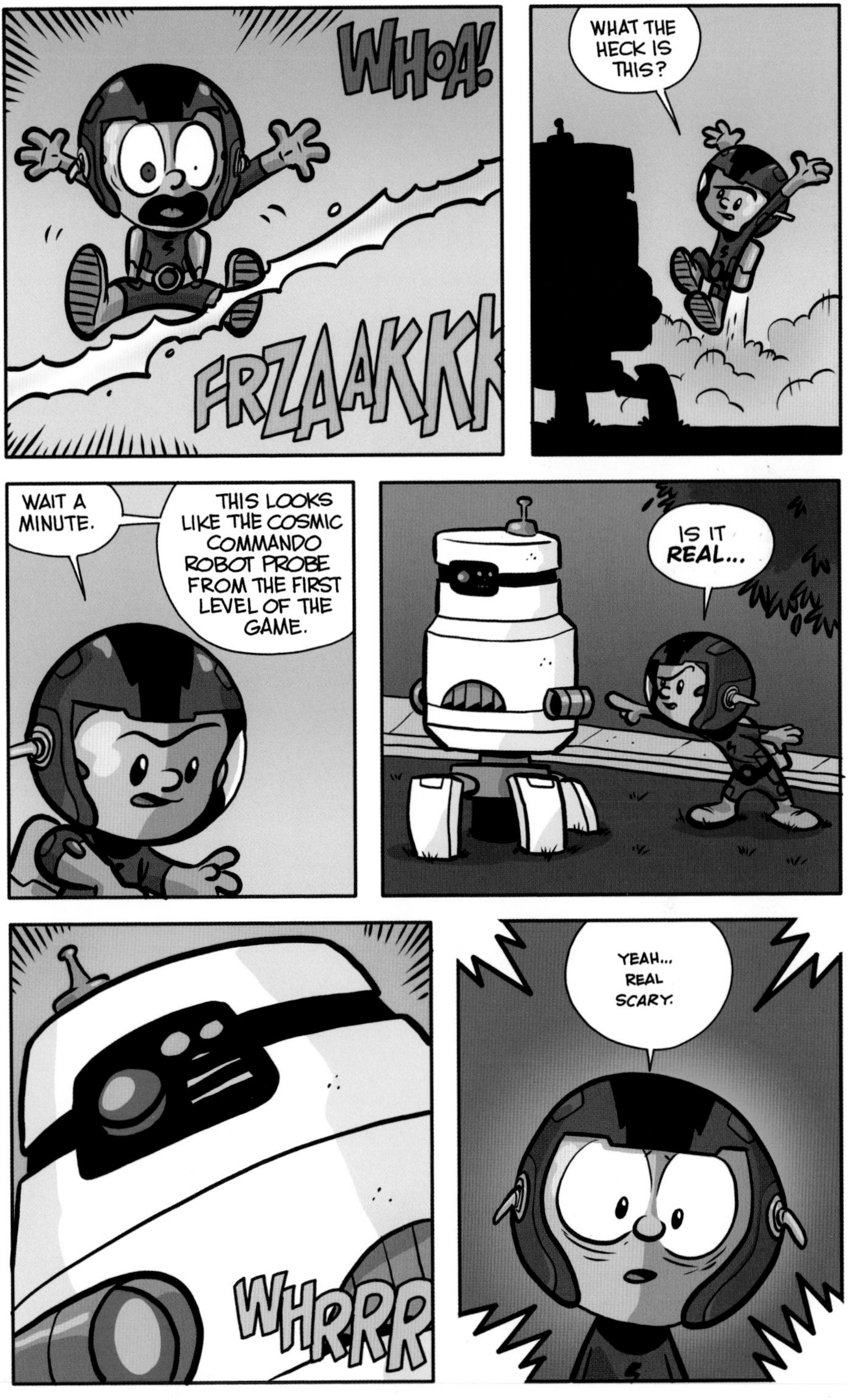
WHOA!
FRZAAKKK
WHAT THE HECK IS THIS?
WAIT A MINUTE.
THIS LOOKS LIKE THE COSMIC COMMANDO ROBOT PROBE FROM THE FIRST LEVEL OF THE GAME.
IS IT REAL...
WHRRR
YEAH... REAL SCARY.

PSHEW
PSHEW
PSHEW
AAAAHHHHH!
KLIK
KLAK
PSHEW
PSHEW
PSHEW

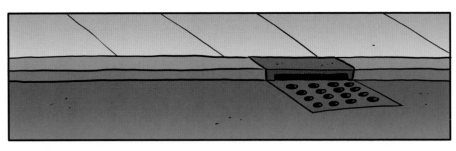

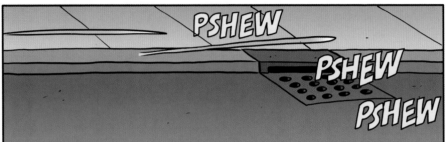

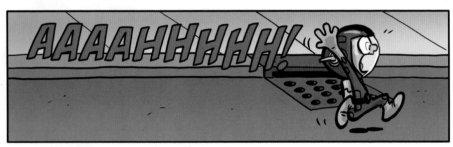

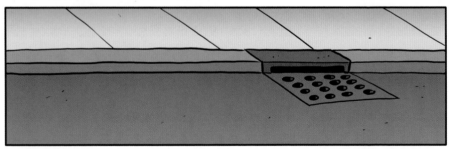

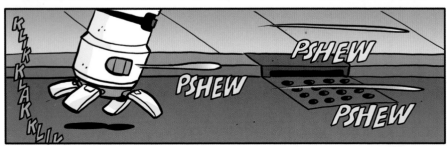

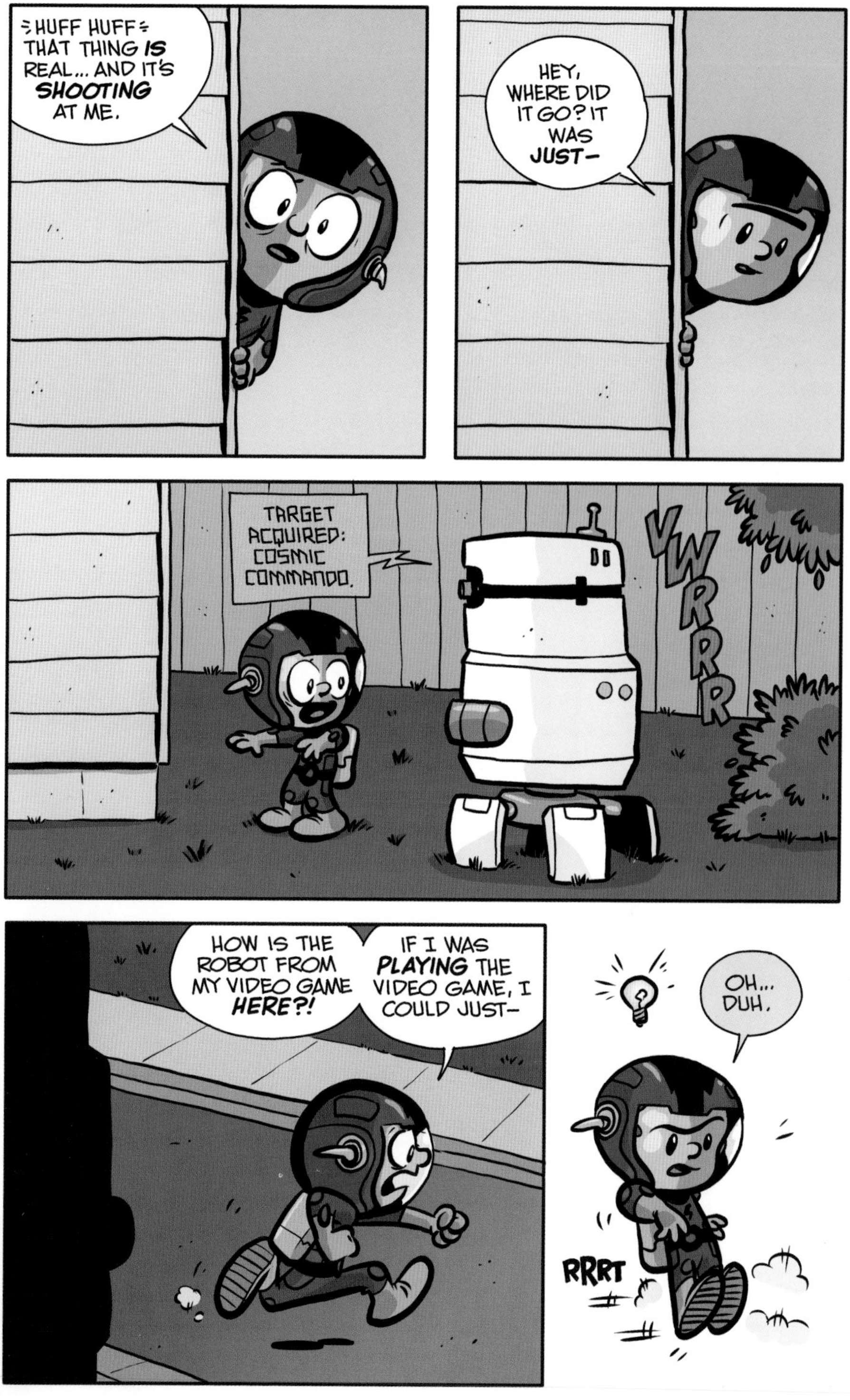
HUFF HUFF
THAT THING IS REAL... AND IT'S SHOOTING AT ME.
HEY, WHERE DID IT GO? IT WAS JUST—
TARGET ACQUIRED: COSMIC COMMANDO.
VWRRR
HOW IS THE ROBOT FROM MY VIDEO GAME HERE?!
IF I WAS PLAYING THE VIDEO GAME, I COULD JUST—
OH... DUH.
RRRT

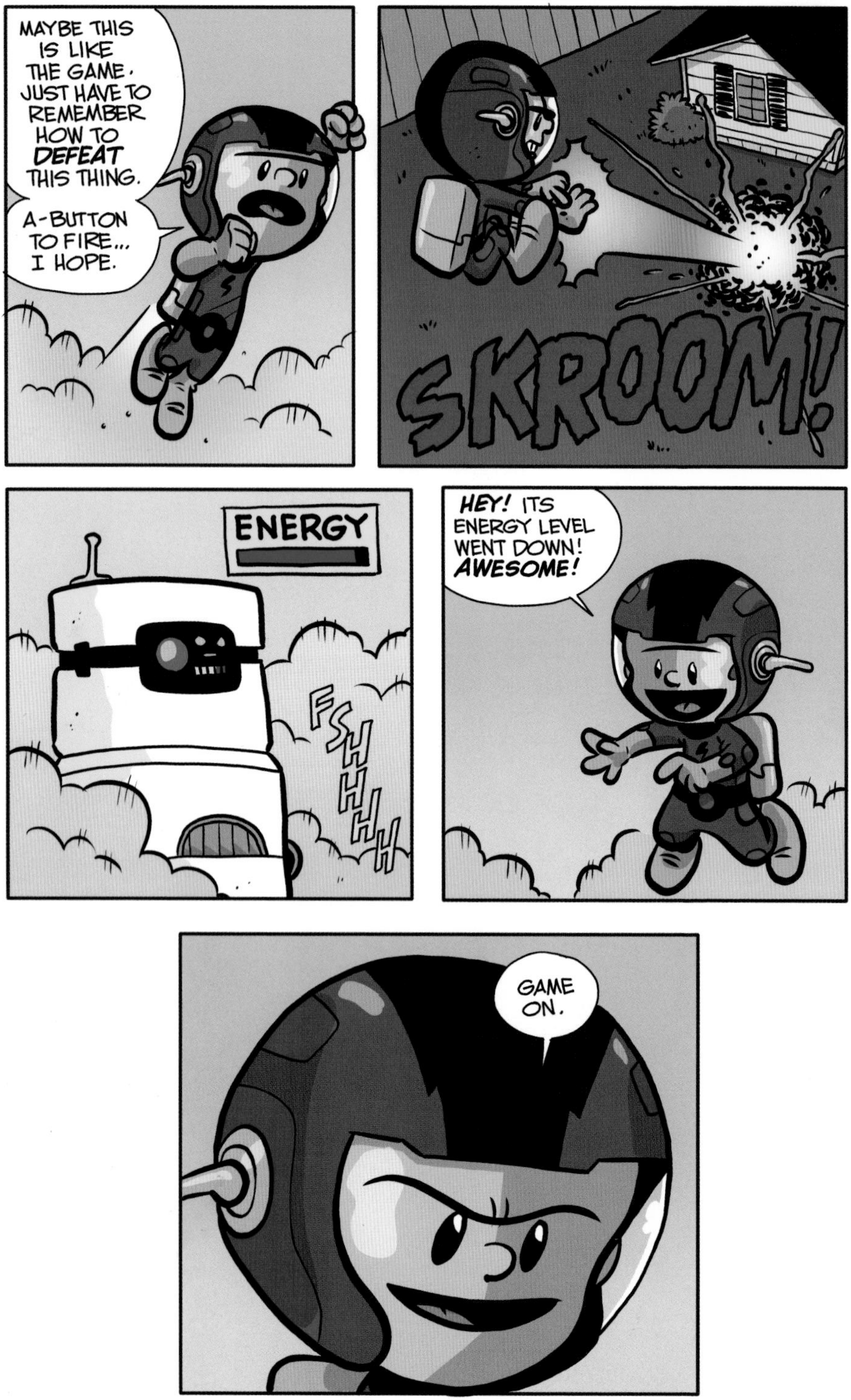
MAYBE THIS IS LIKE THE GAME. JUST HAVE TO REMEMBER HOW TO **DEFEAT** THIS THING.
A-BUTTON TO FIRE... I HOPE.
SKROOM!
ENERGY
FSHHHHH
HEY! ITS ENERGY LEVEL WENT DOWN! **AWESOME!**
GAME ON.

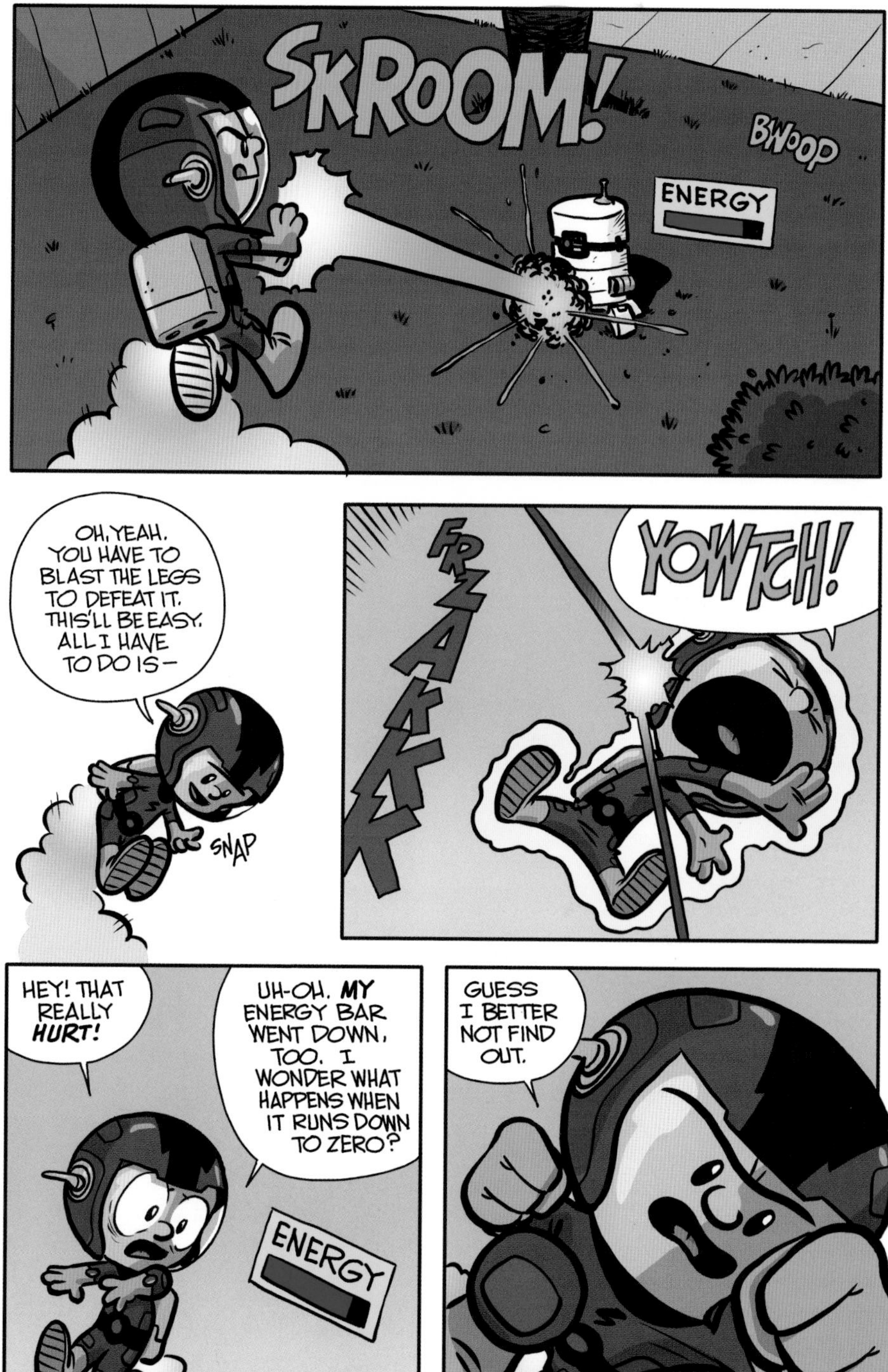
SKROOM!
BWOOP
ENERGY
OH, YEAH. YOU HAVE TO BLAST THE LEGS TO DEFEAT IT. THIS'LL BE EASY. ALL I HAVE TO DO IS–
SNAP
FRZAKKK
YOWTCH!
HEY! THAT REALLY **HURT!**
UH-OH. **MY** ENERGY BAR WENT DOWN, TOO. I WONDER WHAT HAPPENS WHEN IT RUNS DOWN TO ZERO?
ENERGY
GUESS I BETTER NOT FIND OUT.

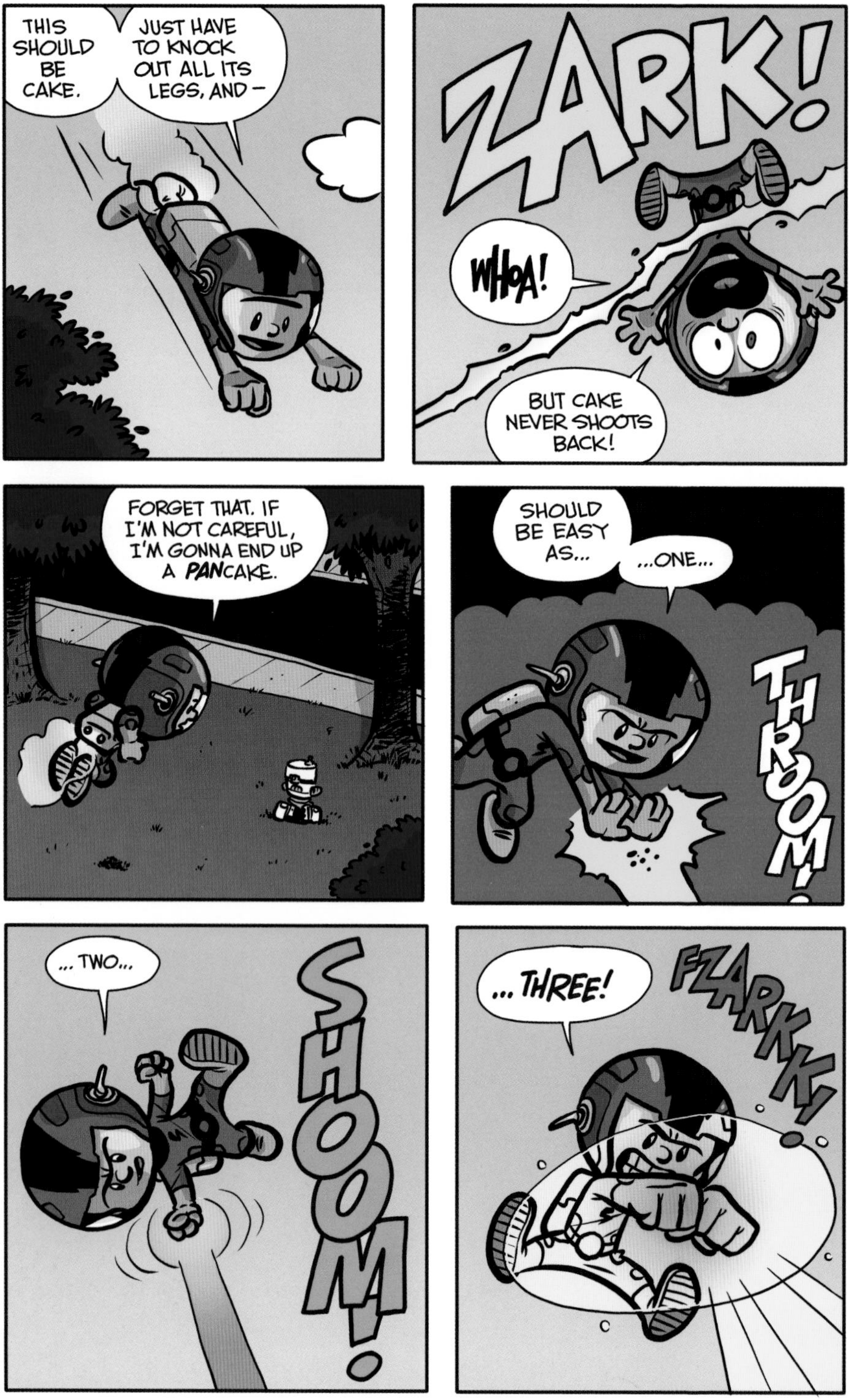
THIS SHOULD BE CAKE.
JUST HAVE TO KNOCK OUT ALL ITS LEGS, AND—
ZARK!
WHOA!
BUT CAKE NEVER SHOOTS BACK!
FORGET THAT. IF I'M NOT CAREFUL, I'M GONNA END UP A PANCAKE.
SHOULD BE EASY AS...
...ONE...
THROOM!
...TWO...
SHOOOM!
...THREE!
FZARKK!

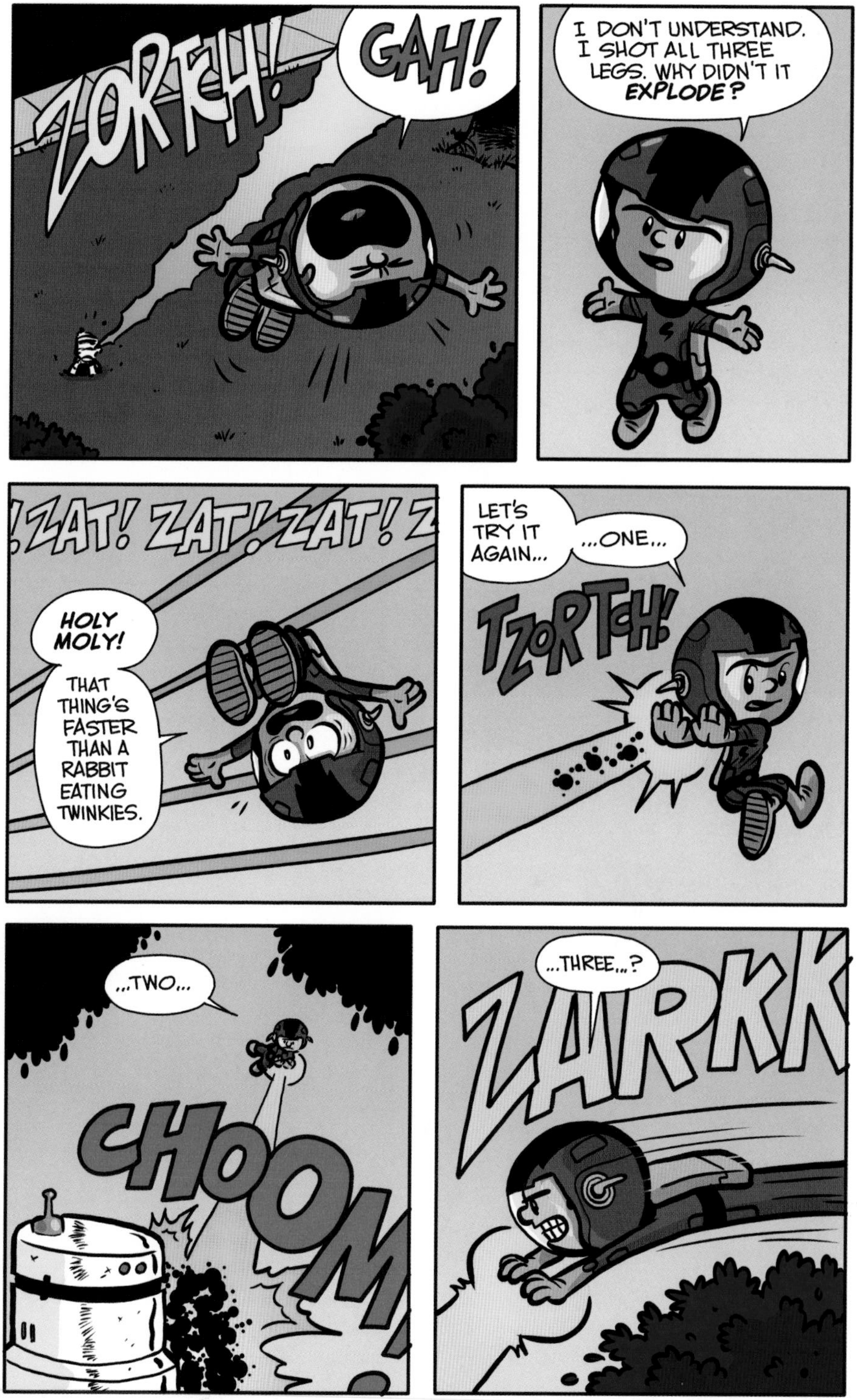
ZORTCH!
GAH!
I DON'T UNDERSTAND. I SHOT ALL THREE LEGS. WHY DIDN'T IT EXPLODE?
ZAT! ZAT! ZAT!
HOLY MOLY!
THAT THING'S FASTER THAN A RABBIT EATING TWINKIES.
LET'S TRY IT AGAIN...
...ONE...
TZORTCH!
...TWO...
CHOOM
...THREE...?
ZARKK

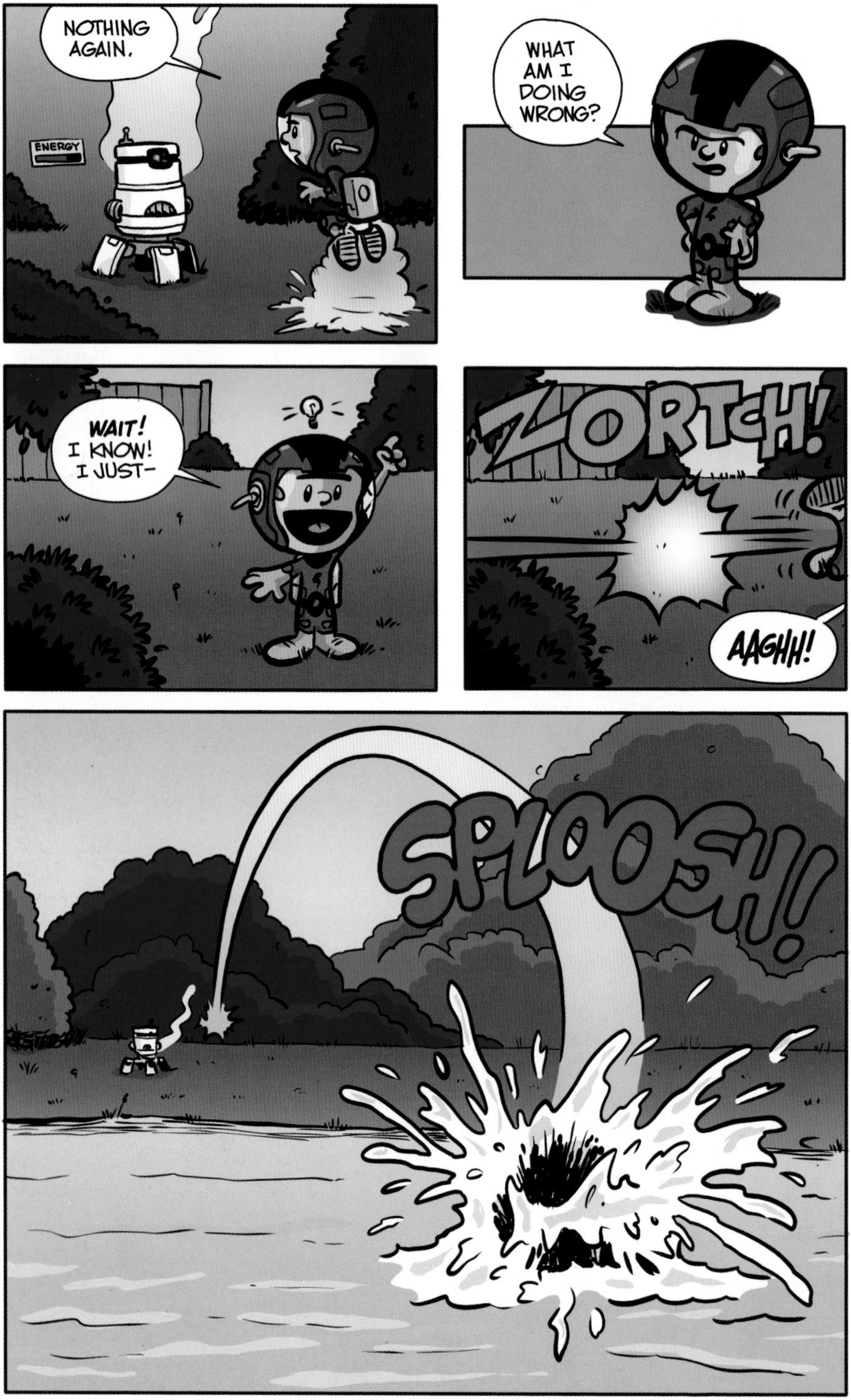
NOTHING AGAIN.
ENERGY
WHAT AM I DOING WRONG?
WAIT! I KNOW! I JUST-
ZORTCH!
AAGHH!
SPLOOSH!

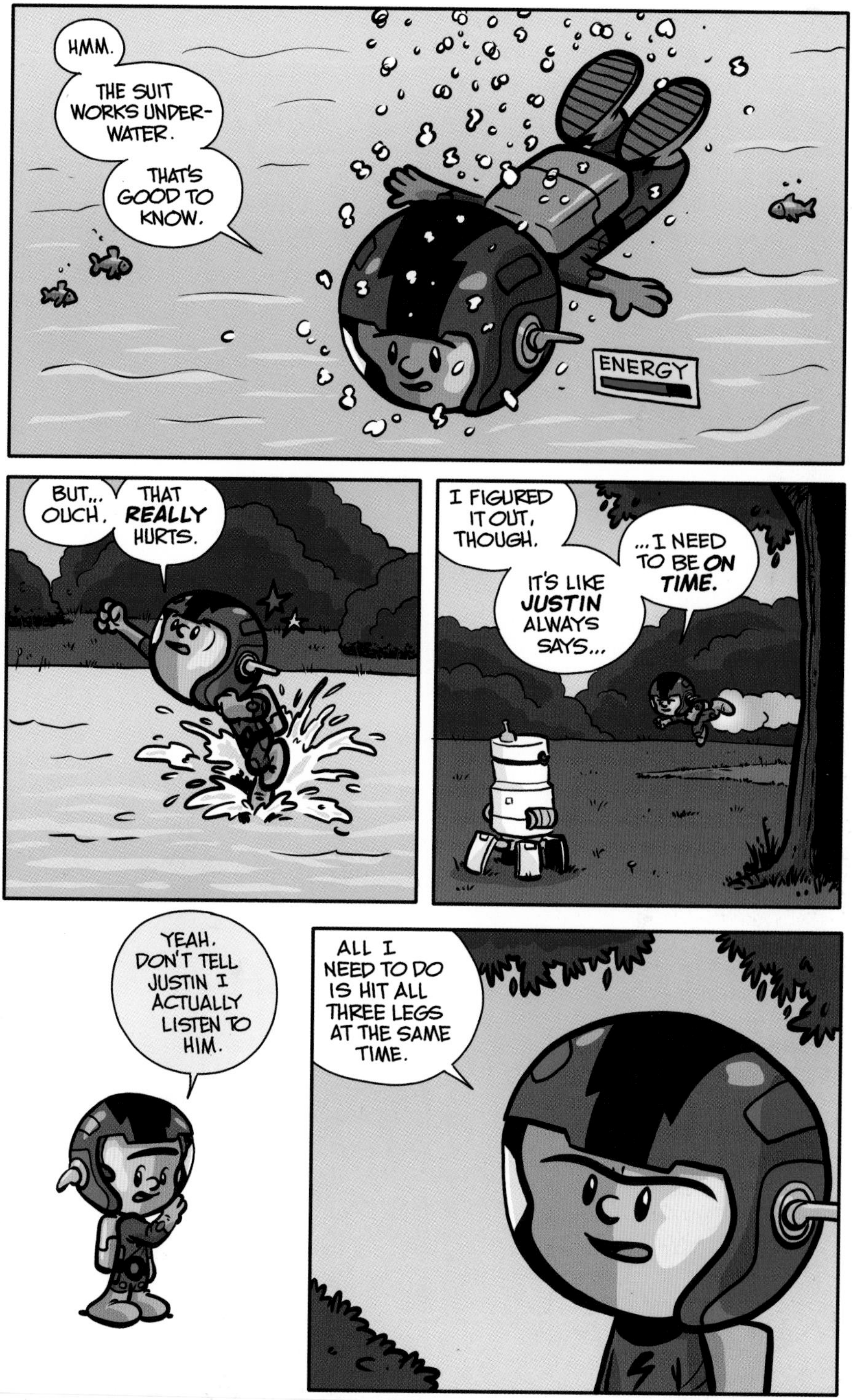
HMM.
THE SUIT WORKS UNDER-WATER.
THAT'S GOOD TO KNOW.
ENERGY
BUT... OUCH.
THAT **REALLY** HURTS.
I FIGURED IT OUT, THOUGH.
IT'S LIKE **JUSTIN** ALWAYS SAYS...
...I NEED TO BE **ON TIME.**
YEAH. DON'T TELL JUSTIN I ACTUALLY LISTEN TO HIM.
ALL I NEED TO DO IS HIT ALL THREE LEGS AT THE SAME TIME.

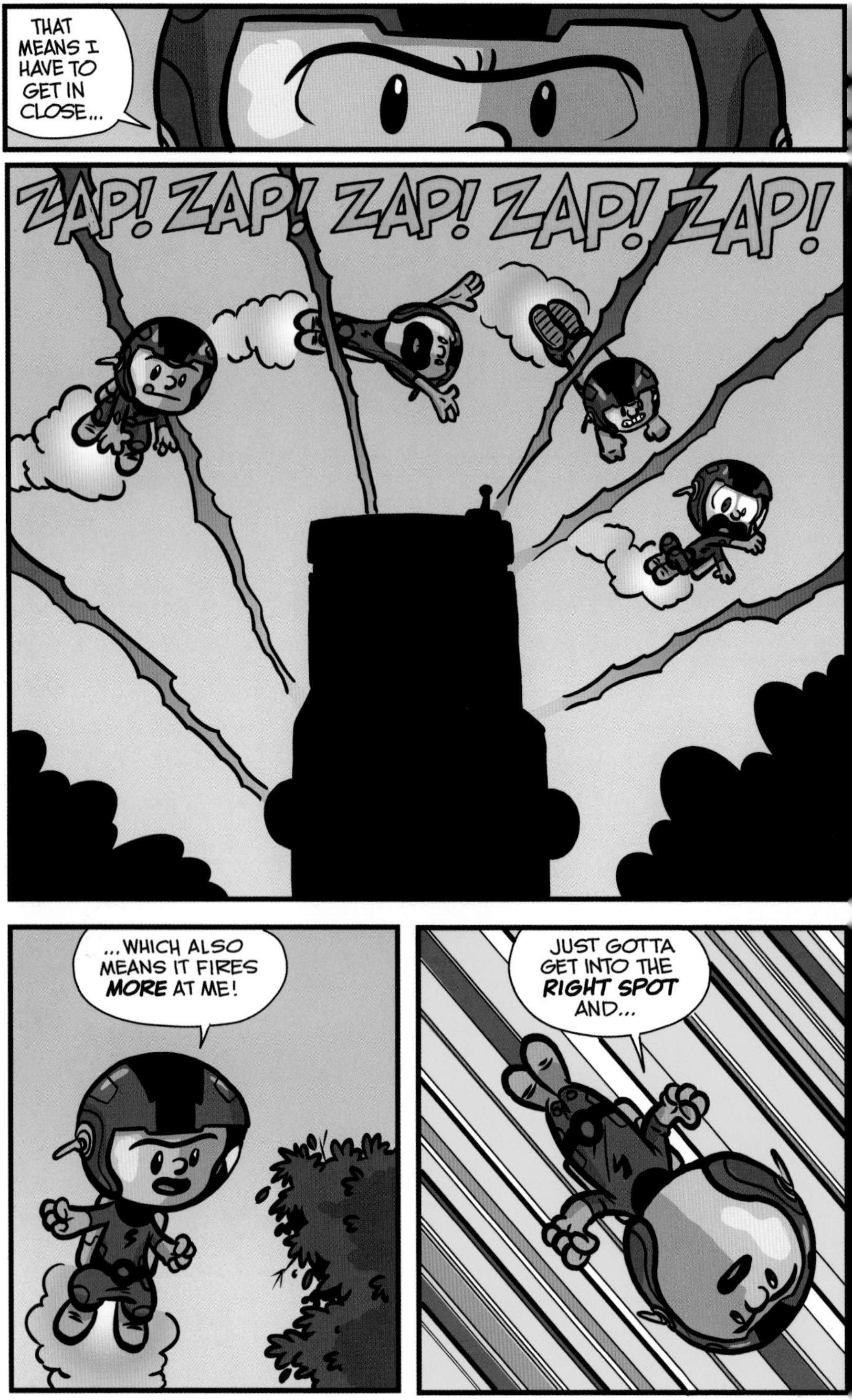
THAT MEANS I HAVE TO GET IN CLOSE...
ZAP! ZAP! ZAP! ZAP! ZAP!
...WHICH ALSO MEANS IT FIRES MORE AT ME!
JUST GOTTA GET INTO THE RIGHT SPOT AND...

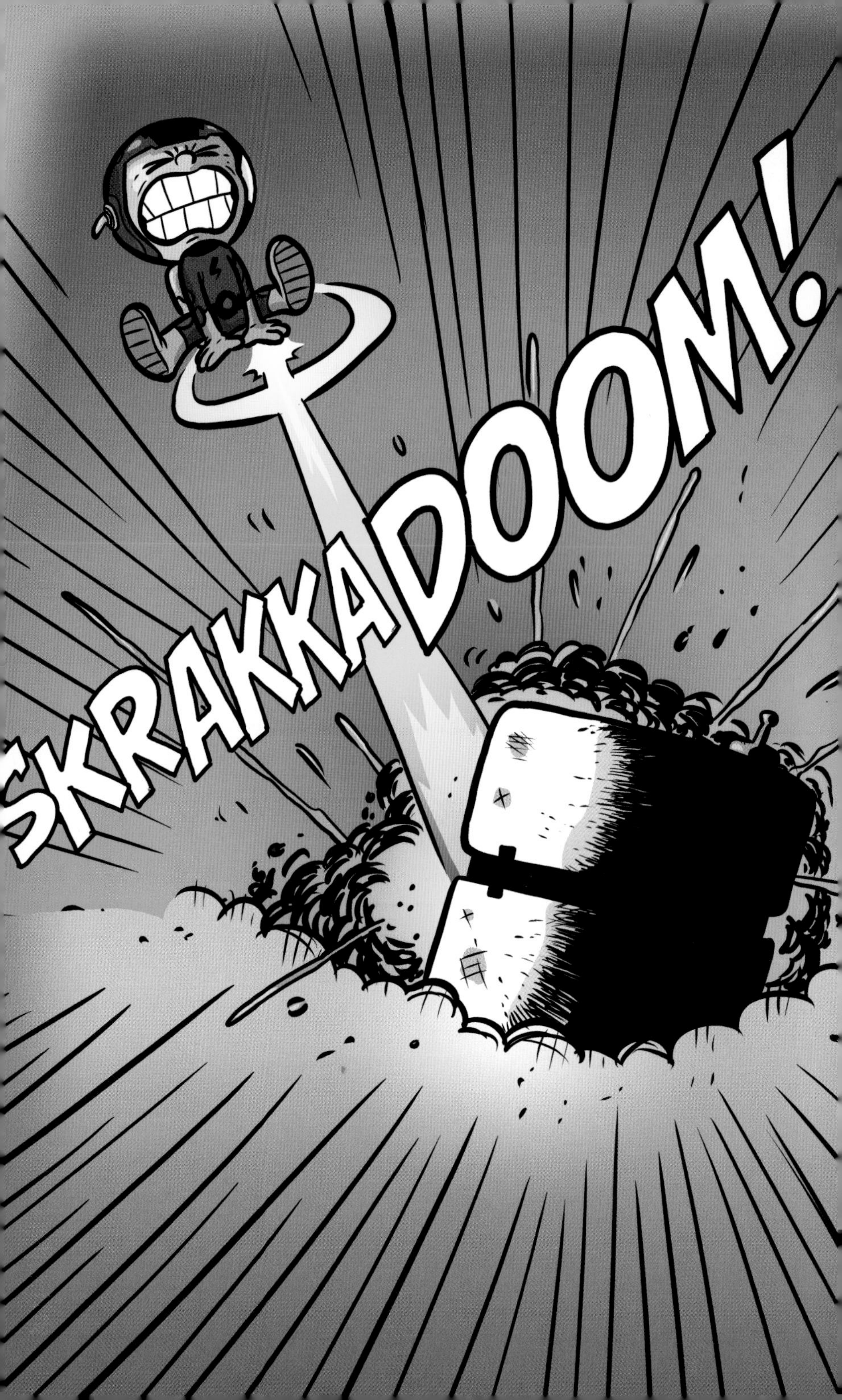
SKRAKKADOOOM!

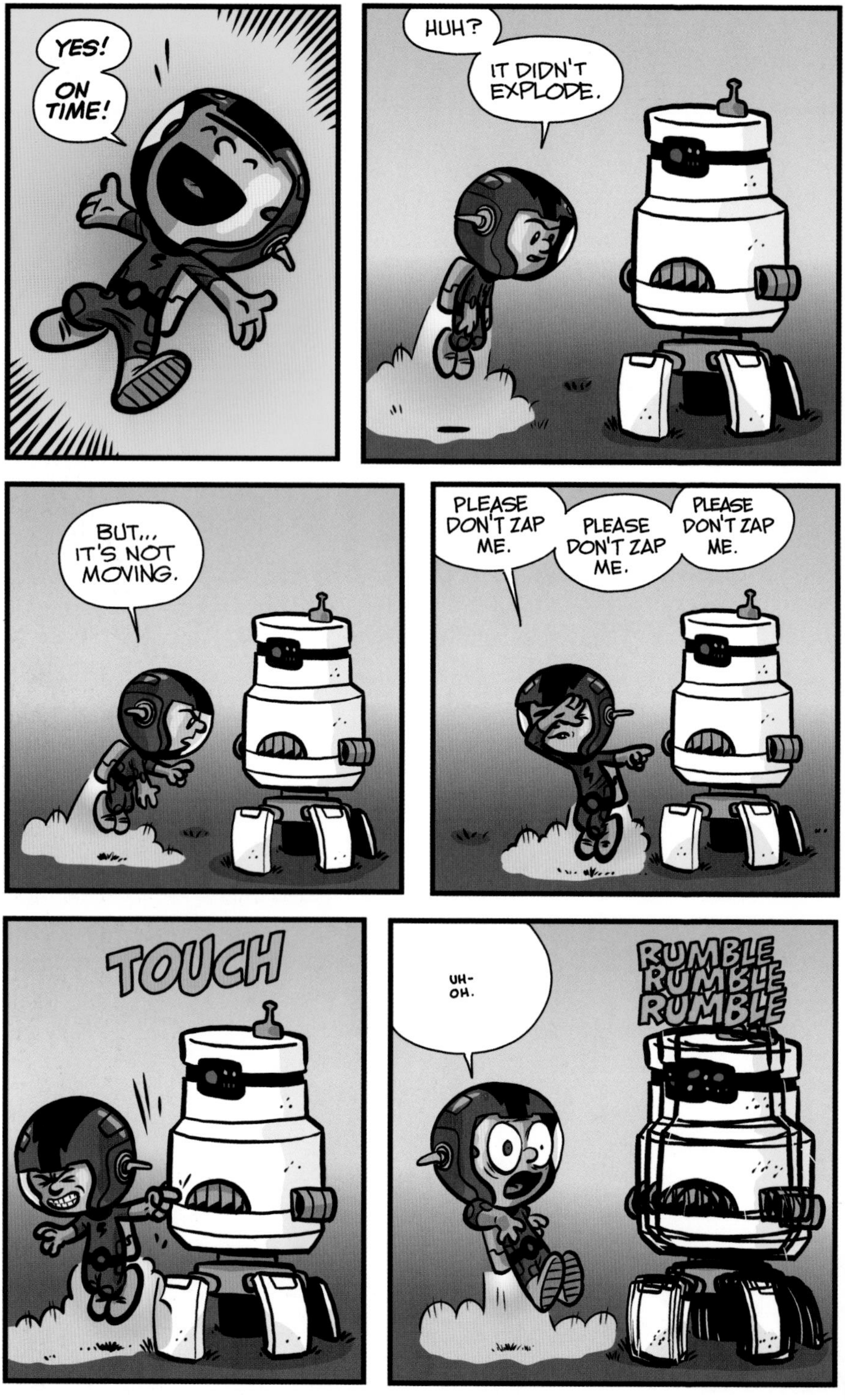
YES!
ON TIME!
HUH?
IT DIDN'T EXPLODE.
BUT... IT'S NOT MOVING.
PLEASE DON'T ZAP ME.
PLEASE DON'T ZAP ME.
PLEASE DON'T ZAP ME.
TOUCH
UH-OH.
RUMBLE
RUMBLE
RUMBLE

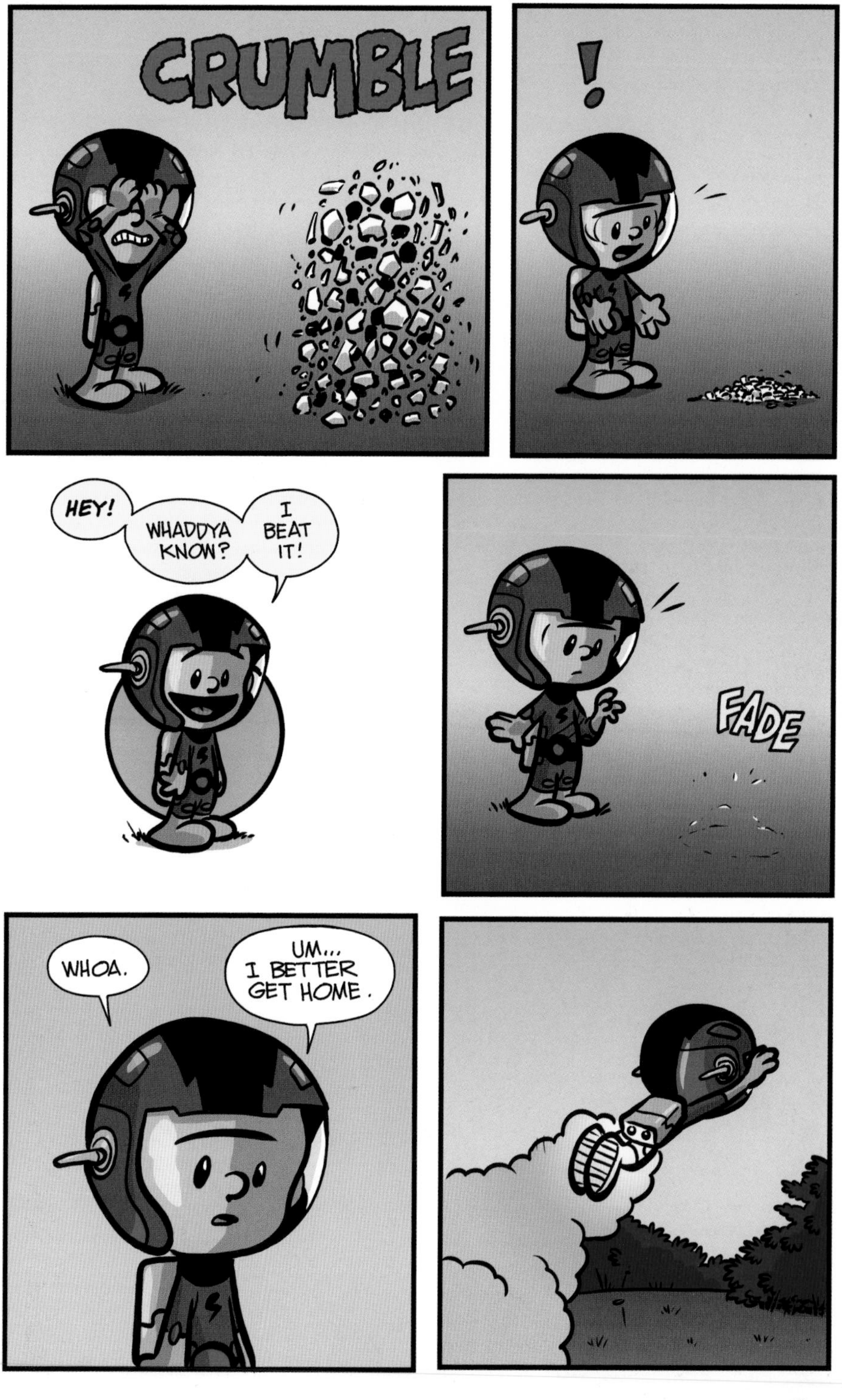
CRUMBLE
!
HEY!
WHADDYA KNOW?
I BEAT IT!
FADE
WHOA.
UM... I BETTER GET HOME.

CUTSCENE

SKORN!

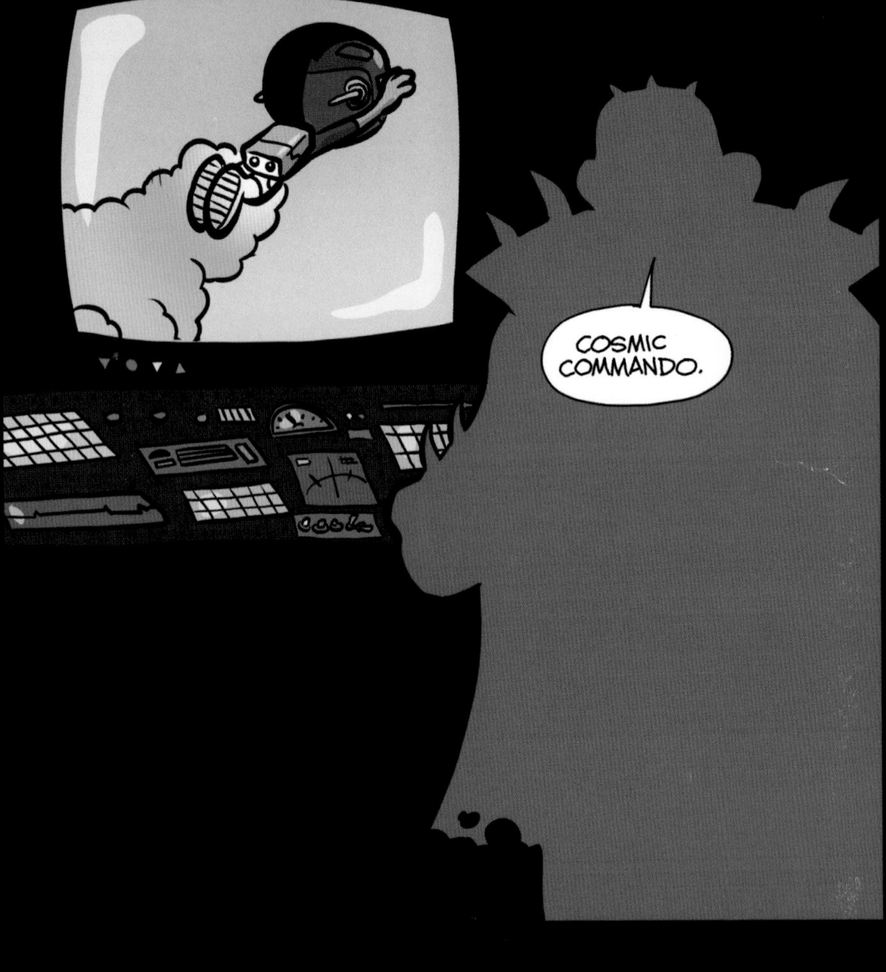
COSMIC COMMANDO.

I THOUGHT I DISPOSED OF THEIR ROTTEN CORPS YEARS AGO.

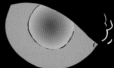

APPARENTLY I WAS *MISTAKEN*.

IT SEEMS I, *SKORN*, HAVE *ANOTHER* BUG TO SQUASH...

... AND, LIKE ALL THE *PREVIOUS* COMMANDOS, THEIR FAMILY AND FRIENDS AS WELL.

CLICK

HAHAHAHAHAHAHAHA!

CHAPTER FOUR

BIG TIME!

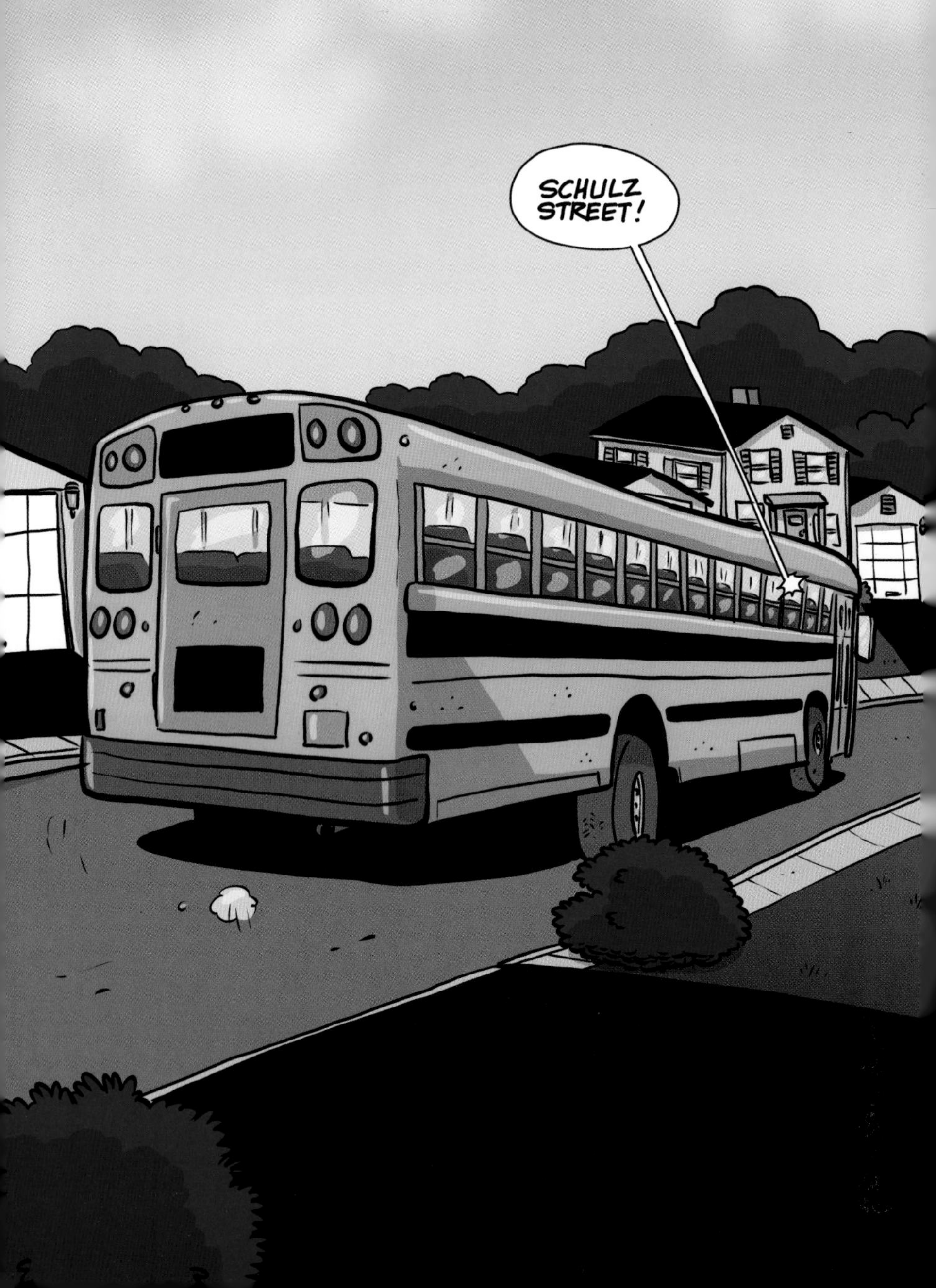
SCHULZ STREET!

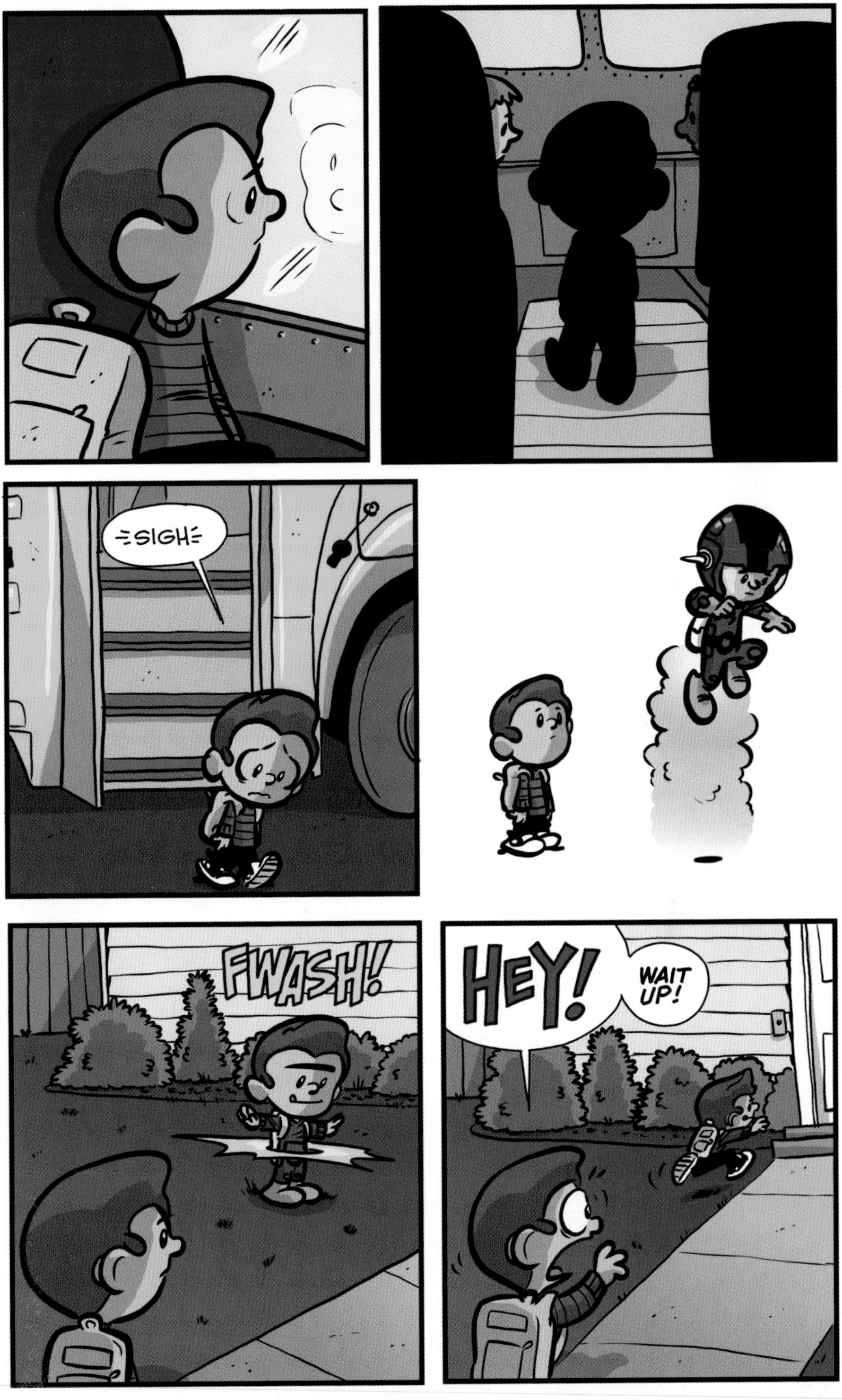
SIGH
FWASH!
HEY!
WAIT UP!

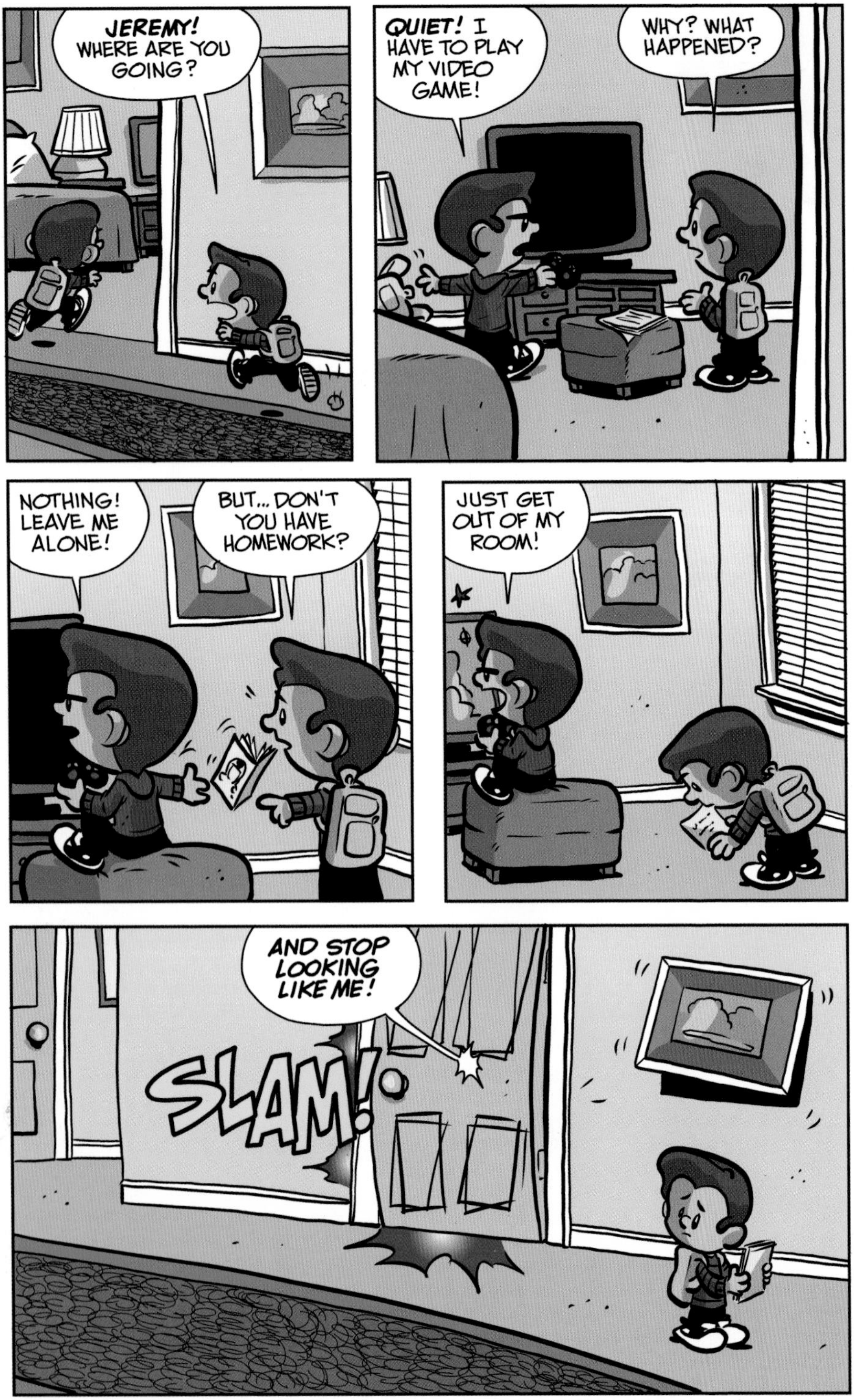
JEREMY! WHERE ARE YOU GOING?
QUIET! I HAVE TO PLAY MY VIDEO GAME!
WHY? WHAT HAPPENED?
NOTHING! LEAVE ME ALONE!
BUT... DON'T YOU HAVE HOMEWORK?
JUST GET OUT OF MY ROOM!
AND STOP LOOKING LIKE ME!
SLAM!

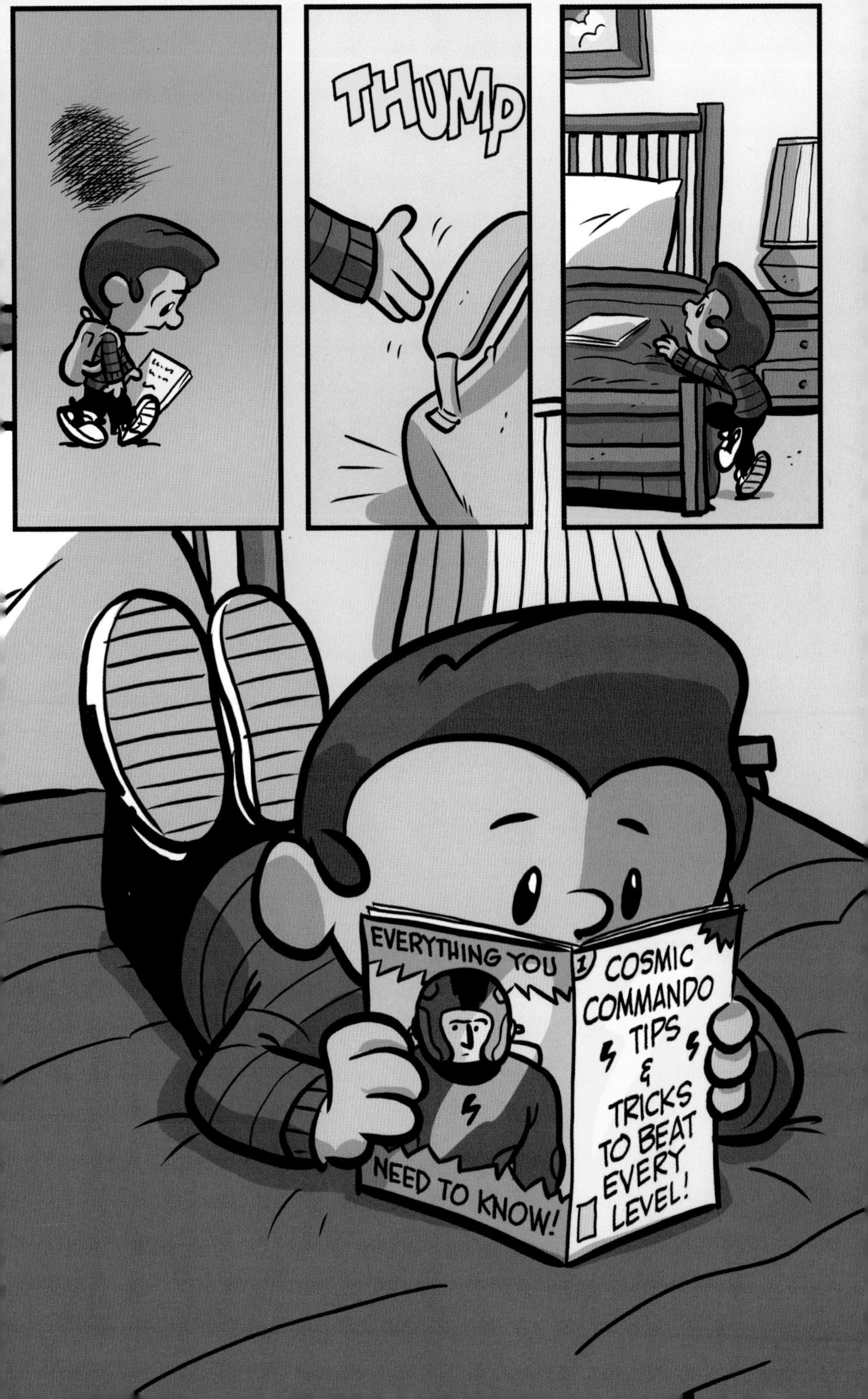
THUMP
EVERYTHING YOU
NEED TO KNOW!
1
COSMIC COMMANDO TIPS & TRICKS TO BEAT EVERY LEVEL!

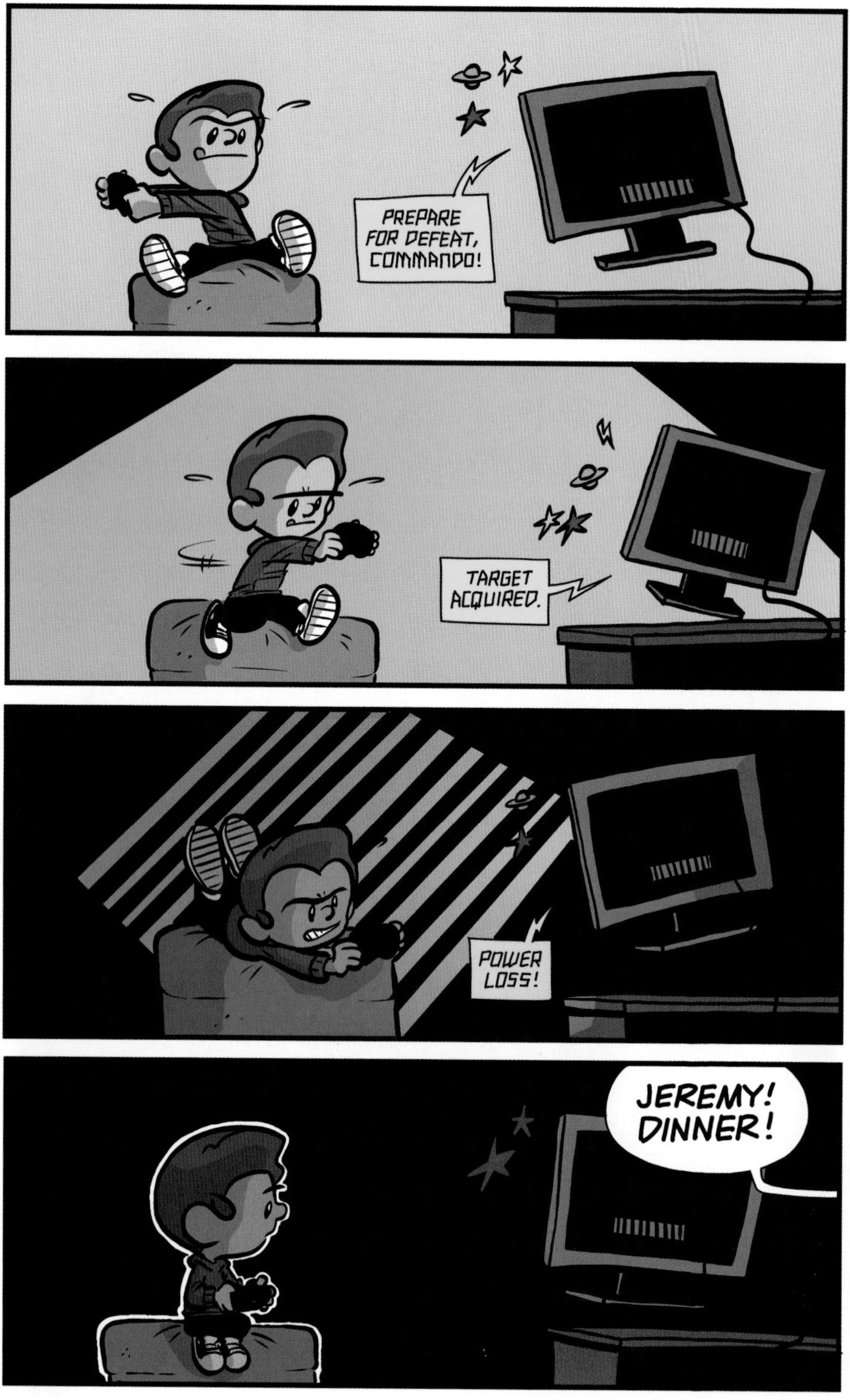
PREPARE FOR DEFEAT, COMMANDO!
TARGET ACQUIRED.
POWER LOSS!
JEREMY! DINNER!

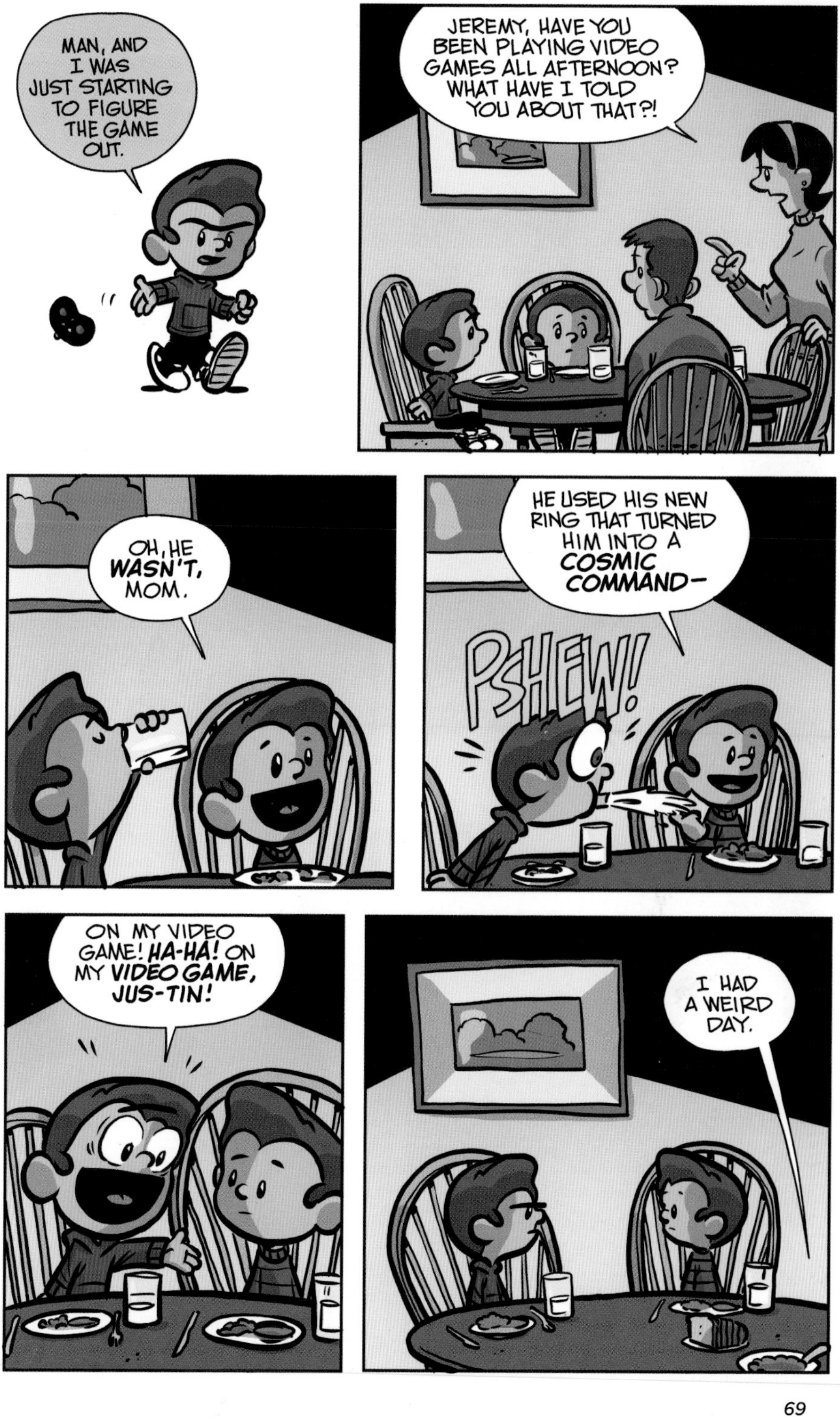
MAN, AND I WAS JUST STARTING TO FIGURE THE GAME OUT.
JEREMY, HAVE YOU BEEN PLAYING VIDEO GAMES ALL AFTERNOON? WHAT HAVE I TOLD YOU ABOUT THAT?!
OH, HE **WASN'T,** MOM.
HE USED HIS NEW RING THAT TURNED HIM INTO A **COSMIC COMMAND–**
PSHEW!
ON MY VIDEO GAME! **HA-HA!** ON MY **VIDEO GAME, JUS-TIN!**
I HAD A WEIRD DAY.

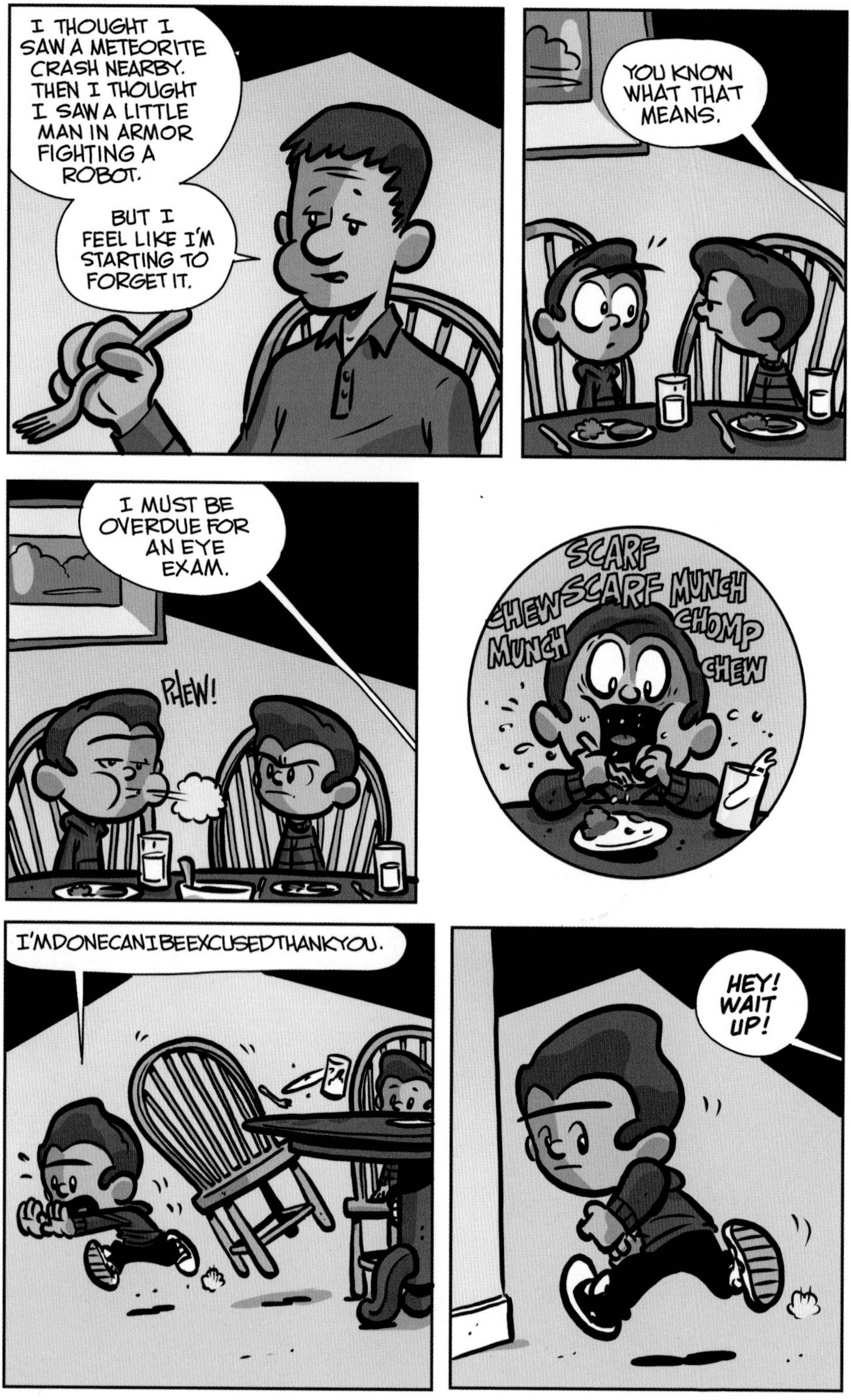

I THOUGHT I SAW A METEORITE CRASH NEARBY. THEN I THOUGHT I SAW A LITTLE MAN IN ARMOR FIGHTING A ROBOT.
BUT I FEEL LIKE I'M STARTING TO FORGET IT.
YOU KNOW WHAT THAT MEANS.
I MUST BE OVERDUE FOR AN EYE EXAM.
PHEW!
SCARF
CHEW SCARF MUNCH
CHOMP
MUNCH
CHEW
I'MDONECANIBEEXCUSEDTHANKYOU.
HEY! WAIT UP!

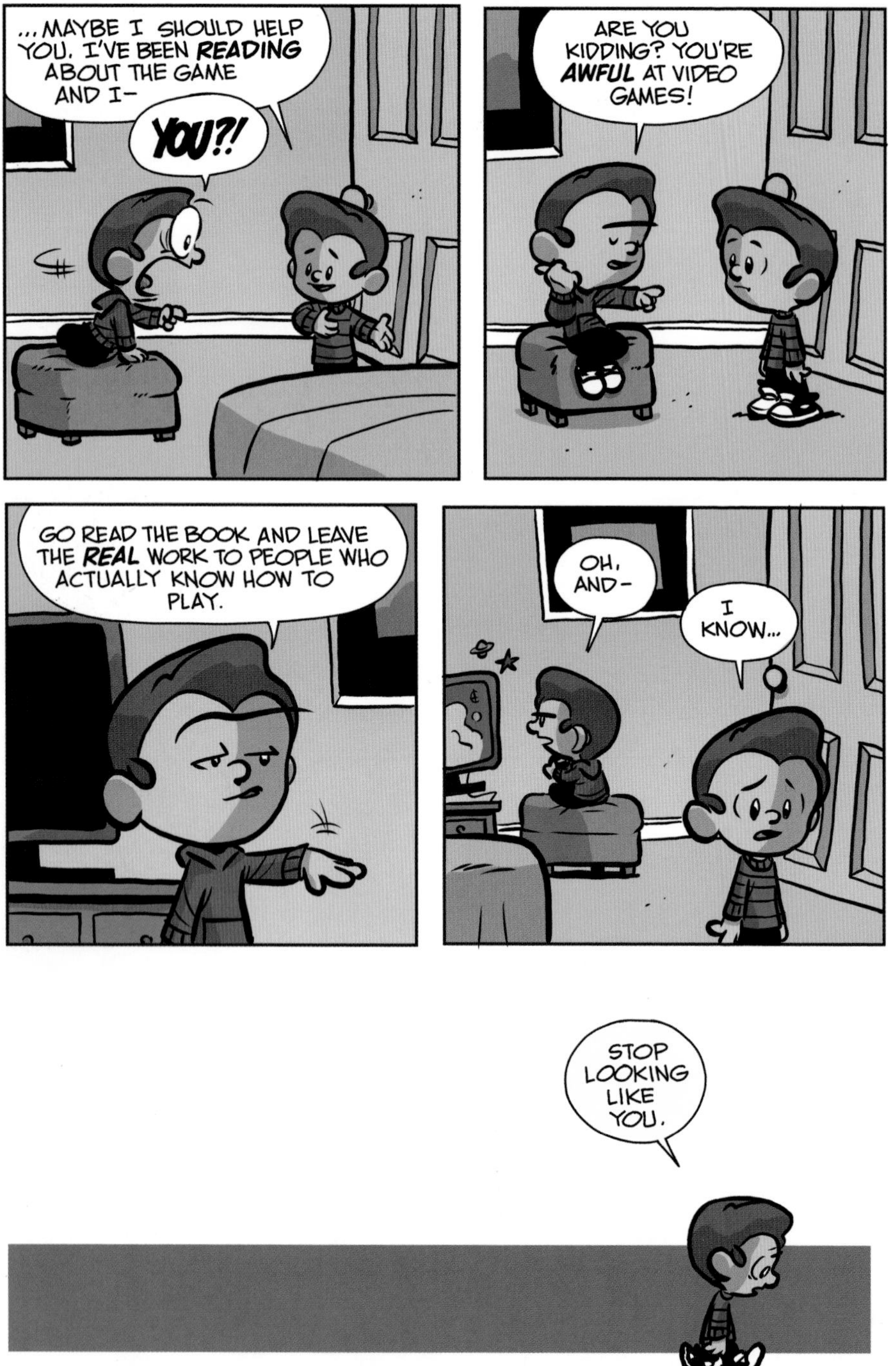
...MAYBE I SHOULD HELP YOU. I'VE BEEN **READING** ABOUT THE GAME AND I-
YOU?!
ARE YOU KIDDING? YOU'RE **AWFUL** AT VIDEO GAMES!
GO READ THE BOOK AND LEAVE THE **REAL** WORK TO PEOPLE WHO ACTUALLY KNOW HOW TO PLAY.
OH, AND-
I KNOW...
STOP LOOKING LIKE YOU.

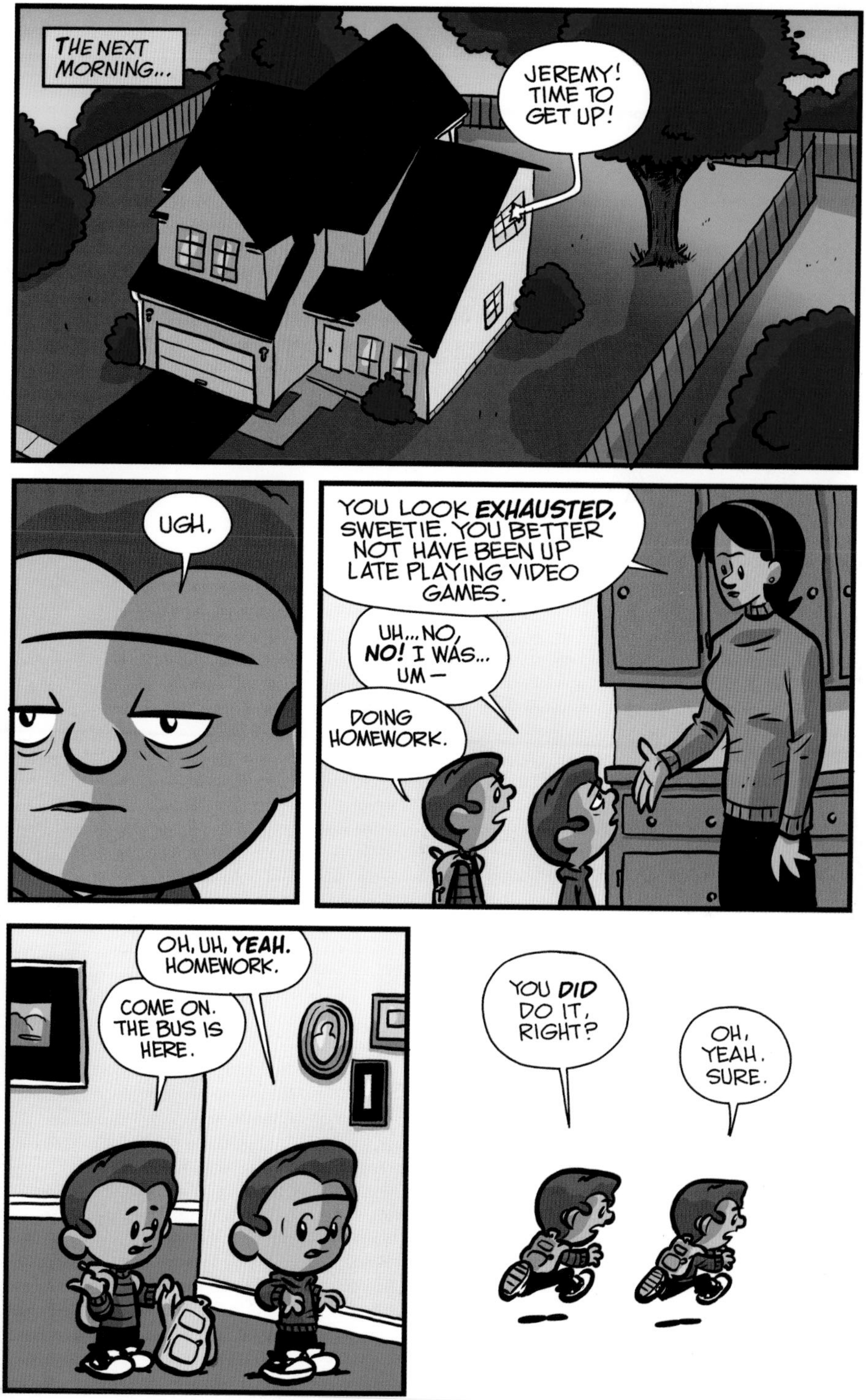
THE NEXT MORNING...
JEREMY! TIME TO GET UP!
UGH.
YOU LOOK **EXHAUSTED,** SWEETIE. YOU BETTER NOT HAVE BEEN UP LATE PLAYING VIDEO GAMES.
UH...NO, **NO!** I WAS... UM—
DOING HOMEWORK.
OH, UH, **YEAH.** HOMEWORK.
COME ON. THE BUS IS HERE.
YOU **DID** DO IT, RIGHT?
OH, YEAH. SURE.

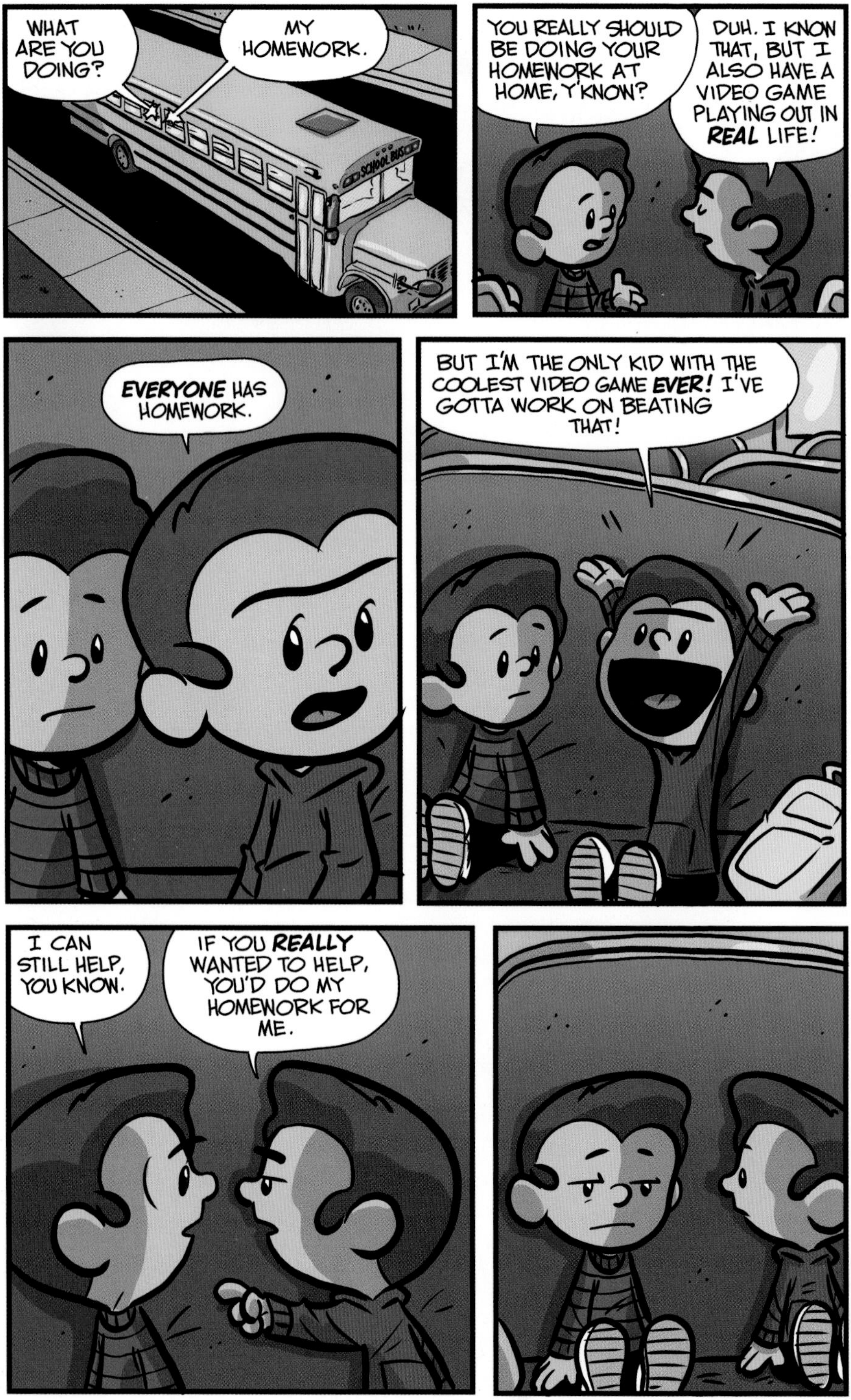
WHAT ARE YOU DOING?
MY HOMEWORK.
SCHOOL BUS
YOU REALLY SHOULD BE DOING YOUR HOMEWORK AT HOME, Y'KNOW?
DUH. I KNOW THAT, BUT I ALSO HAVE A VIDEO GAME PLAYING OUT IN **REAL** LIFE!
EVERYONE HAS HOMEWORK.
BUT I'M THE ONLY KID WITH THE COOLEST VIDEO GAME **EVER!** I'VE GOTTA WORK ON BEATING THAT!
I CAN STILL HELP, YOU KNOW.
IF YOU **REALLY** WANTED TO HELP, YOU'D DO MY HOMEWORK FOR ME.

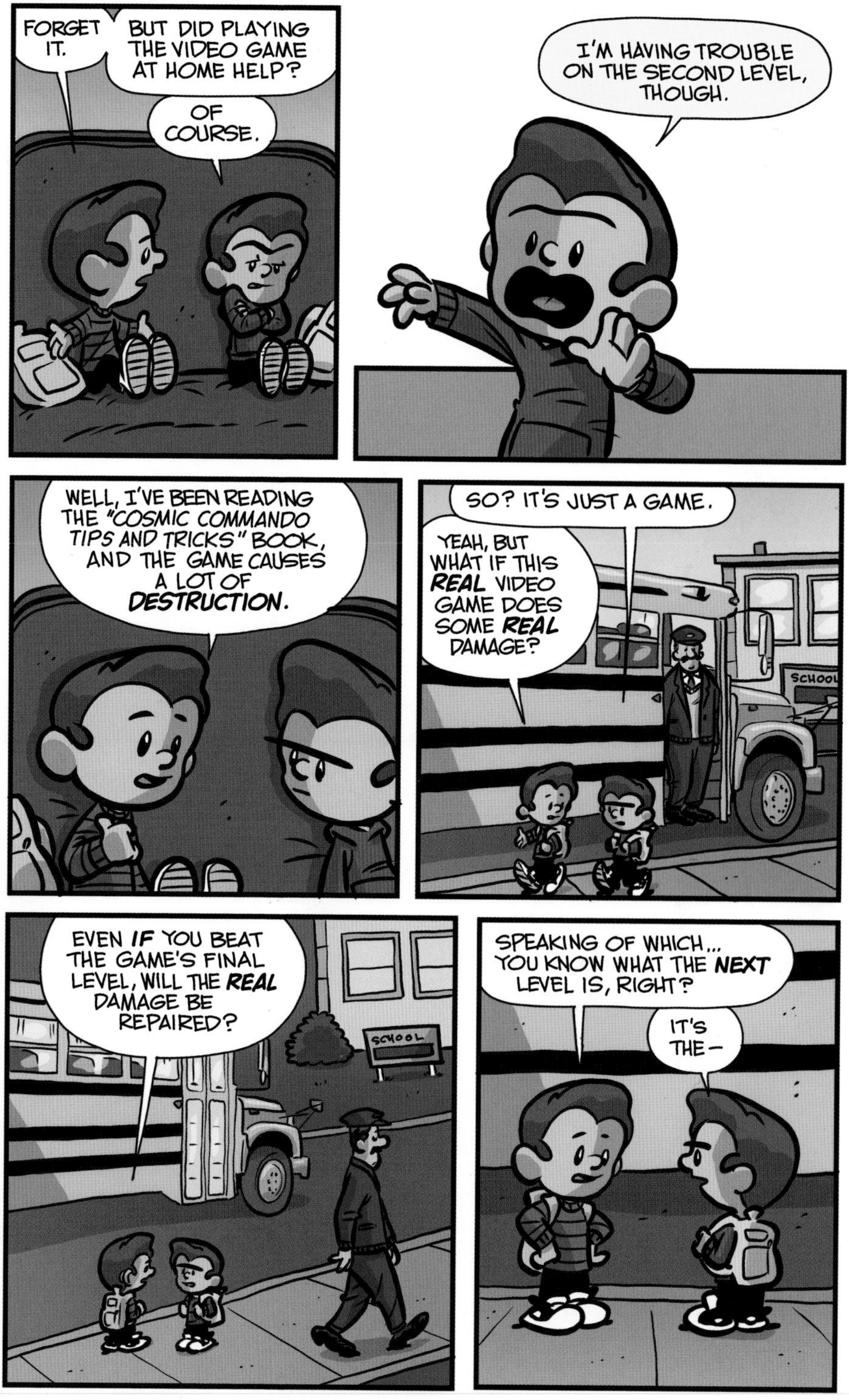
FORGET IT.
BUT DID PLAYING THE VIDEO GAME AT HOME HELP?
OF COURSE.
I'M HAVING TROUBLE ON THE SECOND LEVEL, THOUGH.
WELL, I'VE BEEN READING THE "COSMIC COMMANDO TIPS AND TRICKS" BOOK, AND THE GAME CAUSES A LOT OF DESTRUCTION.
SO? IT'S JUST A GAME.
YEAH, BUT WHAT IF THIS REAL VIDEO GAME DOES SOME REAL DAMAGE?
SCHOOL
EVEN IF YOU BEAT THE GAME'S FINAL LEVEL, WILL THE REAL DAMAGE BE REPAIRED?
SCHOOL
SPEAKING OF WHICH... YOU KNOW WHAT THE NEXT LEVEL IS, RIGHT?
IT'S THE—

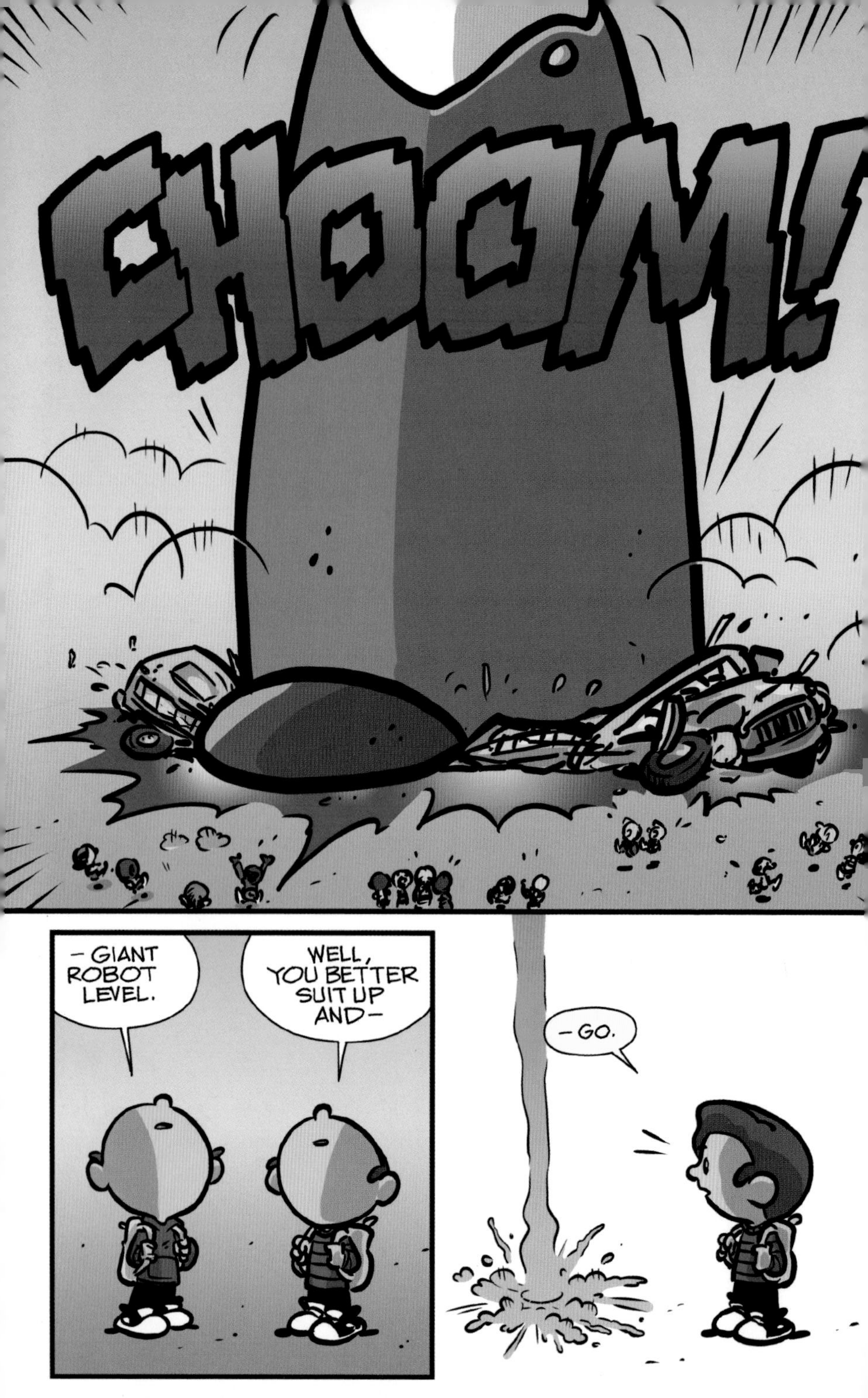
CHOOM!
-GIANT ROBOT LEVEL.
WELL, YOU BETTER SUIT UP AND-
-GO.

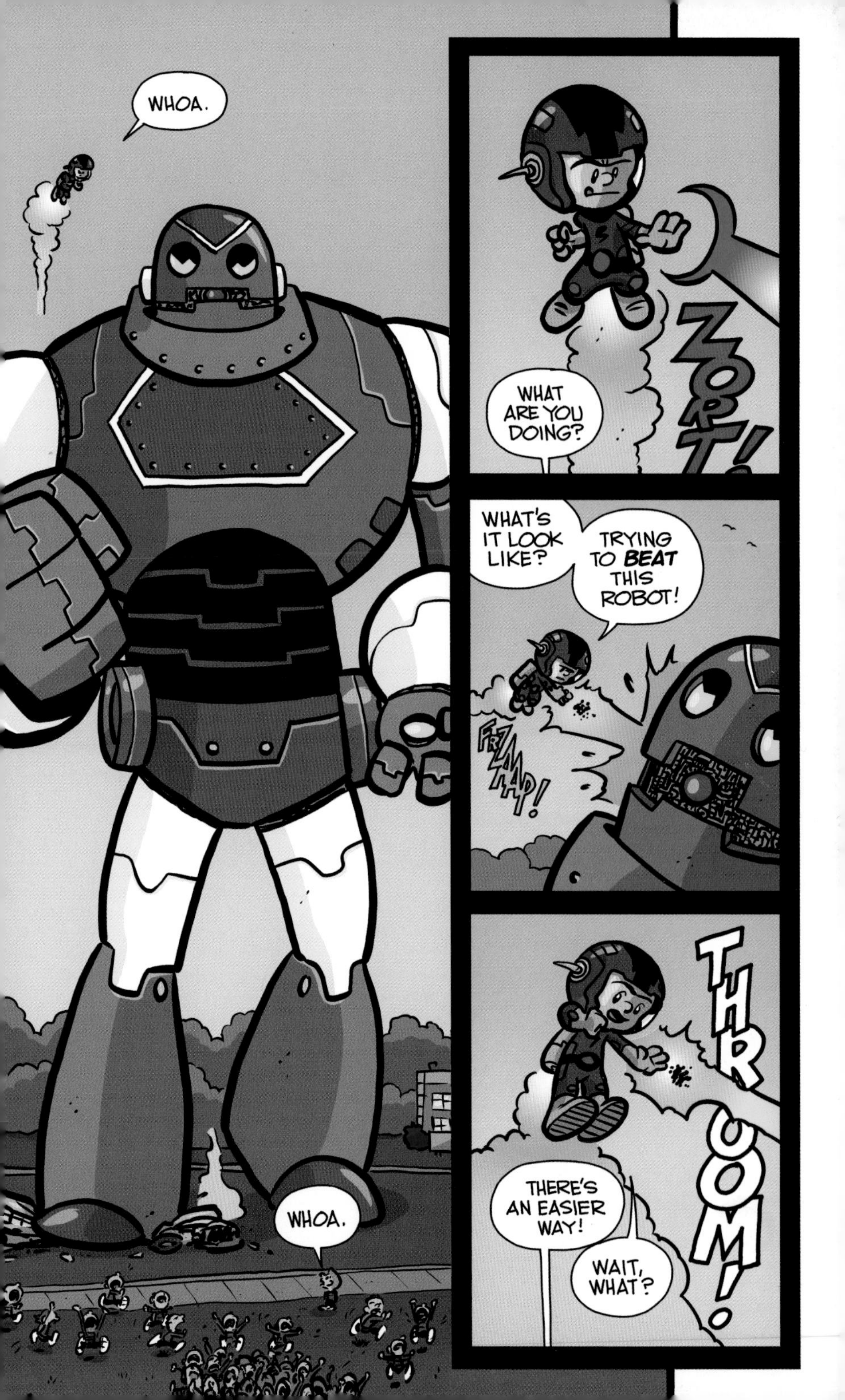
WHOA.
WHOA.
WHAT ARE YOU DOING?
ZORT!
WHAT'S IT LOOK LIKE?
TRYING TO **BEAT** THIS ROBOT!
FRZAAAP!
THRUOOM!
THERE'S AN EASIER WAY!
WAIT, WHAT?

I READ IT IN THE TIPS AND TRICKS BOOK.

THE WHAT?!

THE BOOK YOU THREW AT ME.

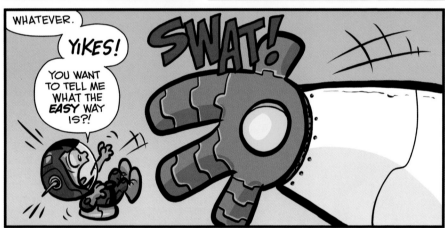

WHATEVER.

YIKES!

YOU WANT TO TELL ME WHAT THE *EASY* WAY IS?!

SWAT!

YOU JUST NEED TO PRESS THE BUTTON ON THE LEFT SIDE OF HIS HEAD!

OH... IS *THAT* ALL?

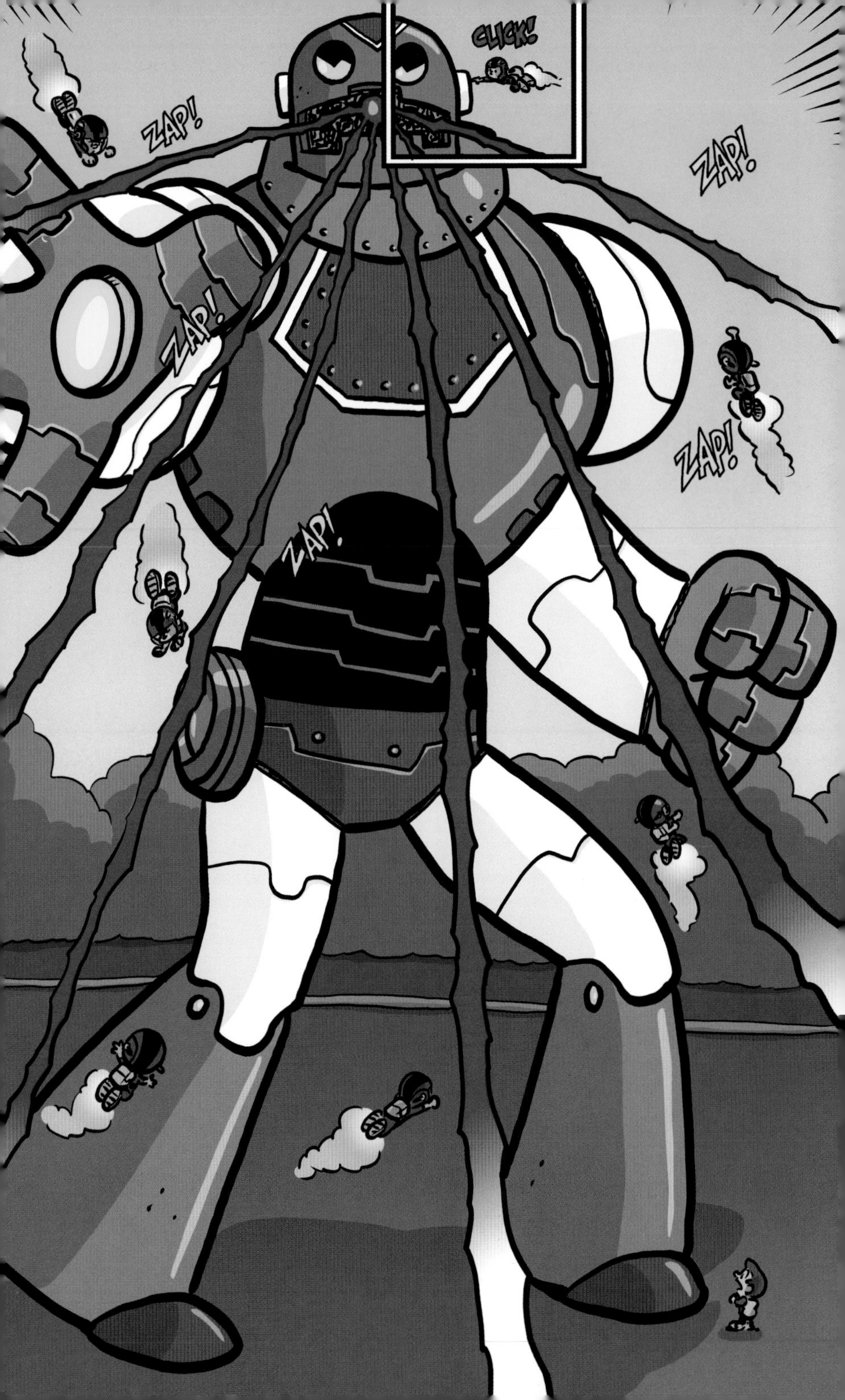
CLICK!
ZAP!
ZAP!
ZAP!
ZAP!
ZAP!
ZAP!

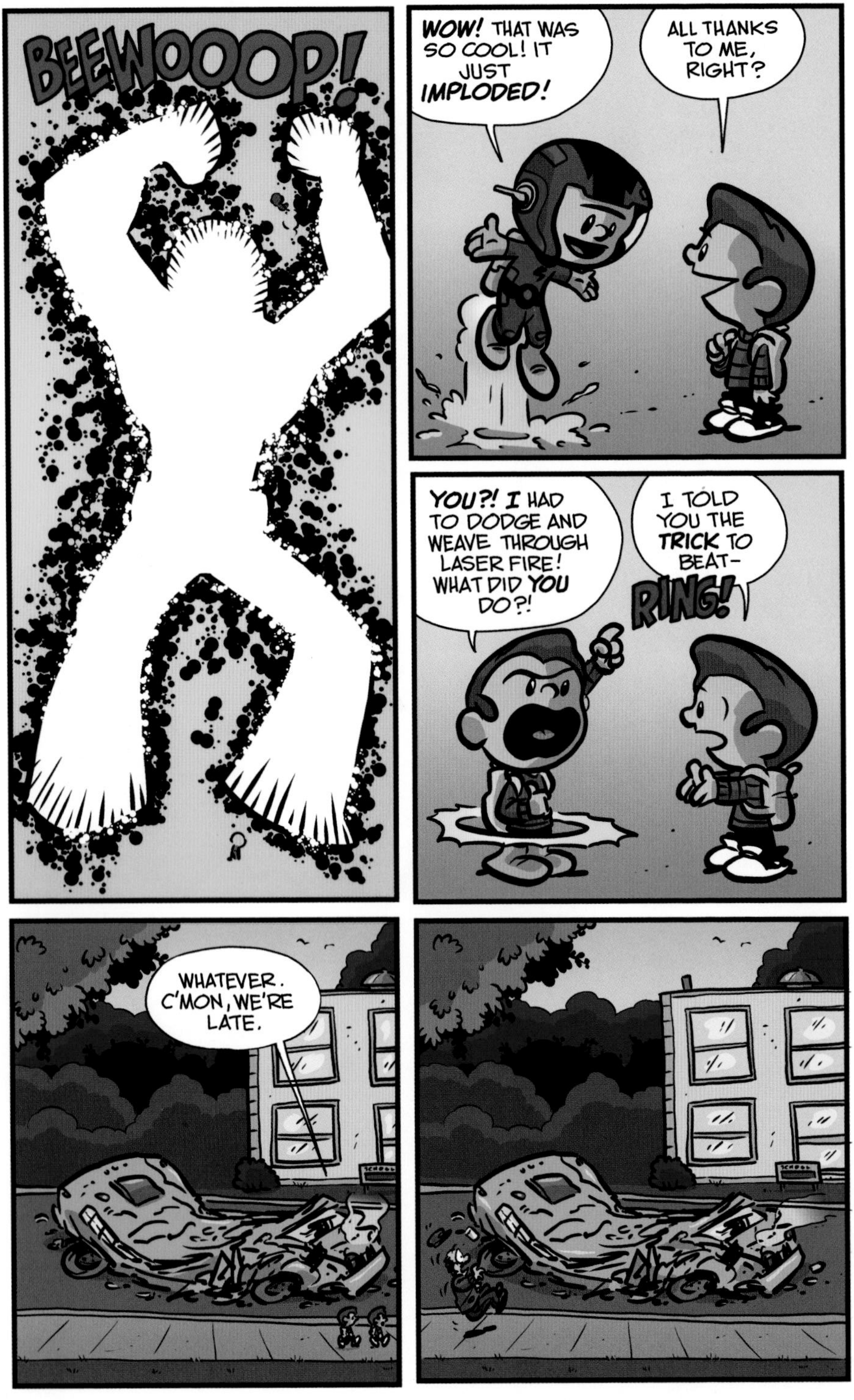

BEEWOOOP!
WOW! THAT WAS SO COOL! IT JUST IMPLODED!
ALL THANKS TO ME, RIGHT?
YOU?! I HAD TO DODGE AND WEAVE THROUGH LASER FIRE! WHAT DID YOU DO?!
I TOLD YOU THE TRICK TO BEAT-
RING!
WHATEVER. C'MON, WE'RE LATE.

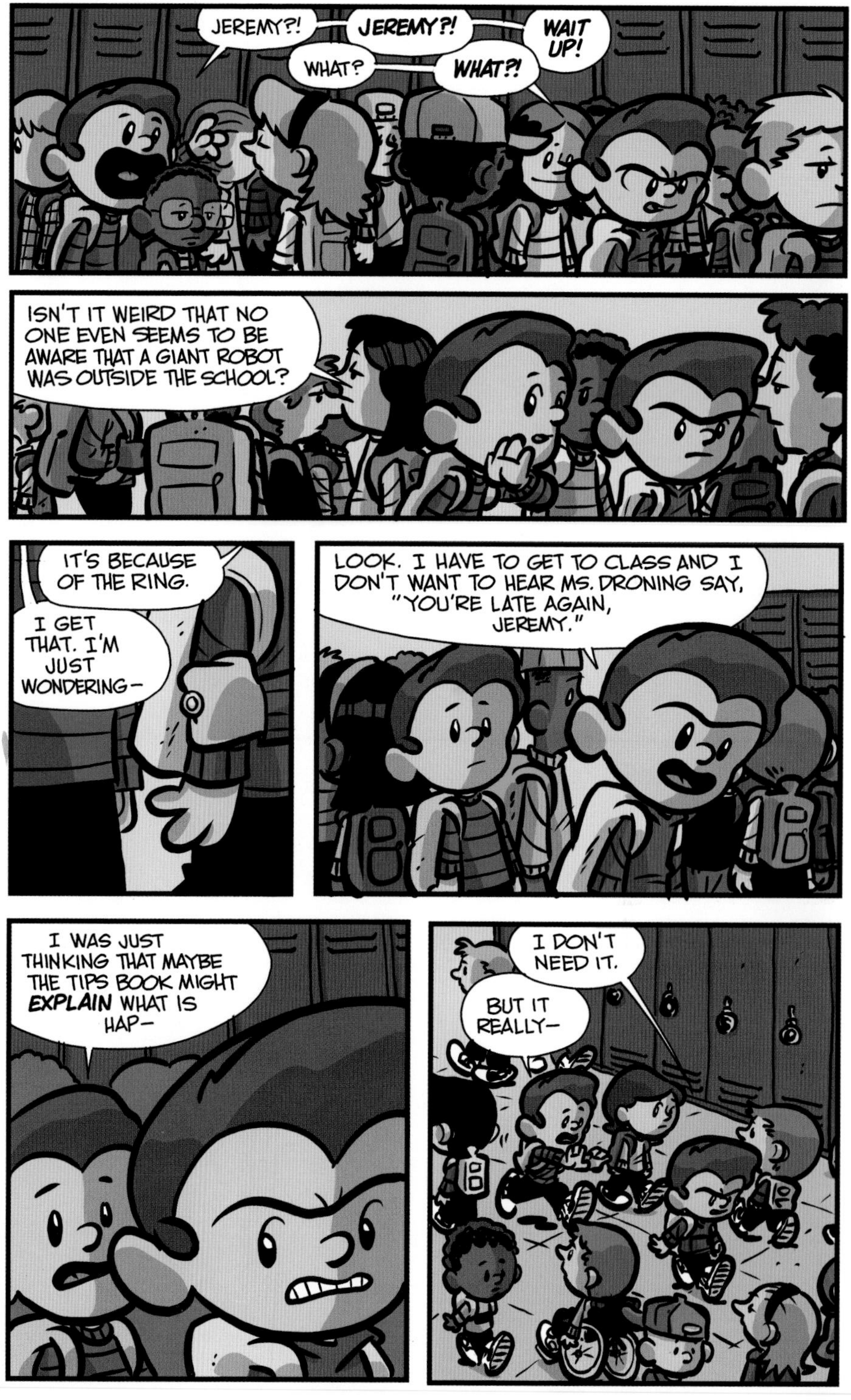
JEREMY?!
WHAT?
JEREMY?!
WHAT?!
WAIT UP!
ISN'T IT WEIRD THAT NO ONE EVEN SEEMS TO BE AWARE THAT A GIANT ROBOT WAS OUTSIDE THE SCHOOL?
IT'S BECAUSE OF THE RING.
I GET THAT. I'M JUST WONDERING—
LOOK. I HAVE TO GET TO CLASS AND I DON'T WANT TO HEAR MS. DRONING SAY, "YOU'RE LATE AGAIN, JEREMY."
I WAS JUST THINKING THAT MAYBE THE TIPS BOOK MIGHT EXPLAIN WHAT IS HAP—
I DON'T NEED IT.
BUT IT REALLY—

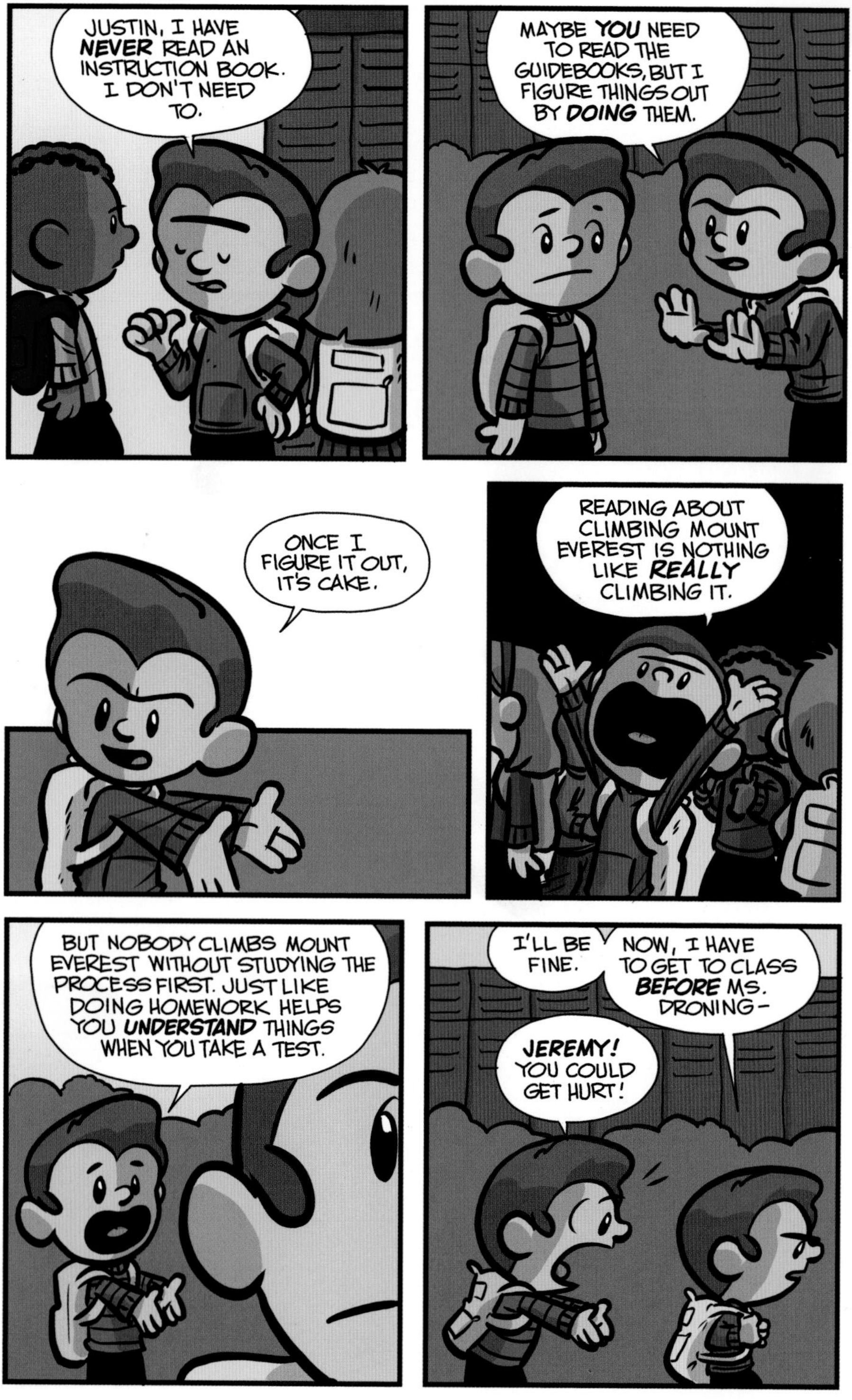
JUSTIN, I HAVE NEVER READ AN INSTRUCTION BOOK. I DON'T NEED TO.
MAYBE YOU NEED TO READ THE GUIDEBOOKS, BUT I FIGURE THINGS OUT BY DOING THEM.
ONCE I FIGURE IT OUT, IT'S CAKE.
READING ABOUT CLIMBING MOUNT EVEREST IS NOTHING LIKE REALLY CLIMBING IT.
BUT NOBODY CLIMBS MOUNT EVEREST WITHOUT STUDYING THE PROCESS FIRST. JUST LIKE DOING HOMEWORK HELPS YOU UNDERSTAND THINGS WHEN YOU TAKE A TEST.
I'LL BE FINE.
NOW, I HAVE TO GET TO CLASS BEFORE MS. DRONING–
JEREMY! YOU COULD GET HURT!

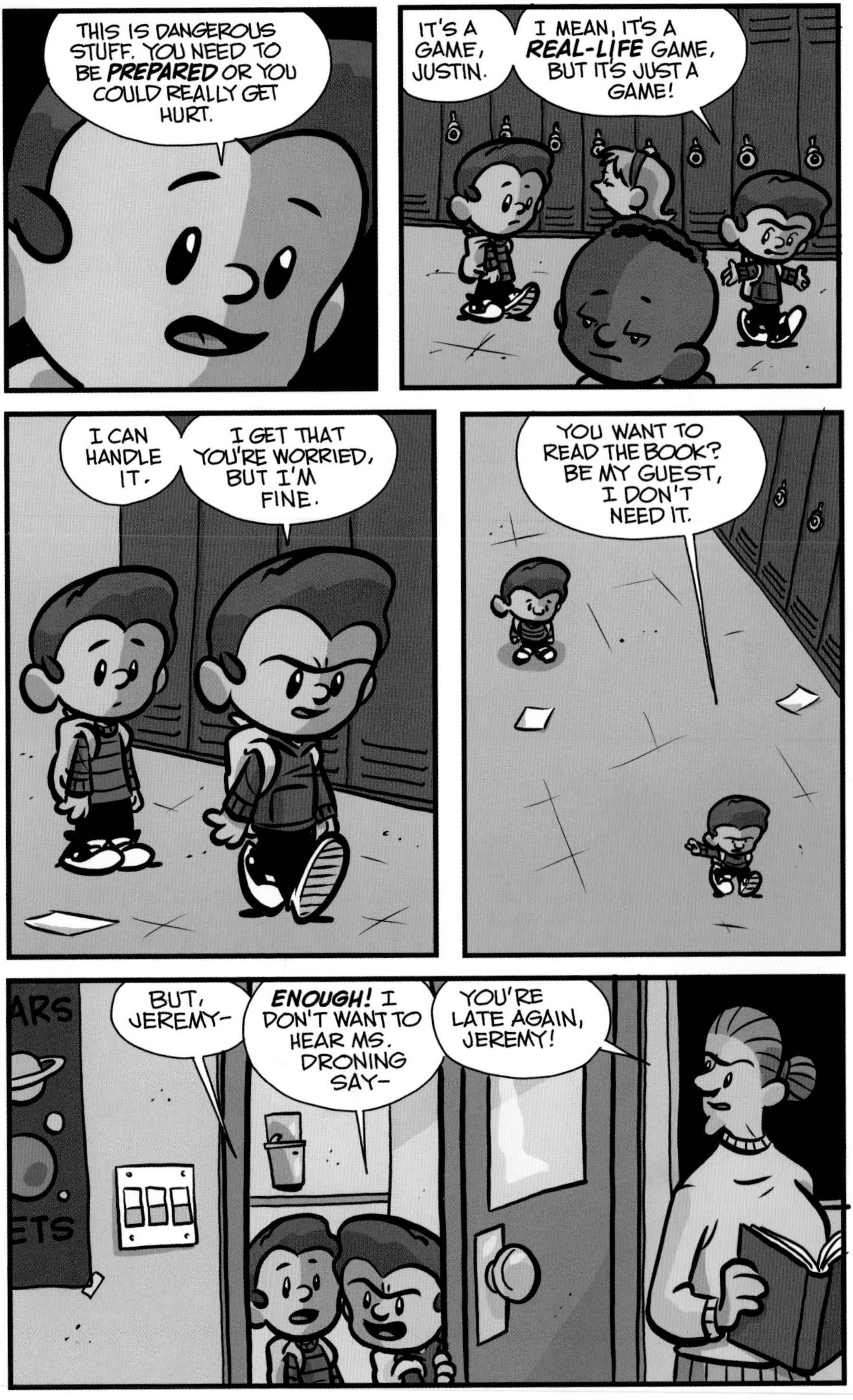

THIS IS DANGEROUS STUFF. YOU NEED TO BE **PREPARED** OR YOU COULD REALLY GET HURT.
IT'S A GAME, JUSTIN.
I MEAN, IT'S A **REAL-LIFE** GAME, BUT IT'S JUST A GAME!
I CAN HANDLE IT.
I GET THAT YOU'RE WORRIED, BUT I'M FINE.
YOU WANT TO READ THE BOOK? BE MY GUEST, I DON'T NEED IT.
ARS
ETS
BUT, JEREMY-
ENOUGH! I DON'T WANT TO HEAR MS. DRONING SAY-
YOU'RE LATE AGAIN, JEREMY!

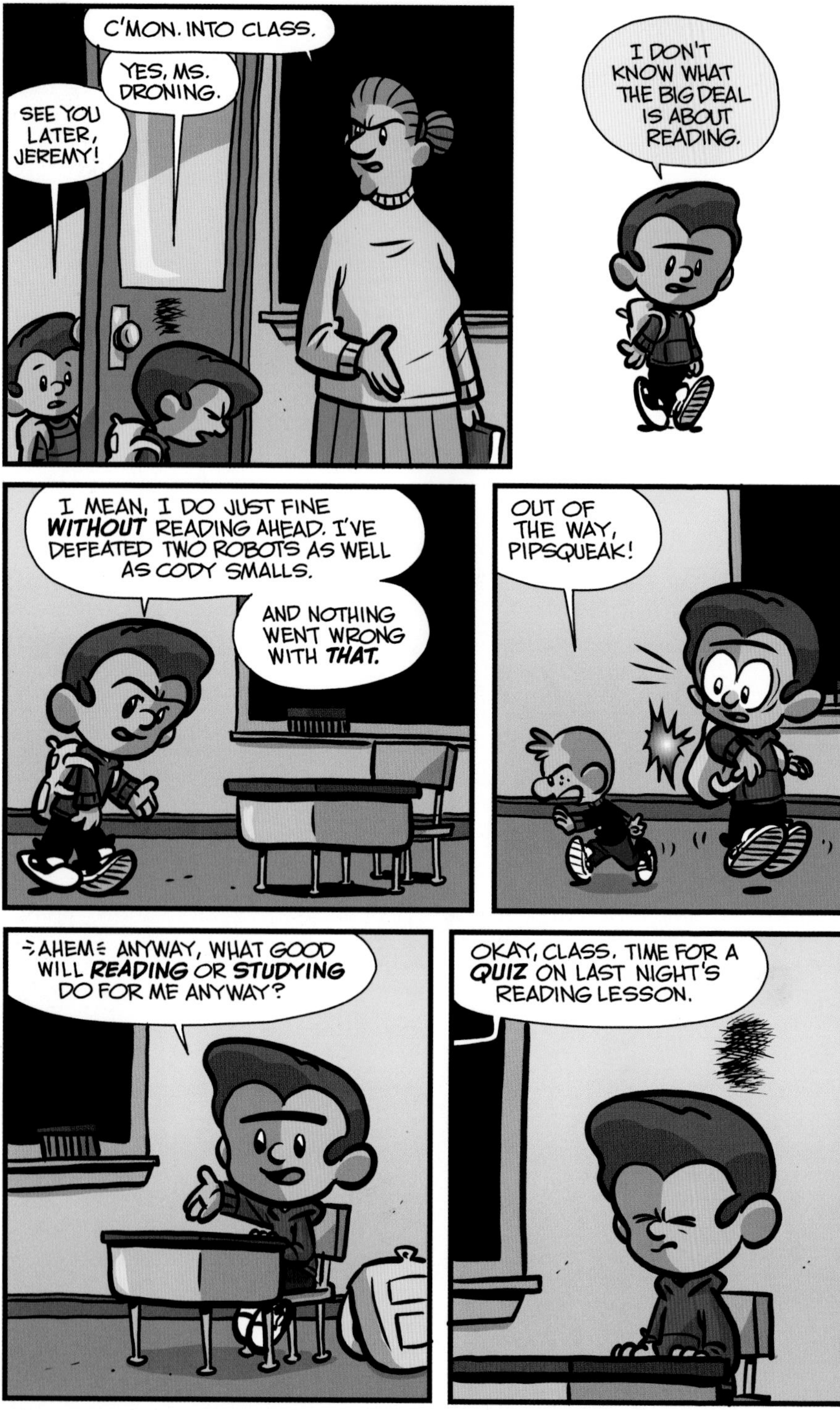
C'MON. INTO CLASS.
YES, MS. DRONING.
SEE YOU LATER, JEREMY!
I DON'T KNOW WHAT THE BIG DEAL IS ABOUT READING.
I MEAN, I DO JUST FINE **WITHOUT** READING AHEAD. I'VE DEFEATED TWO ROBOTS AS WELL AS CODY SMALLS.
AND NOTHING WENT WRONG WITH **THAT.**
OUT OF THE WAY, PIPSQUEAK!
=AHEM= ANYWAY, WHAT GOOD WILL **READING** OR **STUDYING** DO FOR ME ANYWAY?
OKAY, CLASS. TIME FOR A **QUIZ** ON LAST NIGHT'S READING LESSON.

CUTSCENE

SKORN!

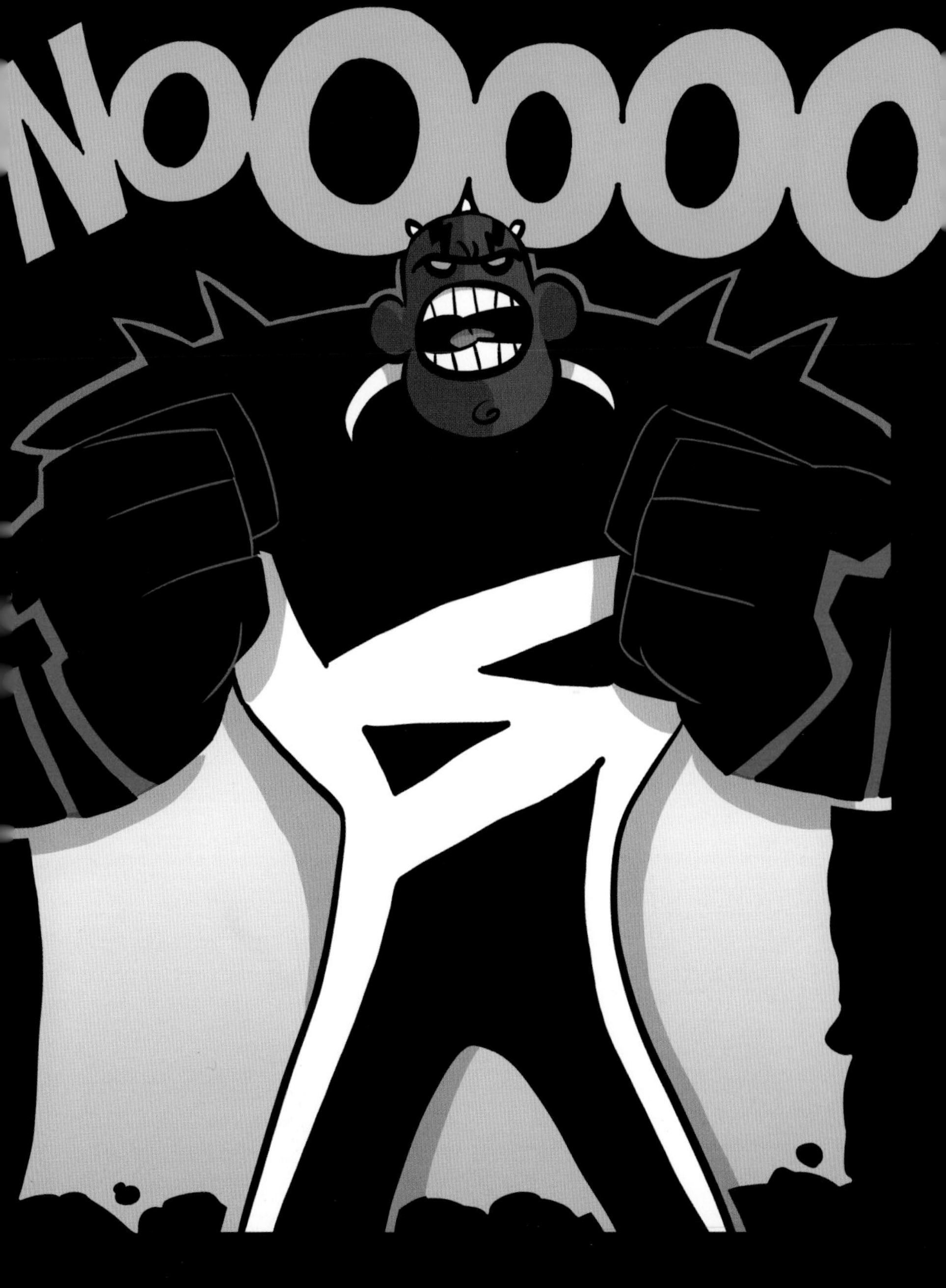
NOOOOO

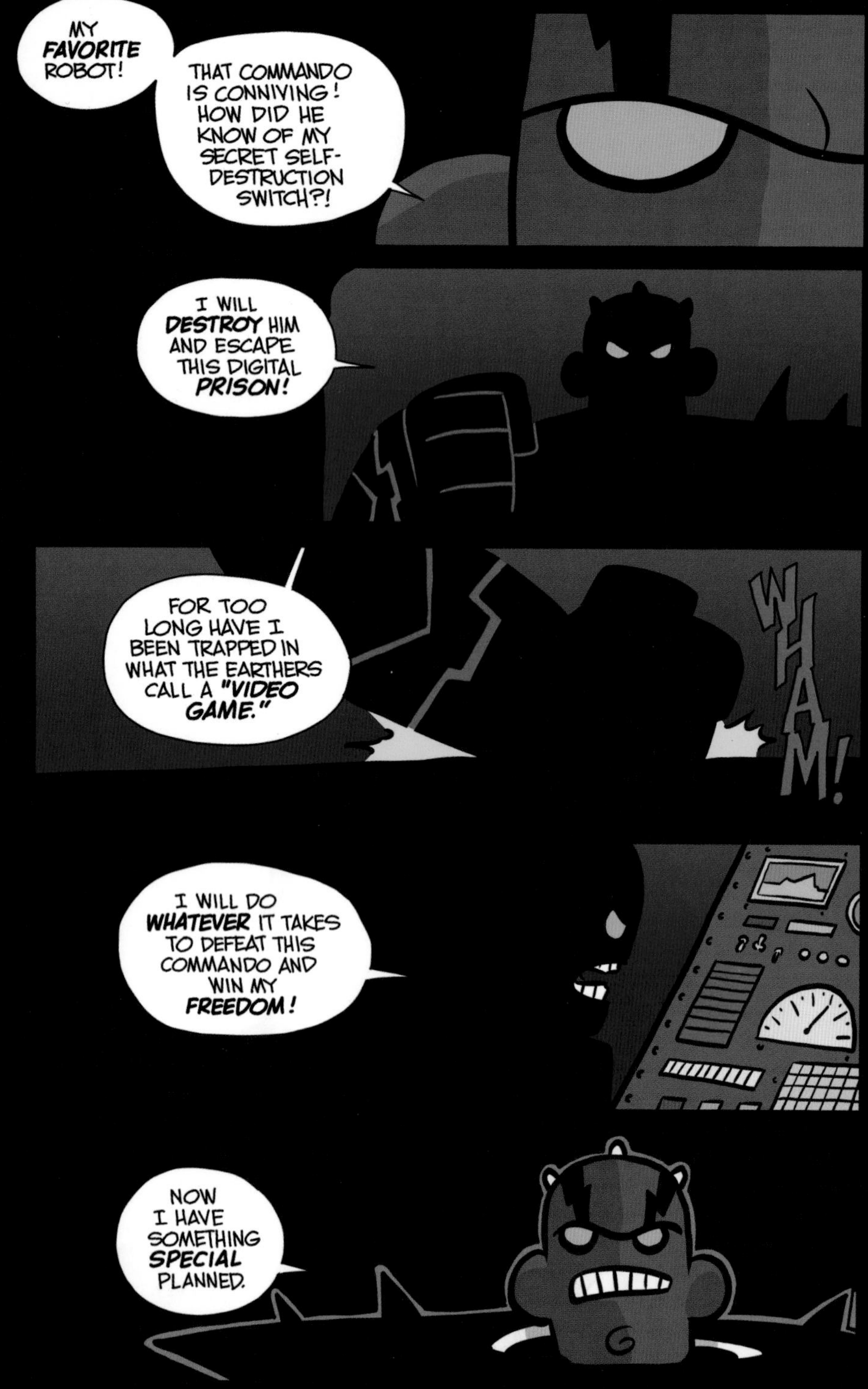
MY FAVORITE ROBOT!
THAT COMMANDO IS CONNIVING! HOW DID HE KNOW OF MY SECRET SELF-DESTRUCTION SWITCH?!
I WILL DESTROY HIM AND ESCAPE THIS DIGITAL PRISON!
FOR TOO LONG HAVE I BEEN TRAPPED IN WHAT THE EARTHERS CALL A "VIDEO GAME."
WHAM!
I WILL DO WHATEVER IT TAKES TO DEFEAT THIS COMMANDO AND WIN MY FREEDOM!
NOW I HAVE SOMETHING SPECIAL PLANNED.

CHAPTER FIVE

LEVELING UP

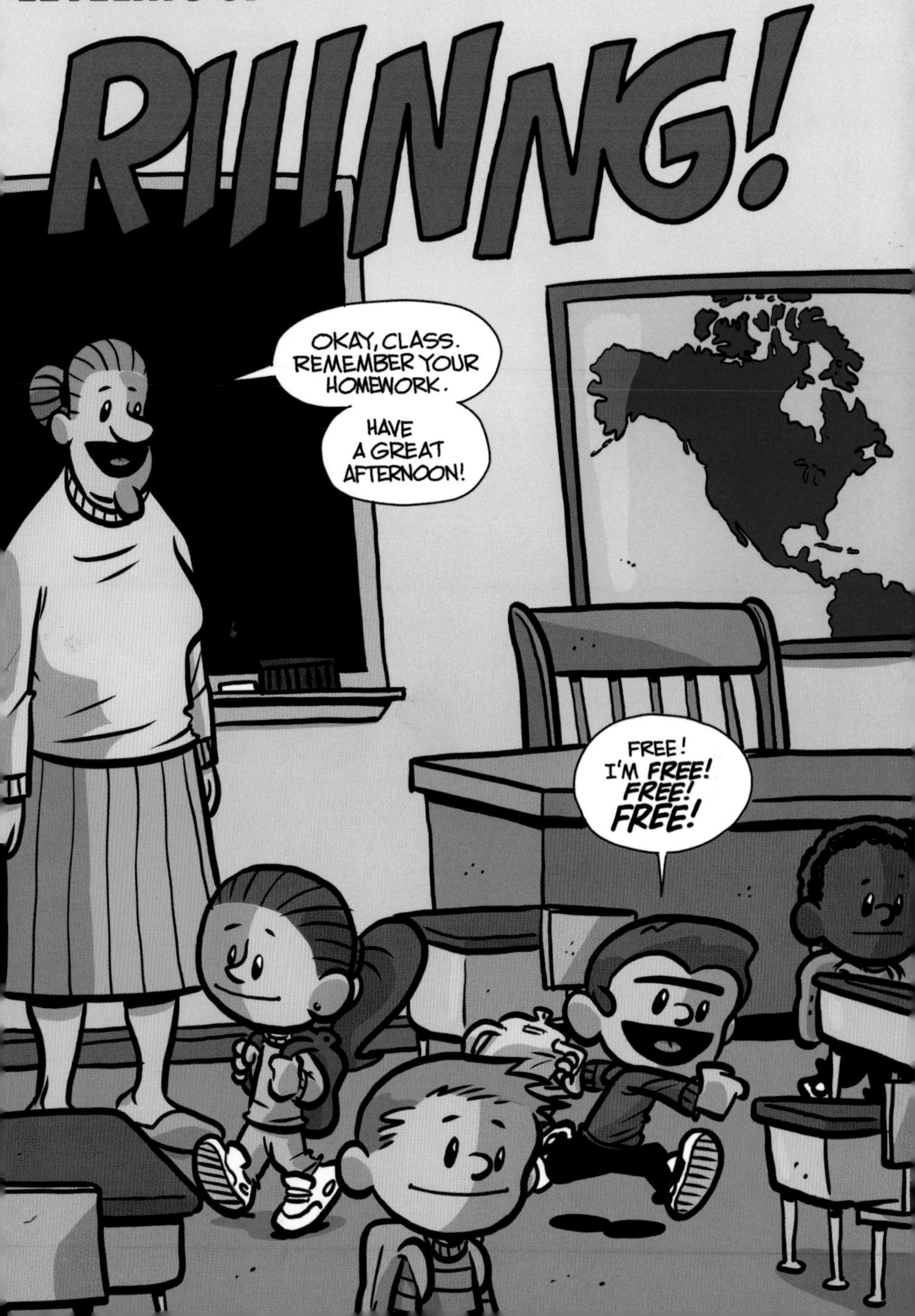
RIIINNG!
OKAY, CLASS. REMEMBER YOUR HOMEWORK.
HAVE A GREAT AFTERNOON!
FREE! I'M FREE! FREE! FREE!

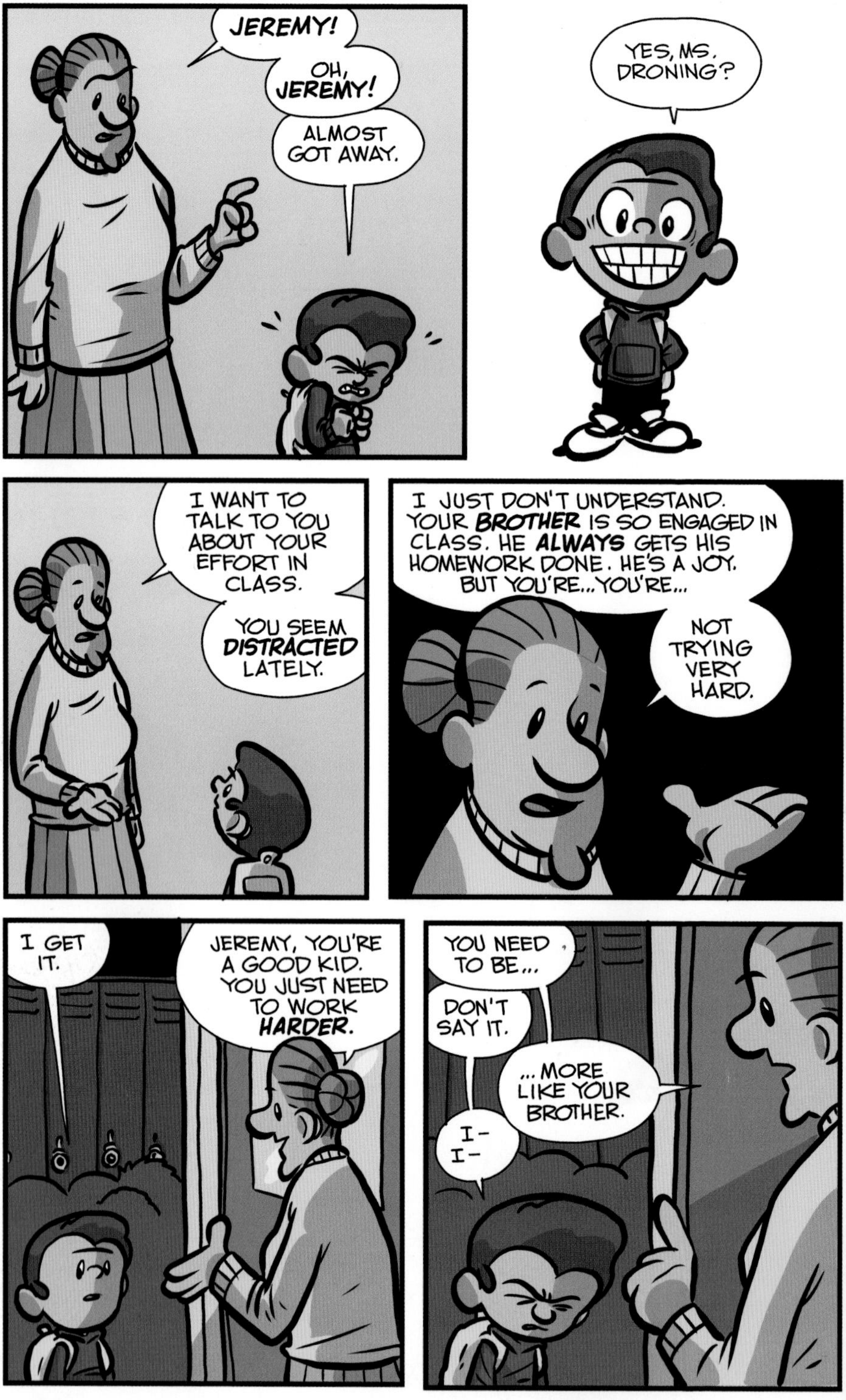
JEREMY!
OH, JEREMY!
ALMOST GOT AWAY.
YES, MS. DRONING?
I WANT TO TALK TO YOU ABOUT YOUR EFFORT IN CLASS.
YOU SEEM DISTRACTED LATELY.
I JUST DON'T UNDERSTAND. YOUR BROTHER IS SO ENGAGED IN CLASS. HE ALWAYS GETS HIS HOMEWORK DONE. HE'S A JOY. BUT YOU'RE... YOU'RE...
NOT TRYING VERY HARD.
I GET IT.
JEREMY, YOU'RE A GOOD KID. YOU JUST NEED TO WORK HARDER.
YOU NEED TO BE...
DON'T SAY IT.
...MORE LIKE YOUR BROTHER.
I- I-

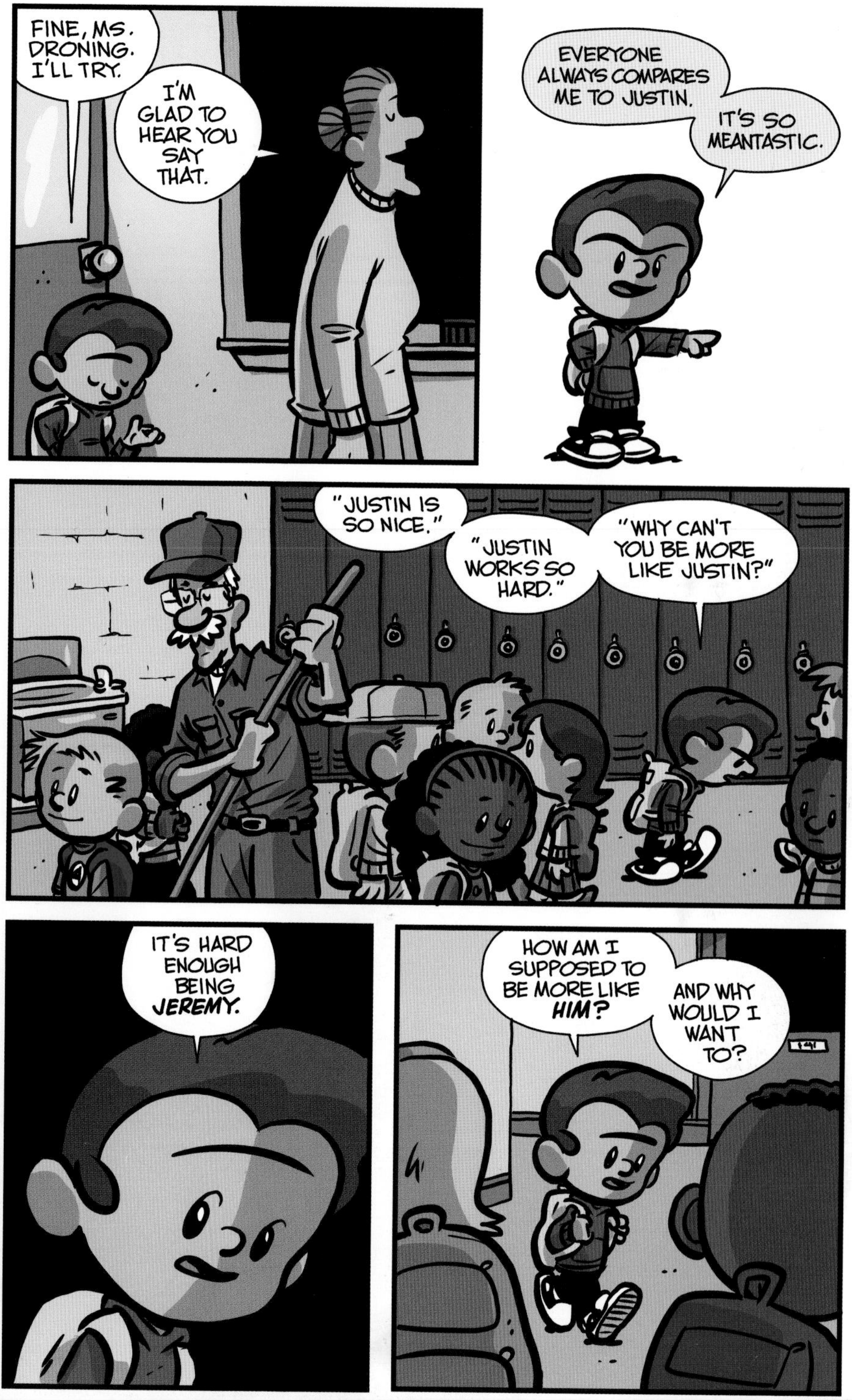
FINE, MS. DRONING. I'LL TRY.
I'M GLAD TO HEAR YOU SAY THAT.
EVERYONE ALWAYS COMPARES ME TO JUSTIN.
IT'S SO MEANTASTIC.
"JUSTIN IS SO NICE."
"JUSTIN WORKS SO HARD."
"WHY CAN'T YOU BE MORE LIKE JUSTIN?"
IT'S HARD ENOUGH BEING *JEREMY*.
HOW AM I SUPPOSED TO BE MORE LIKE *HIM*?
AND WHY WOULD I WANT TO?

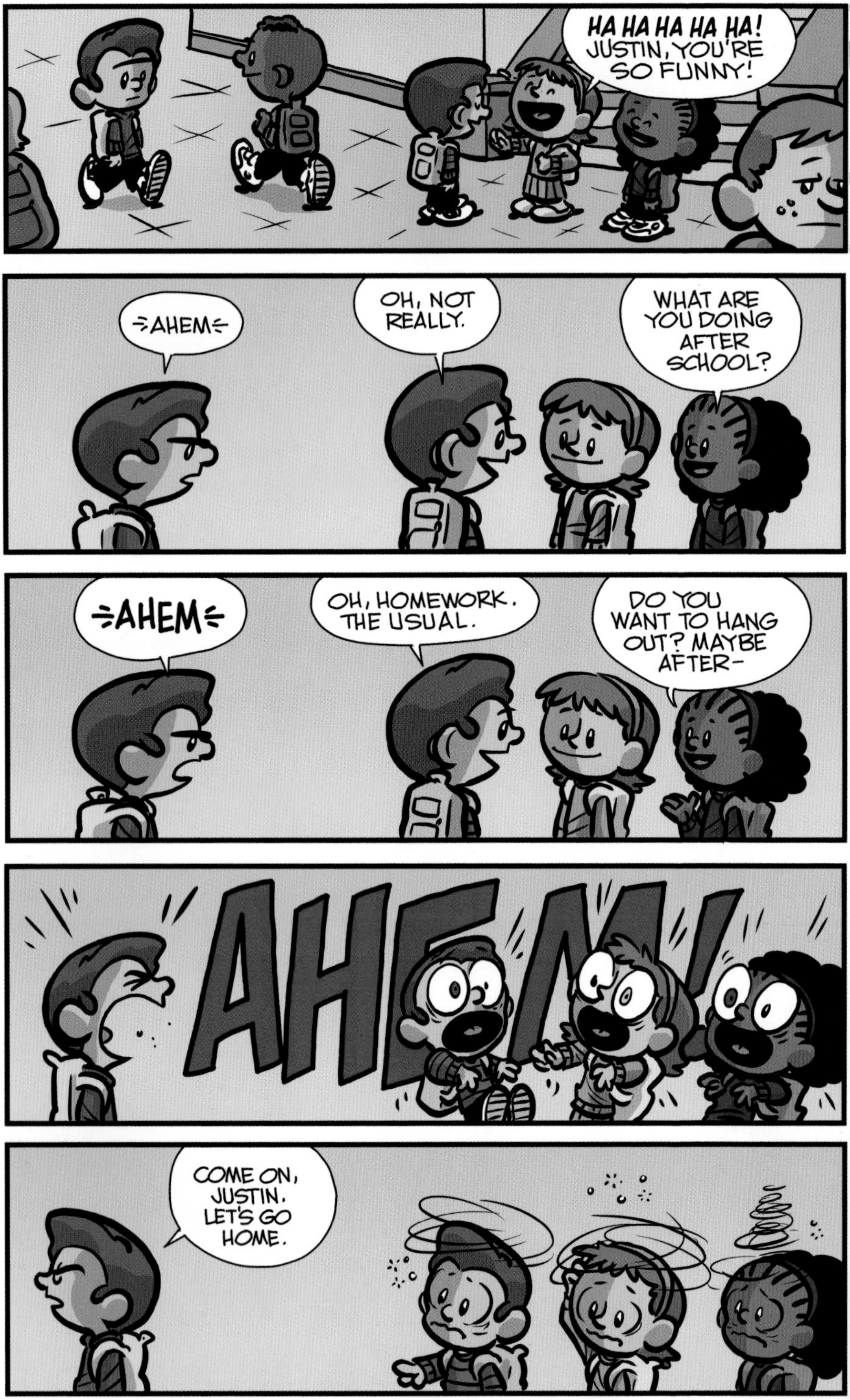

HA HA HA HA HA! JUSTIN, YOU'RE SO FUNNY!
AHEM
OH, NOT REALLY.
WHAT ARE YOU DOING AFTER SCHOOL?
AHEM
OH, HOMEWORK. THE USUAL.
DO YOU WANT TO HANG OUT? MAYBE AFTER-
AHEM!
COME ON, JUSTIN. LET'S GO HOME.

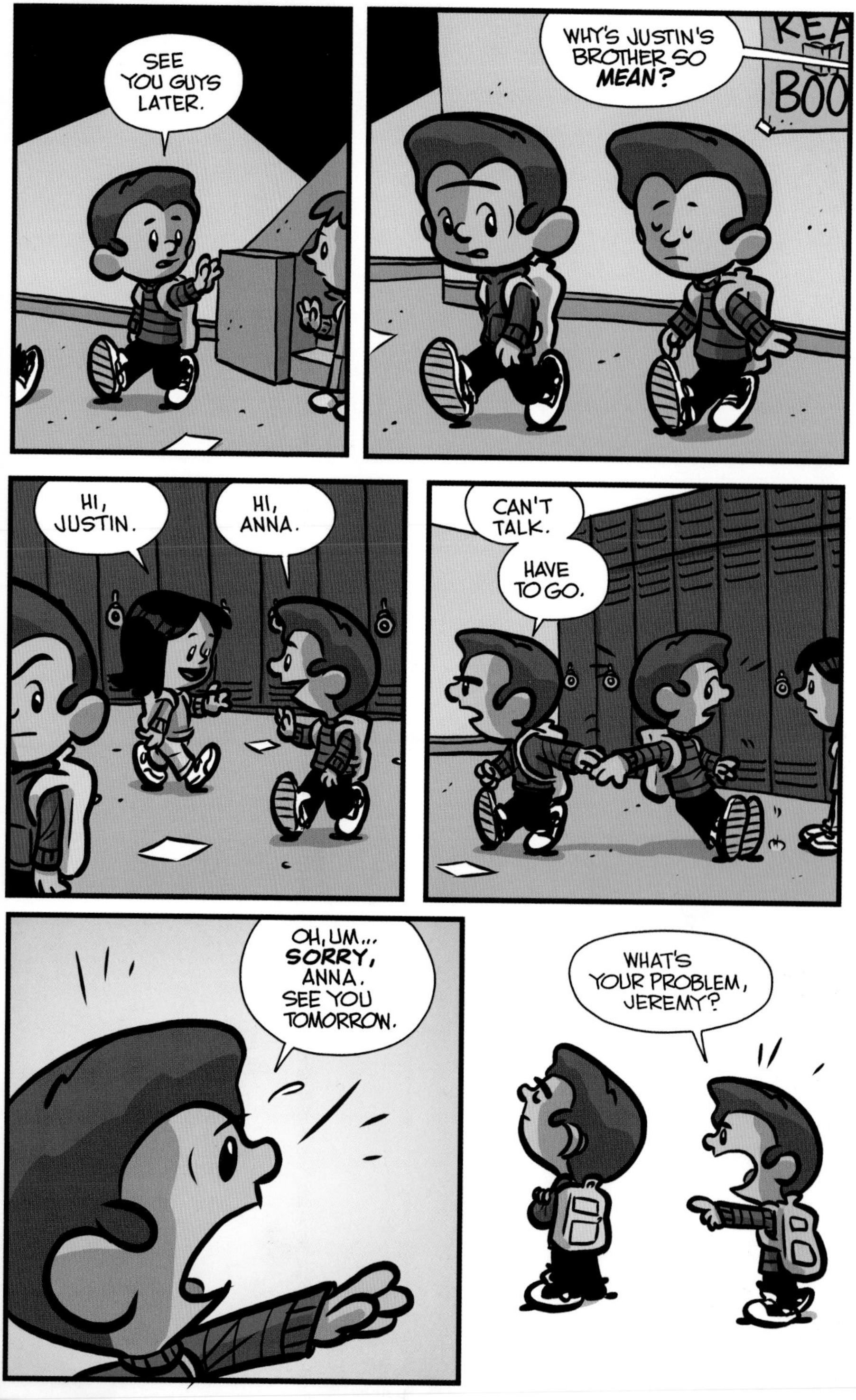
SEE YOU GUYS LATER.
WHY'S JUSTIN'S BROTHER SO **MEAN?**
HI, JUSTIN.
HI, ANNA.
CAN'T TALK.
HAVE TO GO.
OH, UM... **SORRY,** ANNA. SEE YOU TOMORROW.
WHAT'S YOUR PROBLEM, JEREMY?

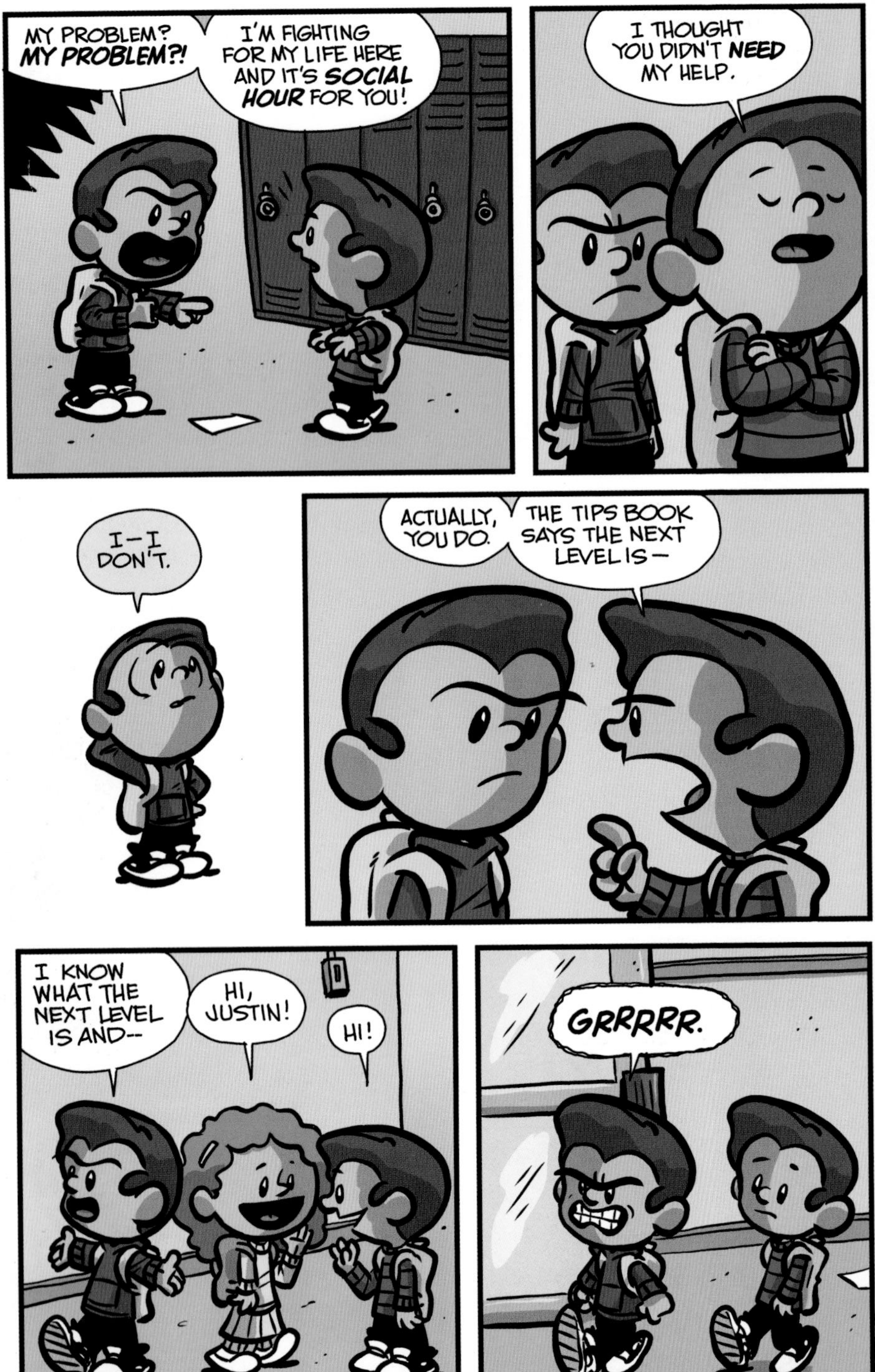
MY PROBLEM? **MY PROBLEM?!**
I'M FIGHTING FOR MY LIFE HERE AND IT'S **SOCIAL HOUR** FOR YOU!
I THOUGHT YOU DIDN'T **NEED** MY HELP.
I—I DON'T.
ACTUALLY, YOU DO.
THE TIPS BOOK SAYS THE NEXT LEVEL IS—
I KNOW WHAT THE NEXT LEVEL IS AND--
HI, JUSTIN!
HI!
GRRRRR.

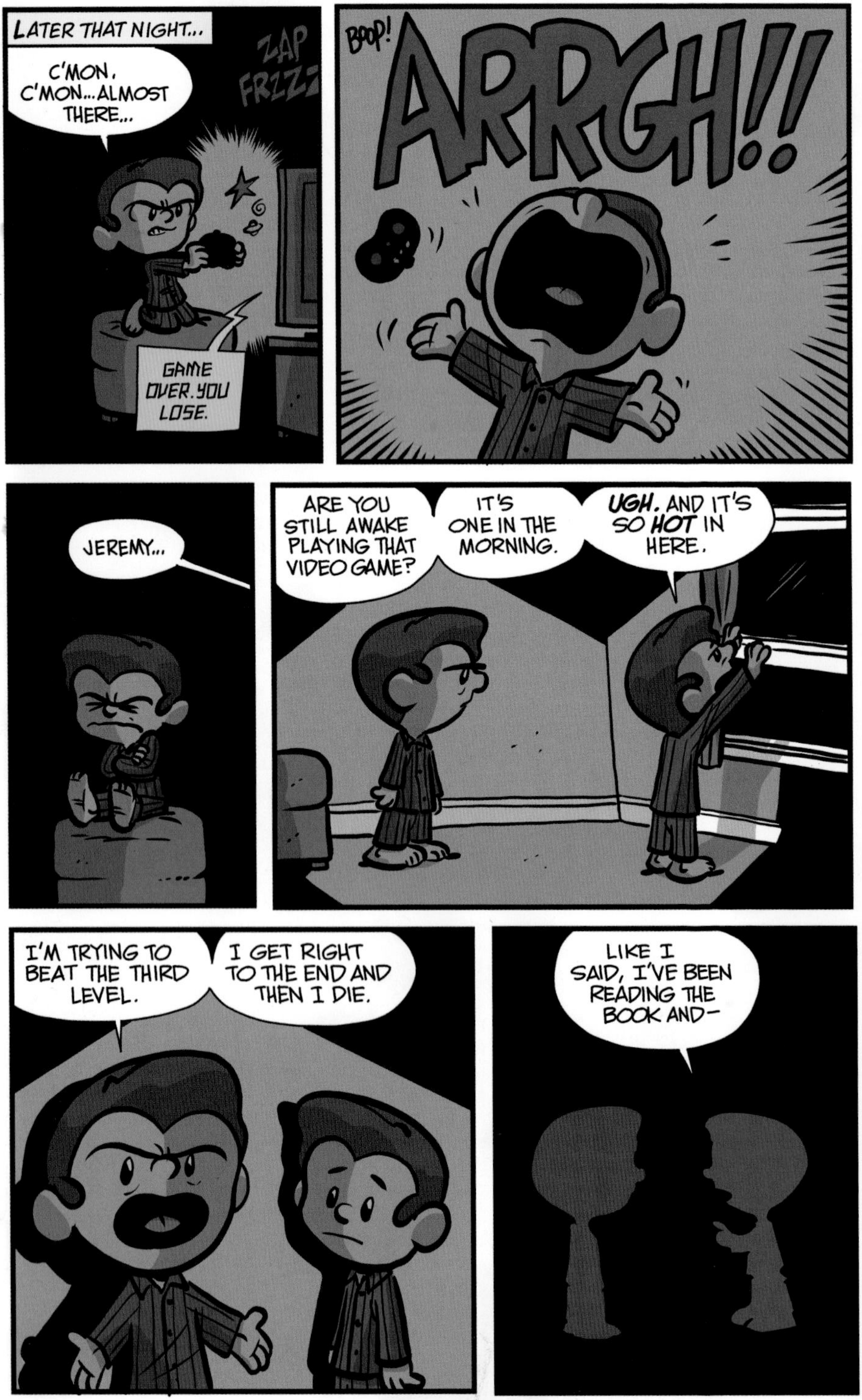
LATER THAT NIGHT...
C'MON. C'MON...ALMOST THERE...
ZAP FRZZZ
GAME OVER. YOU LOSE.
BOOP!
ARRGH!!
JEREMY...
ARE YOU STILL AWAKE PLAYING THAT VIDEO GAME?
IT'S ONE IN THE MORNING.
UGH. AND IT'S SO HOT IN HERE.
I'M TRYING TO BEAT THE THIRD LEVEL.
I GET RIGHT TO THE END AND THEN I DIE.
LIKE I SAID, I'VE BEEN READING THE BOOK AND—

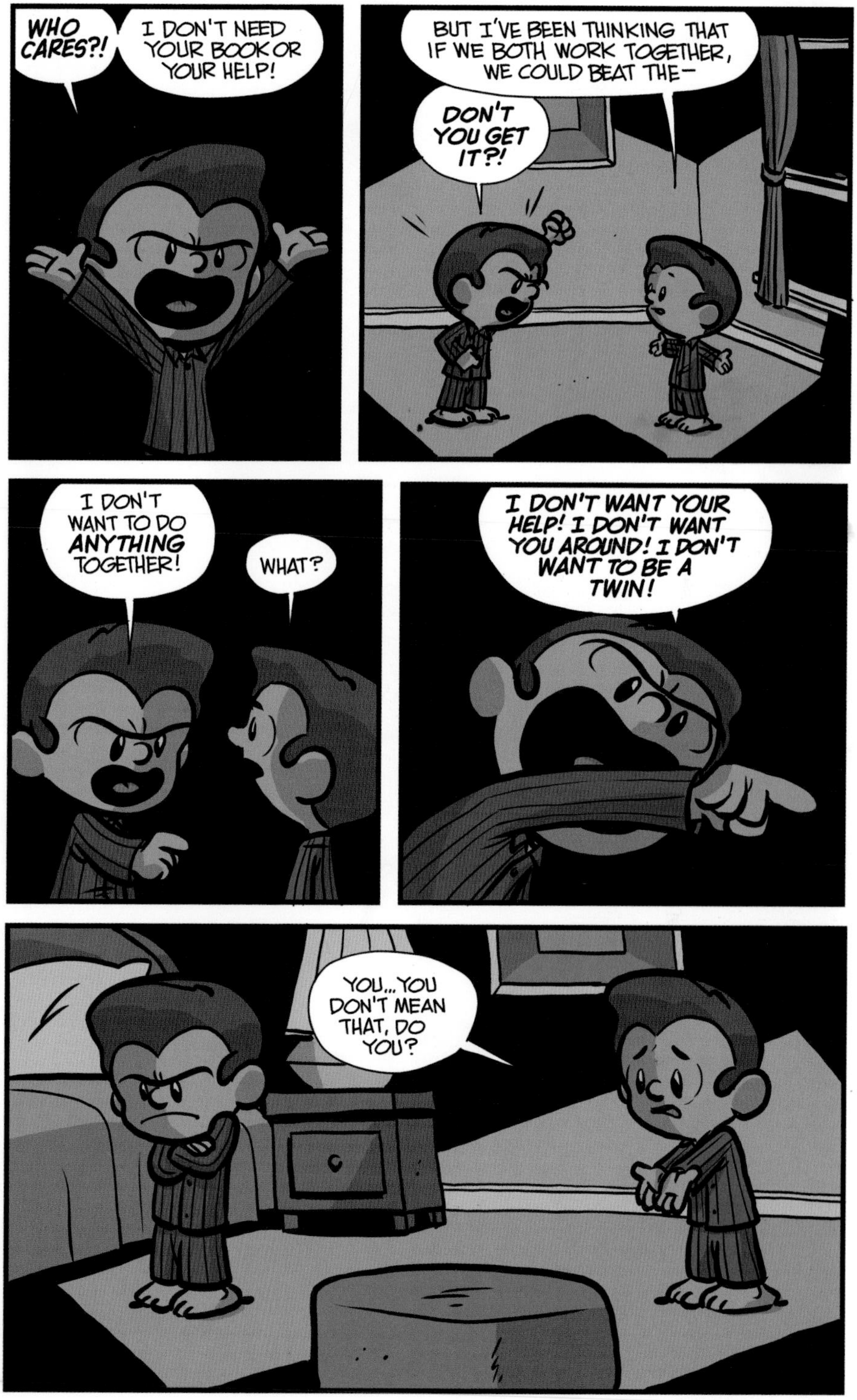
WHO CARES?!
I DON'T NEED YOUR BOOK OR YOUR HELP!
BUT I'VE BEEN THINKING THAT IF WE BOTH WORK TOGETHER, WE COULD BEAT THE—
DON'T YOU GET IT?!
I DON'T WANT TO DO ANYTHING TOGETHER!
WHAT?
I DON'T WANT YOUR HELP! I DON'T WANT YOU AROUND! I DON'T WANT TO BE A TWIN!
YOU... YOU DON'T MEAN THAT, DO YOU?

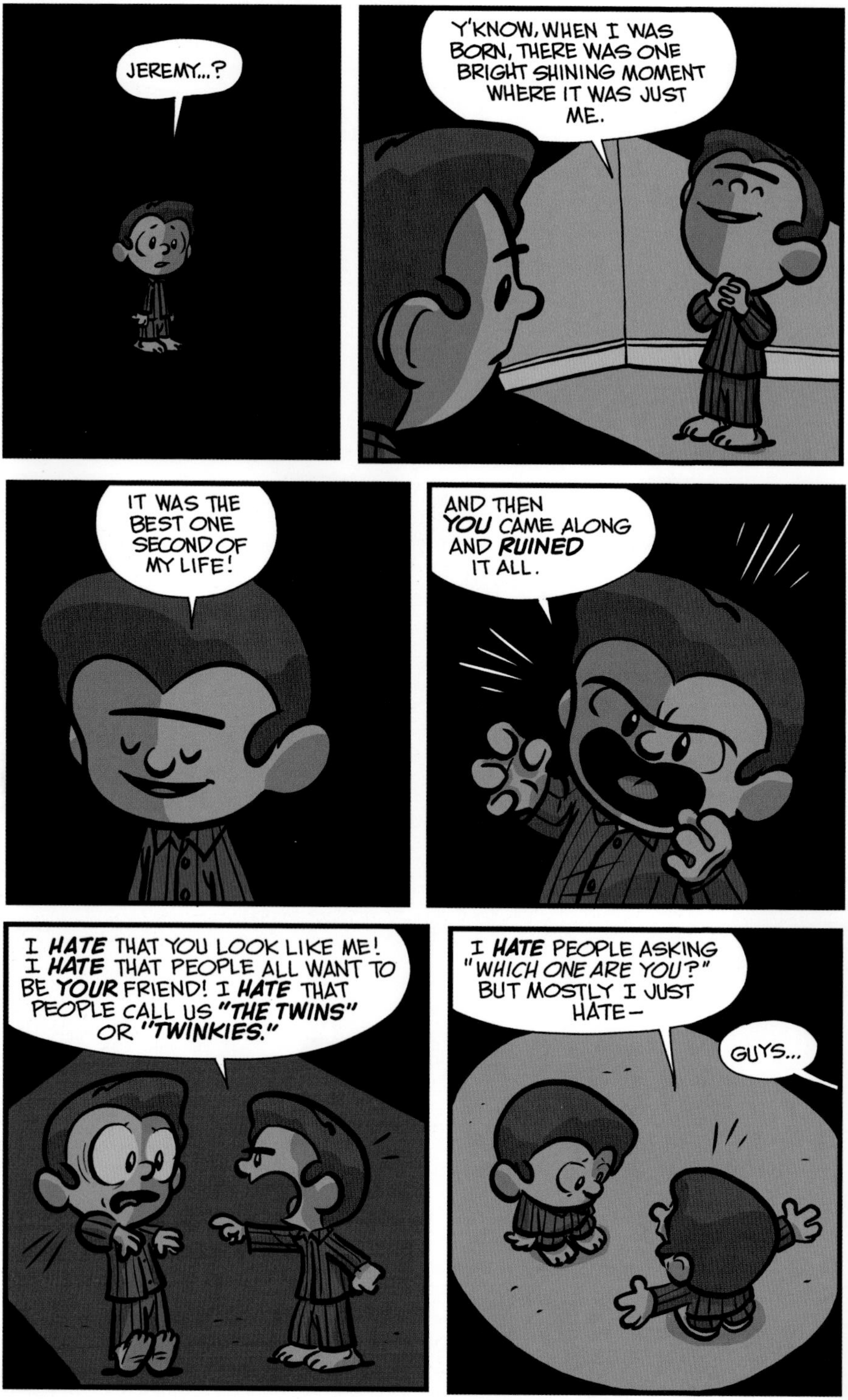
JEREMY...?
Y'KNOW, WHEN I WAS BORN, THERE WAS ONE BRIGHT SHINING MOMENT WHERE IT WAS JUST ME.
IT WAS THE BEST ONE SECOND OF MY LIFE!
AND THEN *YOU* CAME ALONG AND *RUINED* IT ALL.
I *HATE* THAT YOU LOOK LIKE ME! I *HATE* THAT PEOPLE ALL WANT TO BE *YOUR* FRIEND! I *HATE* THAT PEOPLE CALL US *"THE TWINS"* OR *"TWINKIES."*
I *HATE* PEOPLE ASKING *"WHICH ONE ARE YOU?"* BUT MOSTLY I JUST HATE—
GUYS...

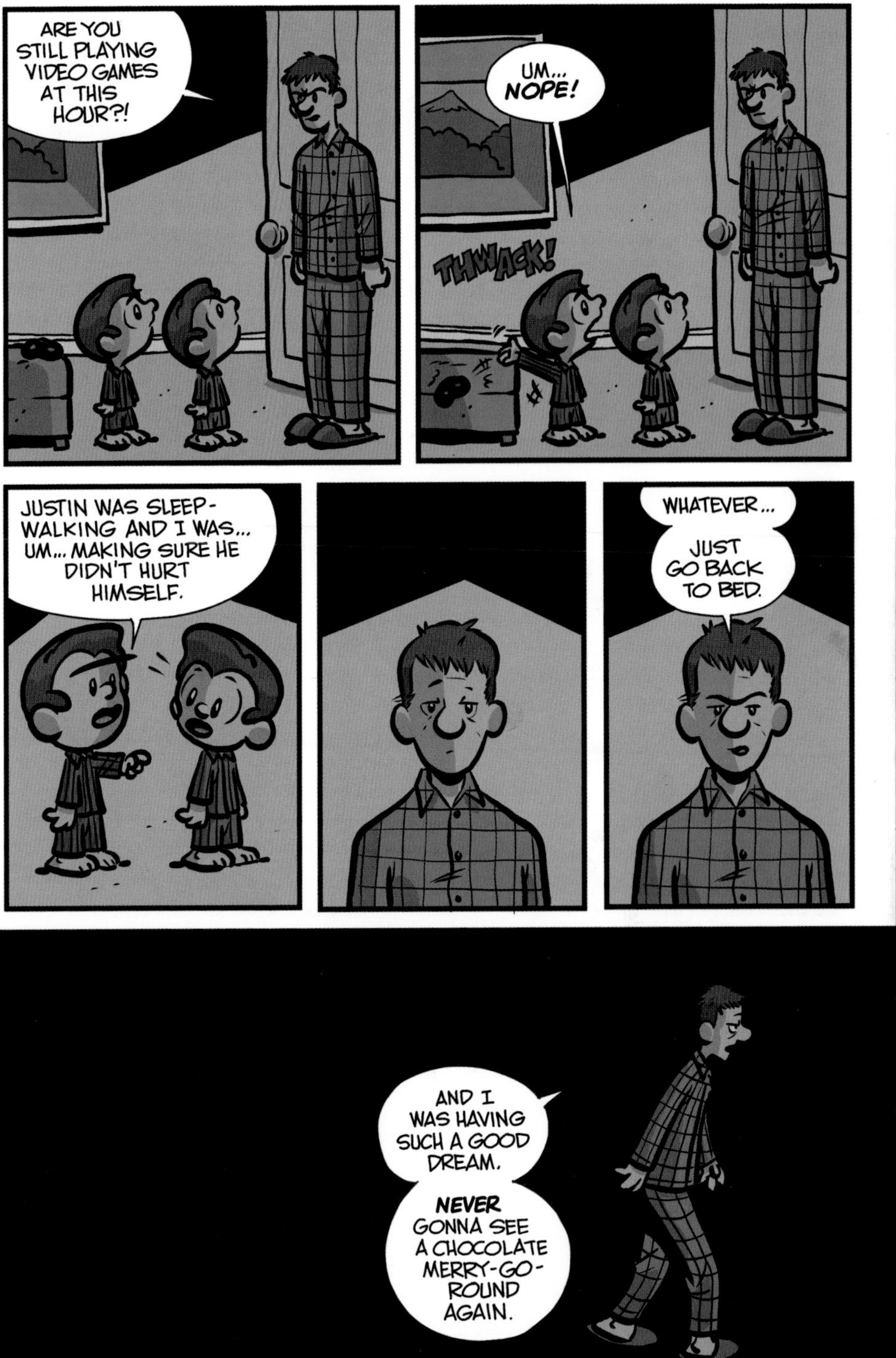
ARE YOU STILL PLAYING VIDEO GAMES AT THIS HOUR?!
UM... NOPE!
THWACK!
JUSTIN WAS SLEEP-WALKING AND I WAS... UM... MAKING SURE HE DIDN'T HURT HIMSELF.
WHATEVER...
JUST GO BACK TO BED.
AND I WAS HAVING SUCH A GOOD DREAM.
NEVER GONNA SEE A CHOCOLATE MERRY-GO-ROUND AGAIN.

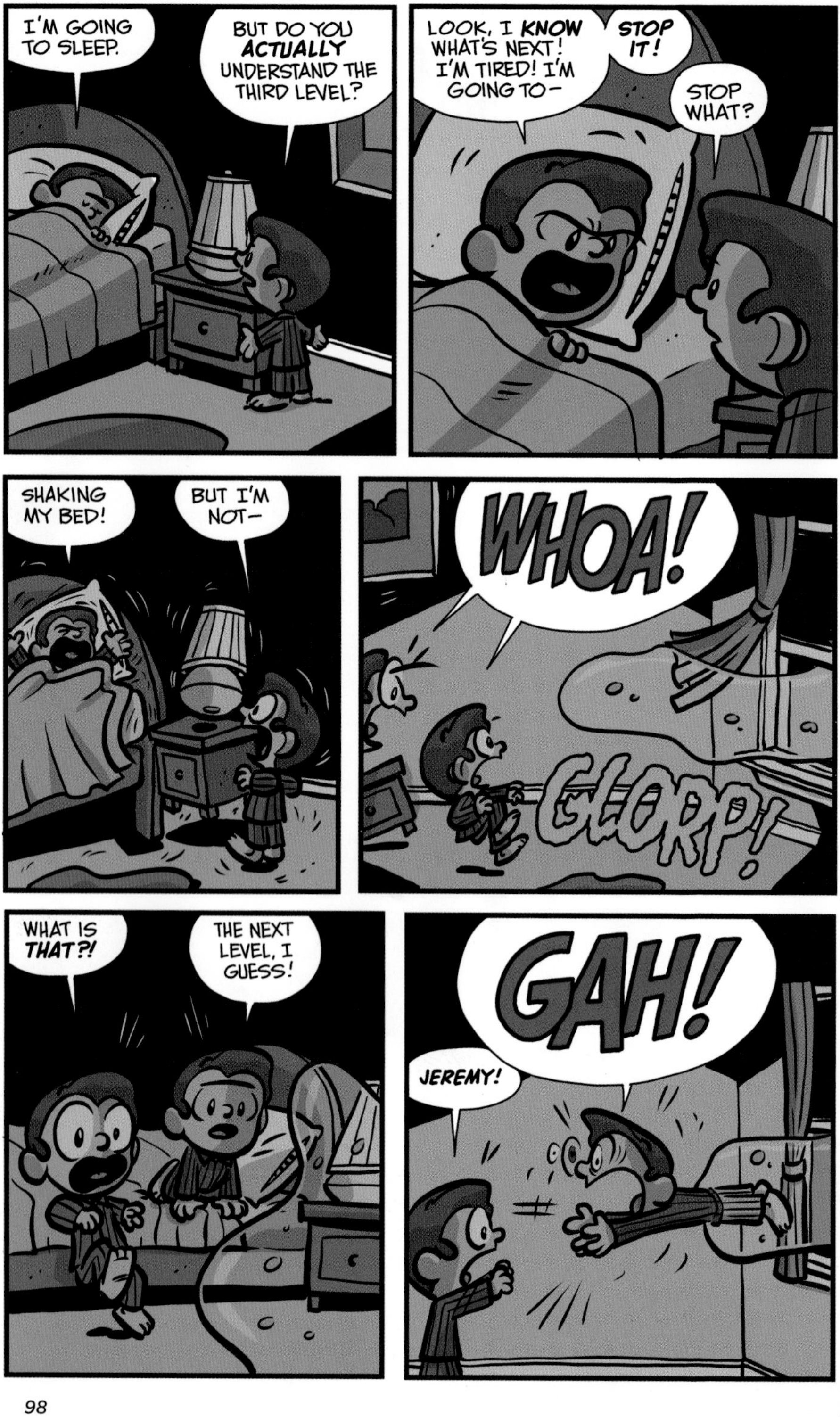
I'M GOING TO SLEEP.
BUT DO YOU ACTUALLY UNDERSTAND THE THIRD LEVEL?
LOOK, I KNOW WHAT'S NEXT! I'M TIRED! I'M GOING TO–
STOP IT!
STOP WHAT?
SHAKING MY BED!
BUT I'M NOT–
WHOA!
GLORP!
WHAT IS THAT?!
THE NEXT LEVEL, I GUESS!
GAH!
JEREMY!

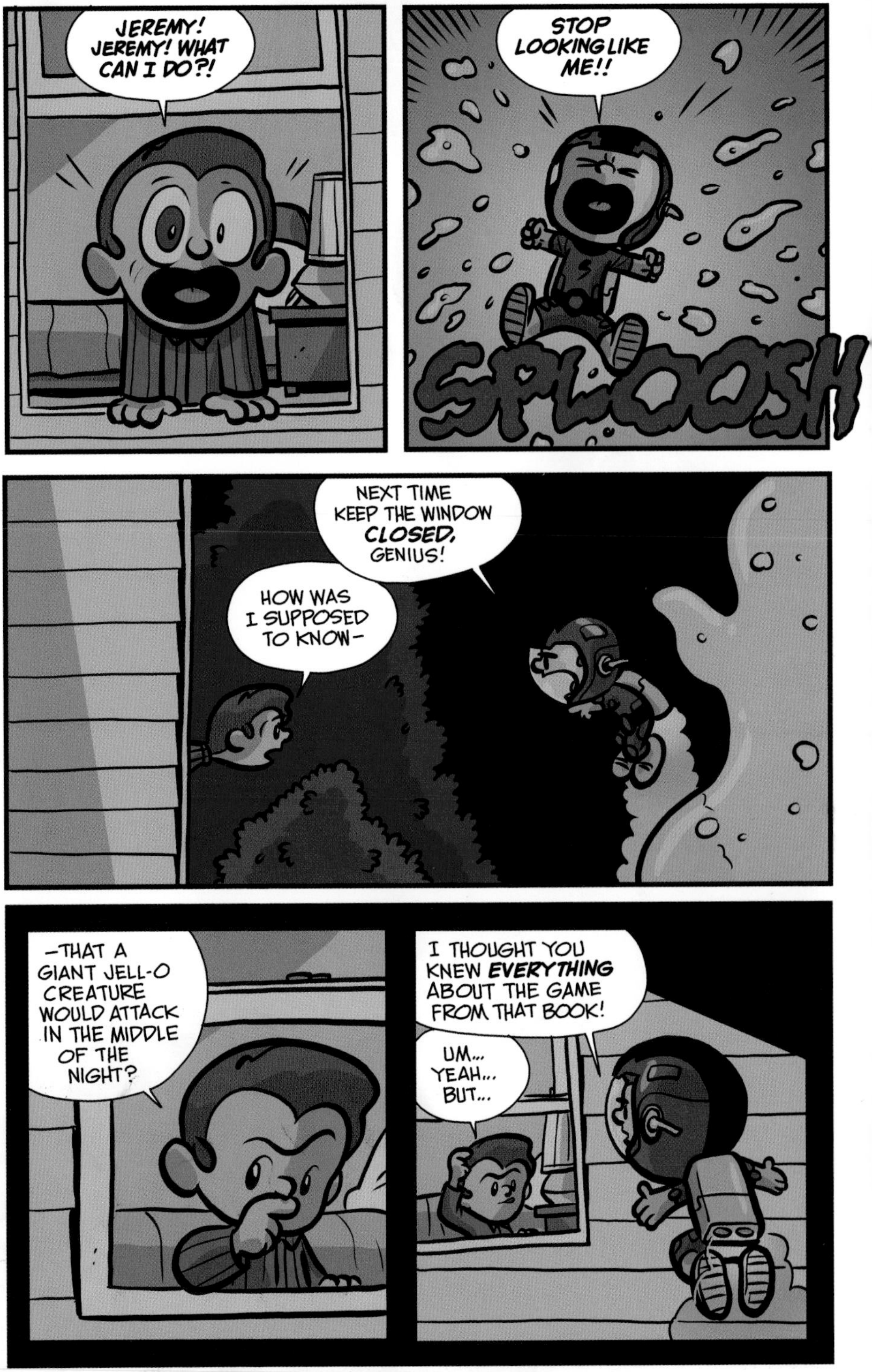
JEREMY! JEREMY! WHAT CAN I DO?!
STOP LOOKING LIKE ME!!
SPLOOSH
NEXT TIME KEEP THE WINDOW CLOSED, GENIUS!
HOW WAS I SUPPOSED TO KNOW-
-THAT A GIANT JELL-O CREATURE WOULD ATTACK IN THE MIDDLE OF THE NIGHT?
I THOUGHT YOU KNEW EVERYTHING ABOUT THE GAME FROM THAT BOOK!
UM... YEAH... BUT...

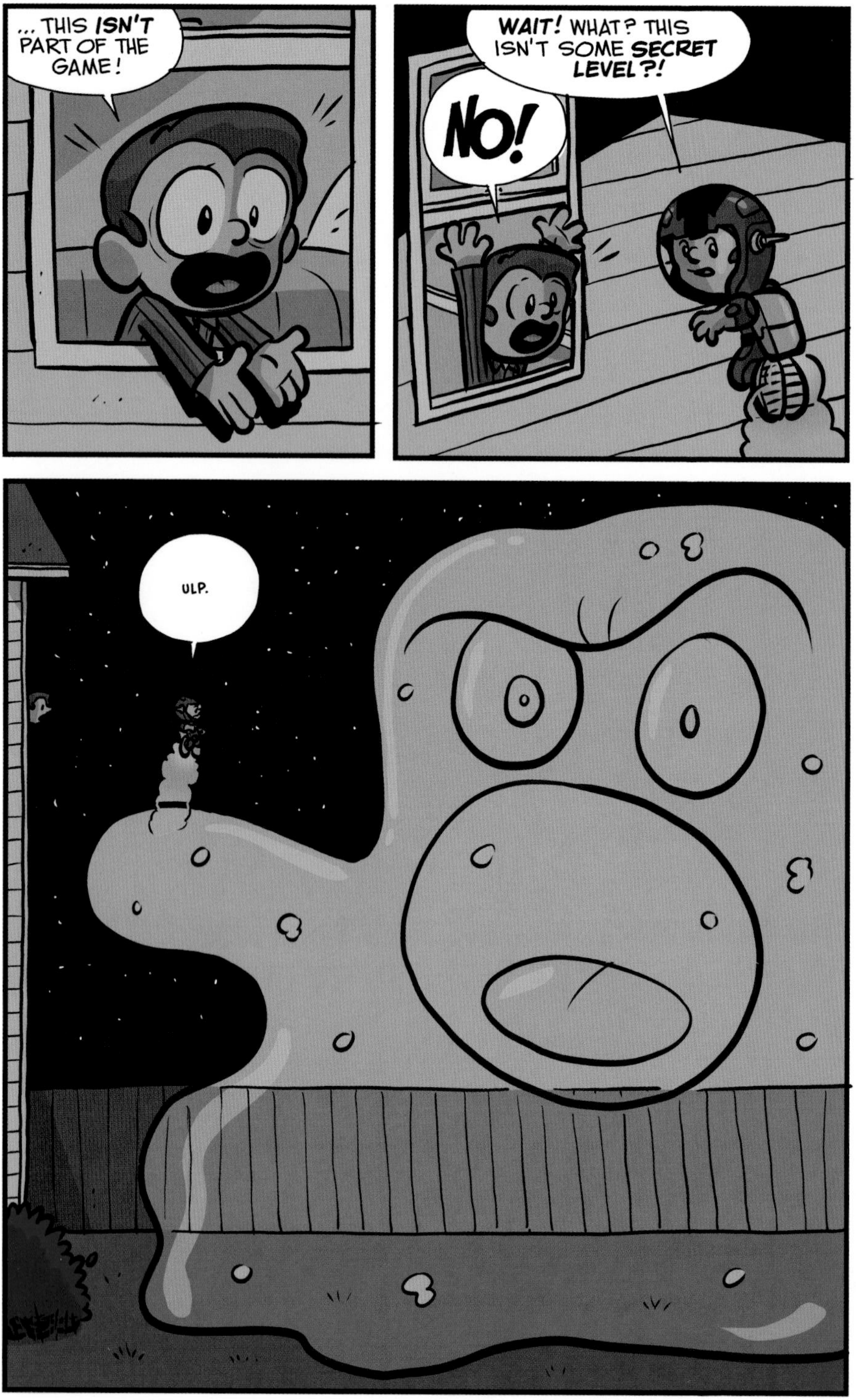
... THIS ISN'T PART OF THE GAME!
WAIT! WHAT? THIS ISN'T SOME SECRET LEVEL?!
NO!
ULP.

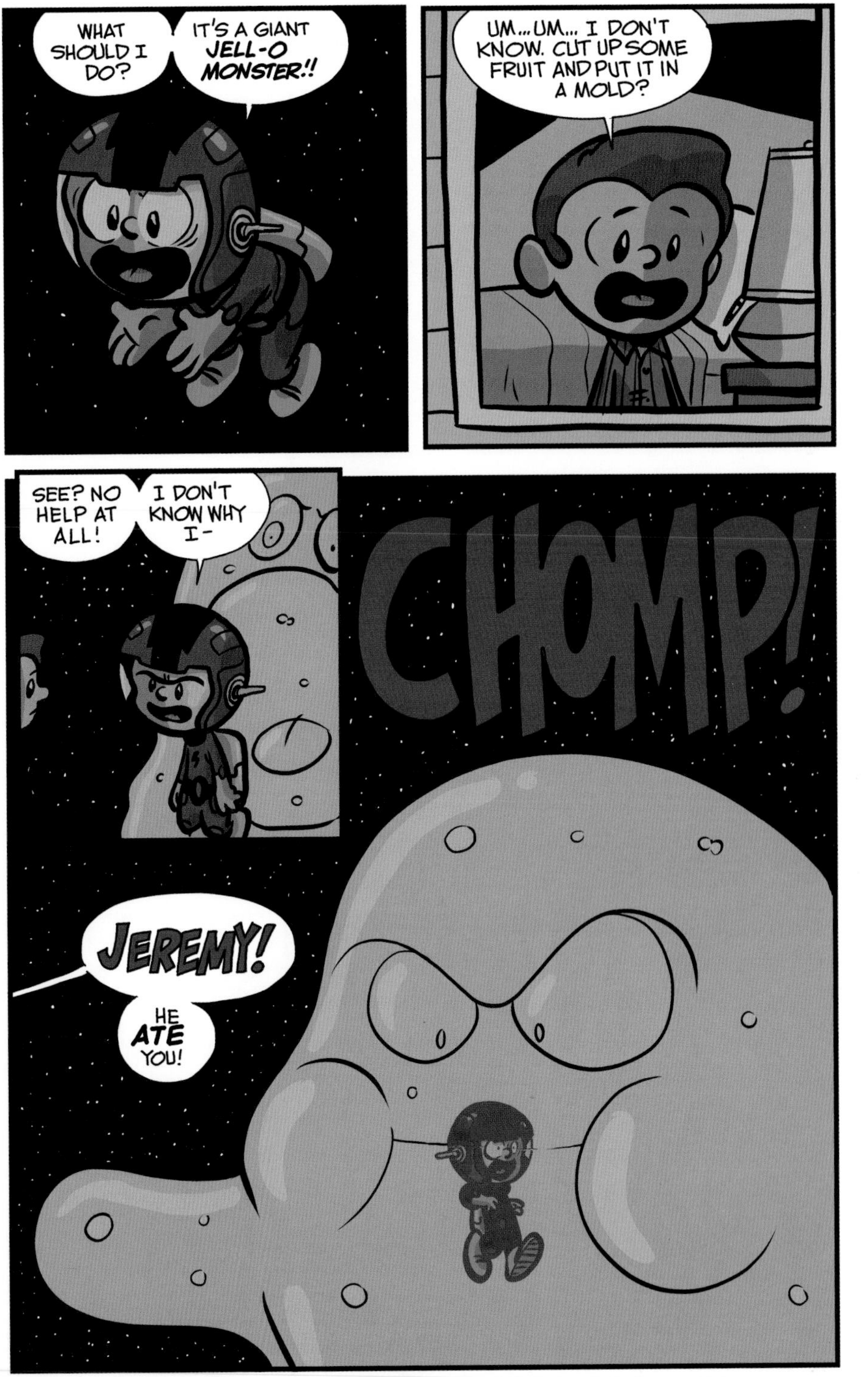
WHAT SHOULD I DO?
IT'S A GIANT JELL-O MONSTER!!
UM... UM... I DON'T KNOW. CUT UP SOME FRUIT AND PUT IT IN A MOLD?
SEE? NO HELP AT ALL!
I DON'T KNOW WHY I-
CHOMP!
JEREMY!
HE ATE YOU!

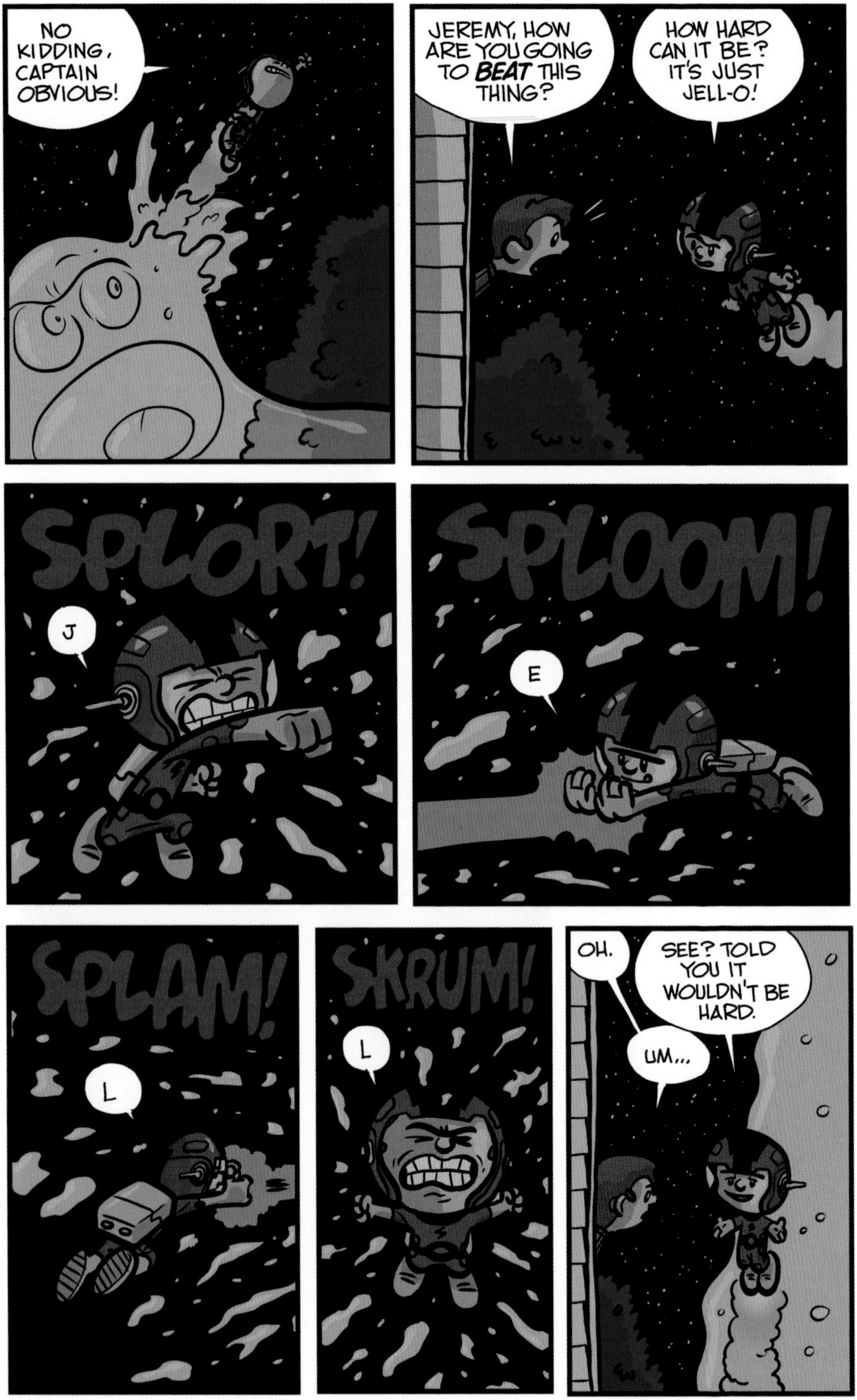
NO KIDDING, CAPTAIN OBVIOUS!
JEREMY, HOW ARE YOU GOING TO BEAT THIS THING?
HOW HARD CAN IT BE? IT'S JUST JELL-O!
SPLORT!
J
SPLOOM!
E
SPLAM!
L
SKRUM!
L
OH.
SEE? TOLD YOU IT WOULDN'T BE HARD.
UM...

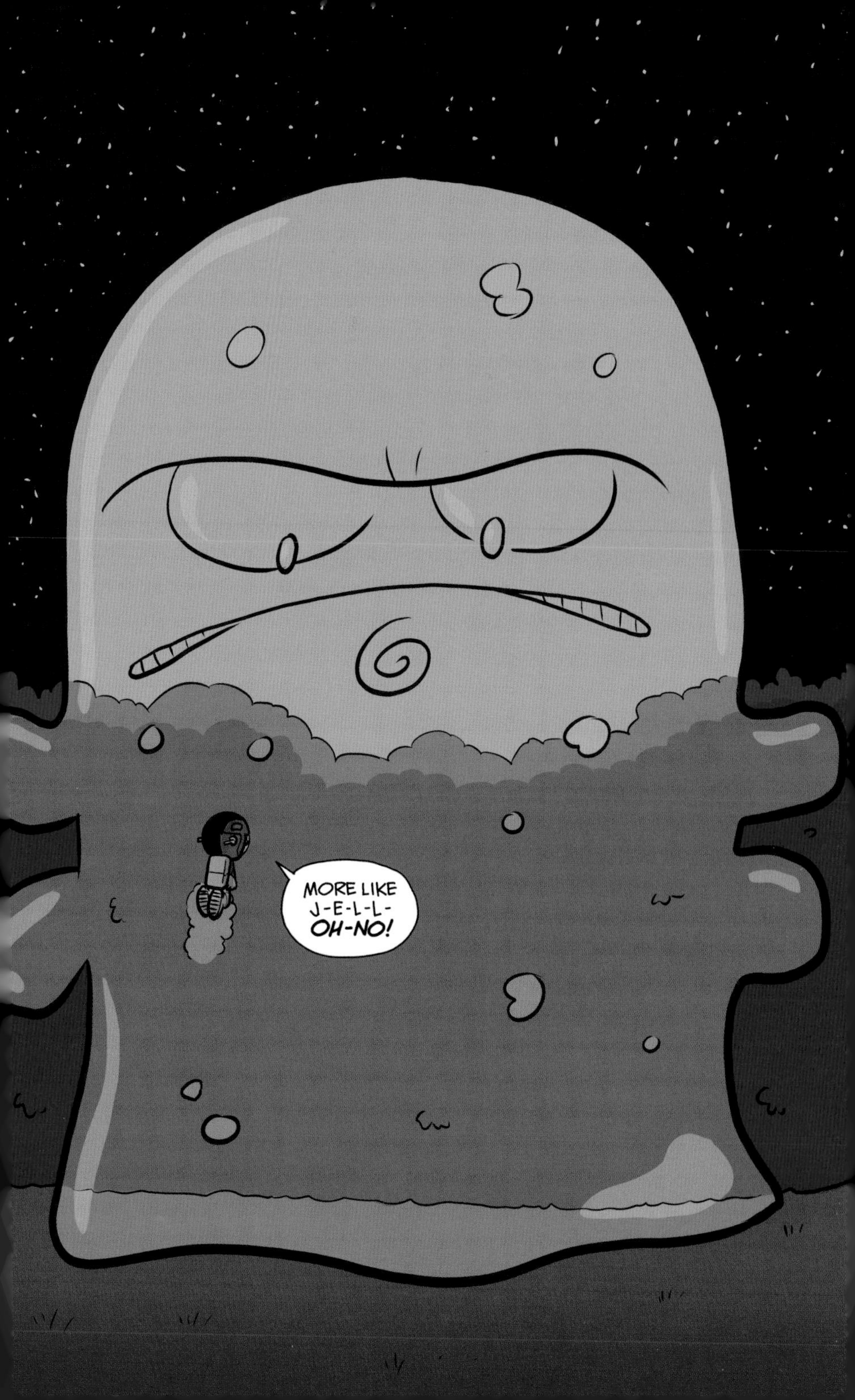
MORE LIKE J-E-L-L-OH-NO!

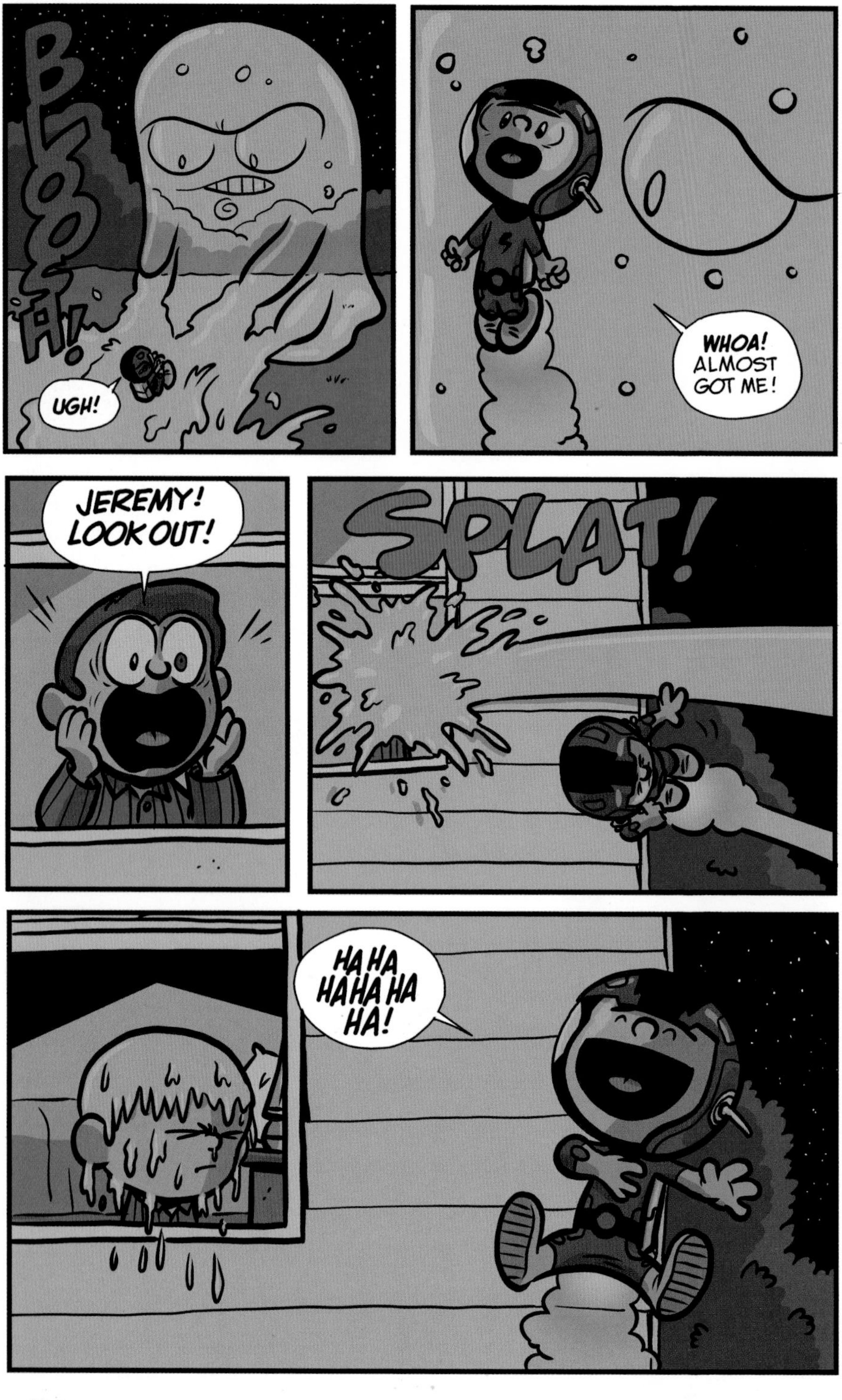
BLOOSH!
UGH!
WHOA! ALMOST GOT ME!
JEREMY! LOOK OUT!
SPLAT!
HA HA HA HA HA HA!

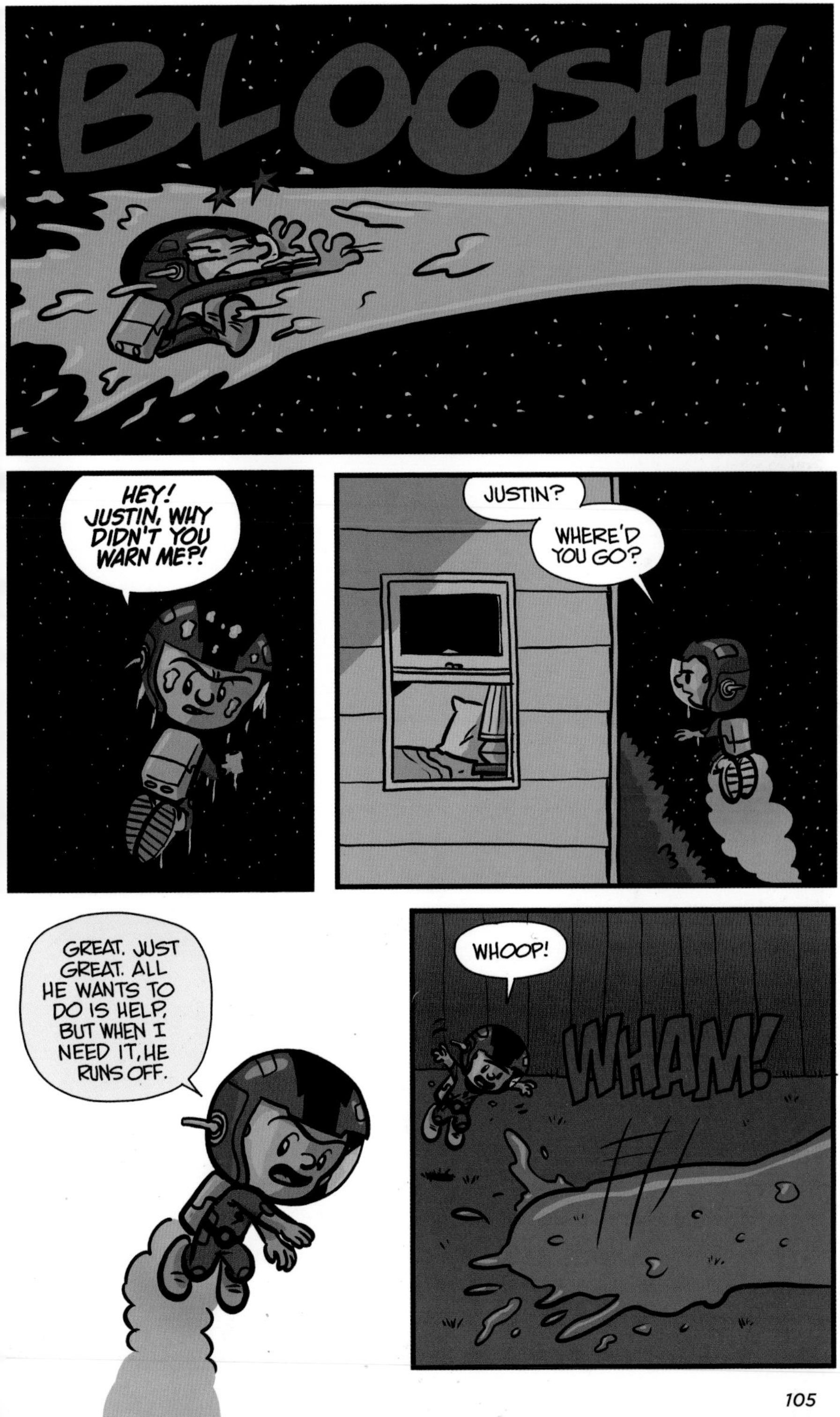
BLOOSH!
HEY! JUSTIN, WHY DIDN'T YOU WARN ME?!
JUSTIN?
WHERE'D YOU GO?
GREAT. JUST GREAT. ALL HE WANTS TO DO IS HELP, BUT WHEN I NEED IT, HE RUNS OFF.
WHOOP!
WHAM!

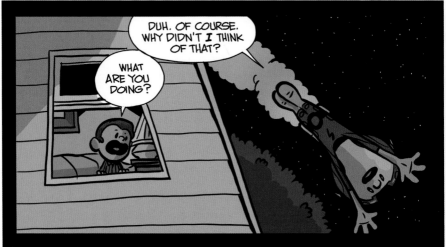

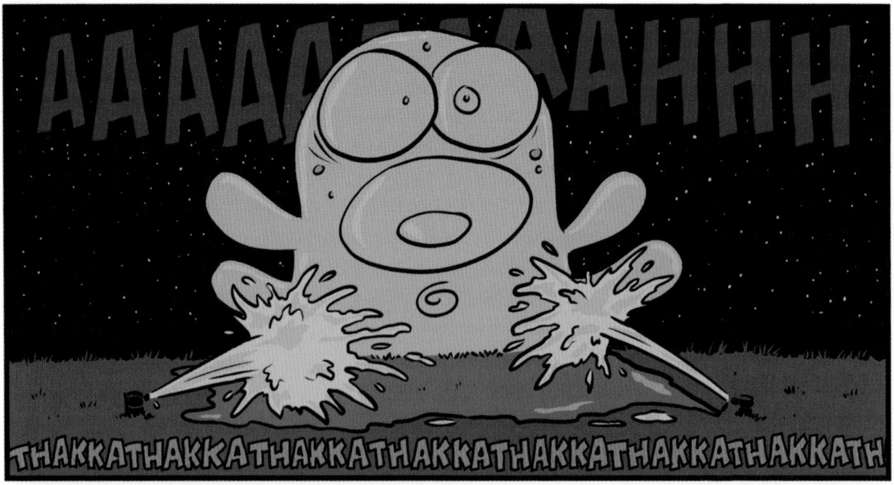
AAAAAAAAAHHHH
THAKKATHAKKATHAKKATHAKKATHAKKATHAKKATHAKKATH

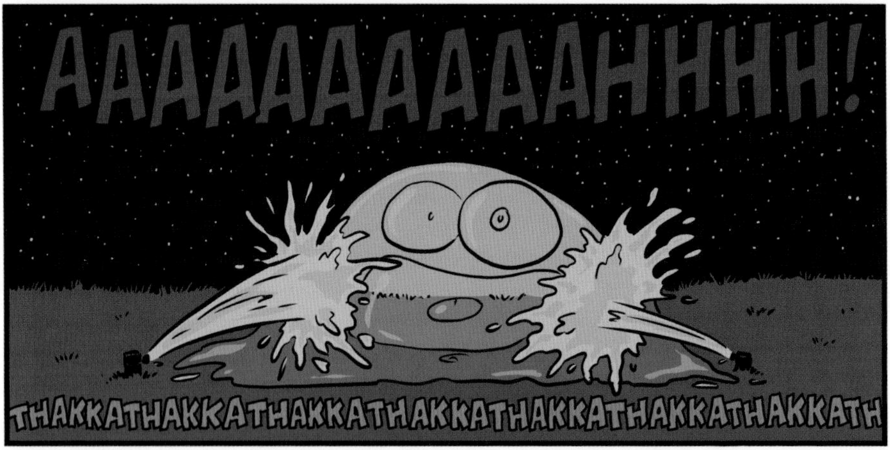
AAAAAAAAAAHHHH!
THAKKATHAKKATHAKKATHAKKATHAKKATHAKKATHAKKATH

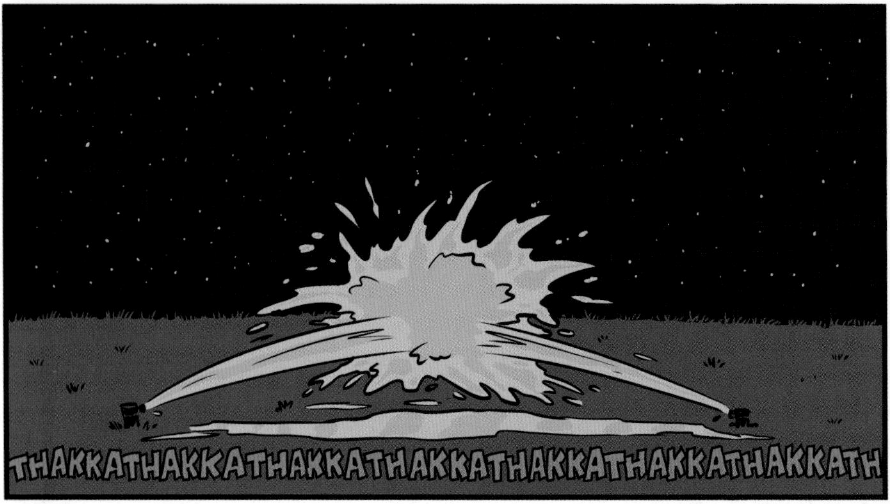
THAKKATHAKKATHAKKATHAKKATHAKKATHAKKATHAKKATH

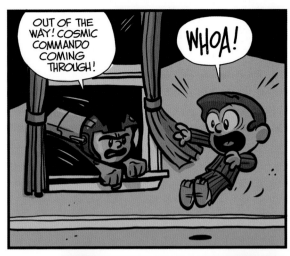

CUTSCENE

SKORN!

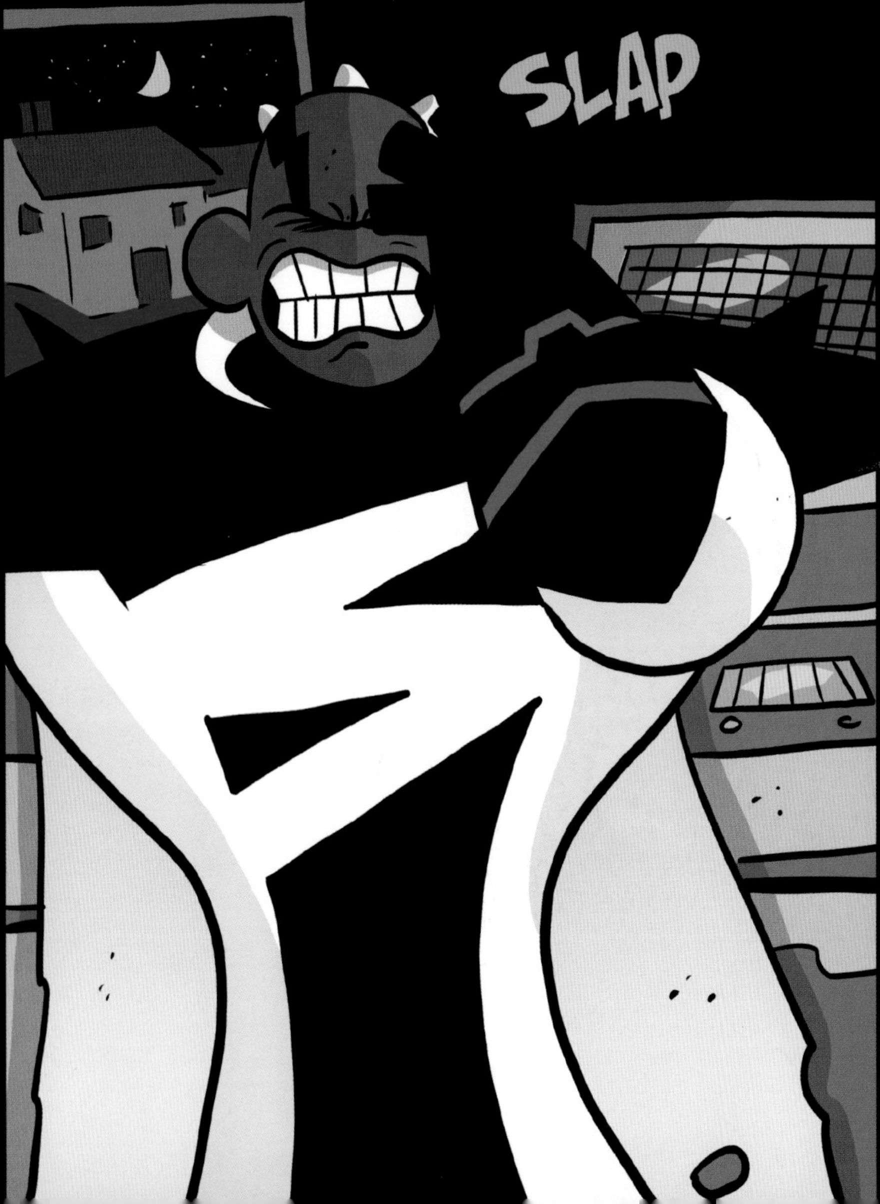
SLAP

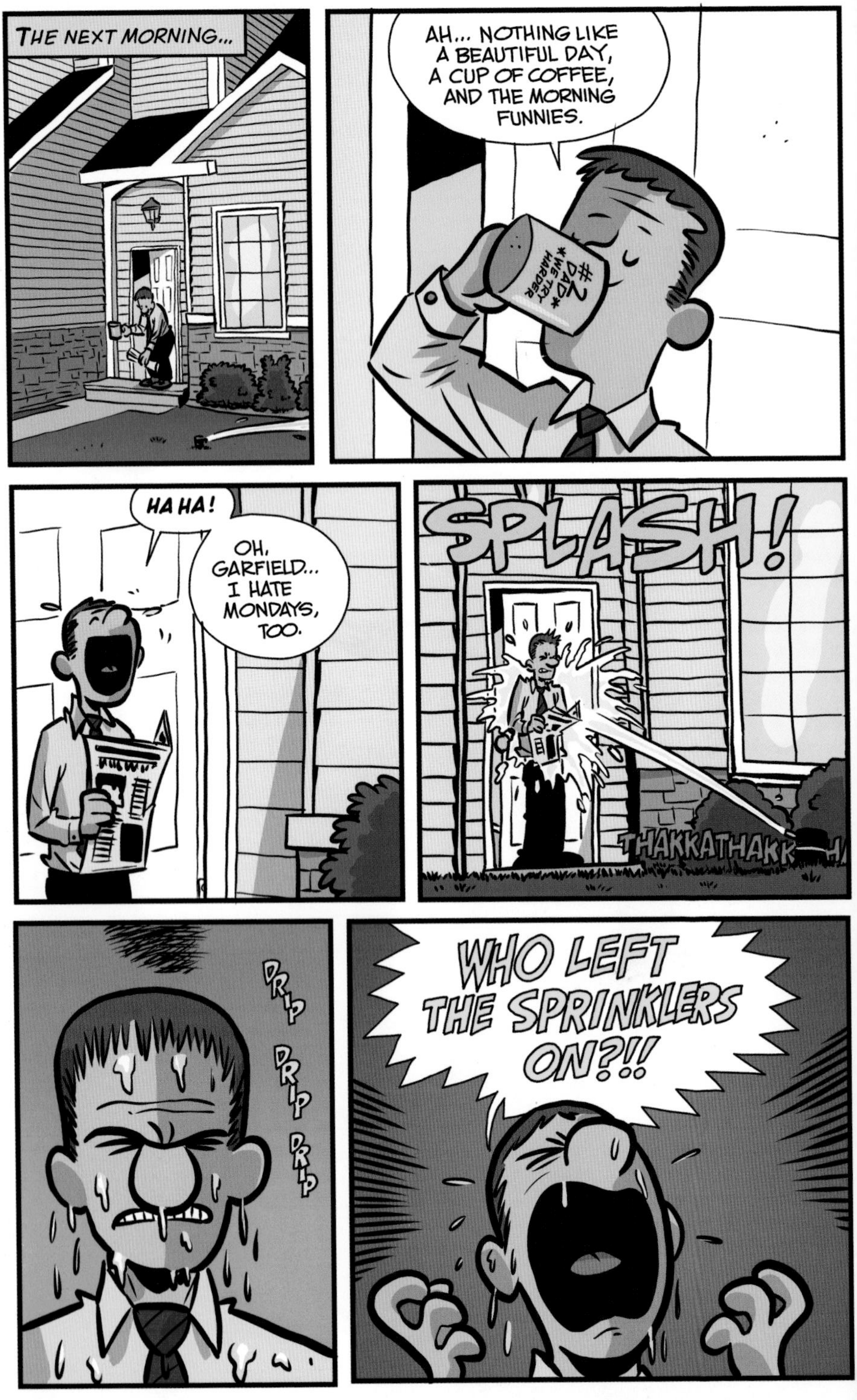
THE NEXT MORNING...
AH... NOTHING LIKE A BEAUTIFUL DAY, A CUP OF COFFEE, AND THE MORNING FUNNIES.
#2 DAD *WE TRY HARDER*
HA HA!
OH, GARFIELD... I HATE MONDAYS, TOO.
SPLASH!
THAKKATHAKK
DRIP
DRIP
DRIP
WHO LEFT THE SPRINKLERS ON?!!

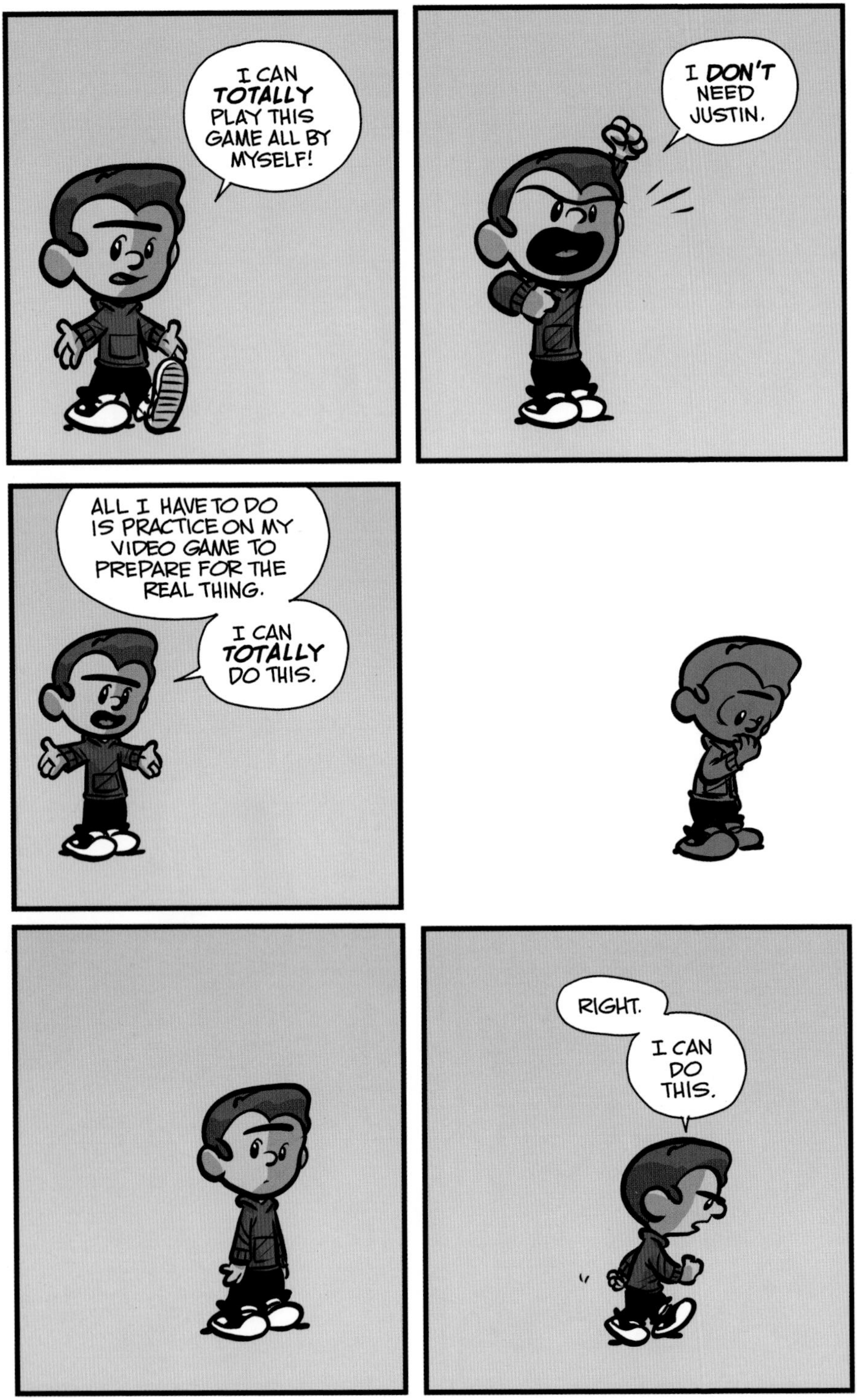
I CAN TOTALLY PLAY THIS GAME ALL BY MYSELF!
I DON'T NEED JUSTIN.
ALL I HAVE TO DO IS PRACTICE ON MY VIDEO GAME TO PREPARE FOR THE REAL THING.
I CAN TOTALLY DO THIS.
RIGHT.
I CAN DO THIS.

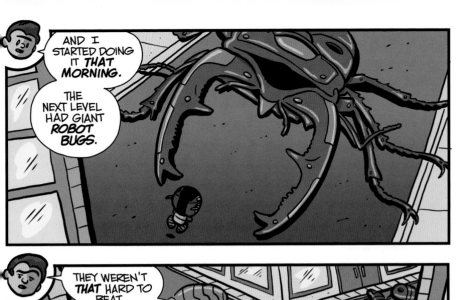

AND I STARTED DOING IT *THAT* MORNING.

THE NEXT LEVEL HAD GIANT *ROBOT BUGS*.

THEY WEREN'T *THAT* HARD TO BEAT.

ALL I HAD TO DO WAS *ENLARGE* A CAN OF BUG SPRAY.

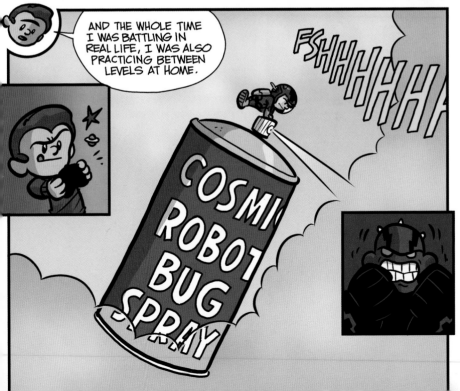

AND THE WHOLE TIME I WAS BATTLING IN REAL LIFE, I WAS ALSO PRACTICING BETWEEN LEVELS AT HOME.

FSHHHHHH

COSMIC ROBOT BUG SPRAY

BUT JUST LIKE IN THE GAME, THE REAL-LIFE BATTLES GOT *HARDER* AND *HARDER*.

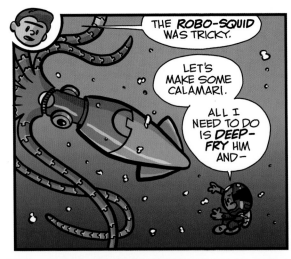

THE *ROBO-SQUID* WAS TRICKY.

LET'S MAKE SOME CALAMARI.

ALL I NEED TO DO IS *DEEP-FRY* HIM AND—

SPLURG!

BLOOP BLOOP

WHAT THE—?!

IF MY BLASTERS DON'T WORK UNDERWATER, WHAT AM I GONNA—

BOOM!

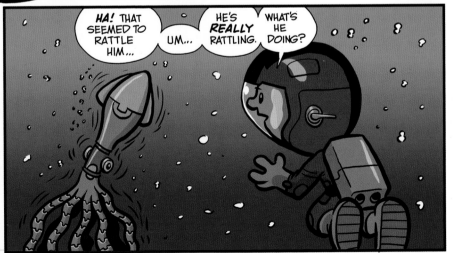

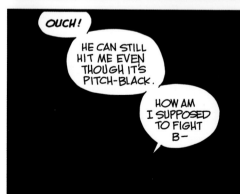

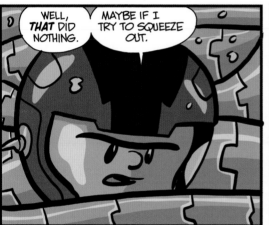

ERG!
ERF!
OOF!
ERGH!
UFF!
MRRG!

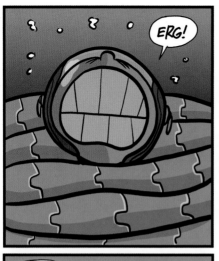

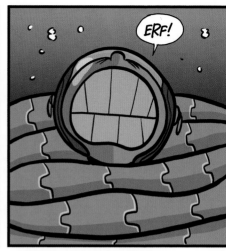

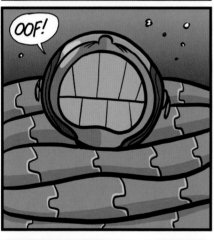

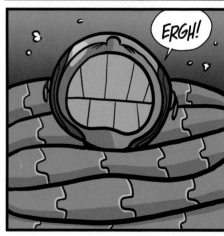

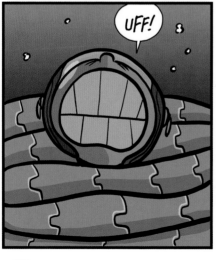

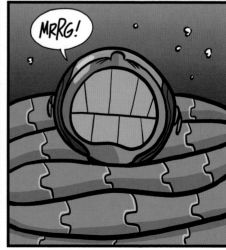

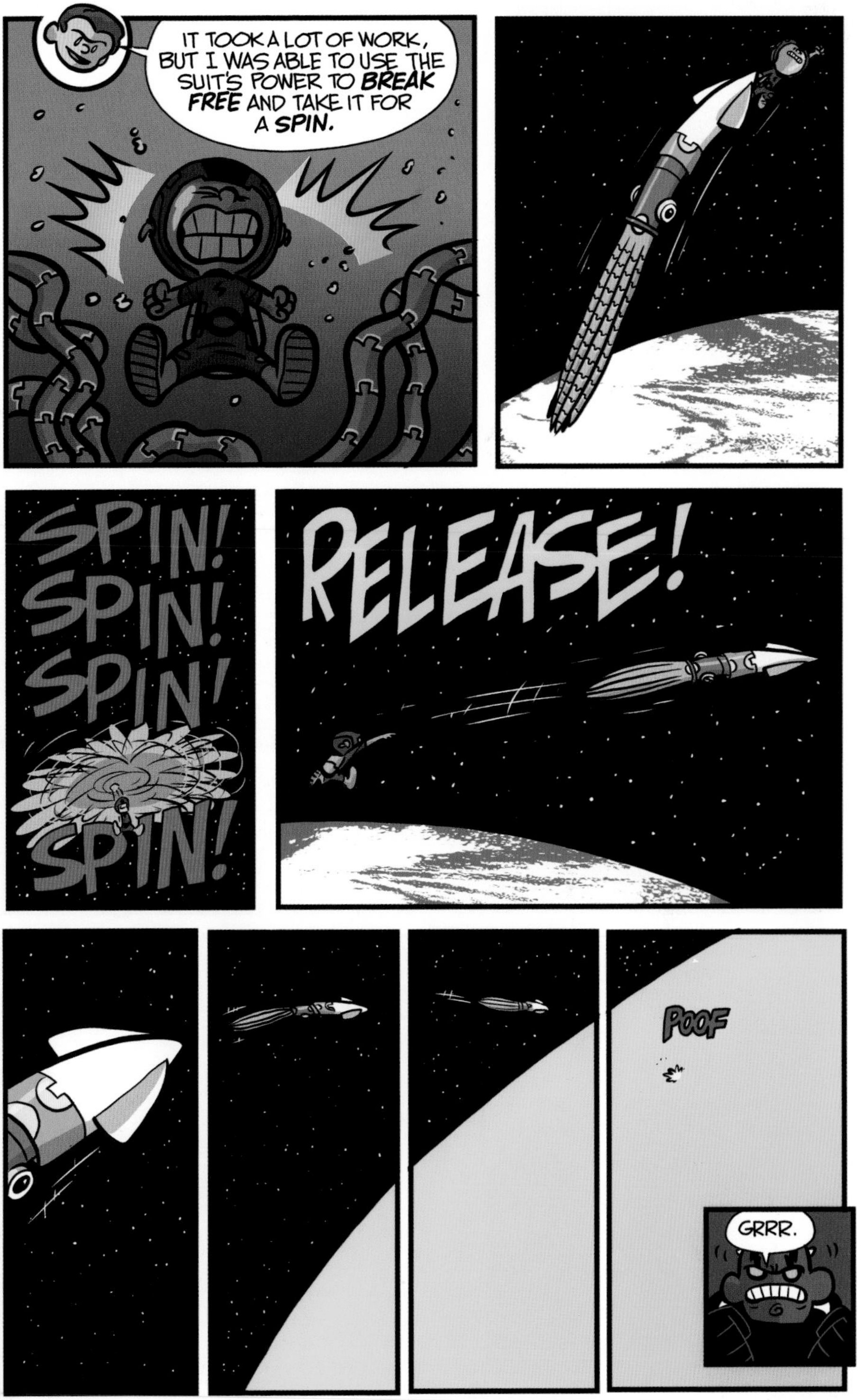
IT TOOK A LOT OF WORK, BUT I WAS ABLE TO USE THE SUIT'S POWER TO **BREAK FREE** AND TAKE IT FOR A **SPIN.**
SPIN! SPIN! SPIN!
SPIN!
RELEASE!
POOF
GRRR.

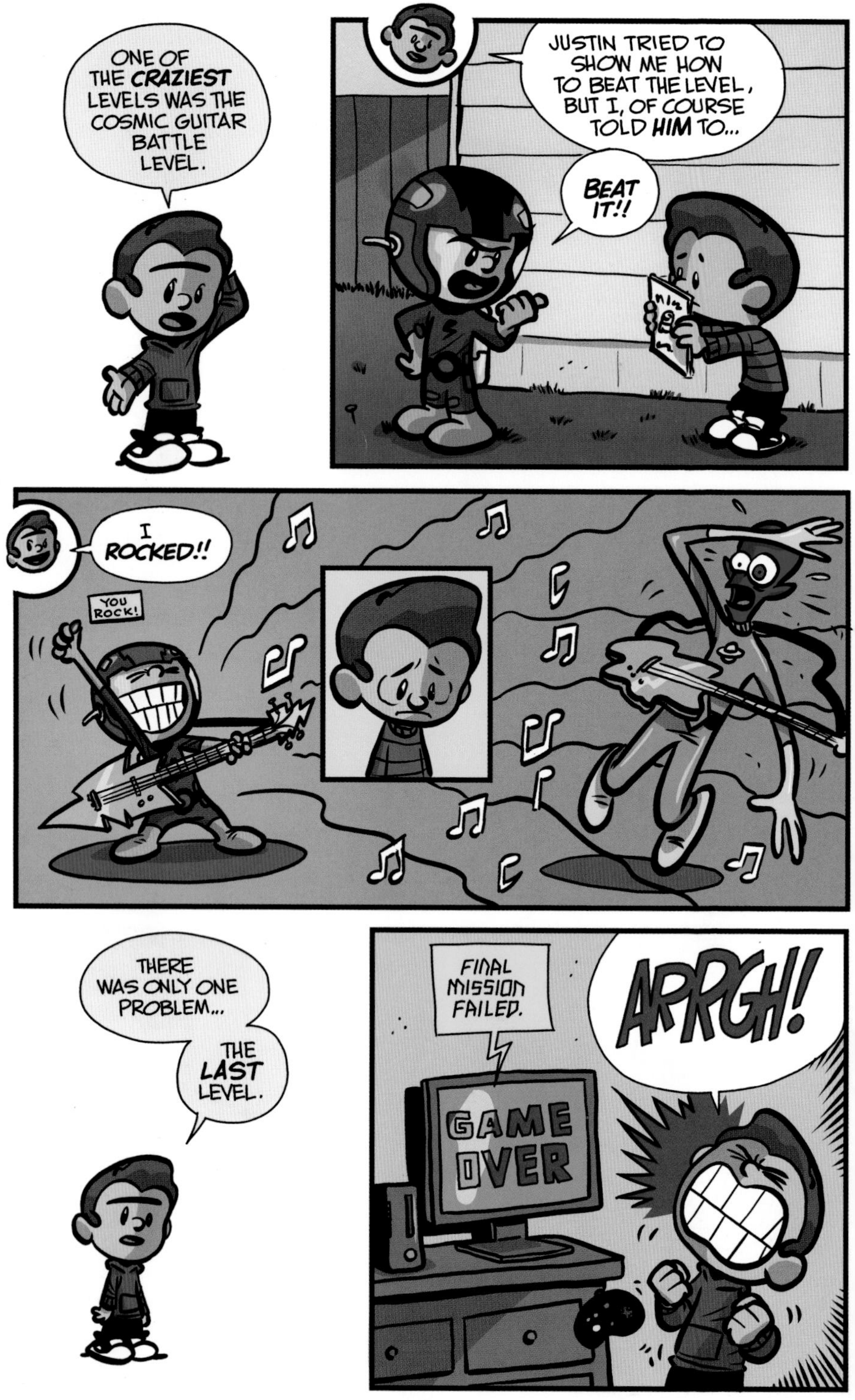
ONE OF THE **CRAZIEST** LEVELS WAS THE COSMIC GUITAR BATTLE LEVEL.
JUSTIN TRIED TO SHOW ME HOW TO BEAT THE LEVEL, BUT I, OF COURSE TOLD **HIM** TO...
BEAT IT!!
I ROCKED!!
YOU ROCK!
THERE WAS ONLY ONE PROBLEM...
THE **LAST** LEVEL.
FINAL MISSION FAILED.
ARRGH!
GAME OVER

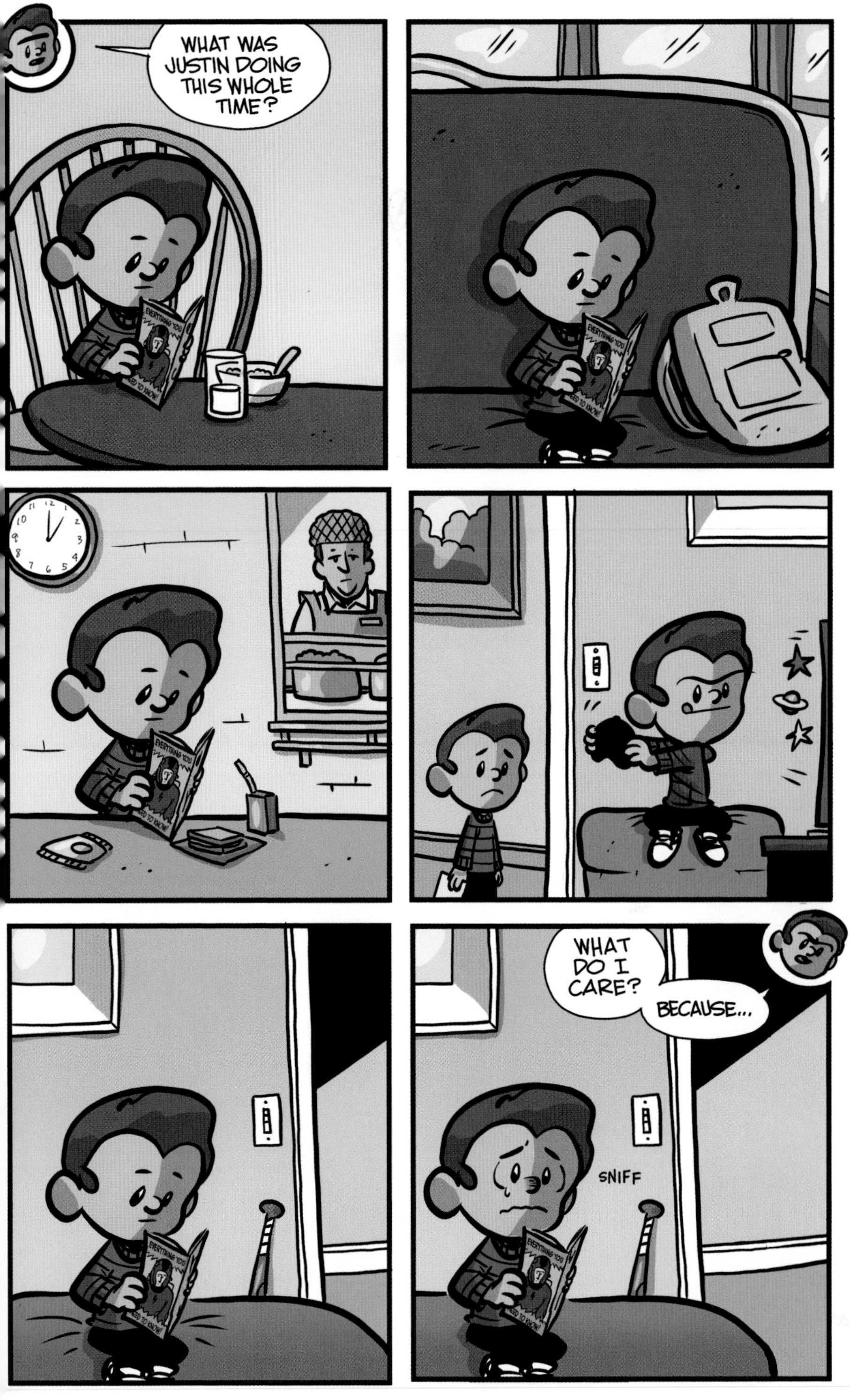
WHAT WAS JUSTIN DOING THIS WHOLE TIME?
EVERYTHING YOU NEED TO KNOW!
SNIFF
WHAT DO I CARE?
BECAUSE...

CUTSCENE
SKORN!

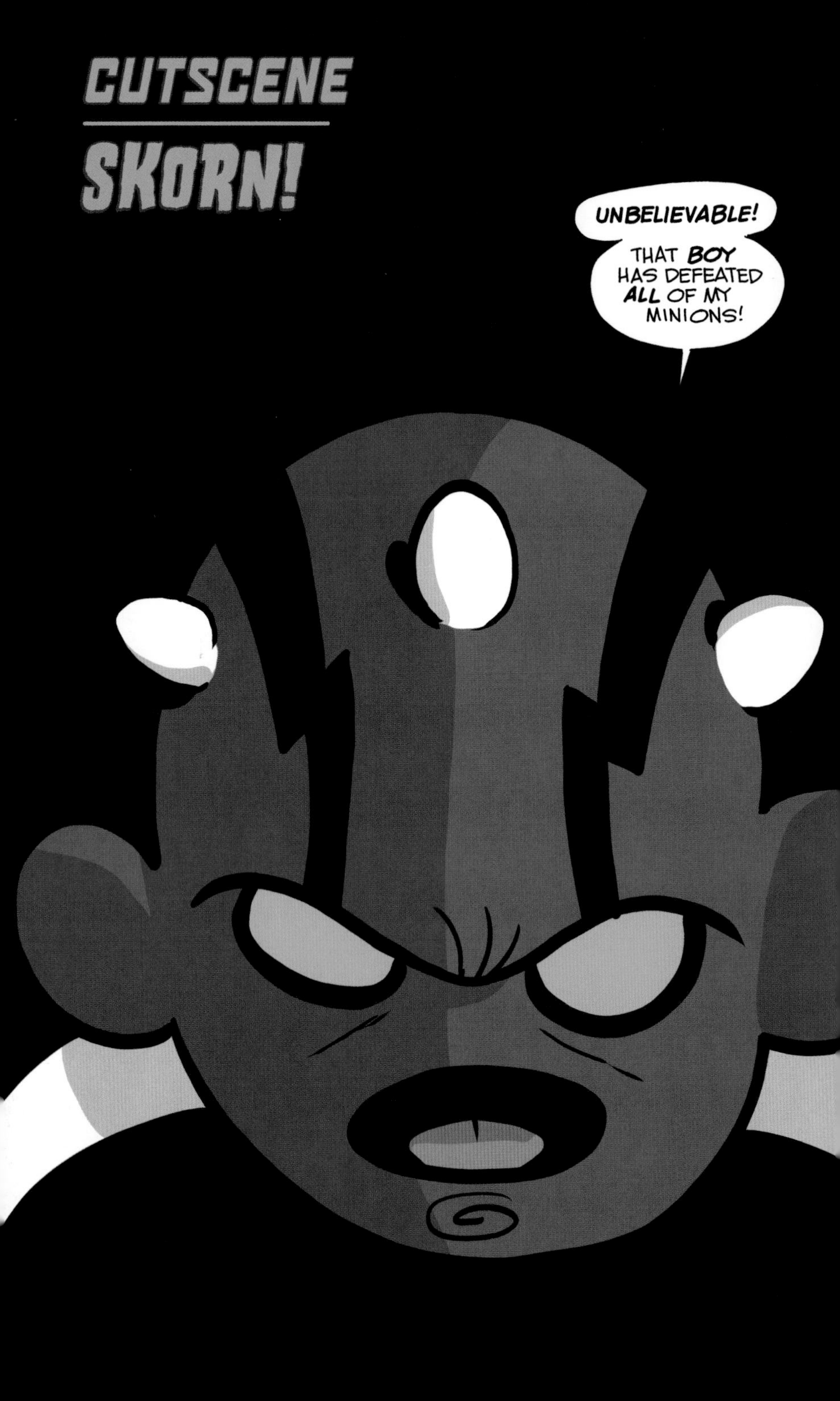
UNBELIEVABLE!
THAT BOY HAS DEFEATED ALL OF MY MINIONS!

CHAPTER SIX

ENDGAME

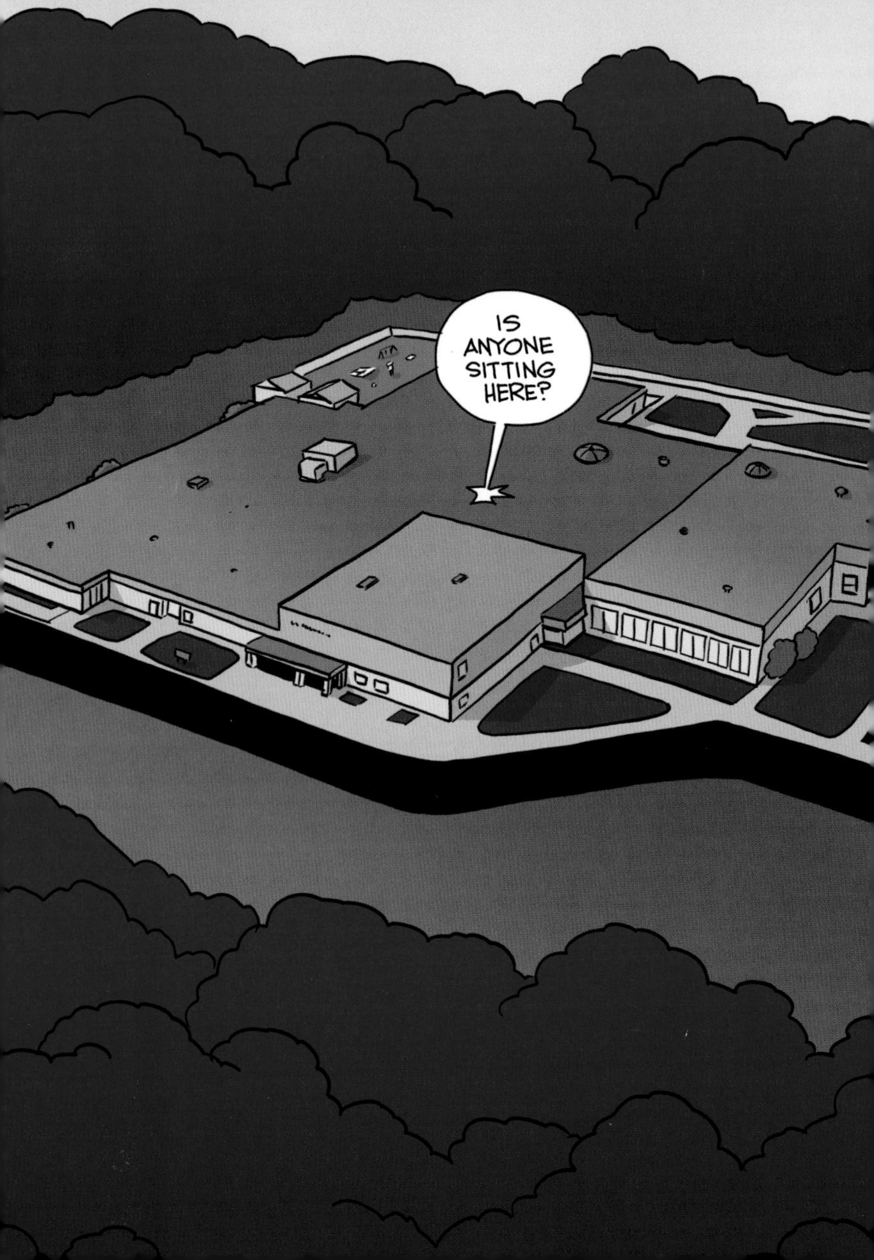
IS ANYONE SITTING HERE?

132

133

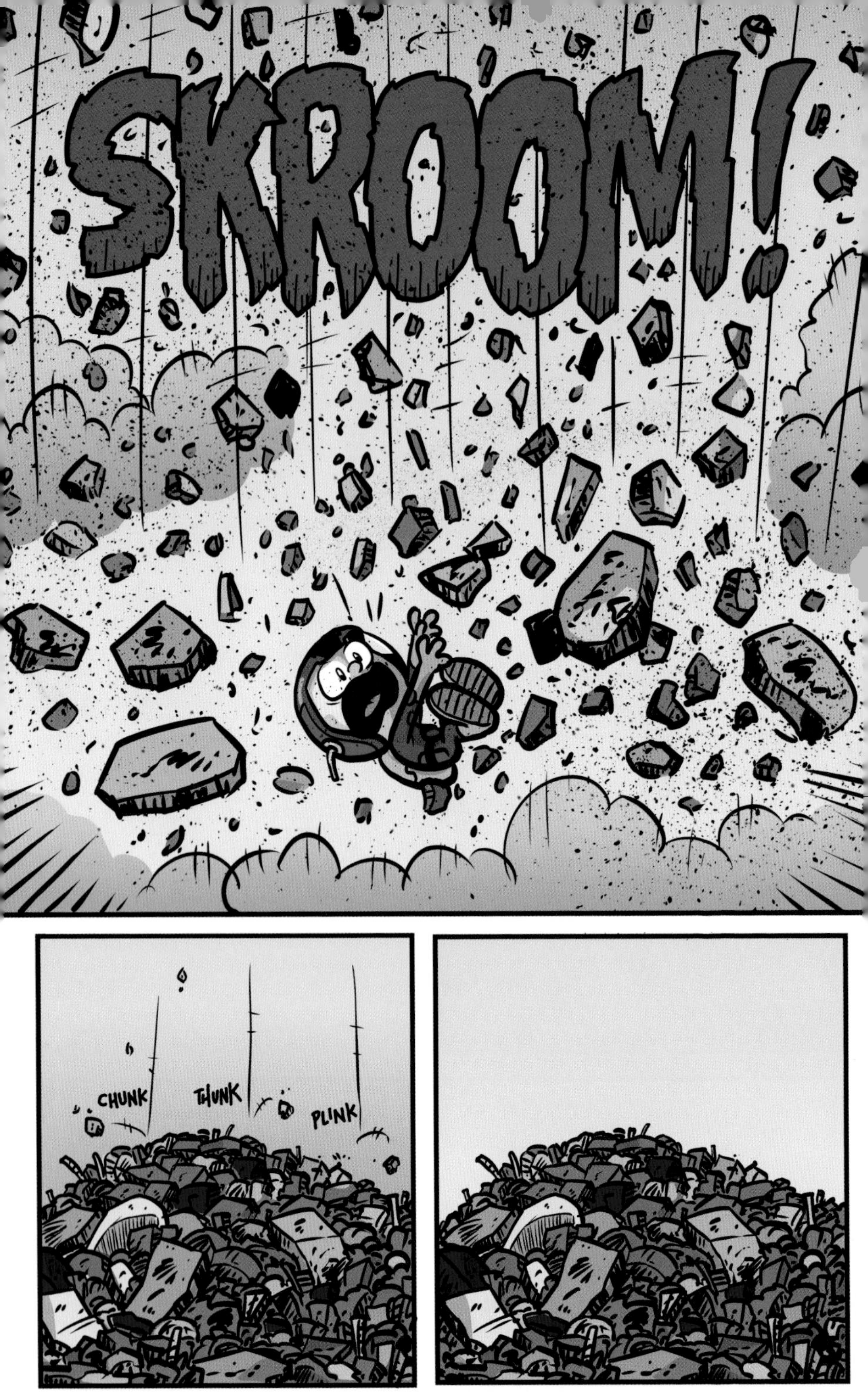
SKROOM!
CHUNK
THUNK
PLINK

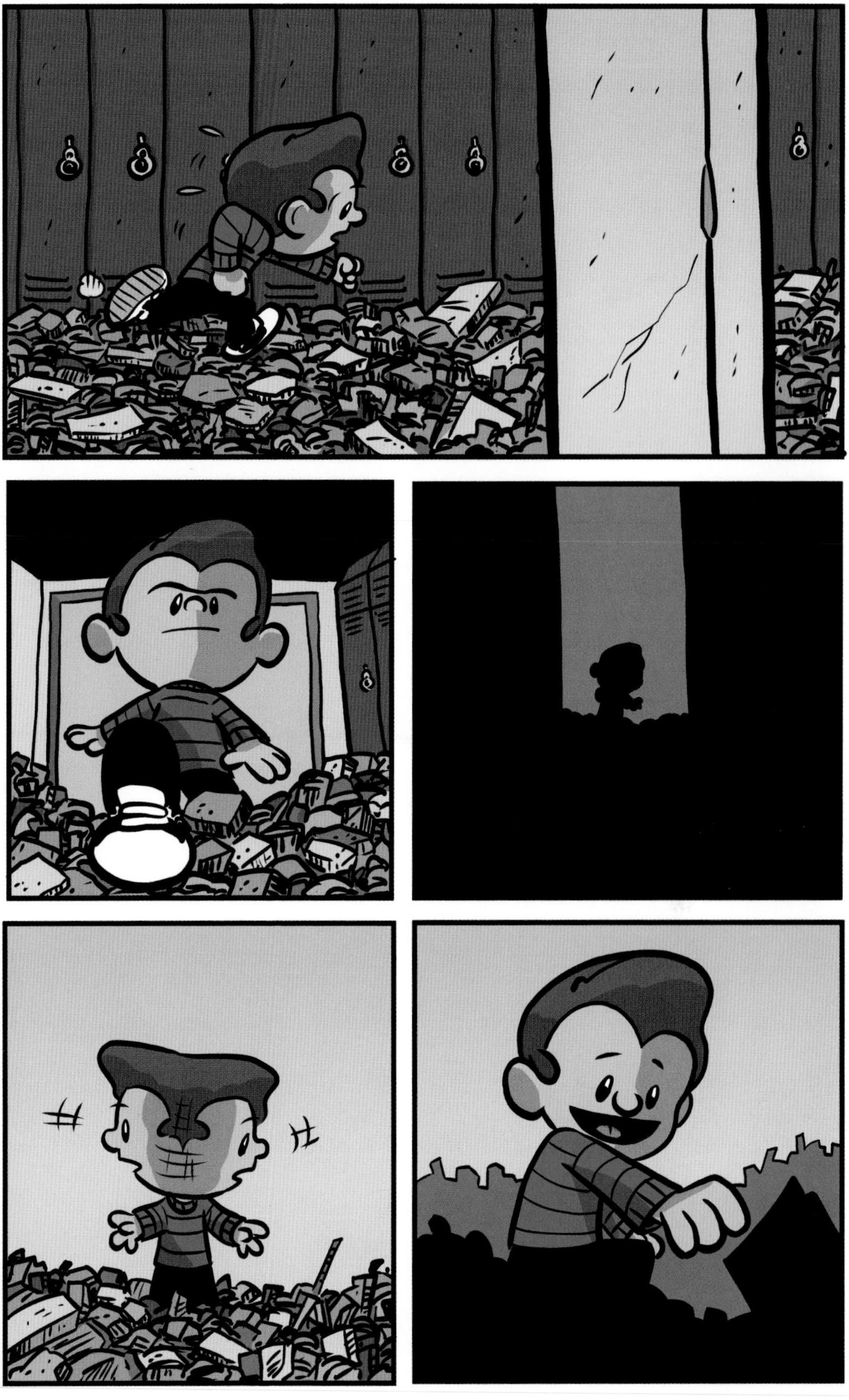

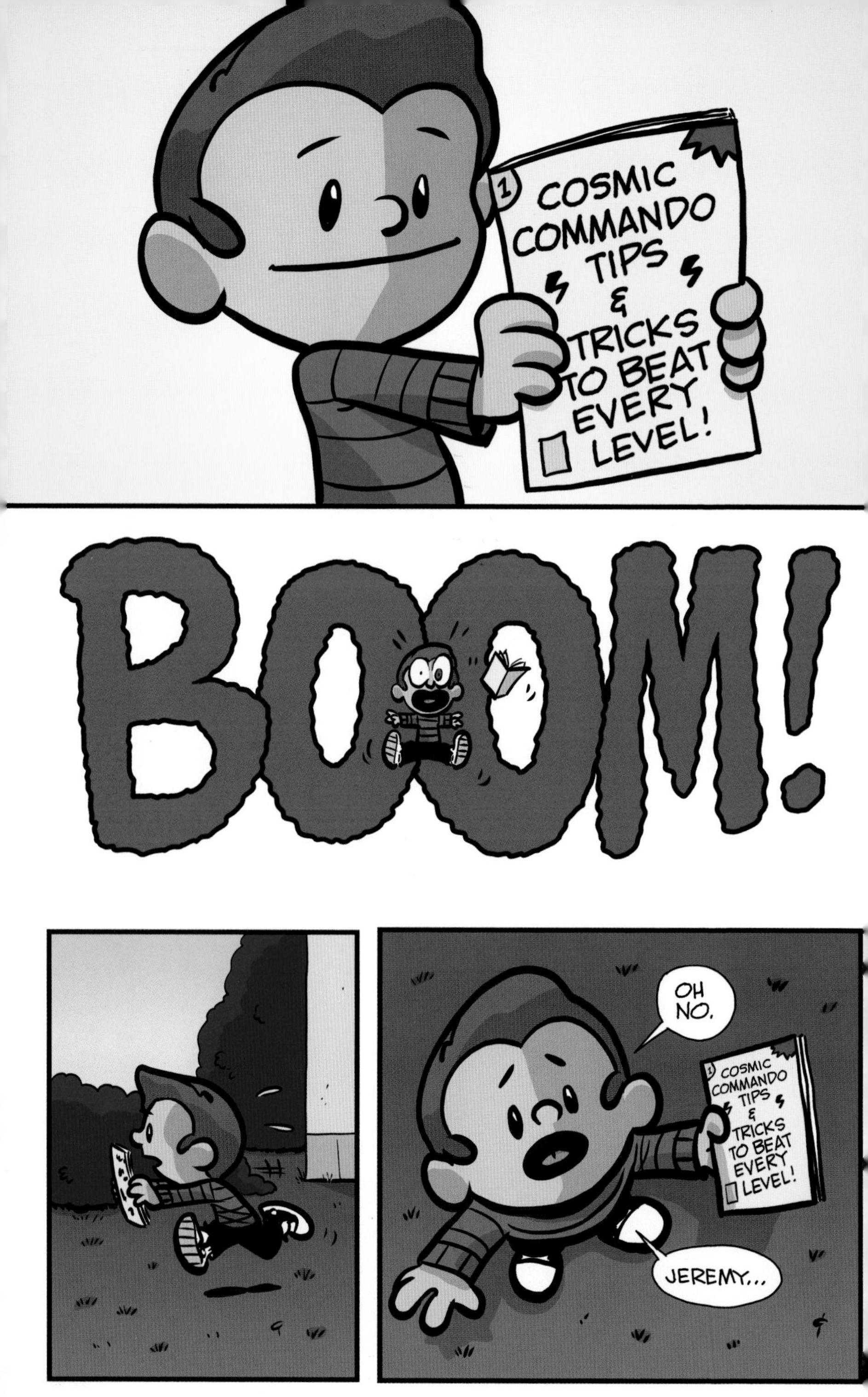

1
COSMIC COMMANDO TIPS & TRICKS TO BEAT EVERY LEVEL!
BOOM!
OH NO.
1 COSMIC COMMANDO TIPS & TRICKS TO BEAT EVERY LEVEL!
JEREMY...

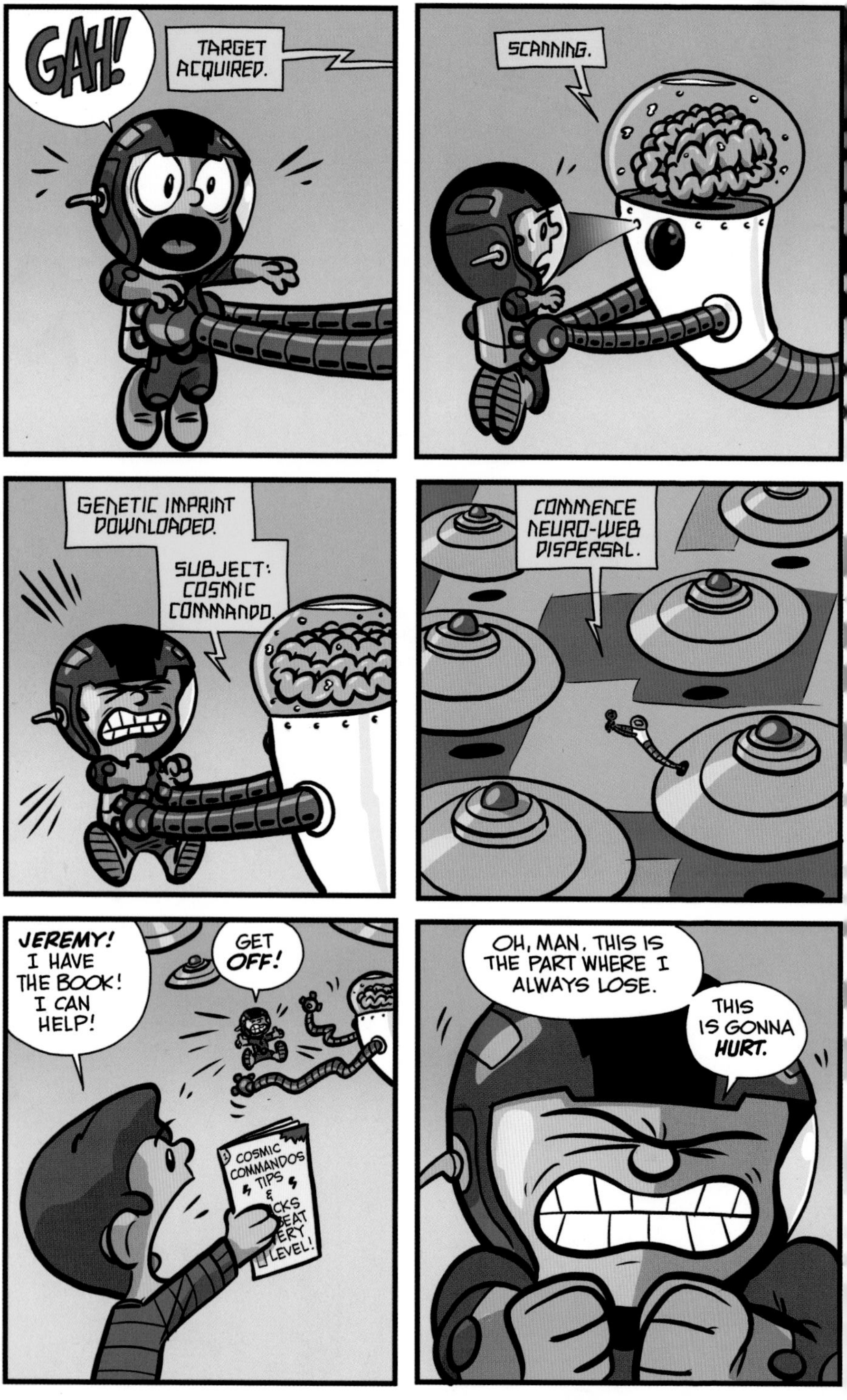
GAH!
TARGET ACQUIRED.
SCANNING.
GENETIC IMPRINT DOWNLOADED.
SUBJECT: COSMIC COMMANDO.
COMMENCE NEURO-WEB DISPERSAL.
JEREMY! I HAVE THE BOOK! I CAN HELP!
GET OFF!
COSMIC COMMANDOS TIPS &
OH, MAN. THIS IS THE PART WHERE I ALWAYS LOSE.
THIS IS GONNA HURT.

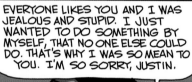

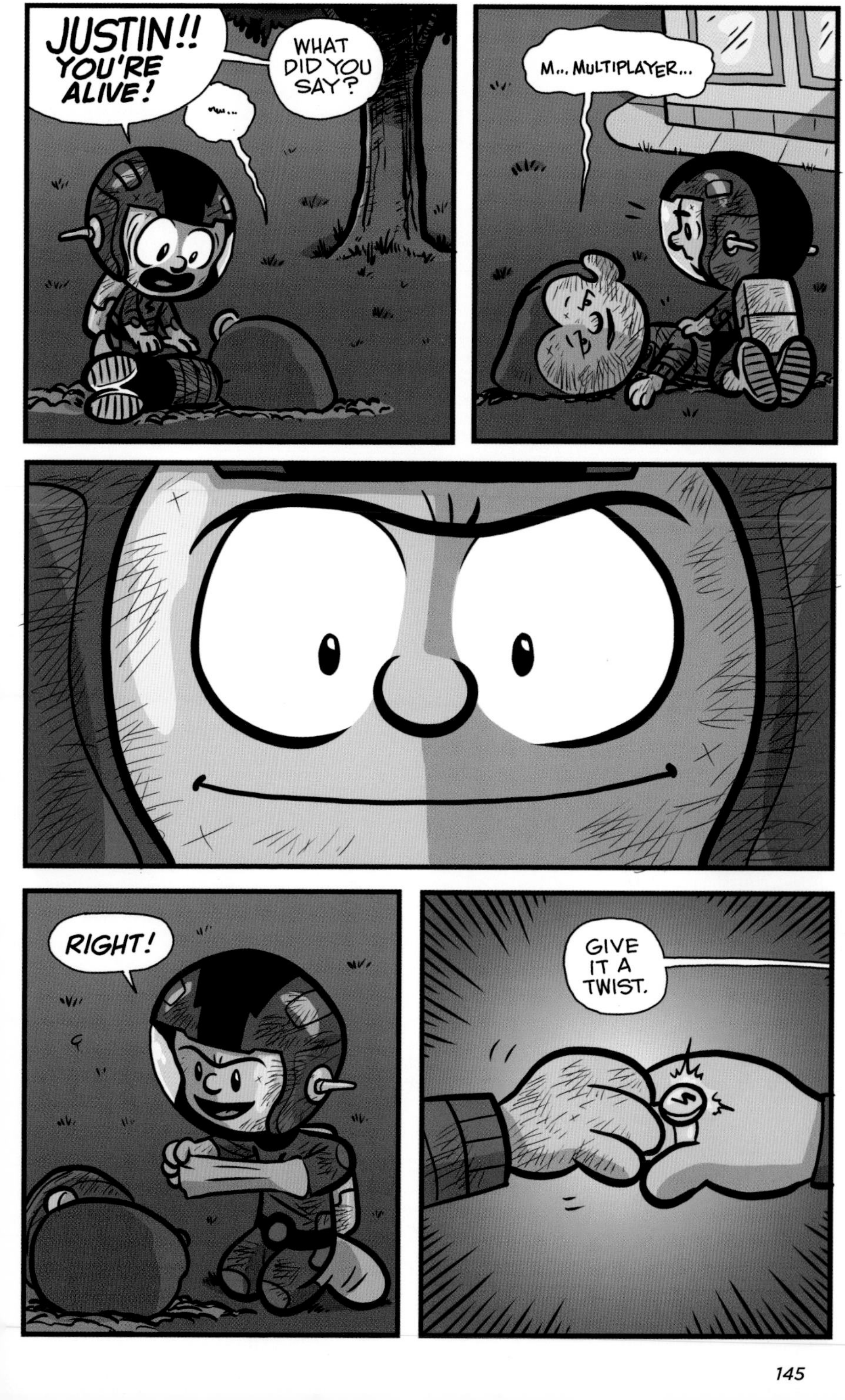

JUSTIN!! YOU'RE ALIVE!
WHAT DID YOU SAY?
M... MULTIPLAYER...
RIGHT!
GIVE IT A TWIST.

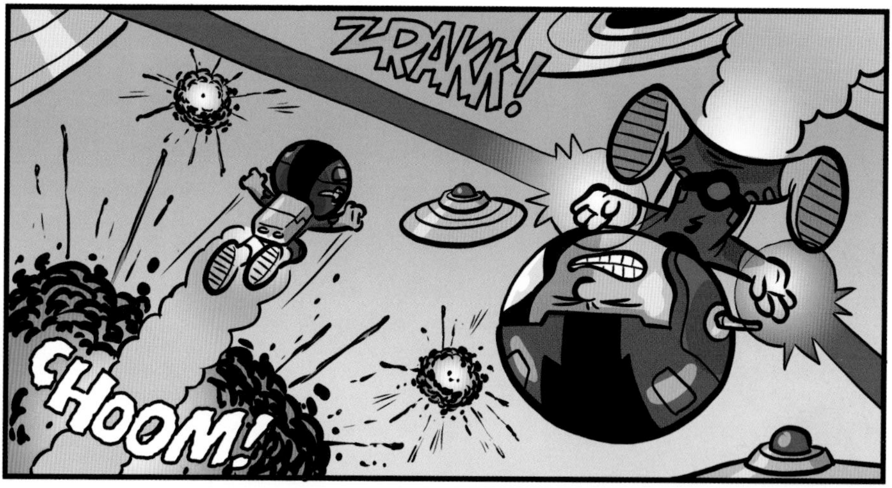
ZRAKK!
CHOOM!

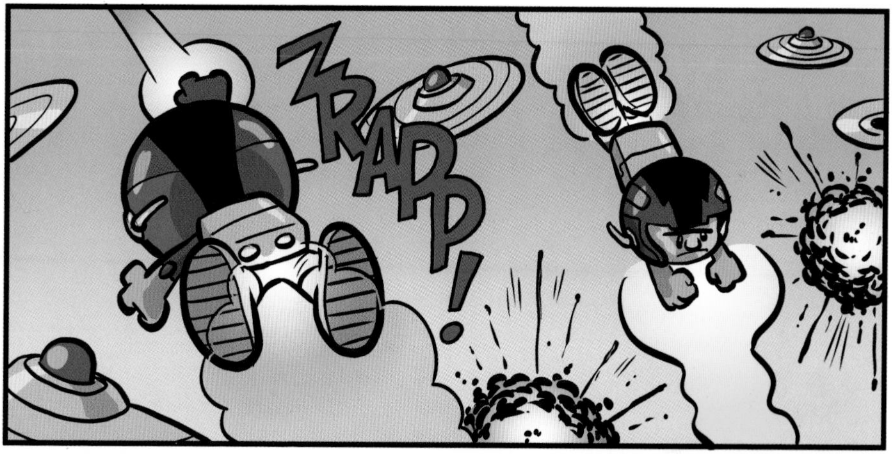
ZRAPP!

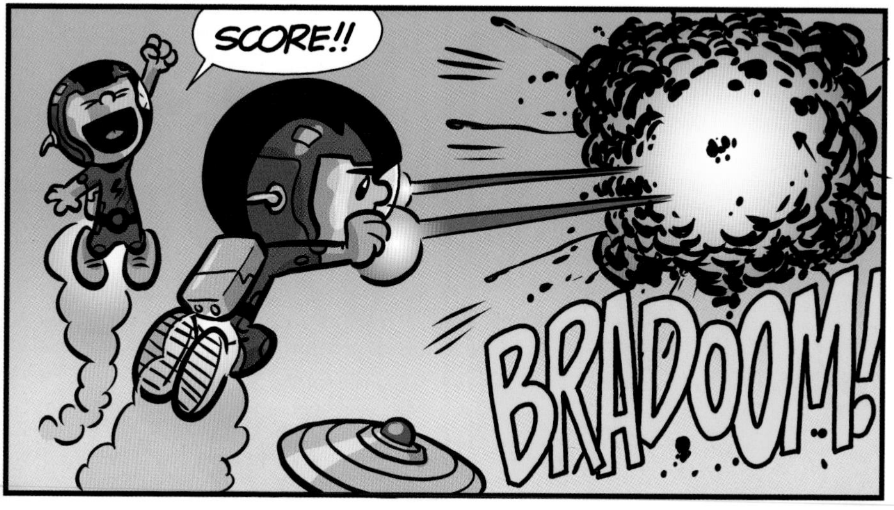
SCORE!!
BRADOOM!

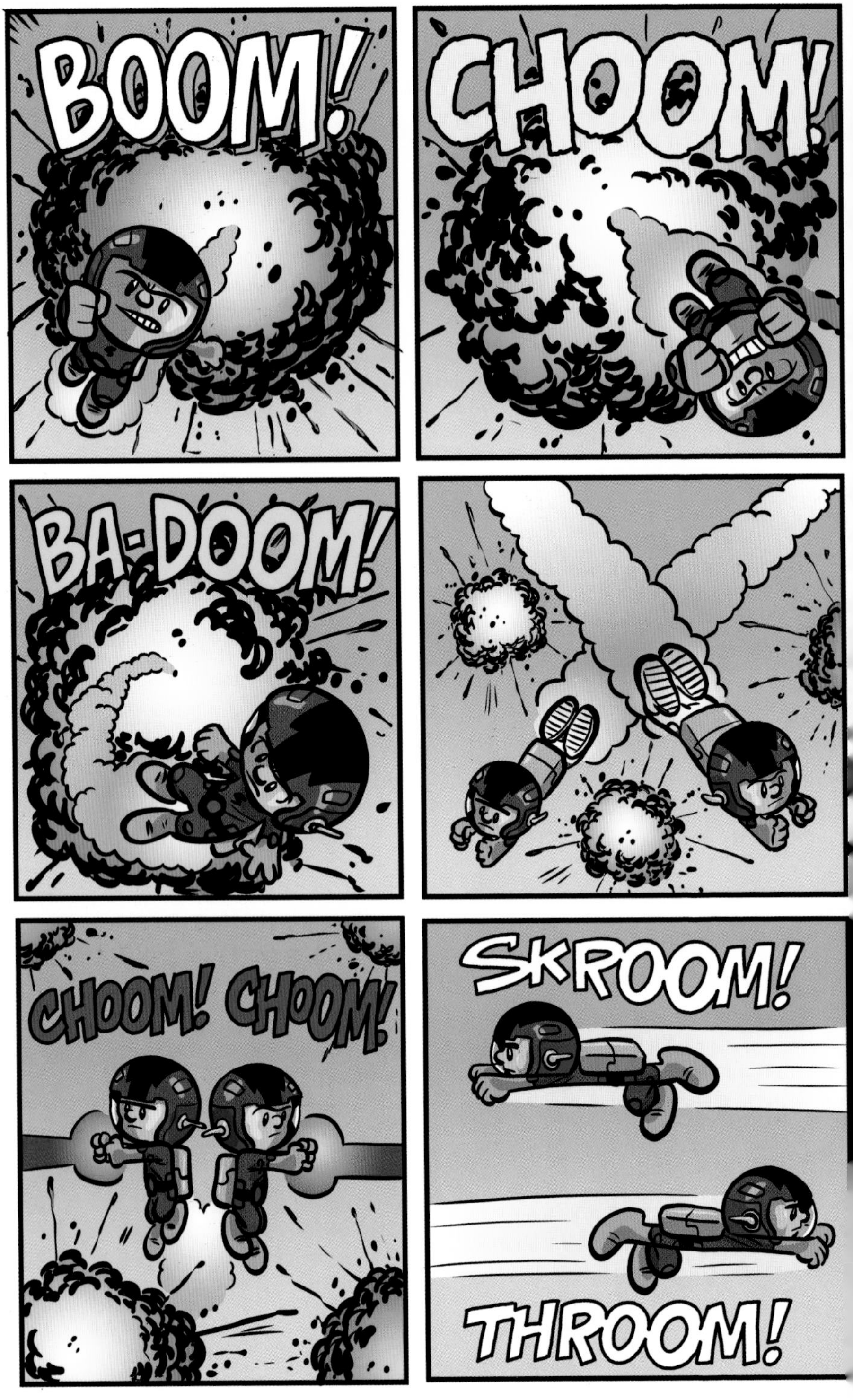
BOOM!
CHOOM!
BA-DOOM!
CHOOM! CHOOM!
SKROOM!
THROOM!

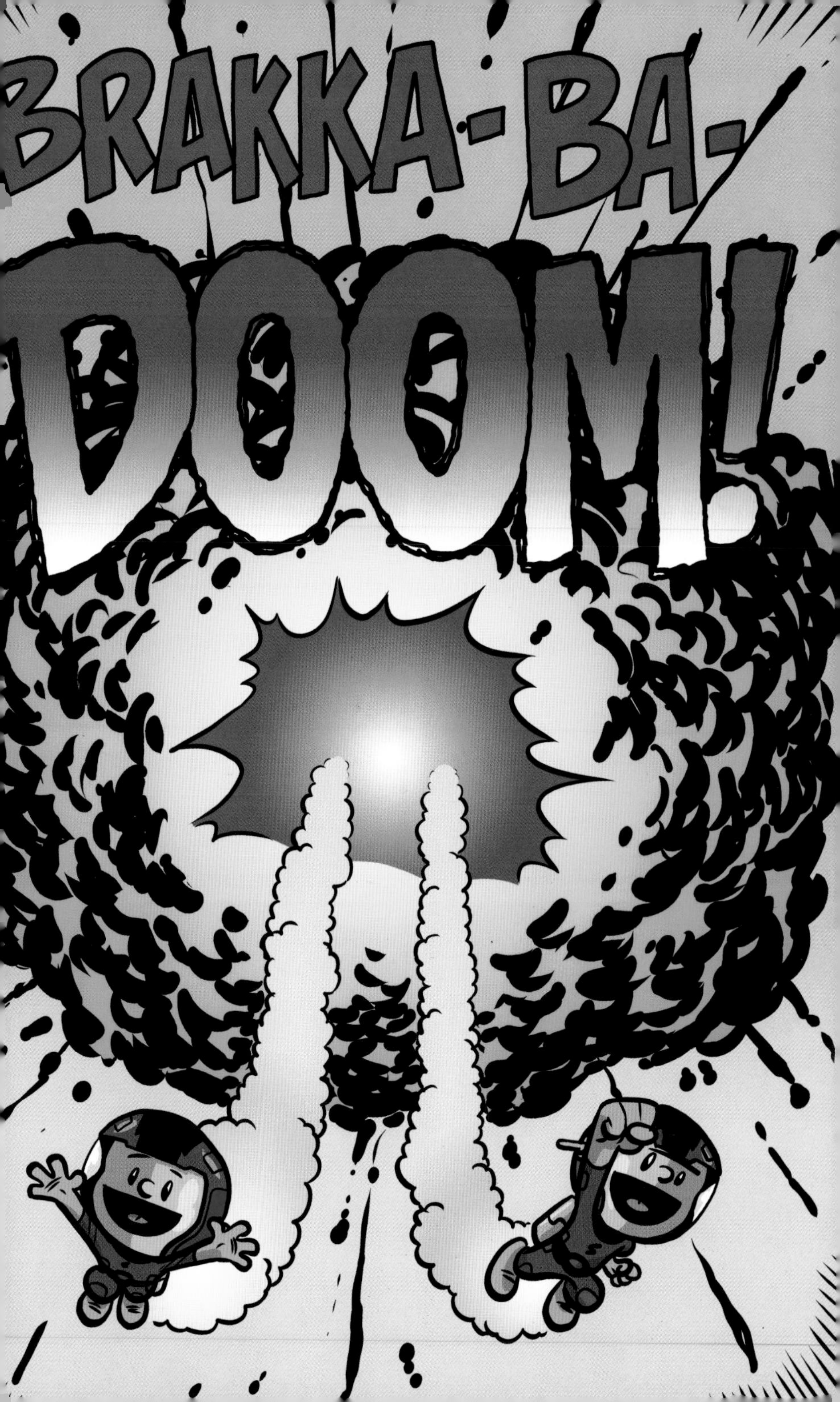
BRAKKA-BA-
DOOM!

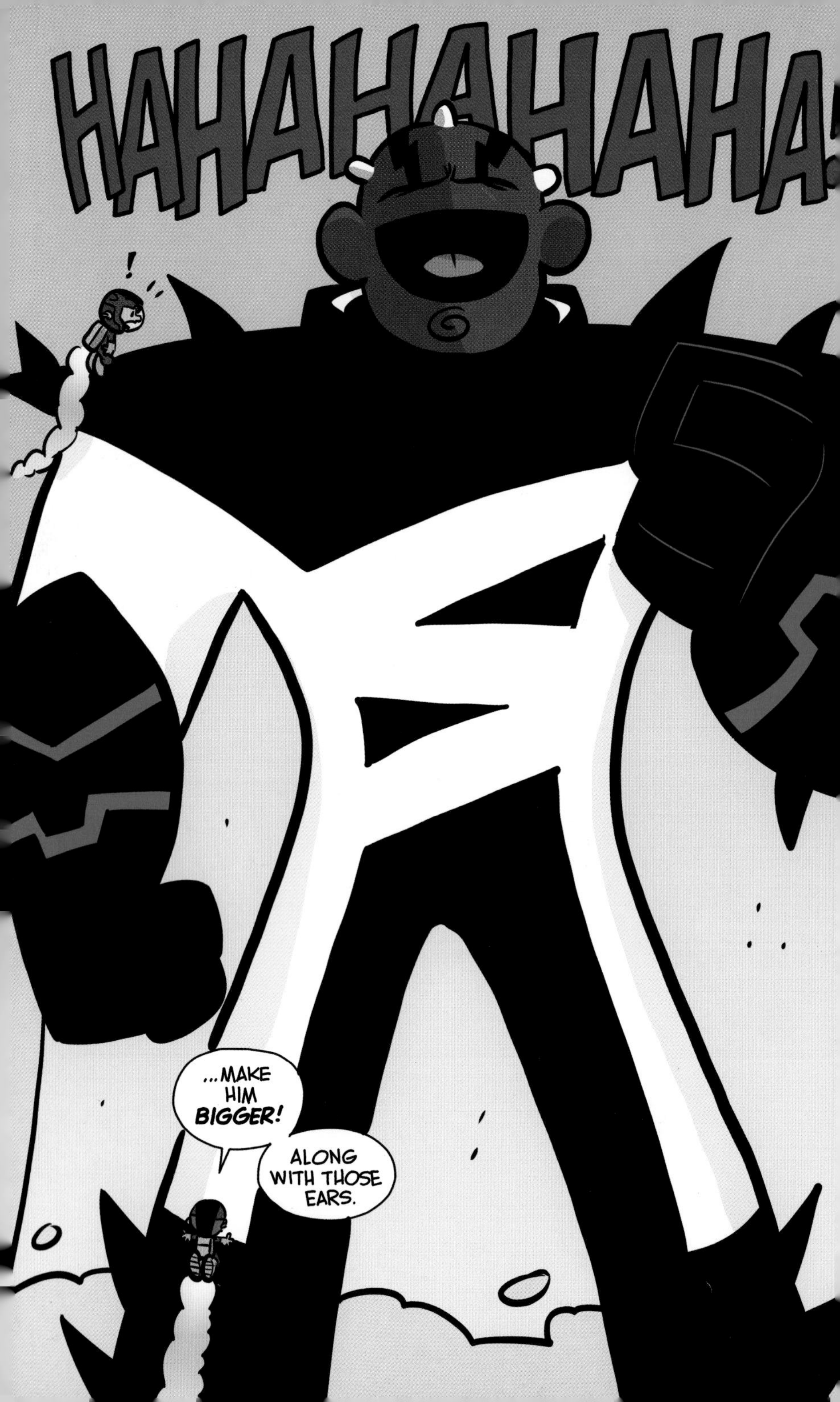

HAHAHAHAHAHA!
!
...MAKE HIM BIGGER!
ALONG WITH THOSE EARS.

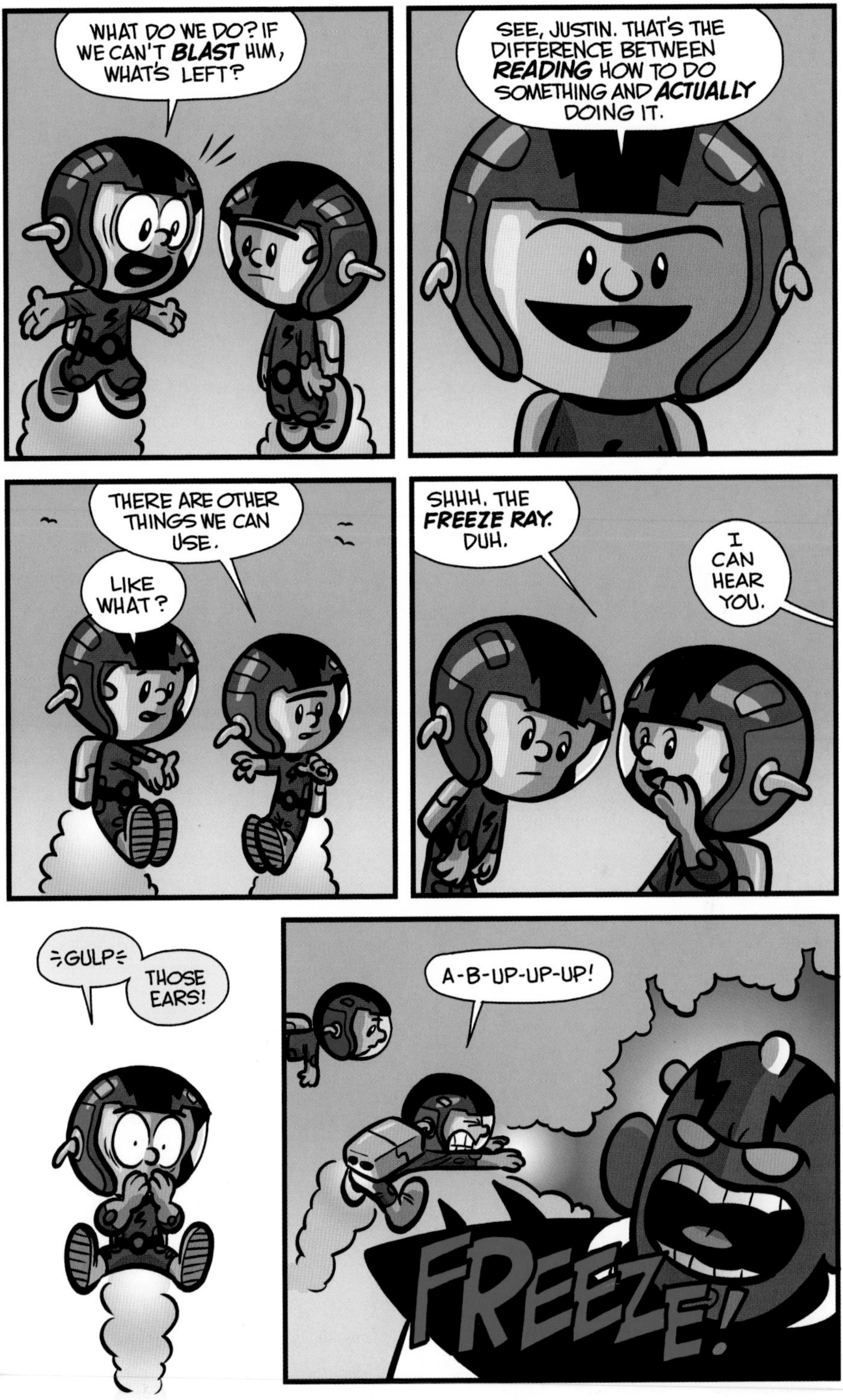
WHAT DO WE DO? IF WE CAN'T BLAST HIM, WHAT'S LEFT?
SEE, JUSTIN. THAT'S THE DIFFERENCE BETWEEN READING HOW TO DO SOMETHING AND ACTUALLY DOING IT.
THERE ARE OTHER THINGS WE CAN USE.
LIKE WHAT?
SHHH. THE FREEZE RAY. DUH.
I CAN HEAR YOU.
GULP THOSE EARS!
A-B-UP-UP-UP!
FREEZE!

159

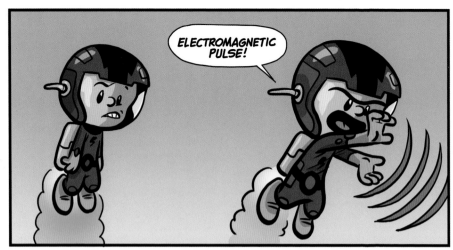

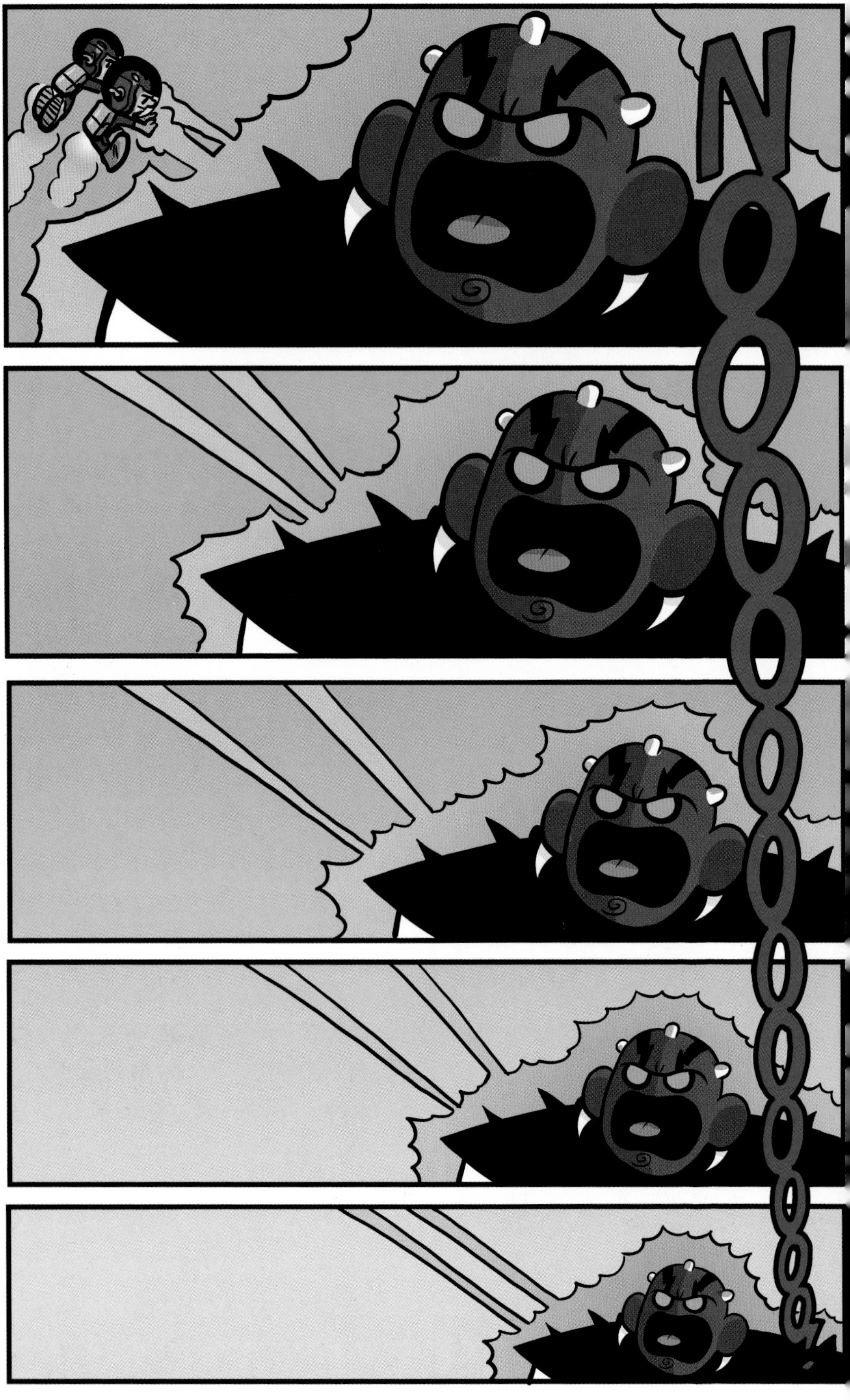
NOOOOOOOOOOOOOOOOOO!

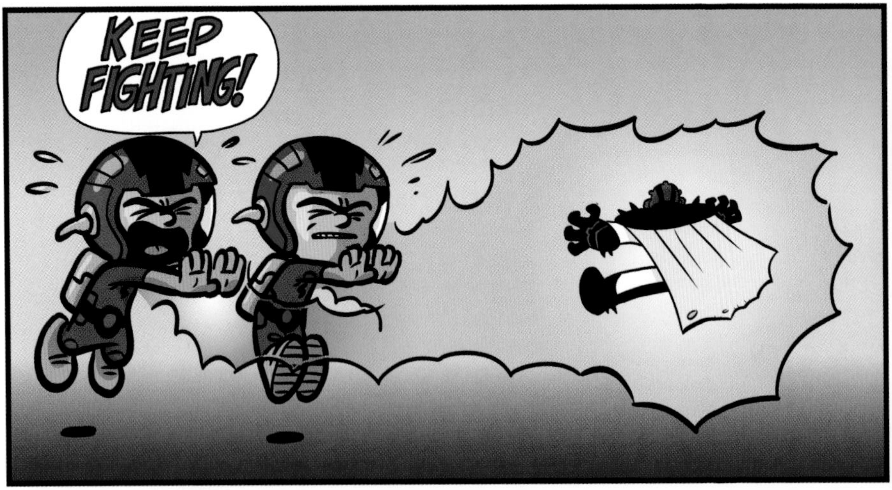
KEEP FIGHTING!

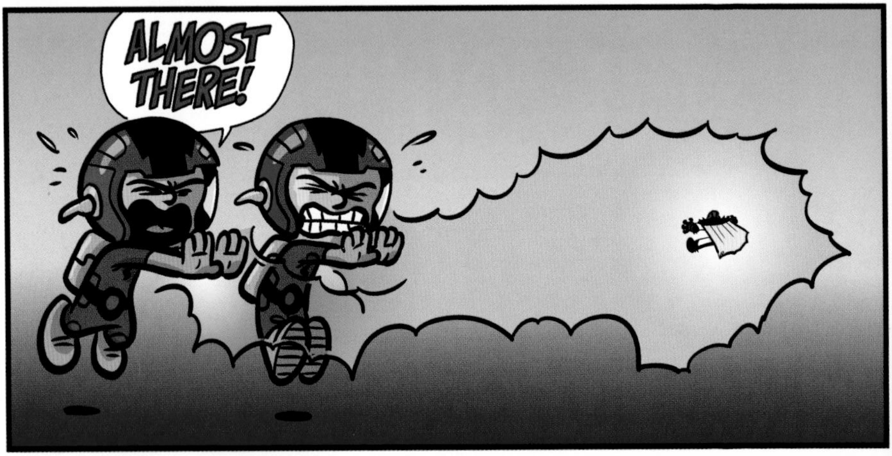
ALMOST THERE!

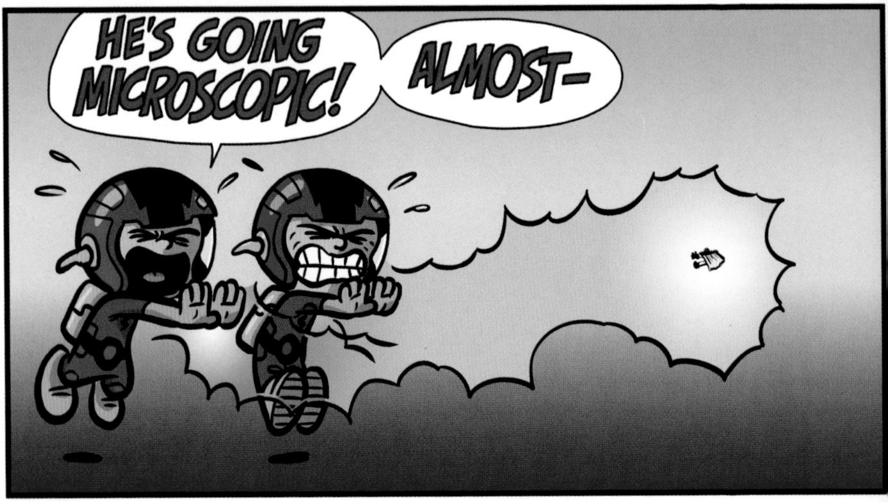
HE'S GOING MICROSCOPIC!
ALMOST-

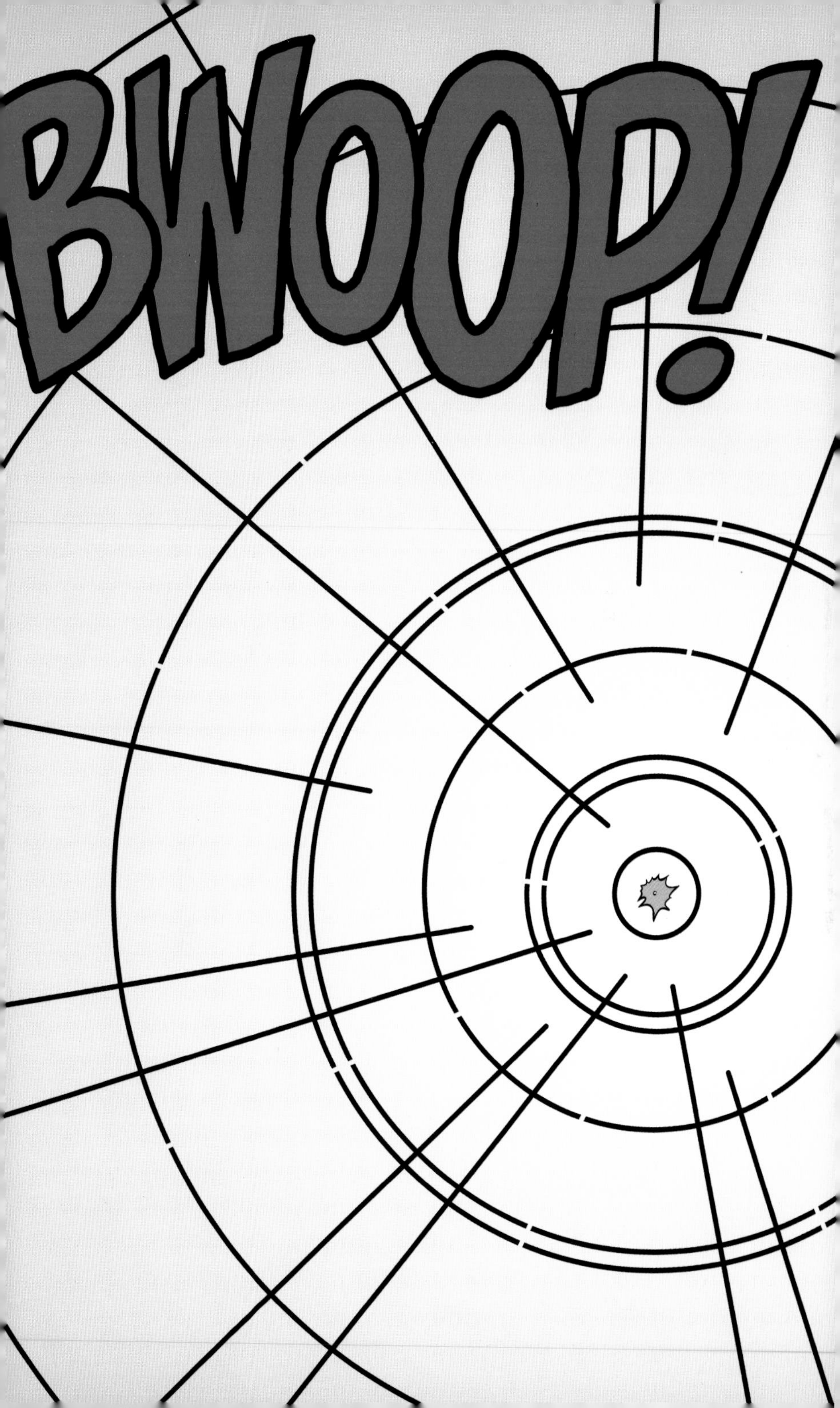
BWOOP!

CHAPTER ⚡ SEVEN

GAME OVER

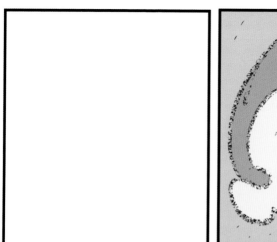

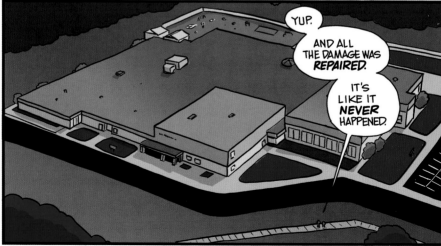

183

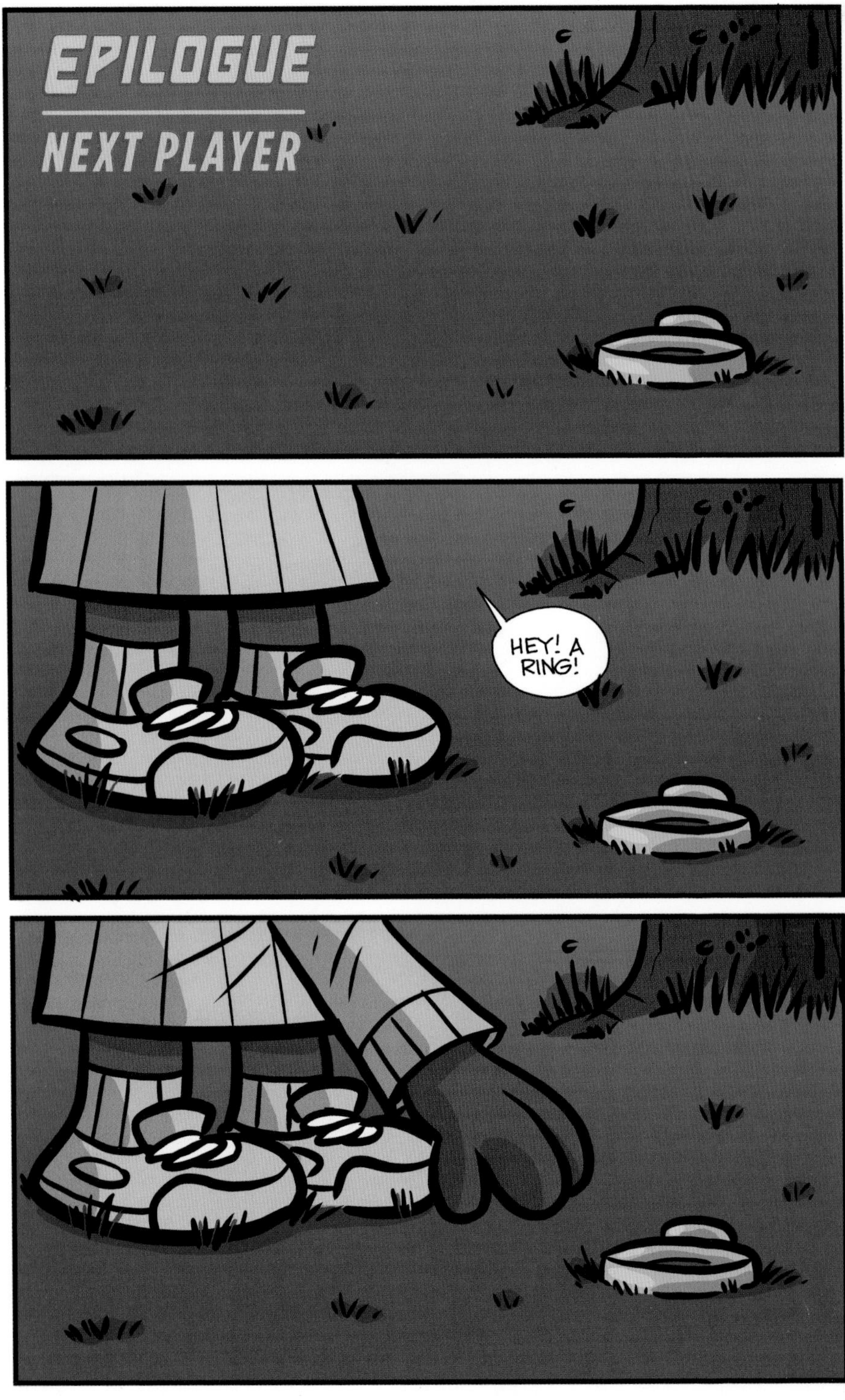
EPILOGUE
NEXT PLAYER
HEY! A RING!